Duets™

**Two brand-new stories in every volume...
twice a month!**

Duets Vol. #95

A return to Morning Glory Ranch! Charming
author Molly O'Keefe serves up not one but two
deliciously funny stories starring the Cook family.
Once again, those Cooks are embroiled in the
sweetest shenanigans in *Cooking Up Trouble* and
Kiss the Cook. Don't miss out on this tasty treat! Be
sure to check out this superb Double Duets volume.

Duets Vol. #96

Two talented authors make their debut this month.
Hannah Bernard, who hails from Denmark, learned
how to write romance by checking out the
eHarlequin.com Web site! Her hard work resulted
in *Catch and Keep*. Tanya Michaels's first Duets
novel will keep every bride-to-be on her toes!
The Maid of Dishonor will have you hanging on
to your husband and rolling down the aisle!

Be sure to pick up both Duets volumes today!

Catch and Keep

"You see, Jake, I've read all about it. I know the techniques and all that." She patted his hand. **"I just need a mouth to practice on."**

A mouth to practice on.

Jake wanted to cry. Instead, he beat his head against the kitchen table. Sitting up, he steeled himself and looked at her soft pink lips. He could do this.

Sarah moved in closer, her head only reaching his shoulders. "Can I just experiment first?"

A tiny frown of concentration formed a straight line between her closed eyes. Her mouth played over his and she began to nibble at his lips. When her tongue snaked out to lick at the corner of his mouth, Jake snapped his head back at the sudden rush of overwhelming arousal he felt. This was going to be harder than he'd ever imagined.

And then Sarah's eyes opened, and that sharp intelligence almost bit at him. *Finally* she was noticing what she was doing to him. *Finally...*

"Do you find it difficult to breathe during French kissing?" she asked innocently as she reached for her pad and pen.

For more, turn to page 9

"My relationships are all business related, not personal."

"Not even with—" Sam bit her lip.

Ethan's green eyes arrested hers. "No. Not even with Jillian. She's sweet, but we don't. "

"You don't click?"

"Right. There aren't any sparks. Do you know that until recently I thought sparks came from carpets?"

Sam overlooked his odd comment. "If there are no sparks, you shouldn't marry her."

"You just don't give up, do you?"

She met his probing gaze straight on. "At least I don't lie to myself. You believe this is what you want?"

"What I want..." He rubbed his thumb slowly over her skin, and a thousand tiny bursts of light pulsed through her. "This marriage is what I need. I don't do things impulsively."

Somehow Sam found enough voice to squeak out the words "Maybe you should."

He leaned forward until he was so close, their breath mingled. "You of all people don't want me acting impulsively right now...."

For more, turn to page 197

HARLEQUIN DUETS

ISBN 0-373-44162-2

Copyright in the collection:
Copyright © 2003 by Harlequin Books S.A.

The publisher acknowledges the copyright holders of the individual works as follows:

CATCH AND KEEP
Copyright © 2003 by Hannah Bernard

THE MAID OF DISHONOR
Copyright © 2003 by Tanya Michna

This edition published by arrangement with Harlequin Books S.A.

® and TM are trademarks of the publisher. Trademarks indicated with ® are registered in the United States Patent and Trademark Office, the Canadian Trade Marks Office and in other countries.

Visit us at www.eHarlequin.com

Printed in U.S.A.

Catch and Keep

Hannah Bernard

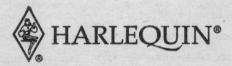

HARLEQUIN®

TORONTO • NEW YORK • LONDON
AMSTERDAM • PARIS • SYDNEY • HAMBURG
STOCKHOLM • ATHENS • TOKYO • MILAN • MADRID
PRAGUE • WARSAW • BUDAPEST • AUCKLAND

Dear Reader,

It's funny about characters. Sometimes they talk to you—and sometimes they don't. Jake and Sarah were stubborn. Before even introducing themselves to me, they acted out their first scene faster than my fingers could type. And then nothing. Not a peep. I waited for them to explain who they were and what they were up to and, for God's sake, *why!* But they weren't telling.

I ate *a lot* of chocolate that month.

The two of them taught me a valuable lesson: don't wait for your characters to speak to you. Just write—and they'll be quick to yell at you when you misquote them.

I hope you enjoy my first Duets novel.

I'd love to hear from you! You can contact me through my Web site at www.HannahBernard.com.

Sincerely,

Hannah Bernard

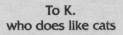

To K.
who does like cats

1

"WELL?" SARAH HAMILTON demanded. Her words were a bit indistinct, coming as they did from somewhere in the region of her toes. "So, what do you think? Will this work?"

"I think there might be considerable trouble keeping…uh…the relevant body parts in required contact."

"Oh. Why?"

"Um, well you see, with the male anatomy in…the proper operational condition, and the female anatomy in this position, there would be some danger of…eh…losing touch, so to speak." If his position had allowed, Jake would have patted himself on the shoulder for his brilliant way with words.

She scrambled off him and knelt on the bed while she scribbled his opinion on a pad.

"Is this an educated guess, or do you have actual experience?"

When he didn't answer, she glanced impatiently at him, and tapped his stomach with her pen. "Jake?"

Jake Benford sat up and pushed one hand through his mussed hair, wondering not for the first time, just how he had gotten himself into this situation. "That's an educated guess. I haven't dated a circus acrobat yet, but I'll be sure to update you on the subject if I do."

"Good," she said absentmindedly. She flipped her pad to a new page, stood up and moved to the small desk where half a dozen books lay open, displaying their colorful photographs and drawings. Jake rolled his eyes as she began studying the text. She wouldn't know sarcasm if it jumped up and bit her in the female anatomy.

It looked like his respite was over. She put the pen back behind her ear where it instantly tangled in her curly dark hair, and turned to him with a let's-get-back-to-work look on her face.

"Okay, let's try this. It looks easier. Stand over there."

Still marveling at the way he had allowed her to boss him around ever since she was two years old, he let himself be dragged to his feet. She pushed him against the wall, then stepped back, frowning. "Drat. Our sizes don't match. This will never work."

Jake folded his arms on his chest and continued standing where told to, while she walked back to the desk and put her glasses on to study the book better. "Right. I'm supposed to be against the wall and you are supposed to hold me up." Frowning, she looked at him, her gray eyes penetrating even through the distortion of the glasses. "Can you do that and still perform?"

"Of course," he said, almost affronted by her doubting tone.

"Mmm... Let's try." She took his place by the wall and pulled him against her. "Okay, how does this work? Do you lift me up?"

Shaking his head in disbelief, Jake wrapped his arms around her and lifted her, then waited.

"Well? What are you waiting for?"

"Your next command, Highness."

"Haven't you done this before?"

He opened his mouth, then closed it again. "I'm not answering any more questions regarding my repertoire of sexual positions."

"Don't be such a prude, Jake. It will help if you can just tell me things instead of me having to look them up constantly. What am I supposed to do now?"

Jake rolled his eyes. "Just hold on. Wrap your arms and legs around me."

She did. "Now what?"

"A demonstration of what comes next would require that we take our clothes off."

"Ah. Okay." She moved experimentally. "Hmm, this doesn't seem very comfortable for either party. Okay, you can let me down now."

"Sex isn't always supposed to be comfortable."

She glanced at him with interest. "It's not? How so?"

Jake laughed incredulously and threw himself into a chair. "Sarah, wouldn't it be simpler if you just found yourself a boyfriend to experiment with?"

"Hey, stay there." Flipping the pages she scanned several pictures before bouncing into his lap, straddling him. "Stretch out your legs." Gingerly, she leaned back until she was lying upside down against his legs. "How about this?"

"Definite potential," he murmured, watching the sleek lines of her body and fighting back a response. "Worth a try." He pulled her back up. "Enough research, okay?"

"Already?" Her hands on his shoulders, she frowned. "There are at least a dozen more positions I'd like to try."

"Sorry, this guinea pig is worn out."

"So soon?" She shrugged and placed the pad against his chest. "Okay, I'll ask you some questions then." She got comfortable on his lap. To his dismay she obviously intended to stay put for a while. "How long does it take?"

"Depends."

"On?"

With tortured amusement, Jake stared into her serious face. "All sorts of things. Use your imagination."

She pouted, but didn't pursue it. "Okay. What's your favorite position and why?"

He shook his head. "Sorry, that's privileged information."

Sarah climbed off his lap and stuffed the pad into the pocket of her cardigan. "I can't believe you're being so prudish, Jake," she said in annoyance. "Let me try just one more thing."

Jake gave up. Anything to get out of here and into a cold shower. Could she really be ignorant of the effect her research had on him? "Fine. Just one more and that's it. It's getting late, anyway. I have a flight to London first thing."

She pulled him to the bed and lay down. "I just want to see how the missionary position works. This shouldn't be too much work for you." She grabbed his hand and pulled until he practically fell on top of her. "Show me how you would move."

"No." She opened her mouth, but he stopped her words with a finger to her lips. "Call me a prude once more, Sarah, and I can't be held responsible for the consequences."

"Fine. I'll do the work then." He gritted his teeth as she moved inexpertly against him, then watched with resignation as her eyes widened in shock.

"Right," he admitted ruefully. "This is turning me on. Sorry."

He expected red-faced embarrassment, but she surprised him by smiling broadly. "This is amazing. I had no idea it was that easy to turn a boy on."

"A *boy?*"

The indignation in his voice went completely unnoticed. She pushed him unceremoniously off of her and sat up, pulling the pad out of her pocket and fetching the pen from behind her ear. "You've been a big help, Jake. I really appreciate it."

Feeling a surge of protectiveness, Jake thanked heavens she had called on him for this task and not some jerk who would have taken advantage of her.

Not that he'd had a choice. She had knocked on his door, a backpack filled with books flung over one shoulder, asking if he could help her research something. The next thing he knew she was sitting on top of him, pad and pencil in hand, asking personal questions about his sex life.

That was Sarah. When she wanted to learn something she approached it with a determination that could only be rivaled by a bulldozer. Although she was twenty-two and to the best of his knowledge had never been kissed, she had no qualms about lassoing him into demonstrating sexual positions to her. Although, thankfully, she hadn't told him to take his clothes off.

Yet.

"How does it feel?"

He had missed something.

"What?"

"Being turned on. What does it feel like?"

As he grasped for words and failed, Sarah's gaze roamed over his body. "I mean, do you feel it all over, or is it only down *there?*" She pointed with her pen, blatantly staring at the body part in question.

"I…eh…" Jake heard himself stutter and gave up trying to speak.

"I don't suppose…" She gnawed at her pen, studying him curiously. "…you'd let me…"

He had a sinking feeling that he knew what was coming.

"…see?"

BEFORE SHE KNEW what had happened, she was being deposited none too gently outside Jake's front door. The door shut firmly, and she heard the click of a lock and the rattle of the security chain.

"Touchy," she muttered, debating whether to knock on the door and ask for her books back. The security chain was really over the top. Did he think she was going to break down the door? His male attributes were hardly *that* interesting.

She raised her hand to knock, but then changed her mind. It could wait until Jake returned from London. It wasn't as if she'd get any research done without his participation.

She trotted around the side of the house and through the backyard, musing over what she had learned. Sex was weird. It was strange enough in animals, but a total enigma in humans. And so complicated, too. Some of the things she had tried with Jake seemed complex enough even without hormonally induced passion and chemically heightened emotions getting in the way. But that was exactly what interested her, the lengths people were willing to go to in their sexual life, and the difference between sexual behavior for people and animals. The interest in many different positions was, almost without exception, peculiar to only the human species. Other animals seemed perfectly content with just one. Why this difference? Was it a question of intelligence and imagination, or did it also have something to do with human emotions?

Jake had seemed insulted that she called him a

boy, she realized belatedly. A slight shiver coursed through her as she remembered the feeling of his body pressed on top of her, but she dismissed it with a quick shake of her head. She had not expected a chemical response in her own body, but when she thought about it, that was only to be expected. All it indicated was that her hormone system was functioning normally and it would wear off.

It was funny, though, how she'd never before noticed how deep the blue of his eyes was. And her fingers had all but itched to run through the darkness of his hair, just to see if it was as soft as it looked.

Hormones worked in mysterious ways.

It was nice of Jake to help her, she thought as she jumped over the fence separating Jake's backyard from her parents'. He'd always been there for her, no matter what. He was such a sweet boy.

Man, she amended with another hormonally induced quake as she entered the darkened house through the back door. Jake was right. He was definitely not a boy anymore.

THROUGH THE KITCHEN window, Jake watched her skip across the dim backyard like the kid she still was, despite her age and vast achievements. He shook his head and hoped his blood would cool down soon. It was much too late for them to be playing doctor. As precocious as Sarah was in some respects, she was way behind in so many others, and it wouldn't be easy leaving her if he ever got that job transfer to Florida.

He'd had a weak spot for her ever since she had toddled to the fence in her birthday suit with a dirty diaper in her hand, gravely handing it over to him. Of course, he had first and foremost been grossed out, but somehow she had wormed her way into his six-year-old heart. Already as a toddler she had latched on to him with all her inherent fierceness. Over the years she had counted on him to guide her through everything from learning to ride a tricycle to driving a car, and his shoulders had all too frequently been wet with her tears.

He'd been shocked, entering high school, to find his little neighbor, four years his junior, at the back of his classroom. Somehow, her uniqueness, the brilliance of the brain behind those clear gray eyes, had escaped him until then. She hadn't lasted long. The large public high school had not been good for her, socially or intellectually. Her age was too conspicuous and despite his efforts to protect her and help her along, the kids continued their relentless teasing. Within a few weeks she had transferred to a private school for gifted children, and before he had graduated from high school, his little friend next door was already in college. At the age of thirteen.

That was almost ten years ago now. Sarah had rushed through a master's degree in chemistry and a Ph.D. in biophysics, and was now a senior researcher at the local university. In her spare time she worked on a second Ph.D. "just for fun," this time in neuroscience.

Jake was still staring at the fence. And now, he

mused, it seemed she intended to learn about sex. From books and, God help him, from him.

He suddenly realized that he had completely forgotten to ask why she was intent on learning about sexual positions and techniques. Was it just general curiosity, or was there a purpose? Was this research for her Ph.D. thesis? He knew her project had something to do with the biology of emotions. Or was she simply using him as a practice dummy before going after some professor who didn't have a clue himself?

The thought was enough to put a scowl on his face. Sarah was an adult, after all. In fact, it was about time she paid some attention to the opposite sex. He was behaving like an overprotective big brother, and he had no business doing that.

He had to admit, though, that his feelings had been far from brotherly not more than an hour ago when she had lain there under him in his bed, or on top of him in the chair. He grimaced. The thought of her using those innocent moves on another man ate at his heart.

He wondered if she intended to use her research in practice. A grin tugged at the corners of his mouth as he imagined Sarah in bed, grabbing her glasses and craning her neck to peek at the notepad on the nightstand. She'd look up one detail and then turn back to him, attention and enthusiasm renewed.

Whoa! He turned away from the window and roughly pulled the curtains for good measure. Where had that come from? Back to *him?* Sarah had no business being naked in his bed, even if the bed in question only existed in his mind.

Especially in his mind. This was Sarah, his best friend and neighbor. The one who came to him for a good cry on his shoulder whenever she put her foot in her mouth or was rejected or ridiculed for being different. Sarah, who once brought over a pile of science fiction videos and a sleeping bag for a sleepover the evening after his parents moved to Florida.

He smiled fondly at the memory and was relieved to find himself on familiar ground again. She'd been sixteen at the time, worried he was lonely and assumed that a healthy dose of Captain Kirk and Mr. Spock would cure that. And they had. Though, he could have done without her three-hour lecture on black holes and event horizons.

He had to admit, although he had lived alone since the age of twenty-one, he had never been lonely with Sarah next door. Their relationship might seem one-sided to some people, but Sarah gave as much as she took. Just in a different way.

Jake glanced at his watch. It was time to get to bed, if he wasn't going to yawn his way across the Atlantic Ocean. He turned off the lights and jogged up the stairs, heading straight to the bathroom to brush his teeth. Then he flipped off the bathroom light and made his way in the darkness to his bed and quickly undressed.

He threw himself face down on the bed, only to find his newfound calm snatched away from him in a split second. What replaced it was a new surge of unwelcome arousal.

Her scent was on the pillow.

He groaned. This was going to be a long night.

"MORNING, CAPTAIN."

Lisa blew him a kiss and winked as she strode into the staff lounge. She went directly to the mirror where she began her preflight ritual of taming her blond ponytail into an elegant knot. "I had a hot date last night. What's your excuse?"

He didn't need to ask what she meant. She had caught him in midyawn. "Believe me, you don't want to know," he mumbled as he gulped down a mouthful of tepid coffee. Lisa had been a member of his crew for three years. Every spare cent she earned in those three years as a flight attendant had gone toward flying lessons, and she was close to realizing her dream of becoming a professional pilot herself.

"What was it?" she asked. "A bad date?"

"Worse."

She gave him a sympathetic glance. "A blind date?" she managed to ask despite the many bobby pins held between her lips.

"Even worse."

"Sounds scary."

He groaned. "It was. I don't want to talk about it. Ask Sarah, if you must know."

"Sarah?" Lisa chuckled, a warm look of affection in her eyes. Jake had been thrilled when Lisa and Sarah had formed a friendship, the first real friendship Sarah had developed with a woman in her life. In fact, her first lasting friendship with anyone other than him. Without knowing, she tended to scare people off. "What did she do this time? Raise genetically enhanced bees and accidentally set them loose on you?"

"Try again."

An elegant eyebrow rose above a perfectly made-up eye as Lisa's mirror image stared at him. "This I gotta hear."

"Well, it won't be from me. I'm not thinking about it, let alone talking about it. I'm seriously considering memory extraction."

Every hair finally in place, she turned around, hands on her hips. "Are you going to make me fly all the way to London and back before I can find out what your genius protégée put you through yesterday?"

"I can safely promise you, Lisa, that this one will be worth the wait." He took another sip of the coffee, then pushed the cup away. "Tell me your story. How was your date?"

Lisa grinned. "Hot," she said coyly. "He doesn't have your inhibitions."

Jake chuckled. Lisa teased him frequently about their one date and how she'd been shortchanged by not even getting a kiss. But, the truth was that they had immediately clicked as friends and nothing more.

"Think it might be serious?"

"Dunno." She fetched herself a cup of coffee, brought it to her lips and grimaced. "We never learn, do we?" she muttered, pushing the paper cup away with one finger. "Anyway, too soon to tell. But he's nice. And terribly cute."

Jake grinned. "Cute is one thing I hope I'll never hear a woman call me."

"They do call you that around here, Jake. For your information, I've even heard gorgeous." She reached out a long-nailed forefinger and thumb and pinched his upper arm. "There's quite a lot of debate about just how much muscle you hide under that shirt. In fact, there has been talk about a reconnaissance mission. Sneaking someone past your line of defense."

Jake shrugged self-consciously. "It's the uniform," he said with a wry grin. "Gets them every time. I could have three eyes and a beard down to my knees and they'd *still* only notice the uniform."

"I do think the constant exposure has made us more or less immune to the uniform. I think they'd prefer you out of it, actually. Of course," she added, "they don't know how irritating you can be."

Jake chose to ignore her last remark. "And just who might 'they' be?"

"Interested?"

Jake shuddered theatrically. "Not in another one of your blind dates, no."

Lisa laughed. "I know, I know. I promised. Never again. I do know, however, that Roxy has her eye on you."

"I know."

"Take it you've been swatting her away?"

"Not my type."

Lisa frowned. "You know, it'd be easier to fix you up if you'd tell me what your type was."

"It's very simple, Lisa. I don't have a type and I don't want to be fixed up."

"You have a not-your-type, but not a type?"

"Yep."

"My job is going to be harder than I thought," Lisa muttered.

"When did my love life become your job?"

"You know what they say," she said as she grabbed her small suitcase and they walked together to the plane. "Hell hath no fury like a woman scorned. Someday I will get back at you for rejecting me. I won't rest until I find you the love of your life and bring you to your knees."

Jake had to laugh. He put his arm around her shoulders and squeezed. "With friends like you and Sarah, my ego gets all the deflating it can take." He chuckled ruefully. "I'm not sure I could handle one more woman in my life."

His mind on his work, Jake went through the motions of preparation and takeoff with the ease of long practice. But once they were smoothly in the air and on course, and he could relax, his thoughts strayed once again to Sarah. She'd caught him off guard yesterday, but she wouldn't again. He'd have to be prepared just in case she had any intention of continuing her experimentation with him. And he'd have to be ready with all the reasons why it was not a good idea. It shouldn't be too hard.

After all, he'd explained the birds and the bees to her. A grin crossed his face as he remembered five-year-old Sarah and her question: "Jay, where do babies come from?" Not feeling up to the task, he had taken her hand and run straight to his mother who knew that if Sarah were to ask her own mother, she was likely to be handed a book. His mother had sat down with them both and let Jake explain things to Sarah, gently correcting him whenever he got a fact wrong and adding information whenever his limited knowledge ran out.

Despite their age difference, the two of them had always been close. He could hardly remember a time when he hadn't been looking out for Sarah. Although, all too often his best had not been enough, he thought with a small frown.

Jake had often thought that for a prodigy it was probably hard to have Sarah's parents. They took her gifts for granted, but didn't guide her in any way. It was as if their daughter was on a separate plane from them, and they seemed to assume that because of her vast intelligence she knew all things better than they, even when she was just a child. She had more or less raised herself. He knew that Sarah had never been able to rely on her parents for advice or guidance, or even simple discipline.

Which probably explained why Sarah had been allowed on sleepovers with him, not only as a child, but also as a teenager after his parents had moved away. A surge of anger hit him hard. Hadn't they been concerned? How could they be sure he wouldn't make advances toward their daughter? It was their job to protect Sarah, but they had always been content to leave that to him, the boy next door.

Jake wasn't at all sure that he liked Sarah's parents. Too many of their duties had been left to him, and he worried that he had not always been able to live up to his role as a surrogate parent, as well as a best friend.

He drew in a deep breath and held it for a moment before slowly exhaling. With her actions last night, Sarah had completely wiped out his role as a surrogate parent, and had damn well nearly done away with the best friend role, as well. A best friend wasn't supposed to think the thoughts he'd been having. As a *best friend* he shouldn't have an almost uncontrollable urge to offer himself up to whatever creative experiments she could think up. And a best friend definitely should not have noticed the shape of her breasts under her shirt as she'd stretched backward over his legs, and his eyes should absolutely not have been drawn to the curve of the faded denim covering her hips.

Still distracted by his thoughts, he jumped when Lisa tapped him on the shoulder.

"You just welcomed our passengers on Flight 3452 to Portland," she informed him, a thin eyebrow raised in a question mark. "Some of our passengers are worried that you don't know where we're going."

Jake groaned and glanced at Karen, his copilot, who shrugged, embarrassed. She hadn't noticed his error. "Thanks, Lisa." He grabbed the microphone again. "Dear passengers, this is the captain speaking. I'm told that I just informed you we would be landing back in Portland. This was purely a slip of the tongue, and I assure you that we are flying in the right direction and will be landing at Heathrow in under five hours." He paused, deciding on how much humor could pepper his apology. "However, should anyone happen to notice the Great Wall of China out their window, please do not hesitate to notify a flight attendant."

Lisa peeked out into the galley and gave him a thumbs-up.

Jake cursed himself. He could not afford to lose his concentration on the job. The lives of several hundred people depended on him. With determination, he pushed Sarah to the back of his mind, though she was never far away from his thoughts.

This was going to be harder than he had imagined.

2

THURSDAY AFTERNOON FOUND Sarah sitting under a parasol in the front of her house, wearing shorts and T-shirt, displaying her pale arms and legs to the spring sun. The weather was getting warmer, and Jake always complained that she never got any color in the summer.

Having memorized almost all of Jake's flight schedules, she was sure she had seen his plane lower for landing about an hour ago. She was hoping he'd see her as he drove past on the way home and drop by. His mood might soften if he saw her taking his advice about spending more time outside. That is, if he was still upset with her.

Her lightning fast brain seemed to slow down to a snail's pace when it came to people and their reactions to her. People were so much more difficult to figure out than chemical equations or the principles of physics. She had only a vague idea about why Jake had become upset with her. What she did know was that she didn't like it. Rarely in their life-long friendship had he ever been angry with her. She bit her lip, then shrugged it off. There was no use in worrying about it. They'd talk about it when he got home. Resolutely, she turned her attention back to the papers in her lap, a rough draft of an article she was writing, and grabbed a red pen from the table.

"Hi, Sarah!"

Before realizing that the voice was the wrong one, she looked up hopefully. The smile only faltered slightly when she saw it was Lisa, not Jake.

Her friend jumped over the low picket fence instead of bothering to open the gate, and then took the liberty of moving a small stack of paper off the second chair and plopped down in it. She helped herself to a cherry tomato from the small bowl of fruit and vegetables on the table.

"Hi, Lisa. I thought I saw your plane come in, but I haven't seen Jake arrive yet."

Lisa glanced up at the blue sky. "Does that thing have Jake and Lisa Coming Through! painted on the bottom?"

Sarah grinned. "No. I knew when you were expected to land back in Portland and the direction the plane was coming from. I extrapolated from there." She winced as Lisa crossed her long tanned legs and set them on top of the table, ruthlessly crushing the open journals.

"So, what did you do to Jake on Sunday?" Lisa asked without preamble, blue eyes aglow with curiosity.

Sarah bit her lip. "He's mad at me, isn't he?"

Lisa shrugged. "I don't know. He seemed more stunned than angry. What'd you do?"

"I just asked him something," Sarah hedged. Lisa's inquiring gaze told her in no uncertain terms that more information was required.

"Spill it."

Resigned, Sarah told Lisa the whole story, watching her jaw slowly drop until her tonsils were clearly visible.

"And then he just picked me up, carried me down the stairs, threw me out and locked the door."

Lisa's mouth closed, her lips quirked, and seconds later she was lying on the grassy ground, clutching her stomach as she howled. Sarah sat still, frowning.

"Oh, my God, Sarah, I can't believe even you would do something like this." Lisa clung to the chair, trying to get back up, but then succumbed to another attack of the giggles and was again rolling around on the grass, apparently in agony as the fits of laughter engulfed her. "Poor Jake," she managed to gasp between fits. "Poor, poor Jake."

Sarah waited a few more minutes until Lisa's howls of laughter had developed into the occasional burst of giggles accompanied by small whimpers of pain. Judging by Lisa's reaction, her fiasco with Jake had been an even worse error of judgment than she had begun to realize. "It wasn't as if I ordered him to do anything," she muttered. "I asked nicely."

Lisa snickered. "And did you give him time to say yes or no, or did you just bulldoze over him?"

Sarah hesitated. "I guess…I bulldozed. A bit."

"Oh, my." Lisa hiccupped. "My stomach is aching. I don't think I've ever laughed this hard." On her side in the grass, she rested her head on her hand and looked up curiously at Sarah. "What about you? Obviously, from your description, Jake…enjoyed it. Didn't you feel anything?"

"Like what?"

"Oh, I don't know." Lisa waved her free hand airily. "An urge to rip his clothes off and have your wicked way with him, perhaps?"

"There may have been a certain physical response," she replied with dignity. "That's something a scientist learns to ignore, whether it's on an emotional or a physical level."

"I see." Lisa moved closer to Sarah. "And did you notify Jake that he would have to be scientific about this and ignore any potential response? Aren't there strict rules regarding the use of human beings in scientific experiments?"

Sarah was embarrassed. And felt just a bit stupid. "I guess I didn't think of his potential reaction. I thought he could just show me…I mean, it's not like he could possibly have any sexual interest in me. I didn't know men could get turned on by someone they aren't even attracted to."

Lisa rolled her eyes as she stood up from the ground, brushing grass from her shorts and T-shirt. Her ponytail danced around as she shook her head in disbelief. "You can be such an idiot sometimes, Sarah. Jake could very well be attracted to you. In fact," she said, grinning, "I think you might have a problem on your hands, now that you've made him see you as a woman instead of a little sister."

Sarah's mouth dropped open. "What do you mean?"

"Just what I said. Jake is going to look at you differently from now on." She leaned across the table and grabbed Sarah's hand. "And, Sarah, I'm asking you this for your own good— When are you going to admit to yourself that you're in love with Jake?"

"What?"

"Come on. I've known you both for three years. It's obvious in the way you look at him, in the way you talk about him. And yes, in the way you trusted him to do that ridiculous exercise with you."

"I don't fall in love," Sarah said wildly. "I'm a scientist. Love is a physical desire to procreate, and I have no intention of procreating in the near future."

"So you just want him for his body?"

Sarah blushed and opened her mouth to protest, but no words emerged.

"Not that I would blame you." Lisa winked. "Jake is a hunk. Plus, he's a terrific person, and I bet he's dynamite in bed."

Sarah stared at her friend, eyes wide open in absolute shock. "Dynamite in…"

Lisa grinned devilishly. "Hey, I dated him, remember. I may not have gotten even a kiss before he had me pegged as just-a-friend, but that doesn't mean I didn't wonder what he'd be like in bed." She stood up and reached across and grabbed Sarah's chin, pushing her mouth closed. "Really,

Sarah, sometimes I wonder if you're from another planet.''

Had anyone other than Lisa and Jake made that comment, Sarah would have been devastated. But now she hardly noticed it. She was too agitated to set things straight. "Jake is my friend, my buddy. I wouldn't think about him like that.''

Lisa chuckled. "You did a hell of a lot more than think that day, Sarah. Boy, if I could have been a fly on the wall.'' She succumbed to a fit of giggles again. "Perhaps next time you'll hire me as a research assistant? I'd be happy to take notes.''

"I don't think there will be a next time," Sarah shot back. "His response wasn't favorable.''

"Oh, I think his response was most favorable.'' Lisa sniggered. "I wish I had someone who didn't know how to say no to me," she added wistfully.

Sarah's eyes widened as something occurred to her. "Do you think he thinks I'm in love with him?''

"I think he will definitely look at you differently from now on and probably assume you're doing the same.''

"Oh, no.'' Sarah rocked back and forth while Lisa didn't even try to contain her glee.

"Don't panic. This may all turn out for the best. Now we just have to figure out a way for you to finish this research project.''

"What research project?''

"Seducing Jake.''

"I don't want to seduce Jake!'' Sarah wailed.

"Sorry," Lisa said relentlessly. "It's too late to back out now. Either you hover in a twilight zone between being friends and being lovers, being awkward around each other all the time, or you take the full step and become lovers." She popped a piece of carrot in her mouth and munched on it. "I recommend becoming lovers. It'll be more fun, and besides, it's about time you got rid of that virginity." She winked. "Even if only for the sake of science."

Sarah looked down the street, then stood up and stuffed all her papers and books into her backpack. "Let's go inside," she mumbled, heading for the door without waiting for an answer. Grabbing the bowl of vegetables, Lisa followed.

"Not up to facing Jake all of a sudden?" she asked, a teasing smile on her lips. She caught up with Sarah just inside the house.

Sarah shook her head. "You're confusing me. I don't know anymore. If you're right and I'm really in love with him, I need to do something about it."

Lisa followed her through the house, up the stairs and into the room. "Whoa! Wait up for us lesser mortals here, will you? I didn't realize you were a champion of speedwalking." She glanced around Sarah's bedroom, then pointed at her bed. "Now, wouldn't Jake look pretty good in there?"

Sarah stared at the bed and didn't blink for what seemed an eternity. Then she carefully sat down at her desk, facing away from the bed. "Jake has been in and out of my bed since he was six years old. It would be ridiculous to find something erotic in that now.''

"Sarah, I could practically see the movie rolling in your mind just now. But I like that remark about doing something about being in love with him.''

"Yes. I'll just stay away from him for a while, and read up on the physiology of love. I'll be able to get it out of my system if I know what is happening.''

Lisa rolled her eyes. "Stay away from him? You should get him in bed again. Naked this time.'' She grinned. "And anyway, you know that absence makes the heart grow fonder.''

"There may be some truth in that,'' Sarah mused. "When people we care for are away, we tend to remember the good things instead of the bad.''

"Yeah?'' Lisa sat cross-legged on the bed. "Tell me the good and bad things about Jake.''

A whimsical smile played over Sarah's face, and Lisa pounced on it. "Bet you can't think of a single bad thing, can you? You're so totally in love with him!''

Sarah shrugged impatiently. "Okay, so you're making a point about mood-congruent memory. It doesn't matter if I am. He's not in love with me, and even if he were, we are not compatible. I'll get over it.''

"Okay.'' Lisa was silent for a while. "You know, Sarah, this makes your research with him even more important. Imagine all the information you could gather on emotional involvement in sex.''

Sarah peered suspiciously at her friend. "Are you suggesting I have sex with Jake just for research?"

"Well, I think it could be good for both of you. Especially if there were sparks flying between you that one time. Is there some law about not mixing research and pleasure?"

"Well, you have to remain objective."

"But what if you're researching pleasure? You also have to explore subjectivity, don't you?"

"That's true," Sarah allowed, then shook her head firmly. "Stop it, Lisa! I need to think about this and you're just confusing me."

Lisa's mouth curved into a wicked grin. "Fine. Discussion postponed, but by no means forgotten."

"EMERGENCY!" STILL IN HER uniform, but with her hair freed from the tight knot and scrunched into the usual ponytail instead, Lisa rushed into the lab and grabbed the arm of white-coated Sarah. She glanced around and noticed the half a dozen lab technicians and students who had all stopped their work to stare at her. "Hi there, gang. I'm Lisa." She curtsied and sent a glowing smile to all, then dragged Sarah, still holding a vial in each hand, out of the lab and into the gloomy gray corridor.

"What's wrong?"

"It's serious." Lisa grabbed Sarah's upper arms as if to prepare her for the worst. "Jake has a date tonight."

"Oh." The small word belied the sting in her heart. Of course Jake had dates. She had learned to ignore the stabs of jealousy they caused. Jealousy was a strange emotion. She had tried to analyze it, but it didn't make much sense in her situation. Jake wasn't hers except as a friend. He was not mate material, so why did she suffer the primitive impulse of wanting to scratch out the eyes of any other female who approached him?

"This is bad, Sarah. I know her. It's Roxanne. A *redhead*." She pronounced the word redhead as she would "scorpion" or "wasp." "She reels men in, keeps them on a leash for a few weeks, then dumps them. And now she has Jake in her sights."

"I'm sure Jake can take care of himself," Sarah said reasonably.

Lisa put her hands on her hips and glared at her. "So, you're just going to let her have him? Isn't he worth a fight?"

"What do you want me to do? Let her catch me and Jake practicing the Kama Sutra with our clothes on again?"

"That wouldn't deter her," Lisa said. "I was thinking something more aggressive. Roxy isn't the type to wait until the third date to sink her claws into him." She poked Sarah's chest with a long pink fingernail. "You caused Jake to become sexually frustrated, and therefore vulnerable to Roxy. If you want to prevent your friend from getting hurt you need to ruin their date tonight to make sure they don't end up in bed. Then you can make your move over the weekend."

Sarah looked with resignation at the now contaminated vials and then mixed them together. White smoke filtered out, leaving the vials empty, and Lisa took a step back, peering at the emptied glass containers with a look of utter distrust.

"Do I want to know what you people are doing in there?"

"Don't worry, it's not very toxic," Sarah said, putting the vials in the pocket of her lab coat as she turned back to the door.

"Not *very* toxic?"

"I need to get back to work. I'll have to take a rain check from masquerading as a waitress so I can spill red wine all over Jake's shirt." She paused with one hand on the door handle. "Besides, I won't be making any 'moves' on Jake this weekend or any other weekend."

Lisa ignored almost every word she had spoken. "Bet you'd make a cute waitress in that white coat, but I have a better idea." She grabbed Sarah's elbow as she made a futile effort to reenter the lab. "You still have that cat, don't you?"

"Yes," Sarah said cautiously.

"Well…it just so happens that Roxanne is allergic to cats."

"So?"

"Really allergic. She had to quit her last job because a co-worker had a cat and she kept sneezing all day long."

"So?" Sarah repeated.

"You just make sure that Jake cuddles that cat of

yours before he goes off on his date, and he will be effectively inoculated.''

"No..."

Lisa grabbed her by the bulky sleeves of the lab coat and shook her. "This is important, Sarah. It'll be your fault if that vixen manages to seduce him tonight. Do you want to lose Jake for good? Either you go for him now, or you lose him. This could be your only chance.''

"Lisa, Jake isn't mine to lose. You are being overdramatic and blowing this all out of proportion...."

"Which of us has more experience with male and female relationships?''

Sarah bit her lip. "I don't think that one serious relationship makes you an expert.''

Disregarding the first three words of her sentence, Lisa rested her case. "Right. Well, I'm telling you, this has to happen. He's picking her up at six. Knock on his door with that cat at five-thirty. That way he won't have time to change his clothes, even if he wants to.''

"No."

Lisa's back was already to her, as she briskly walked down the corridor. Shaking her head, Sarah reentered the lab. In her humble opinion, that cat idea was just as crazy as anything she had ever dreamt up herself.

She'd just pretend this had never happened.

"WELL, IT'S ALMOST HALF past five already. Time for my show."

"Mom!"

Her mother looked at her, startled. "What did I say?"

Sarah groaned. "I was trying to ignore the time."

"I'm sorry, dear, I didn't know." Her mother sat down on the sofa and turned on the television.

Sarah had been resolutely sitting in the rocker in the living room, her nose stuck in a book as she concentrated on not thinking about Roxanne, Jake, her cat or any combination thereof. For good measure, she had left her watch in her room and was sitting with her back to the large grandfather clock in one corner.

But she hadn't counted on Mom and her shows and now she was excruciatingly aware of every ticking second.

Sarah sighed. Her concentration broken, she couldn't get the words on the page to make sense anymore. Instead, she counted them. Four hundred eighty-seven. She counted the letters. Two thousand six hundred fifty-five.

The commercials were over. Jake would be leaving on that date any minute now.

Her stomach twirled in a most annoying manner. She knew that it was simply stomach acids responding to the irritating workings of her autonomic nervous system, but it really did feel like her intestines were deliberately trying to tickle her liver and spleen.

Lisa was right. She *was* guilty of causing Jake sexual frustration. And knowing that he wasn't a one-night stand kind of man, it would be wrong if her actions caused him to fall into bed with a woman just to slake his lust. She frowned in sudden consternation as a new thought occurred to her. Lisa had said that this woman played the field. He might even catch something from her! Potentially something life-threatening. If Roxanne seduced Jake tonight and he caught a deadly disease from her, it would be Sarah's fault.

Torn, she bit at her knuckle. Perhaps she could just go over there and remind him to have safe sex?

Something soft touched her bare ankle and then "exhibit one" jumped into her lap. Green eyes stared into hers as if saying: "Well? Aren't we supposed to be somewhere?" Then the cat yawned, displaying two rows of sharp white teeth.

Before she could think it through, Sarah threw the book on a table and grabbed the cat. She ran up to her room and back down, then out the front door without even stopping to put her shoes on.

JAKE WAS UNDER NO illusions about why he accepted Roxanne's invitation. She had asked him out before, but he had always found an excuse. The aggressive redhead was not his type, and besides, he tried not to date women he worked with. But he knew why he had agreed to go out with her this time. To take his mind of something else. *Someone* else.

Sarah.

He knotted his tie quickly then stared at himself in the mirror. His tie was askew, and he had only combed his hair with his fingers, but he didn't care if he looked less than perfect. Had Sarah any idea what she had done to him? He'd hardly slept at all since she had knocked on his door. What little sleep he did manage was even worse, because it was filled with delectable dreams of the two of them together, trying out everything in her books, and a few additional things. In his dreams they weren't wearing clothes or glasses and there were no cold showers.

He hadn't seen her since dumping her outside his front door last Sunday. Well, he had *seen* her, riding her bike past his house on her way to work and back, but she hadn't dropped by as she normally did at least every other day. And, truth be told, he had avoided her, too. That would have to come to an end, though.

If she didn't come see him soon, he'd have to go over there and talk to her, he grimly acknowledged. He couldn't allow a little thing like carnal lust to come between him and his best friend.

The doorbell chimed and he automatically glanced at his watch. He was picking Roxanne up in half an hour, so it couldn't be her. He strode to the door, still worked up.

There on his doorstep was the guilty-looking imp holding her cat, barefoot with goose bumps covering her arms.

Perhaps she wanted to come along on the date, he

reflected with dry sarcasm. She might be hoping to learn from observation as well as participation. She'd be disappointed, though. He hadn't planned on doing anything with Roxanne that could possibly benefit Sarah's sex education.

"Hi, Sarah."

"Hi, Jake."

She rocked back on her heels, staring up at him. He'd thought he knew just about every facet of Sarah's personality, but this was a new expression for her. A mixture of guilt, innocence, guile and... awareness.

Oh, hell. Had their circus act awakened something in her as well? Was that why she had stayed away, and not because of embarrassment or awkwardness? Jake leaned against the doorjamb, suddenly weak. He wanted his little buddy back.

Sarah still hadn't spoken. She was fiddling with the cat's ears. Then she suddenly handed it over. "Would you hold her for a moment?"

"Uh..." Jake was not given opportunity to reply. The cat was in his arms, the paws on his shoulder. The darn thing was purring and he reluctantly scratched behind the ears.

"What's up, Sarah?"

"Nothing. I'm worried about Dead-or-Alive. Don't you think she looks sick?"

Jake looked at the creature. It looked more or less the same furry, spoiled thing as it always had. It hadn't changed since Sarah had brought it home as a scrawny neurotic kitten four years ago.

"I don't think so. What's wrong with it?"

"Her."

"Her what?"

"Dead-or-Alive. She's a she, not an it."

Jake rolled his eyes. "Okay, what's wrong with *her?*"

"I don't know. I just thought she didn't look well. She's been acting different ever since the kittens were born."

Dead-or-Alive squirmed in his arms, purring louder as she stuck her nose in his armpit. She didn't seem to have a care in the world, let alone be suffering postpartum depression. Jake lifted the beast away and deposited her back into Sarah's arms. He grimaced. There was cat hair all over his shirt. He pulled the pristine handkerchief out of the pocket of his jacket and used it to brush most of the cat hair away. He shrugged into his jacket and stuffed the handkerchief in a pocket.

"Looks fine to me. Take it to the vet if you're worried. If you can wait until tomorrow, I can come with you. Gotta run now, I have a date."

"I know," she said, somewhat sadly. She hugged him, the cat complaining loudly as it got caught between them. Then she turned around and snuffled away. The cat threw him a menacing glance over her shoulder.

Jake cursed, then went after her, and turned her around with one hand on her cat-free shoulder. "I'm sure she's okay, Sarah. If you're really worried, I'll give you a lift to the vet on my way. If not, we'll take her in first thing tomorrow.''

Her smile was tentative, again a mixture of something he didn't quite recognize. ''Thanks, Jake. I'm sure she'll be fine until tomorrow.''

''Okay. I'll see you then.'' As he often did, he leaned forward and kissed her quick on the forehead. This time, however, her skin seemed to imprint itself on his lips, and her scent filled his nostrils. He cursed under his breath as he strode to his dark blue Mazda and unlocked it. He wouldn't allow himself these feelings. She trusted him and he would never ever betray that trust.

''Jake?''

He turned around to see her standing close to the fence, the cat weaving eights around her ankles.

''You always practice safe sex, don't you?''

The curse that slid out of his mouth was too soft for her to hear, but as his palm slammed none too gently down on the roof of his car, his body language was obviously readable. Dr. Sarah vanished over the fence and into her house as quickly as her bare feet could carry her.

3

ROXANNE GREETED JAKE AT the door wearing a scarlet dress and an even more scarlet shade of lipstick. Jake had to admit that she was strikingly beautiful, if you liked that type. She welcomed him with an enthusiastic kiss on his cheek. A kiss that would have landed elsewhere had he not turned his head just enough to avoid it, but not enough to offend. As she linked her arm through his, he had the irrational feeling of being a fly cautiously feeling its way through a spiderweb.

"Oh, I'm sorry. I smeared you with lipstick," Roxy said with a flirty smile. Jake grinned politely back and reached into his pocket for the handkerchief to wipe the lipstick off. As he pulled up the piece of cloth, something hidden in its folds fell to the floor. Jake bent to pick it up but Roxy beat him to it.

"You must have been a Boy Scout," she purred, looking up at him with a grin. Puzzled, Jake raised an eyebrow in a question.

"Always prepared, isn't that right?" Roxy held out her hand, palm open.

Jake stared into her palm flabbergasted. It wasn't

a brand he had ever bought, but there was no mistaking what the two small foil packages contained.

Roxy moved closer and pulled his jacket open, then slid the incriminating evidence into the inner pocket, her hand lingering on his chest. "You better hold on to that, Captain, you never know when you might need them." She winked, causing him to take a step back. If he was reading her correctly, Roxy's reputation as a fast player was no exaggeration. He opened his mouth to proclaim his innocence, but closed it again. Nothing he could say would make this episode any less embarrassing or misleading than it already was. He settled for a shrug and what he hoped was an enigmatic smile.

Sarah. Sarah and her safe sex advice. She must have slipped the condoms into his jacket pocket when she'd hugged him at the door. His frown deepened as instead of thinking up an appropriate punishment for her, he began to wonder why the hell Sarah would have condoms anyway. Had her research progressed further than he'd thought? Was that why he hadn't seen her all week? Was she already experimenting on someone else? She couldn't be. Could she?

She better not. She really, really, better not.

He postponed the thought for a while. He had other problems to contend with. Roxy was still the picture of flattered ego, obviously convinced he was desperate to end the evening in her bed. He'd have to work on a gentlemanly excuse.

They walked to the car and he forced a cheerful

smile on his face as he opened the door for her. They were attending some sort of gallery opening at a large cultural center downtown. He had only paid vague attention to the details when she had described them to him.

As he pulled away from the curb, Roxy began her usual barrage of self-centered small talk. At the first red light she sneezed abruptly, once, then four times in quick succession.

"Bless you," Jake muttered, glancing to his side.

Roxy sneezed again, then started sniffing and coughing. She searched frantically in her handbag for something. Jake handed her his lipstick-stained handkerchief. She grabbed it gratefully and kept sneezing.

A few turns later, she was wheezing along with the sneezing, sniffing and coughing.

"Are you ill?" Jake was becoming seriously concerned. She had been fine just a few minutes ago, and now it was as if she could no longer breathe. She furiously turned her handbag upside down on her lap, but didn't seem to find what she was looking for.

"What do you need? Pills? Water?"

The wheezing noise got higher and she grabbed desperately at his arm.

"Doctor…" she croaked. "My…asthma…"

"Okay…" Jake slowed down the car and tried to think. They were still on familiar streets, close to the exit he took normally on his way to work. There was a hospital near the airport. He quickly turned the car around and a few minutes later they were at the emergency room. In her state, Roxanne was quickly admitted.

Jake spent the next hour reading old magazines. The choices being mainly gardening and women magazines, he learned how to fight crabgrass in an ecologically sound way, and 101 things to drive a man wild in bed.

"Oh, my."

Jake glanced to his side. The old woman sitting next to him, swaddled in shawls and a thick knitted sweater despite the warm weather, was staring at his magazine.

"Excuse me?"

She nodded at the page. "Number seventy-eight. I wouldn't have minded knowing that half a century ago, I tell you. It would have come in handy on several occasions."

Jake glanced at number seventy-eight and chuckled. "If that was the first thing you missed, I'd say you've done pretty good so far." He grinned back at the wrinkled face and winked. The wink was promptly returned.

"How far before you missed a thing, young man?"

Jake shook his head slightly. It was possible, after all, to get into bizarre situations without Sarah in the immediate vicinity. He read the list again. "Um. Number three, I'm afraid," he confessed. The old woman tsked, then reached out and grabbed the magazine from him. She looked furtively around before ripping the two pages out and handing them to him. "Take this. You should give it to your redhead. She needs to learn how to please her man."

Jake laughed. "I appreciate the sentiment, but she's not *my* redhead."

"I see." The old lady nodded sagely. "Isn't there another woman in your life then, who could use this important information?"

Jake held the pages out and stared at the neatly formatted list. "I do know a woman who would appreciate such precise directions in a bulleted list, yes."

A gnarled finger pointed at number ninety-three. "Do you think she'd do that?"

He studied the explicit instructions. "Is that even physically possible?"

"Oh, yes it is. It most certainly is. At least it was, back in 1940." She cackled. "I admit, young people's stamina isn't what it used to be."

Chuckling, Jake folded the pages and smiled at the self-satisfied grin on the old woman's thin lips. He held out his hand. "Jake Benford. Pleased to meet you."

A surprisingly strong hand gripped his. "Amelia Taylor."

"What brings you here, Mrs. Taylor? You look the picture of health to me."

"Oh, yes, I'm fine. As fine as you can be at eighty-eight. And call me Amelia." She moved closer to Jake. "It allows my halfway senile mind to imagine you are a young beau courting me."

Jake smiled. "Amelia. Are you waiting for someone, then?"

Amelia shook her head and leaned toward him to whisper furtively, "No. I just come here for the company."

"Really?"

"I live in the retirement home across the street." She snorted. "They call it a retirement home, but judging from the action over there, most of my fellow geriatrics seem to be under the impression that it's a graveyard." She gave a big sigh. "That may indeed be the next stop, but I see no reason to start packing. Eternity will be long enough to be dead." She tapped on his knee with her knuckle. "But enough about me. I'm practically history already. Tell me about the young lady who likes lists. Have the two of you done anything from that one?"

"Well..." Jake glanced over the list again. "To tell you the truth, we've pretty much covered twenty-three through twenty-eight, but we had our clothes on at the time."

"That sounds frustrating."

"You have no idea," Jake stated grimly.

"Is that why you're out with not-your redhead?"

He shrugged reluctantly. "I guess so." On an impulse he reached into his pocket and pulled the condoms out. "Sarah, that's the one with the lists, she even slipped these into my pocket before I left. She wants to make sure I have safe sex."

"Ohh..." Amelia stared into his palm, fascinated by what she saw. "You know, I've never seen one of those up close. Do you mind... Could I just take a look?''

Jake stared at her face for a moment, then handed her one and stuffed the other one back in his pocket. ''Be my guest. I hope you'll make good use of it.''

Amelia cackled. ''Oh, I will. The nurses will have a fit finding this in my purse. They go through it regularly, you know.'' She snorted. ''I don't know what they imagine they'll find. And speaking of those devils, they will be frantic if I'm not in time for my sleeping pill.'' She stood up carefully and Jake followed, supporting her frail weight on his arm. ''It was very nice meeting you, Jake,'' she said, grinning up at him. ''I wish you luck with your list-lady.'' She grabbed a cane from beside her seat and hobbled slowly past him and out the door.

Intrigued, Jake looked out the window as she laboriously made her way across the street and into a tall gray building. He returned to his seat still smiling at the spirit of the old woman. He chuckled to himself and carefully placed the ripped-out pages in his jacket pocket. If Amelia wanted Sarah to have that list, Sarah would have that list.

All in all, this hadn't been a bad evening, he thought cynically, then chastised himself for his cold thoughts. Roxy was sick, and all he could think about was how glad he was to get out of their date and how much he'd enjoyed spending the evening talking about sex with a senior citizen.

Roxy finally emerged all makeup gone. She was pale. Jake stood up and walked toward her, but she held up an arm to keep him at a distance. "You don't have a cat, do you?" she asked carefully, her voice nasal.

"A cat? No." His heart sank as he remembered. "Uh, but my neighbor has one. And I petted it just before I picked you up." His hand in his hair, he stared at her. "My God, was that an allergic reaction to the cat hair?"

Her lips tight, Roxy nodded and headed for the entrance. Keeping a prudent distance, Jake followed, trying not to think about the cat hair–infested handkerchief he'd given her when she first started to sneeze. "I'm sorry. I'd heard about your allergy, but I didn't imagine it was that bad. And it didn't cross my mind when I held Dead-or-Alive."

"Dead-or-Alive?"

"The cat's name. You see, it's named after the cat in the famous Schrödinger paradox. Put a cat in a box with a vial of poison and a Geiger counter with a radioactive atom. If the Geiger counter is rigged to break the vial of poison when the atom decays, and there is in a certain space of time an equal chance of it decaying or not, you can't know until you open it whether the cat is dead or alive."

Roxy didn't look impressed.

"Um, anyway, so in fact, the cat is either dead or alive, or it's actually dead and alive at the same time."

"I sincerely hope it is closer to dead," Roxy hissed, and headed for the cab queue. "See you around, Jake."

Jake stood for a while, hands in his pants pockets, and stared after her cab. Ouch. That had been a disaster. And it probably hadn't been in the best of taste to educate Roxy about quantum mechanics at that precise moment. Then he shrugged and headed back to his car. In the morning he'd send her some flowers, as a gesture of apology. He grimaced as another thought occurred to him. He wouldn't send any flowers. With his luck Roxy would be allergic to them as well.

He slid behind the wheel of his car and brushed at the front of his shirt, still finding the occasional cat hair. The pale display of the dashboard clock told him it was only half past eight. He started the vehicle. Well, since both he and the car were contaminated he might as well go to Sarah's house and get that obnoxious creature to the vet.

Her cat, too.

SARAH PACED THE FLOOR. Since coming home she had gone online and searched the medical databases for information about cat allergies. What she discovered frightened her, and now she was becoming more and more concerned. It really had been an irresponsible thing to do. The worst-case scenario was death. Of course, statistically it was extremely unlikely, but just in case that parallel universe thing was real, she didn't want to be a murderer in any of them.

Her fingers tangled in her hair as she fisted her hands near her temples and tried to concentrate.

What could she do? Jake hadn't mentioned where they would be going, so she had no way of tracking them down and no idea which hospital was nearest to them. Should she call the emergency rooms and see if anyone had been brought in, suffering acute allergic reaction to *felis catus?*

Downstairs, the doorbell rang, but she ignored it, knowing her mother would get it. A few moments later, there was a knock on her door, then it was opened.

Jake.

Searching his face for the bad news, she walked hesitantly toward him.

"Jake? Is everything okay?"

"Yeah." He rubbed at his chin and smiled weakly. "Your cat gave my date a severe allergic attack, but she'll be okay."

"I'm so sorry."

"It's not your fault, Sarah. You couldn't have known."

"Well…" She hesitated. As much as she longed to confess, it would cause more trouble than good. And she would get Lisa in trouble as well. "Is she mad at you?"

Jake flung himself down on her bed before remembering their fragile new status, but stayed put anyway. He'd frequently been in Sarah's bed over the years. That silly incident couldn't be allowed to ruin their easy friendship.

"I don't know. She didn't seem too pleased, but

then again she wasn't exactly feeling well. She might forgive me tomorrow.''

Sarah sat down at her desk, another sign of their new phase, he thought regretfully. Before, she would have sat on the bed opposite him, feet crossed as they earnestly discussed everything from fuel consumption for fighter jets to the latest movies.

''She might be conditioned not to like you now. You know, connecting you with being allergic.''

Jake grinned. ''Well, actually I wouldn't mind too much if she ended up allergic to me. I didn't really want to go on that date anyway.''

''She's not your type?''

''No.''

Sarah chewed her lip.

''What is your type, Jake?''

He grabbed her stuffed moose and set it on his stomach. ''That seems to be the question of the week. Why do you want to know?''

''Just wondering.''

Rubbing the moose's horns together, Jake turned his head sideways on her pillow and sent her a smile that turned her insides to butter. ''I think you've ruined me for every other woman. I'm always kinda disappointed when on the first date they don't give me a lecture on the human genome.''

He looked so good in her bed, Sarah thought wistfully. His tie was loosened and his hair was all mussed. Her fingers were just itching to tangle themselves in there. She supposed she should be taking advantage of those hormonal surges, taking notes and introspecting, but she just felt like looking at Jake. Touching would be even nicer, but he'd probably jump out the window if she did. "It's sweet of you to say that, Jake."

"Sweet, that's me." He grinned at her, still playing with the moose's ears. A furry thing walked haughtily into the room, pushing the half-closed door open, and reminded him why he was here in the first place. "I just came by to see if you still wanted to take the cat to the emergency vet."

"No. No, I think she's fine."

"You're sure?"

Squirming inside, she nodded, cursing Lisa and her crazy schemes. She was no good at lying, and even if she could get away with lying to everyone else, Jake was the one person who knew her inside and out. Desperate to change the subject, she cast around in her mind for something to say, but Jake beat her to it.

"I know why you came to my house before."

Her heart nearly stopped, then began to beat again in relief at being found out. It was better that he knew. "You do?"

"Yeah." Jake suddenly went still. "Wait a minute—the cat was just an excuse, wasn't it? There really isn't anything wrong with it?"

"Her," Sarah corrected. "No. I'm sorry, Jake, I—"

"You went to all this trouble just to make sure I had safe sex?"

Sarah squirmed, but Jake took it as a gesture of embarrassment, not guilt.

"I don't know if I should be grateful or furious with you, Sarah. I can and do take care of myself."

"I'm sorry," Sarah muttered.

He fished the condom out of his pocket and tossed it her way. Her hand shot up and caught it midair.

"Just one?"

Jake nodded. "Yep."

She stared at the packet then back at him, a question written across her face. He rolled his eyes, but decided to put her out of her misery. "No, you idiot, we didn't have a quickie in the car before she succumbed to her allergies. I gave the other one to an old woman at the emergency room. She wanted to shock her nurses." He reached into his pants pocket and pulled out the folded pages from the magazine. "She wanted you to have this."

Sarah peered at the page he was holding up. "Roxanne wanted me to have this? Why?"

"Not Roxanne. The old lady. I told her you liked lists." Jake folded the pages into a paper airplane and threw it toward Sarah. It swerved to the right, but Sarah just managed to catch it before it flew out the opened window.

"She recommends number ninety-three, by the way."

Sarah unfolded the airplane and took one look at number ninety-three. Jake shook his head at the speculative look on her face. "Forget it. Just forget it." He quickly switched to a more pressing matter.

"Why do you have condoms around? Are you having sex with someone?" He managed to stop himself from adding the word "else."

"No. Not yet."

Filing the "not yet" away for later scrutiny, Jake continued his questioning. "Why do you have them, then?"

She shrugged defensively. "Well, you never know. Better safe than sorry."

"You didn't..." He narrowed his eyes to stare at her. "You bought them after your little experiment last weekend, didn't you?" He sat up on her bed, looking adorable with that furious look on his face while still clutching her moose to his chest. "Jeez, Sarah, you're not even considering going that far, are you? With me?" He looked horrified.

"Of course I'm not!" Sarah denied vehemently. "But I am a scientist and I wanted to be prepared for every conceivable contingency." The box had been a "present" from Lisa and had been accompanied by a lecherous wink, but Sarah suspected that information would do nothing to calm Jake's nerves.

"Every conceivable contingency..." Both hands raked through his hair and the moose fell forgotten to the side. "Sarah, you're crazy. Absolutely bonkers. You don't want to have sex with me."

Weird as this conversation felt to her, Sarah had to bite her lip to hide a grin at the abject terror painted over his face. "Why not?"

"You just..." He gestured madly. "You just don't."

"I would like to try it sooner or later. You'd be the perfect man to show me."

"You...me...sex..."

"You're stuttering, Jake."

"I know I'm stuttering!" he exploded. "That's what happens when you bring up you, me and sex. It's absurd. Just absurd!"

"Oh. The way you responded to me last week, I thought perhaps it wouldn't be so repugnant to you."

"It's not repugnant to me." Jake cursed a blue streak, his hands curled into fists at his sides. "Sarah, you know I hate when you put words in my mouth."

"So you could imagine sleeping with me?"

Could he ever. He had spent four journeys over the Atlantic doing just that. He closed his eyes and tried with pure willpower to slow the frantic beating of his heart. This was Sarah. He was used to her eccentricities, and he was used to talking her out of things. He'd just have to calm down, and explain to her that best friends didn't jump into bed together just for the heck of it. He'd have to ignore his over-active imagination, and explain to her that best friends just didn't have lover status in each other's minds.

Or did they? His eyes snapped open.

"What about you, Sarah?" She looked puzzled, so he elaborated. "Have you really been thinking about that, or is this just another one of your ideas?"

She blushed. Her whole face turned utterly red

and she looked away. Jake felt as if someone had slammed a fist into his stomach.

"Well," she said, slowly and carefully. "I have been studying the biology and psychology of sex, and if you must know, during my reflections I have frequently relied upon you as the hypothetical partner."

Translation: She had been fantasizing about him. Feeling suddenly weak, Jake nevertheless found the energy to stumble out of her bed. That was one place he should not be right now.

She was grinning. Jake stared at her, still clinging to the bedpost to prevent himself from sliding into a heap on the floor. "What's so funny?"

"You're so cute when you're panicking, Jake. Absolutely adorable. I have this weird urge to just pick you up and cuddle you and tell you everything will be just fine."

"Were you…" He stared at her. "Were you just putting me on? No. You don't even know how to do that."

"I'm learning," Sarah replied wickedly.

Jake was still staring at her, his expression now suspicious. "Just how much of all this was a joke?"

Sarah had opened her mouth to confess just how little of it was a joke when there was a brisk knock on the door.

"Your mom let me in, Sarah. How did it go— Oh, hi, Jake."

"Lisa," he acknowledged.

Lisa looked between them. Sarah just knew that

she was debating whether to leave things to progress at their own pace or to give them an ever so slight push in the right direction.

"I thought you were going out with Roxy tonight, Jake."

"I was. It was cut short." He saluted them both. "I'll see you ladies later."

Sarah jumped up and followed him downstairs to the door. "Thanks a lot for worrying about Dead-or-Alive, Jake. I really appreciate it. And I'm sorry about Roxy and the allergy and the condoms and everything..." She let her words trail off.

Jake smiled and tucked a stray curl behind her ear. His fingers lingered at her jaw. "It was very sweet of you to worry about me, Sarah, but I can take care of myself. Save your condoms for..." His brows drew together and his eyes clouded up with confusion again. "Just save them," he whispered and exited without a backward glance.

Wistfully, Sarah watched him vanish before she ran back upstairs. "I feel really bad about this," she burst out upon entering her room. She began pacing the floor, a small frown marring her brow. "I think I should confess."

"You will do no such thing!" Lisa ordered, busily retouching her makeup while balancing a tiny mirror on her knee. "Things are going just fine."

"Just fine?! I could have killed Jake's date!"

"Nonsense," Lisa said breezily, applying a heavy coat of mascara. "Roxy will be fine. She probably used the opportunity and snared a date with a doctor or two." She grinned at Sarah. "Now, Dr. Sarah, let's plan stage two of Jake's seduction."

"I'm not sure I want to," Sarah sighed. "Jake seemed really upset after my experiment. I don't think he'll be very open to further attempts."

Lisa pointed at her with a tube of bloodred lipstick. "You don't realize what a strong hold you have on Jake. If you play your cards right, you can get that man to do anything you like." She snapped her mirror shut and tossed it into her purse, along with the small makeup kit. "You've got it made, Sarah. Now you just have to figure out what it is you want from him."

Sarah's palms felt damp. She rubbed them on her jeans, then curled her fingers into the back pockets.

"Don't move!" Automatically, Sarah obeyed. "You probably didn't notice, but this pose, Sarah, has Jake all in knots. He can't even figure out where to put his eyes when you stand like that."

"What?"

Lisa pointed to her chest. "He wants to look there, but doesn't allow himself to because he's such a gentleman. And, of course, because you two have convinced yourselves that you only have a platonic, brother-and-sister friendship. Use that pose. It will completely mess up his ability to think straight. We want him befuddled."

Sarah glanced down at the small mounds of her breasts under the cotton T-shirt and blinked at the very thought of them having the power to befuddle

Jake. Before she could formulate a question, Lisa continued.

"Okay, when you got him into bed, that was because you were researching a book you're planning to write?"

Sarah nodded. "Yes. It's about the difference in sexual behavior in humans and other animals." She shrugged. "I was wondering about the positions people use for sex. I felt I needed to try them out, just superficially."

"Good. Do you feel your personal research for that book is complete?"

"Of course not. I haven't tried much of anything myself. But I won't do that to Jake again. I'll just have to do without it."

Lisa shook her head. "No, you don't. You're going to research kissing next."

"Kissing?"

Lisa rolled her eyes. "You know, that thing people do with their mouths touching and you're wondering where on earth they put their noses."

"I know what kissing is," Sarah quipped.

"Well?" Lisa leaned forward. "Humans are the only animals that kiss, aren't they? There would be a big chapter on kissing in your book."

"Yes, there will be, but actually, some primates—"

Lisa didn't let her finish. "You didn't kiss Jake that day, did you?"

"Of course not!"

"Good. That's your assignment for tomorrow."

"Kissing Jake?"

Lisa gave her a dry look. "Does the idea seem so repulsive to you?"

"No," Sarah admitted. "It sounds most intrigu-ing, in fact," she added, blushing slightly.

Lisa grinned. "Yeah, that's one kissable guy, eh? So what you do next, is go over there and ask him to help you research those kisses."

"I can't do that!"

"You've already had him in several interesting positions, why shouldn't you ask him to allow you to kiss him?" She rolled her eyes. "It's innocent enough, Sarah. It's not like you're asking him to cut out any vital organs and donate them to science."

Sarah pulled on a lock of hair. Using Jake was appealing both personally and professionally, but she still wasn't sure how she felt about the whole thing. "It's…unethical, isn't it?" she asked uncertainly.

"Unethical? Not if you ask him and he knows what he's getting into. And you still need to do that research, don't you? How are you going to write that chapter on kissing if you've never kissed a man?"

"You have a point," Sarah conceded. "But I can't use Jake like that."

"You're not using him! You're doing research, just like before. It's no big deal. He's just doing you a favor as a friend."

Sarah felt quite out of her depth. "Do you really think it'll be okay? That he'd do that for me?"

"Of course he will. Absolutely."

4

"No! ABSOLUTELY NOT!"

Sarah's eyes were the color of a winter sky as she gazed at him from the other side of the table. Two seconds ago they had been sitting side by side at the rickety table in his backyard, sharing a packet of cookies and a large pitcher of cold milk, a ritual from their childhood. He had been relaxed, secure in this familiar habit. And Sarah had almost become his little buddy again, as they'd lazily discussed Dead-or-Alive and the new homes she needed to find for the kittens.

Then she had ambushed him again with those crazy ideas of hers, making him jump out of his skin and seek refuge on the other side of the chipped wooden table. He felt only moderately safer standing there with that barrier between them. The things she did to him with her eyes should be illegal. And she wasn't even trying.

He felt out of breath.

"I thought you were over this nonsense, Sarah."

"Nonsense?"

The gray eyes were still wide open and Jake shuddered at the thought that he might be bringing tears to them.

"I'm not talking about your book! I'm referring to this idea about using me to practice on."

"Can you think of someone else?"

"No!"

The idea of Sarah practicing anything with someone else was almost as disturbing as the idea of her practicing on him. He softened his voice. "Not that any man wouldn't be delighted to kiss you, Sarah, but it's not something that should be done for research or practice. It's done only if you mean it."

Sarah looked confused. "I don't understand, Jake. You tried all those positions with me. Compared to that, this should be a piece of cake. It's just kissing."

Jake raked a hand through his hair in increased agitation. "Forget it, Sarah. You are not practicing kissing on me. No way. Use your...hand or whatever teenage girls practice on."

"I'm not a teenage girl, Jake."

God, did he ever know that.

He sat down, and tried to calm himself. Words. They were the key. He needed to find the right words to explain this to her, and she'd realize what a ridiculous idea this was. "Listen to me, Sarah. Kissing is...intimate. It's not something that should be practiced. It's something that should happen between two people when the time is right and there is chemistry between them."

Hardly believing the fatherly lecture he'd just

given, he watched disappointment eclipse her eyes, but steeled himself against it. He couldn't agree to her absurd scheme. It would jeopardize their friendship, one of the most important things in both their lives.

"Okay," Sarah said at last, swiping the last cookie and standing up. "Thanks anyway, Jake, for considering it. I appreciate it."

She walked away, head down and hands fisted deep in the pockets of her jeans—a sure sign of her being deep in thought. As she disappeared behind the fence, he felt a wave of uncertainty, which then escalated into full-blown panic. What now? Would she go to someone else?

"Aw, hell." He ran after her through the ankle-high grass, and jumped the fence with ease. "Sarah!"

She was nowhere to be seen, but her mother leaned out the kitchen window. "She's out front, Jake. I saw her just pass."

He thanked Ellen, then ran after Sarah, catching her just as she was mounting her bike.

"Wait, Sarah! Where are you going?"

"To the lab," she answered, staring at him. "Thought I'd get some work done."

To the lab. Experiments and research had suddenly taken on an ominous meaning in Jake's mind. Just what was she going to do in that lab?

"What will you be doing?"

She shrugged. "Nothing much. Just some regular

lab work to save me some time next week. I'll get some experiments running.''

He bet. Get some experiments running. Probably some bozo's hormones as well. She'd be taking notes and concocting theories, and in her innocence turn some guy on, just as she had him. Only difference was, this one might not understand her innocent intentions. She could get hurt. He'd be damned if he'd let that happen.

He walked closer and grabbed the handlebars, keeping her bike steady. She put her feet on the pedals, trusting him to keep her upright. Their moves were easy, almost instinctive, born of old habits.

''Will there be other people at the lab?'' A male, he meant. Any male with lips that she could use for her fiendish purposes. If so, he was going to make sure she didn't go anywhere close to campus over the weekend.

Her narrow shoulders lifted in a shrug, and she thrust her hands in the back pockets of her jeans, and leaned back, for a moment drawing his attention to her breasts. He snatched his gaze back up and couldn't quite believe it when he felt himself blush.

''I don't know if anybody will be there. Probably a few. People come and go on weekends. Depends on what they are working on.''

He bet her co-workers would be willing to put in quite a bit of overtime for Sarah's special project. A tide of protective anger washed over him. They would not take advantage of her innocence. She had always been his protégée; he would continue to watch over her. He would protect her if it killed him, no matter if he lost both his dignity and his sanity in the process.

"I've changed my mind," he said quickly, before he could regret it. "I'll…mentor you. Today."

She didn't smile and his heart slammed painfully against his ribs while he waited, his hands clenched around the handlebars of her bike. Had she changed her mind, too? Did she prefer someone not so close to her? Had she finally understood his reluctance and agreed with his reasoning? He wondered uneasily if she would allow him to chaperon instead, if she insisted on finding another guinea pig. He'd find some way to "accidentally" incapacitate the bastard before anything happened.

"Thank you, Jake," she said solemnly, dismounting and chaining her bike back to the tree. He breathed out, not sure if the sound he made was a sigh of relief or a whimper of terror.

Sarah rubbed her hands together as if she didn't quite know what to do with them, then put them back in her pockets, forcing him again to purposefully avoid looking below her chin. "I really appreciate it. When should we do it? Now? Or tonight?"

Tonight was out. A cozy cover of darkness was definitely out. So was a bedroom, a sofa, a couch and the grass in the backyard—in fact any place where a horizontal position was possible, and quite a few places where her books could have them in several other positions.

In fact, he couldn't think of a single safe place or time.

He wondered how she'd feel about kissing a man handcuffed to a cold shower.

"Well, not here," he muttered. He folded his arms on his chest, feeling absolutely foolish. This was what came of befriending geniuses. They messed with lesser minds such as his until nothing but a puddle of weird sensations was left between his ears.

She grabbed his hand, sending lightning bolts through his body with that simple touch. "Let's go to your house. Then Mom won't interrupt us."

Feeling all of fifteen years old, palms sweating and heart pounding, Jake allowed himself to be led through her backyard, where her mother waved cheerfully at them through the window. They went over the fence and into his house. Once inside, Sarah dropped his hand. She looked nervous. Well, she bloody well should look nervous, Jake thought indignantly. She was messing with his heart, his brain and his body, and the least she could do was be a bit nervous.

He finally realized the meaning of "butterflies in the stomach."

"Oh, God, Sarah, we need to talk."

He grabbed her hand again and led her into the kitchen, chastely placing them on opposite sides of the kitchen table. He took a deep breath, as if oxygen could be his salvation.

"Sarah, this scares me." If all else fails, try honesty. That did get her attention. "You're my best friend. I've known you all your life. I don't want this to ruin our friendship."

"Why would it have to ruin it?"

How could he explain it to her? Jake stared at his hands, lying there on the kitchen table. Treacherous things, they were all but trembling in anticipation, wanting to get at that soft skin, stroke up her arms and up her neck, entwine in her hair. And his lips! He didn't even want to think about what his disloyal lips wanted to do. And he was absolutely *not* going to think about what any other parts of him were up to.

"You see, Jake, I've read all about it. I know the techniques and all that." She patted his hand in a way that was probably supposed to comfort. All it did though, was push his blood pressure slightly higher. "I just need a mouth to practice on."

A mouth to practice on.

Jake wanted to cry. Just put his head down on the kitchen table and howl until men in white coats came and took him away in a straightjacket. Slowly his head tilted forward until his forehead was resting against the tabletop. Yes, that was it. That was just what he needed. A nice, quiet room in an asylum, far from inquisitive geniuses who wanted to use him as a mouth to practice on. He could learn to play chess, solve crossword puzzles with a crayon and practice whistling Beethoven's Fifth Symphony from beginning to end. It would be a good life.

"Jake?"

Once, twice, he beat his head against the table, then sat up straight and resigned himself to what he had to do. Steeling himself, he looked at her lips. They were pale pink, not full, but not thin either. Just right, in fact. She never wore lipstick, or any other makeup for that matter. He liked that. No messy stuff.

Okay. He could do this. Almost all his life he'd been doing weird things for Sarah. What was a kiss or two? He'd just be cold and clinical about this. If he could be just a mouth, she could be just a mouth. Nothing more.

"Jake?"

Of course, it would have helped if he'd thought to postpone this, and paid a hasty visit to the dentist. He should have thought of that. This would be a piece of cake with his mouth, hell, his whole face anaesthetized. Perhaps he could even have had a few other spots knocked out of commission while he was at it.

"*Jake!*"

Startled, he moved back, his chair scraping on the tiles. "What?"

"You seem extremely apprehensive about this."

He laughed. Or maybe he cried. It was difficult to tell these days. Then he stood and held out his hand. "Okay, Sarah. Come here. Let's get it over with."

That was more like it. Decisive. Controlled. Nonchalant. And it actually worked. She did as he said and came to stand in front of him, without so much as a single argument.

"Standing up?"

Darn. It had been too good to be true. There came two argumentative words.

"What's wrong with standing up?"

"Don't people usually kiss sitting down or lying down?"

She'd like that, wouldn't she? "No. I have it on good authority that in fact 53 percent of all kisses are performed with at least one partner in an upright position."

"That can't be an accurate..." She broke off. "Oh. You're joking."

Jake's heart melted at the familiar sight of her sheepish smile as she belatedly got his joke. He couldn't help grinning back at her. "My brilliant humor never fails to dazzle you."

She laughed softly. "I like your jokes, Jake. I really do. It just takes me a while to get them."

"Let's just get to this kissing thing, Sarah. What do you want me to do?"

Even though she was no longer a kid, she was still so tiny. The top of her head only reached his shoulders and she had to lean her head back to look up into his face.

"Can I just experiment first? You only need to stand there."

Jake only stood there, still as a statue. He tilted his head slightly forward so she could reach him more easily. In his mind, he calculated the distance from Portland to London in kilometers, while Sarah's lips moved slowly, softly over his. Her hands rested lightly on his shoulders, but they nevertheless sent waves of tingling heat coursing through him.

There was something to be said for technique learned from books, he acknowledged in surprise. She was not as clumsy as he had expected and the soft innocence of her kisses moved him, even through the concentrated conversion of miles to kilometers. He held his breath; her scent messed with his ability to do arithmetic.

"You're very tense, Jake. Are you sure you're okay with this?" She moved a few inches away from him.

Jake used the opportunity to gulp down a fresh supply of oxygen. Okay. Straight talk. Make sure she knows what she's up against.

"You do know that this might turn me on, Sarah. That's what kissing does to people. Hell, I guess that's why they do it in the first place."

She nodded. Her cheeks were slightly flushed. Was this farce finally beginning to embarrass her? God, he hoped it did before he made a total fool out of himself.

"Sarah… You can't just ask any man to do something like this with you and not expect them to react. They will react. And they might think you're a tease if you don't follow through on what they believe you have promised."

"Oh. Do you?"

He stepped back, and shoved both hands through his hair. "No, Sarah. I know you. I know your crazy little mind and your weird ideas and your absolute determination to find things out firsthand. But you can't do something like this to anyone else. Not unless you mean it. Do you understand?"

"Yes. Can we continue now?"

Continue. Right. She must have barely scraped the surface of all the techniques she wanted to try. And here he was, all afire after only a few simple touches with their mouths. Bitterly, he wondered which one of them was the greenhorn here.

"Yes. But you have to understand, Sarah, I may be your friend, but I'm also a man. I can control my actions, but I can't control the way my body responds—"

Sarah's answer was to pull him out into the hallway toward the stairs. She stepped on the first one, bringing her closer to his level.

"This way I don't get a crick in my neck," she explained. He didn't even have time to nod before her arms were wrapped confidently around his neck and she was leaning into him. Shocked at the overwhelming feelings full body contact roused, Jake grabbed her waist and held her away, but when she tightened her grasp on his neck he gave up and allowed their bodies to touch. She'd felt his arousal before and it hadn't shocked her. In fact, he thought grimly, knowing her, she just might be using it as an indicator of her success.

He didn't close his eyes this time. The images that

played behind his lids were even more dangerous than having Sarah's face so close to his.

And besides, he had completely forgotten the formula for converting miles into kilometers.

A tiny frown of concentration formed a straight line between her closed eyes. Her mouth continued to play over his and now she began to nibble at his lips. When her tongue snaked out to lick at the corner of his mouth, he snapped his head back at the sudden rush of overwhelming arousal.

Her eyes opened, and that sharp intelligence almost bit at him. "Do you find it difficult to breathe during French-kissing?"

His vocal cords were paralyzed. He couldn't answer, and she shrugged after seeing his frozen stare. "Well, we'll find out." Her hands warmed his cheeks, and then her mouth was assaulting his, sparking off a cascade of feelings that escalated into a fire that zipped through his every nerve. She was hesitant, yet curiously explored his mouth, and by reciting the alphabet backward Jake was able to keep his participation passive. That was until she ran her tongue against his in a long smooth stroke.

He lost control.

He entwined his arms around her, and pulled her roughly against him. One hand was entangled in her hair, tilting her head as he plundered her mouth. *Sarah, Sarah, Sarah.* His heart pounded her name into every part of his body and the mating of their mouths was not nearly enough.

Only when her hand grabbed at his chin, pushing him away softly, but urgently, did he manage to draw back.

She was smiling. His regret only half-formed, the apology died on his lips as she laughed. "I'm sorry, Jake, I'm such a novice yet. I couldn't breathe anymore."

Neither could he. His breath came in rapid rasps and his body was still on fire. Would anyone blame him if he picked her up and carried her to his bed and kept her there until hell froze over?

He would, he acknowledged with a tortured groan.

Hadn't that incredible kiss affected her at all? He looked at her, and took in the high color of her cheeks, her heavy breathing—although that could be attributed to a lack of oxygen—and the furious pulse beating in her throat.

He put his finger against the fluttering at the base of her throat and counted her rapid heartbeats while he calmed himself enough to speak. Then he looked into her dark eyes, serious, determined.

"Do you know now what it feels like to be turned on, Sarah?"

"Yes," she whispered, a dazed smile in her eyes. "I feel it in so many different places. In fact, it tingles all over. It's wonderful."

He took a deep breath. "Do you understand now why this isn't a good idea between friends?"

She nodded. "I think I know what you mean. I

will never be able to look at you the same again, knowing you can make me feel this way.''

''Yeah…'' His voice trailed off as he was torn between regret and a strange sense of pleasure.

''But it's not always like this, is it?''

He shook his head.

''The chemistry has to be right.''

''Yes.''

''So we have chemistry, then.''

''That we do,'' he muttered.

''Jake?''

''Yes, Sarah?''

''Can we kiss some more?''

Jake shook his head slowly. He had to stop this insanity now. They'd already crossed an invisible line, but perhaps things could still be salvaged. ''I don't think that's a good idea if we're going to save our friendship.''

Her disappointment was almost his undoing, but he resisted the temptation to kiss the frown away. She had learned her lesson. It had come at a cost for them both, but she had learned it.

As she opened the front door, he stopped her with one hand on her arm.

''Sarah.''

''Yes?'' Her eyes held hope. As if she was wishing for him to pick her up and carry her back inside. He bit back his impulses and forced the words out.

''Don't…don't try to find a mouth to practice on. Either find someone you care about, or don't find anyone at all.''

She smiled, sending a bittersweet arrow of renewed desire to the center of his heart.

"Thanks, Jake."

"NOW, DON'T WE LOOK red-faced and well-kissed," Lisa cackled, and squinted up at her. She was lying in the middle of the lawn, all tanned arms and legs, bisected by a white T-shirt and white shorts.

"Lisa?" Disoriented, Sarah rubbed at her mouth with the palm of her hand, certain that Jake's kiss must be printed there for all to see. "What are you doing here?"

"It's a lovely day. I came to see if you'd want to go to the park for a picnic or something. I was just in time to see Jake digging his heels in as you dragged him away. So, I figured sticking around might be rewarding." She grinned. "Looks promising so far. Nice color in your cheeks. Have you done your research?"

Sarah shrugged. "Sort of, yes."

"Goody!" Lisa sat up and hugged her knees to her chest. "Tell all. Did the earth move?"

Sarah rubbed at her red cheeks. "As visible by the reaction of the small blood vessels in my face, my adrenaline levels did rise significantly."

Lisa squealed and rubbed her hands together. "Translation from Sarahese—the earth moved. What about Jake? Did the earth move for him?"

"His pulse shot up incredibly high. His temperature seemed to increase also and his breathing patterns were interrupted. This activity must be quite dangerous if your blood pressure is too high. The whole autonomic nervous system goes haywire."

Lisa chuckled. "Music to my ears. Did he say anything?"

"He told me to find someone I care about to practice on."

Lisa frowned. "How blind can that man be? That's exactly what you're doing."

Sarah knelt down next to her friend and absently picked at the grass.

"Well, we won't be doing it anymore."

"What?"

"We won't. He says he doesn't want to risk our friendship, and I agree."

Lisa glowered. "Well, both of you will be risking *my* friendship if you don't come to your senses. The two of you belong together. You adore one another, he's about the only person who can follow your train of thoughts, and you strike sparks off each other. What more do you want?"

"Friendship."

"Being lovers doesn't exclude being friends. Okay. We'll call it quits on the lessons and go to plan B." Lisa beamed at her.

"What's plan B?" Sarah asked hesitantly, sinking down on the grass by a tree. She wrapped her arms around her knees. "I don't even remember having a plan A. In fact, I think this is all becoming a big mess. Jake doesn't even kiss me on the forehead anymore." She rested her head on her knees. "I miss that."

"Don't worry." She reached over and patted

Sarah's shoulder. "We'll soon have him kissing you in some much more interesting places."

Sarah blushed fiercely, and Lisa chuckled at her. "That's right, Dr. Sarah, keep your mind in the gutter," she grinned.

"I don't know, Lisa. He was so serious when he told me how this could ruin our friendship." She tore at a blade of grass. "I think I do love him, Lisa."

Her friend was uncharacteristically silent and Sarah looked up at her. "I'm in love with Jake. That's…" She searched for words, but couldn't find the right one to express how she felt. "I don't know. I need to get over him."

"Get over him? Why? I think the two of you would make a great couple."

Sarah shook her head. "No. Besides, he's not in love with me. And as for me, it's just the hormones speaking. I shouldn't have started this whole mess in the first place. Jake was right all along. We have a special friendship. If I don't get over him soon, this will just ruin our friendship."

Lisa didn't look convinced. "And just how are you going to get over him?"

"Stay away from him for a while," Sarah replied promptly. "And read up on the biology and psychology of love. I told you—if I understand why I'm feeling like this I'll be able to get over it."

Lisa shook her head. "The worst thing you can do is stay away from him, Sarah. Absence makes the heart grow fonder, remember?" She looked over at Jake's house. "If you really want to get over him, the best thing to do is spend a lot of time around him."

"What?"

"It's true. Hang around Jake a lot, and you'll soon get over him."

Sarah pondered divorce statistics and the seven-year itch. "That does make sense, Lisa. Reality can whip those rose-tinted glasses right off. People can get saturated with each other's presence—that's what you mean, isn't it?"

Lisa was beaming. "Right." She rummaged in her purse for one of her ubiquitous miniature chocolate bars and bit half off. "And this is urgent. If you're going to stop this, and I don't really agree that you should, you need to stop it before you fall even deeper in love. Let's see. What reason can we give you for constantly going over there?"

As if sensing her imminent participation in the evolving plot, Dead-or-Alive ran across the grass between them, followed by two tiny black-and-white kittens trying to catch their mother's tail.

Lisa snapped her fingers, then pointed at the three felines. "The cats! Ask him to watch the cats for you for a while! Then you can be there all the time, feeding and playing with the cats while you get over Jake."

Sarah picked up one kitten and stroked the tiny head. "Doesn't really make sense, Lisa. Why would I ask him to take care of my cats?"

A mischievous smile emerged on Lisa's lips.

"How about if you've got a visitor who has an allergy?" She giggled. "I mean, by now Jake knows all too well how bad allergies can be."

Sarah played with the kitten on her lap, deftly avoiding the sharp claws. "I suppose I could do that," she mused. "Aunt Eleanor is coming for a visit, so it would only be half a lie anyway." She glanced out the window to Jake's house. "This can't be allowed to mess up our friendship. I need to get over him quickly."

Lisa smiled. "This way everything will work out for the best. It'll be perfect. I guarantee it."

5

FOUR DAYS LATER, Jake felt safe enough to drop by Sarah's house after he came home from his last flight. He was intent on reestablishing the close and uninhibited friendship they had shared before.

Sarah was in the garden, a concentrated frown on her face as she wrote on her laptop. She hadn't noticed his approach, and he paused by the gate, studying her. Seeing her brought on a familiar sensation in his chest, one that kept getting stronger and stronger. He hadn't quite identified it. It was a mixture of caring and possessiveness, an urge not only to protect her, but to make her happy, too.

The gate was closed, but not latched. He pushed it open and jogged over the grass toward her. He was in no hurry to label his emotions yet, but when she looked up and sent him a brilliant smile, then jumped up and hugged him, it suddenly seemed urgent to know what he was doing.

He pushed the feeling away, and hugged her back, trying to convince himself this was just a regular friendly hug, like the ones he had given her hundreds, hell, thousands of times before. He bent his head to kiss her on the forehead, but then pulled back. Better not risk anything. She looked up at him, and there was a look in her eyes that he recognized as disappointment. She had been expecting their regular kiss-on-the-forehead, and she should have gotten one.

He just didn't quite feel up to it yet.

He cursed under his breath when she stepped back and put her hands in her back pockets. He'd have to find a way to talk to her about this pose. It was impossible for him to keep his eyes under control and his thoughts out of the gutter when she did that.

"How was London?" she asked. He felt her gaze take in his clothes and he stood up a little straighter. He was over the stage of basking in the overabundance of appreciative looks women sent him when he was wearing his uniform, but Sarah had never seemed impressed before.

She seemed impressed now, and for some reason that thrilled him more than all the interested glances he had received from other women over the years.

"Rainy and cloudy," he replied, "I didn't really see all too much from my hotel window."

"Oh," she muttered. She was still looking him over, her eyes slowly moving over his body from top to toe. He almost felt like squirming, yet he felt absurdly happy at her obvious pleasure in what she saw.

"You're staring, Sarah," he teased her. He leaned against the apple tree and folded his arms on his chest.

"I'm sorry. I've just never noticed how great you look in that uniform."

Well. She was nothing if not straightforward.

"Thank you." He took a bow, not quite sure how to respond. He took refuge in humor. "A pilot's uniform is a known babe magnet."

Sarah grinned. "Does that make me a babe?"

Jake froze and just stared at her. Was she *flirting?* With *him?*

His emotions catapulted from shock to wrath in a split second and his frown was intimidating enough that she took a step back and stared warily at him. Who had taught her to flirt, anyway? He hadn't, that's for sure, and it better not be any other member of his sex. And she better not flirt with anyone else, either. They'd get the wrong idea.

Just like he was. Plenty of ideas filled his head, and although they felt deliciously right, they were *definitely* very wrong. He could never be Sarah's lover. Their friendship was first priority. They must both protect that.

"I was just joking, Jake." Sarah was frowning, and he realized he was scowling at her. "I know I'm no babe." Her voice was tinged with resignation.

He recovered. "It's not that, Sarah. I was just…thinking." He paused, then opened his mouth to elaborate, but she was no longer looking at him. She was smiling at someone behind him, and he turned around.

His first instinct was to punch the guy in the face,

but he managed to curb it. This was the very prototype of the kind of man he'd imagined Sarah collaborating with in her labs, right down to his glasses, briefcase and corduroys.

And to top it all off, the man had the audacity to have lips, too.

Jake frowned and hoped he looked threatening. He stepped between the man and Sarah, but with determination arranged his features in a bland smile when the man looked at him.

"William!" Sarah pushed Jake aside to accept a pile of papers from the Nerd with Lips. "Thanks for dropping that by. I missed them the minute I got home."

"I thought you might," William answered, then held out a hand to Jake. "William Rogers. I'm one of Sarah's lab rats."

Jake didn't even crack a smile at the man's joke. He knew all too well what Sarah put her lab rats through. Hadn't he been one himself? Sarah should put the two of them in a cage together and let them fight it out. He clenched his fists at his side and sized the other man up. Yeah, he could take him. Easily. He put his arm possessively over Sarah's shoulder. Something was burning deep in the pit of his stomach, and he firmly labeled it as protectiveness. This man would not be allowed to hurt Sarah.

William's gaze moved between them, and a faint smile hovered on his lips. He didn't seem at all uncomfortable. Jake removed his arm from Sarah's shoulders, and cursed himself. He was jumping to crazy conclusions, and what business did he have staking his claim on Sarah anyway? *Just friends, just friends, just friends,* he chanted wordlessly.

Sarah pinched his arm lightly, and he realized that William was still holding out his hand.

"Jake Benford." He shook the man's hand, disappointed when he failed to make William wince with his strong manly handshake.

"I guessed that from your uniform tag," William said, gesturing at his clothes. "Nice to meet you. Sarah's told me a lot about you."

"She has?" Jake looked suspiciously at William and then at Sarah. Just what had Sarah been telling William about him? Did they share research notes? Were the kisses he'd shared with Sarah described in a report somewhere in that guy's briefcase?

His paranoid musings, not to mention his plan to grab the briefcase and make a run for it, were interrupted by a new addition to the impromptu garden party.

"Bill! How good to see you again!" Lisa bounced over the fence, ponytail flying and slapped William on the back.

William's features took on a long-suffering look, and he pushed the too-long hair out of his eyes with an impatient gesture. "Miss Walters. It's William, please. Dr. Rogers, even. Or if you really can't pronounce either, 'hey you' will do fine." He pushed the glasses up on his nose and glared at Lisa. "Just don't call me Bill. Ever."

Sarah looked between the two. "Have you met?"

"We bumped into each other when I came to your lab the other day," Lisa explained, linking her arm through William's, who quickly disengaged himself and stepped away. Unperturbed, Lisa sent him a brilliant smile. "I got lost in that maze of corridors, and Bill here kindly showed me out."

"William. And how anyone can get lost inside a lab with only one door, I fail to understand. Even our most backward mice do better than that."

Lisa winked at him. "I can never resist a cute monkey. That failing has gotten me in trouble on numerous occasions."

William glared at her. "Because of your insistence on feeding at least five miniature Snickers to our chimp, he was hyperactive for two days and impossible to work with."

"I know a fellow suffering chocoholic when I see him," Lisa retorted. "The poor thing kept reaching toward my purse, whimpering. How could I be so cruel as to turn away?"

William opened his mouth, then closed it again and shook his head. He raised his hand in a farewell and strode away. Lisa stared after him speculatively, and when he was out of earshot she nudged Sarah with her elbow. "He's cute. He needs a haircut and some new clothes, but he's cute. Can I have him?"

Sarah looked at her in bafflement. "William?"

"Yeah. Why that look of horror? Is he married or something?"

"No, he's not married." She thought for a while.

"And no 'something' either, I think. He spends a lot of time at work."

"Goody." Lisa rubbed her hands together. "He finds me irresistible, did you notice?"

Jake shook his head. "He seemed to find you utterly irritating, Lisa."

"I know men," she said airily. "That's just a front. He wants me. He just doesn't know it yet." She gave Jake a pointed look. "Men are funny that way. It's not enough to rub their nose in it, you actually have to spell it out for them, and then teach them to read." She took Sarah's arm and led her into the house, waving to Jake over her shoulder. "We need to do some girl talk, Jake. Bye!"

"Bye," Jake said to the closed door. Lisa could have William. He couldn't imagine two people more different, but at least that would ensure that the man would stay clear of Sarah.

His Sarah.

SARAH TRAILED AFTER Lisa, who strode confidently up the stairs and into her room.

"Did you notice that?" Lisa asked triumphantly. "Jake was jealous of Bill. When I got there, he had all but grabbed a marker and written 'Taken' on your forehead."

"He did seem pretty possessive," Sarah acknowledged, very unsure how to feel about that. What was Jake thinking? Was he being possessive as a friend, or was he sharing those illicit feelings she was battling herself? And if so, what were they going to do about it? She sighed. Life had become extremely complicated all of a sudden.

"Did you talk to him about your cats yet?"

Sarah shook her head.

"Well? Why not?"

Sarah sank down into her chair and grabbed a pen. She always felt more at ease with a pen between her fingers. "I've been thinking. What if Jake feels the same way about me?"

Lisa grabbed a passing kitten from the floor and cuddled it. "Yeah. What if?"

Sarah frowned. "That's not supposed to happen. I'm not someone for Jake. He needs a real person to fall in love with."

Lisa put the kitten down on the floor and glared at Sarah, hands on hips. "Didn't you promise me and Jake you'd stop referring to yourself as not a real person?"

Sarah looked away. She frequently felt that she was lacking. Jake and Lisa had been very insistent, last time she had voiced those emotions, that being different was a part of individuality and that she was just as real as anyone else.

She knew they were right, but her feelings often betrayed her. And when she thought about the possibility of having a real relationship with Jake, the first thing that came to mind was how difficult it would be for him. She had been causing enough trouble for him all her life.

Lisa had made a great point though, regarding her suggestion to get over Jake by spending time with him. She wasn't sure that would do the trick, but it was bound to work the other way around. If Jake was starting to feel something more for her than the deep affection of a friend, being around him would work to quench those feelings in him, even if it failed to work for her.

She couldn't lose.

"I NEED A FAVOR."

Uh-oh. Jake squirmed and looked suspiciously at her. He should have known this was coming. If he had any sense at all, he'd already be running away. First positions, then kissing, and his imagination was doing a great job at painting possible future scenarios in his mind. At least he'd had the sense not to let her into the house. Not that the doorstep didn't have potential too, but it did have its limits.

"What sort of favor?" he asked cautiously, sending up a prayer to the God of Platonic Relationships. As long as it didn't involve body contact, he'd agree to anything.

"I need you to adopt my cat for me. Just for two weeks or so."

He relaxed. "No problem." Then he frowned as he realized exactly what he had been agreeing to. "Wait a minute. Your cat? And the kitten, too? You were keeping one of the kittens, weren't you?"

"Yeah." She pointed toward the fence, where something was moving between the trees. "Remember Bohr, the gray one? He's a very loving and sensitive kitten. You have to treat both of them well."

Jake sighed. "Why do you need a cat-sitter?"

"Well, you see, Aunt Eleanor is coming for a visit. She's allergic." Sarah didn't look him in the eye, but stared sideways at the kitten who was carefully approaching them, its eyes fixed on Sarah's shoelace. "You know how bad allergies can get, Jake. It would really help if you'd allow the cats to stay here."

"I don't even like cats." This was a protest he had made hundreds of times over the years, and one that was utterly unconvincing considering how he had the arrogant creatures purring in five seconds flat.

"How can you not like cats?"

"They make messes. They scratch the furniture. The smell of the litter box is horrible. There is cat hair everywhere. Do I need to go on?"

Bohr had finally gathered the courage to attack the shoelace, and Sarah picked the little hunter up and cuddled him to her chest. "Don't listen to the mean man," she muttered to the furry ball. Then she held it out toward him. "Can you say to his face that you don't like cats?"

"I most certainly can." He looked the cat straight in its wide green eyes. "Hi there, buddy. It's nothing personal, but I don't like—" Bohr was reaching toward him with one small paw.

"Oh, look, he likes you!" The creature was suddenly sitting on his shoulder, the tiny gray tail brushing over his chin.

"...cats," he finished. "Sarah, remove it before— Ouch!'' The kitten inserted at least twenty sharp claws into his shoulder before jumping down behind him and running into the house.

Sarah cooed. ''See, he's smart too. He already knows that this is where he'll live.''

Jake cursed, rubbing at his shoulder. ''How do you tell a cat where it lives? Won't it run right back to your place?''

''He,'' Sarah corrected. ''Food. Cats are kinda stupid that way. They stay where there's food.'' She frowned. ''Come to think of it, that's not stupid at all. It's pretty smart if you're thinking about surviving.''

''Food. Right. What do they eat? Or is that thing—'' he waved a hand ''—breastfed or something?''

''Cats have teats, women have breasts,'' she informed him calmly. ''And no, Bohr is no longer suckling. But you don't have to worry about the food. I'll drop in daily and feed them, if that's okay with you. You won't be here half the time to feed them anyway.''

Jake scowled at her for a while, then turned on his heel and strode into the kitchen, beckoning her to follow him. He fetched something from an upper cupboard, then handed it to her in his open palm. ''Here, take the key. You can come and go as you like.''

A small spark of static electricity jumped between them as she picked up the key from his palm.

She smiled. "Amazing thing, electricity, isn't it? Physics is fascinating."

"I suppose so," he muttered. He didn't think that spark had much to do with physics and everything to do with chemistry. The two of them could probably fill a whole table of the elements just by themselves. "Where do the little beasts sleep? Do I need a box or something?"

Sarah shook her head. "They sleep anywhere, and are more than likely to find their way to your bed during the night."

"My bed?" He swore softly. "I'm not sharing my bed with two cats."

Sarah's eyes were unreadable. "Whatever you say, Jake. If you close the door, they won't get in there anyway."

JAKE DID CLOSE THE DOOR for the night. However, after a series of pitiful meows he didn't have the heart to shut them out any longer. He shuffled to the door and opened it a crack, and the cats beat him to the bed. The two small bodies hogged more than their share of the bed, and Bohr seemed intent on using his toes for hunting practice.

That kitten must be hyperactive, he thought, waking up for the millionth time with a furry beast stuck to his big toe. He grabbed Bohr and held him above his face. All he saw in the darkness was a kitten shaped shadow. "You are not one tiny kitten," he informed the animal, "you are a whole army of miniature tigers in training."

Bohr answered with a purr, and Jake dropped him by his mother's side, and wrapped the covers carefully about his own feet. He drew the line at allowing them under the covers, but he could live with them purring close to his ear.

After all, Sarah would never forgive him if the creatures were returned suffering post-traumatic stress disorder.

Sarah didn't sleep particularly well. Used to the warmth of at least one cat in her bed, she constantly woke up to imaginary tails flicking her face.

As soon as she saw movement in Jake's kitchen, she hurried over there, and quickly knocked on the door before letting herself in with her key.

"Jake?" she called out.

"I'm in the kitchen."

She hurried to the kitchen to find Bohr crouched by the door, stalking some invisible enemy. She scooped him up and cuddled him against her face, relishing the feel of his soft fur against her cheek. "I missed you!" she cooed. "Did you treat Jake well?"

"He did," Jake drawled, standing barefoot by the counter with a mug in his hand, wearing faded old jeans and a white T-shirt. "More or less. I may have some missing toes, but nothing more serious. His mother, however, was a different story."

"What did she do?" Sarah noticed the look on Jake's face and her hand went to her mouth. "That bad?"

Jake gave her a grim look. Without speaking he

put his mug down, then pulled the T-shirt out of his jeans and lifted it, revealing a flat stomach and muscular chest, already slightly tanned from the time he'd spent outdoors this spring.

Oh my. Suddenly boneless, Sarah had to lean against the wall for support. He was absolutely beautiful. Funny, she must have seen him half-naked hundred of times before. Why hadn't the sight punched her in the stomach like this before?

"I didn't know you worked out," she said weakly, her hungry gaze roving over him from his chest to the waistband of his jeans, her fingers itching to follow suit. His shoulders were still hidden by the white fabric and she was quite shocked at the sudden urge to rip the T-shirt off him just to get a closer look.

"Huh?" He looked confused, then pointed at his midriff. "I didn't undress so you could ogle my body, Sarah. See this?"

Sarah forced herself to look past smooth tanned skin and finely delineated muscles. It wasn't easy, but she managed at last to see what he was talking about. Two sets of ugly red scratches were covering his middle, just below his chest. The pattern looked familiar.

"Dead-or-Alive did that?" she asked in resignation.

"That beast came in through the window sometime during the night, and jumped down on me." Much to Sarah's regret he began tucking the shirt back in. "That cat must weigh twenty pounds, and the jump down is over four feet. And as if the impact wasn't enough, it had to use its claws on me, too.''

''She,'' Sarah corrected. ''I'm sorry. Did you get that disinfected?''

''No, I didn't bother. I just took a shower and washed it with soap.''

''You need to disinfect that, Jake. You never know what sort of nasty stuff could have gotten in the wound.'' She grabbed his hand and dragged him upstairs to the small bathroom.

''Sit down on the edge of the tub,'' she ordered as she stretched to fetch the medical kit from the top of the cabinet. She opened it and placed it within reach, then turned to Jake and grabbed the edge of his T-shirt to pull it up over his head.

I'm definitely not undressing him because I want to complete the picture and get a look at his shoulders, she firmly told herself as she kept her eyes averted while she flung the shirt over the towel rack. There was just no need to get disinfectant on that clean white shirt.

Then she turned back to him, and couldn't help herself. She stared. She had frequently rested her head against him, often sobbing her heart out in some trivial adolescent angst. How could she have touched him and not felt all what she was feeling now? Unable to stop herself, she put her hand on his shoulder, just rested it against his warmth, then took a deep breath and held it.

Lisa's plan better work. And work soon.

Jake turned his head and looked at her. ''Sarah?''

Self-control in, lust out. Sarah bit her cheek hard to punish herself and snatched her hand off him. She sat down beside him and dumped the bottle of disinfectant and some bandages in his lap. All sorts of strange thoughts were flying through her mind and she bit the other cheek to punish herself again.

Lust was refusing to stay out. Darn hormones. There was no limit to their power over people. Even over her cool and calm scientist's mind.

"This is going to sting a bit," she said, avoiding his questioning gaze. She soaked some cotton in disinfectant. Hesitating only a second, she then pressed the cotton ball against the small wounds, while allowing her other hand to rest on the warmth of his shoulder. She was storing the resulting feelings away for later analysis. His skin felt as smooth and warm as it looked. Her hands were itching to move, to caress rather than press clinically against him, to stroke down his back and up his neck into his hair.

Sarah swallowed and pulled her hand away. All in all, she was thinking some very strange thoughts and having some very strange feelings.

"Sting a bit?" Jake managed between clenched teeth. "It feels like you're pressing a burning match against me."

She grasped the opportunity for innocent conversation gratefully. "Do you know why it burns?"

He shook his head and she launched into an explanation.

Jake listened halfheartedly. His attention was too focused on the small and delicate wisps of hair framing her face. He wanted to trace the strands with his fingers, lay gentle kisses down her throat, and when she'd look up at him with her irresistible look of innocence and curiosity, he would—

Sarah looked up in surprise, holding a ball of cotton in the air. "Hey, I'm not done!"

Moving as far away as he could into the tiny bathroom, Jake grabbed a couple of bandages and roughly slapped them on the small wounds.

"I'm fine," he said roughly. "Thanks. Prognosis is good. I'll definitely live."

He willed his body to calm down so he could turn around and show Sarah he wasn't upset. She was always quick to jump to conclusions about such things, even though he was rarely annoyed with her. Well, until recently, anyway. He looked over his shoulder. She was looking at him, but not with the worried look of are-you-upset-with-me. Rather, she was staring at his naked back with a look that in anyone else would have signified pure unadulterated desire.

With a sinking heart he decided that he didn't even want to think about what it signified coming from Sarah.

He grabbed his T-shirt and quickly pulled it on, grinding his teeth when he heard what sounded suspiciously like a moan of disappointment.

The God of Platonic Relationships was obviously not in a happy mood today.

They went into the living room and found the kitten clawing at the window and trying to catch the flies. There was something different about it. Jake walked to the window for a closer look.

"Hey, Bohr didn't have white paws last time I saw him."

"Didn't he?"

Jake cast Sarah a wary look and his suspicions were confirmed. She was trying to look innocent and failing miserably. "No. And he had a gray tail, not a black one."

"Are you sure?"

"Of course I'm sure. The thing was flicking my face with its tail all night."

"All cats are gray in the dark."

Jake looked at her and felt a smile sneak onto his lips, completely without his approval. "You're right about that. But it doesn't change the fact that your cats are changing color on me. So, anything you want to tell me?"

Sarah bit her lip, then shrugged. "Okay. That's not Bohr. That's Edison. I kind of helped Dead-or-Alive move them over last night."

Jake saluted Edison. "Okay. So there are two kittens left, not one? And they're both staying at my house?"

"Sort of," Sarah confessed.

Two bundles of fur chased each other across his floor. Both of them had white tails, without an inch of either black or gray in sight. Jake stared at them for a while before moving his gaze gradually to Sarah. He did it slowly so she'd have to squirm a bit.

"Is there anything *more* you'd like to tell me?" he inquired politely, treating her to his very strictest stare.

She was squirming. Good. "Jake, meet Einstein and Marie Curie. She's the only girl in the litter, remember? You saw the whole bunch when they were newborn."

Jake rubbed his forehead. "First you tell me there is one kitten, then two, and now it's *four?* Plus the mom, so that's *five* cats?"

"It's the foot-in-the-door method," Sarah muttered, at least having the grace to look abashed. "It's a well-known phenomenon. If you ask people a small favor first, they are more likely to agree to a bigger favor later. But they would never have agreed to the bigger favor if it had been asked first."

Jake picked up two kittens and went hunting for the other two. "Obviously, people are suckers."

"That's what I'm counting on," she replied, smiling at him as he picked up two more kittens and then placed them one by one on the sofa beside her, naming each one in turn.

"Edison, Einstein, Bohr, Marie Curie. Is that it, or can I expect more visitors in my bed?" He flicked Bohr's tail with a finger. "No wonder you seemed like a small army last night, little guy. You *were* a small army."

One more furry creature came streaking into the room, jumped onto the sofa with its siblings and began to sharpen its tiny claws. Jake looked up at the ceiling in frustration.

Sarah patted his arm. "This is the last one, I promise." She picked the kitten up by the scruff of his neck, and silently ordered him to charm Jake. "His name is..." She hesitated and then smiled. "Jake Junior?"

Jake put out his hand and took the animal. "I know the mothers carry them like that, but I always worry that they can't breathe."

Sarah smiled secretly as he began stroking the kitten in that okay-I'm-just-doing-this-so-you-won't-bite-me manner.

"Okay. The updated number is Edison, Einstein, Bohr, Curie and Jake?" He sent her a look of distrust. "You think that naming your kitten after me is going to make me forgive you for planting *six* cats in my house?"

His voice was softer already. Jake Junior was working his magic. "It's only for a little while, Jake. Aunt Eleanor sneezes all the time with the cats around. I don't really have anyone else to ask."

"Okay," Jake relented as Junior poked a pink nose into his ear. "But only on a trial basis, and only if you stop by every morning to feed them and clean the litter box. If it doesn't work out, your aunt will just have to sneeze her way through her vacation."

Mission accomplished. Sarah smiled broadly. "Thanks, Jake." She scooped up Bohr and kissed the top of his head. "I'm sure they'll behave themselves. All six of them."

6

SARAH WAS AT JAKE'S DOOR bright and early the next morning, carrying bags of cat food and kitty sand. She rang the doorbell and instantly his voice bellowed from inside. "It's not locked. Come in."

Jake was staring at himself in the mirrored corner in the living room, looking none too pleased with his appearance. Come to think of it, he did look rather odd. Gorgeous, but odd. She looked him up and down, trying to see what the problem was. He turned around, muttering a curse, and saw her.

"Hi, Sarah. See what your beasts have reduced me to?"

Sarah was finding it hard to keep from laughing. She had finally figured out what was strange about him today. He was wearing his flight uniform, but the pants were black and his jacket blue. The contrast was glaring, not to mention the texture of the fabric clashed.

Jake cursed. "I'm doomed. Even you, with your nonexistent fashion sense can see that I look like a complete idiot." He gestured at his pants and to a pair of jeans lying across the back of the sofa. "Well, it's either this or jeans. One of your darlings had a little accident on my only clean pair of uniform pants. Lisa is picking me up in just a few minutes and there's no way I can clean and dry them in that time." He looked in the mirror again and shook his head in disgust. "Jeans have to be better. At the very least it couldn't possibly look worse."

"I'm sorr—" The sentence trailed off into a giggle.

Jake gave her an injured look, as he hurriedly removed the offending pants and reached for his jeans. "You're obviously very sorry, cat woman."

"I am. I really am." Another giggle belied her words. "I've never known them to do that before. Kittens take to the litter box naturally. Aunt Eleanor's cat has had kittens three times and they've always been trained from the sixth week."

Belatedly, she realized what she had revealed. She took a quick glance at Jake's face, and her hope that he hadn't noticed her slip was brutally extinguished. He had paused with one leg inserted in the jeans and was staring at her.

"Aunt Eleanor's cat, Sarah?"

Her muscles tensed at the dangerous calm in his voice. Then he straightened and allowed the jeans to fall forgotten to the floor.

"I assume you're talking about the Aunt Eleanor who's been staying with you? Poor Aunt Eleanor who has such a bad allergy that all cats have to be banished from the house?"

With each word he had moved a fraction closer, looking most intimidating, even with bare legs above black socks and shirttails flapping around his thighs. Sarah inched closer to the door, just in case she'd need an escape route.

"You mean I've been tolerating your *six* cats in my bed and your aunt doesn't even have an allergy?"

All she could do was nod.

"Okay." Jake took a deep breath and to her relief he stopped advancing toward her. He sat down, folded his arms on his chest and stared at her like a stern principal. "Now, keep in mind that I am just a simple pilot and not a rocket scientist and try to explain it to me. Why?"

"I wanted to spend more time with you," she whispered, unable to tell him anything less than the truth, even if it wasn't the whole truth. She couldn't reveal her real motive. She couldn't let Jake know she was trying to fall out of love with him. "This was the perfect excuse."

Jake's expression flashed from irritation to surprise to rueful realization in a split second. "Spend more time with me? Hell, Sarah, you didn't need a whole undercover operation to spend time with me. You've never needed any excuse to be with me." He stared at her for a long moment then reached out. "Come here."

She took his hand and allowed him to pull her into his lap. He stroked the curls away from her face and then pulled her chin up to look into her eyes. "You're as confused about this as I am, aren't you?"

There was no need to ask what "this" was. She swallowed, then nodded, her body stiff as she tried to stop herself from melting into him. Her skin was on fire where his fingers cradled her chin. Her nerve endings were picking up things that she was sure should be far below her sensitivity threshold.

His eyes were beautiful, the pupils large and surrounded by a ring of deep blue, and for some inexplicable reason the anatomy of the eye was now turning her neurochemistry haywire. When his face moved closer, she could hardly remember how to breathe, but her hands moved of their own accord, up his chest and neck, to stop only when they were holding his face. A big tremulous sigh escaped from her lips when his mouth was so close she could feel his breath.

"Jake, are you ready...oops. Excuse me."

Jake jackknifed to his feet, leaving Sarah to stand wobbling beside him.

"I'm sorry for interrupting," Lisa said, backing out of the room and pulling the door closed. Jake grabbed the edge of the frame and stopped her, and without speaking motioned her back in the room.

"Really, Jake, there's no hurry. The door was open so I walked in, but I'll just wait outside."

Muttering something neither woman could hear, Jake raked both hands through his hair, mussing it up, and then strode out of the room and toward the front door.

Sarah put out a hand and leaned against the table,

not quite trusting her legs. Her head was still reeling from the potential of a kiss that hadn't happened.

Lisa's grin could have spanned continents. "Well, well, well. Things are progressing beautifully, I take it?"

"Ehhh... I...we...um..."

Her friend's eyes were sparkling dangerously. "Jake got your tongue?"

Sarah glared at her, finally reclaiming her voice. "Very funny," was all the scathing retort she could muster. Before she could think of something better, bare-legged Jake strode back into the room and snatched his jeans off the floor.

"Well?" he growled at Lisa as he put them on in record time, then put his hands on his hips and glared at her. "Are we going or not?"

Lisa chuckled. "Our passengers won't know what they missed, Jake. You've got really sexy legs."

Jake shook his head in disgust and strode out of the house. Lisa winked at Sarah. "You'll tell me all when we get back," she whispered. From outside, the car horn sounded impatiently, but Lisa paused. "Sarah, you might have to speed up the getting-over process."

Sarah was still dizzy. "What?"

"Jake got a transfer."

Sarah almost gasped with shock as she realized what Lisa was saying. She knew Jake had applied for a transfer almost a year ago, when his father had suffered the heart attack. He'd wanted to move to Florida to be closer to his parents. It was something she hadn't thought much about at the time, and he hadn't mentioned anything about it since then.

Lisa looked at her impatiently as the horn blasted again. "Well? Are you just going to let him leave? It might be time for some drastic action."

"When…when is he leaving?"

"I don't know. He probably doesn't know yet that the transfer has been approved. I have a friend in the personnel department who told me."

Sarah said nothing.

"Well?" Lisa asked, increasingly impatient. "Aren't you going to do something?"

Sarah looked up. "Yes. I'm going to do something."

Lisa smiled. "Great. See you when we get back." She hugged Sarah and finally responded to the summon of the car horn.

Alone at last, Sarah carefully sat down on the sofa. Jake was going away. Moving halfway across the country. She might never see him again. Not only was she in love with him, but he was obviously feeling something too, even if it was just confusing physical attraction.

Yes, she was definitely going to do something about this.

She was going to seduce Jake. There was absolutely no logical reason not to do that before he went away. At best, it would get this thing out of both their systems, and at the worst she would at least have the experience under her belt.

And besides, she really wanted to.

FOUR DAYS LATER, JAKE WAS back home. He was almost disappointed to find his house empty of cat litter boxes, saucers of milk and little tigers. He sat down in the living room and ruefully looked at his discarded pair of pants on the ironing board. He was almost at the stage of finding that incident funny. Almost.

He'd done a lot of thinking while he'd been away. What he was feeling for Sarah was not disappearing. And she was definitely feeling the same attraction.

They *could* stop fighting this thing, and see what happened. Their friendship was at risk, yes. But it was also in jeopardy if they continued on this way.

A sound at the window distracted him from his musings and he rose to check its source. A gray kitten stared pathetically at him from behind the pane.

Jake opened the window and Bohr leapt inside. He rubbed himself against Jake's hand, complaining loudly over the cruel and unusual treatment of being refused access to his preferred home.

"Have you been locked outside, tiger?" Jake murmured. "I was just thinking about giving your mistress a call." He took a deep breath, even though he was just confiding in a kitten. "I was going to stop all this mucking around and ask her out on a date. Preferably today, so I won't have time to panic about it." He looked out the window, up at Sarah's bedroom window. She'd be at work now. "I could pick her up when she's finished at work, and maybe take her flying in the Piper and then dinner or something. She's never flown with me before, you know. I should have asked her that a long time ago, anyway. What do you think? Is dinner pushing it?''

Bohr rubbed his head into Jake's palm, then mewed. Jake chuckled. ''Yeah, a date is quite a novel idea, isn't it? What do you think she'll say?''

The kitten sat and started washing its face. Jake fell back down into the sofa and after a few minutes of procrastination reached for the phone with determination. If he called, he wouldn't be distracted by her—her smile *or* her body. He could be calm and rational, instead of stuttering incoherently—he seemed to be doing a lot of that these days.

He rapidly dialed the number for Sarah's office, then clenched his eyes shut as he waited for her to pick up. Better get it over with while he still had the courage.

SARAH PUT THE PHONE DOWN, feeling slightly faint. Jake had sounded strange as he'd asked if she'd have dinner with him tonight, but that was not her main concern. Her stomach clenched and she leaned over her desk taking deep, calming breaths. It was what he planned for them to do *before* dinner that terrified her.

Ever since Jake had first expressed his wish to be a pilot, she had kept her fear of flying from him. She had been in an airplane only once, as a small child, and she had found the whole experience terrifying. To make things worse, she'd been alone and hadn't even had an adult to cling to for those frightening two hours.

As Jake progressed through his studies, finally to become an airline captain, she had never let on about her fear. She knew very well how irrational and silly her fear was. Shame had prevented her from ever admitting that fear to Jake, who braved the skies daily without any anxiety at all.

After he bought the Piper in partnership with two of his colleagues, he'd offered to take her up a few times. She'd always found an excuse.

So far. Sarah groaned. Jake's voice had been hesitant, unsure, and her heart had started pounding as soon as she'd picked up the phone. And she had said yes. She had committed to flying with him, and not just flying as she'd done before, in a huge aircraft with a crew of twenty and hundreds of passengers. No, she was flying inside a small tin can with barely room enough for one passenger.

She stood on shaking legs and reached up into her top shelf for a book she knew was supposed to be there, somewhere. Then she sat back down at her desk, and pushed papers and miscellaneous stuff out of the way to make room for the slim volume. She took a deep breath and opened the first page.

Self-hypnosis for Beginners.

THE SELF-HYPNOSIS DIDN'T seem to be working.

Sarah sat in Jake's plane, barely breathing. Muscles she hardly knew she possessed ached from the pressure her terrified body was putting on them. She took a deep breath and worked on unclenching each muscle, keeping her eyes unfocused so she wouldn't see out the window. The ground was still only ten feet away, but it was the principle of the thing.

"Okay!" Jake said cheerfully. "We're ready to go."

He started the engine. Sarah's heart picked up speed, until it was racing so fast she could hardly count the individual beats. She froze, chanting in her head statistics about plane safety, specifics of aeronautical engineering, and all those things that should be calming and reassuring. With determination, she arranged her facial muscles into a smile. Mind over matter. It was absurd to be afraid of flying.

The plane started slowly along the runway. Just like a car, Sarah reminded herself. Just driving. *Just like a car.*

"Ready?" Jake asked and she forced herself to smile at him, managing a few seconds without paralyzing fear at seeing the excitement on his face. He wanted to share this with her, the magic of flying that he had so often told her about. She would conquer her fear for him. She *would.*

Jake sent her one last smile, and then his face became serious and businesslike as he busied himself with the controls and communications with the flight tower. She looked at the controls herself, scanning buttons and levers and gauges. Most of them she knew, or could deduce their function. She had read most of Jake's books and manuals from when he was learning to fly, and she rarely forgot anything she'd read. Her panic subsided as she familiarized herself with the controls. At the top, near the window, a row of gauges indicated the status of various functions.

For a split second, her gaze wandered a few inches upward.

Suddenly she couldn't breathe. Blue sky. Gauzy white clouds. And the green of the ground somewhat more than ten feet away, and receding fast. Her mouth opened in a desperate attempt at breathing or screaming—she wasn't sure which was more important.

It didn't matter. No sound emerged.

Then the world vanished into welcomed blackness.

THEY WERE UP. JAKE laughed aloud as he looked sideways, but his laughter was cut short at what he saw.

Sarah was slumped sideways in her seat, held upright only by her belt.

Ice trickled down his spine. "Sarah!"

No response. Her head was lolled to her side, facing him, her face pale and lips slightly parted. His heart thudding, he put the plane on autopilot and reached for her, checking her pulse and breathing. He held his own breath, then released it with relief. Her vitals were fine. Regular pulse, normal breathing. What was wrong with her? What could have happened? He racked his brain for any logical explanation. He was fine himself, and all the gauges were normal. The air pressure in the cabin was normal, nothing out of the ordinary there. They weren't even high up yet.

Adrenaline pumped through him with renewed force as he dismissed several possible explanations. There was nothing wrong with the atmosphere in the plane. That meant there had to be something wrong with Sarah. What could have happened?

Although loath to let go of her limp hand, he let her be while he resumed control of the plane and changed course, heading back to the airport. Sarah didn't move at all as he requested permission to land. Eternity seemed to pass until he was finally given the clear. No landing—not even his first one— had brought such relief.

He quickly undid Sarah's seat belt and lifted her out of the plane, grabbing the first aid kit as well. "Sarah?" He patted her cheek, hoping the slight breeze would wake her up. He felt utterly useless. Did anyone use smelling salts any longer? Would there be something like that in the first aid kit? He rummaged inside and found something that at least smelled awful, then held it under Sarah's nose.

The fist around his heart unclenched a bit as her eyelashes fluttered, then her eyes opened. The first look at the blurry confusion in her eyes knocked the truth into him.

He loved her. Completely, as deeply as it was possible for a man to love a woman. How could he ever have mistaken that love for a friendly affection, for a brotherly love?

Her blank look around brought him back to reality. A slightly different reality, with the future all of a sudden aiming in a certain direction. But the fact remained that Sarah wasn't well. She had fainted, and he didn't know why.

She looked blankly around. "Jake? What happened? And why are you putting disinfectant on my nose?"

"Good question," Jake said grimly. "You passed out, that's what happened." He picked her up again and marched toward the exit. He would secure and lock up the plane later. What was important now was getting Sarah to a doctor. Since she had woken up, he would drive there himself. It would probably be quicker than an ambulance, anyway.

"I fainted?" She buried her head in his shoulder. "That's so embarrassing! I'm sorry, Jake."

Jake didn't reply. He wanted to get her to the doctor as soon as possible. Once he had her somewhere private, where they wouldn't be disturbed, he wanted to tell her he loved her.

"I can walk, Jake. I'm fine, really. Put me down."

"You're not walking. Save your strength. We're going to the emergency room."

"Emergency room?" Sarah squeaked. "I don't need a doctor. I'm fine. I fainted, that's all."

"People don't faint without a reason, Sarah. Don't even try to protest. We're seeing a doctor."

He slid her into the car, fastened the seat belt for her and drove to the emergency room, ignoring her protests that increased in volume the closer they got to the hospital. Once there, he was at her side of the car before she even had time to undo her seat belt, and he lifted her out. He glanced around for a wheelchair, and finding none, marched with her in his arms toward the entrance.

Sarah was still not taking his advice about conserving oxygen. Instead, she was wriggling in his arms, trying to get down. "Jake, you're being absolutely ridiculous! I'm fine, I don't need a doctor and I can most certainly walk by myself."

"Don't take this the wrong way, Sarah, but shut up. You scared me sick." He stalked to Reception and waited impatiently for a woman with an infant to be ushered off to the waiting room.

"We need a doctor," he told the nurse tersely. "She fainted."

The nurse motioned for them to sit down while she did the preliminary paperwork. "How are you feeling now, dear?" she asked Sarah, looking her over.

"Fine. Actually, I'm really okay. I don't need a doctor at all."

"Don't listen to her. She could be delirious for all we know. She went out cold without any reason. She needs a doctor."

Sarah groaned, as the nurse nodded briskly at Jake, obviously trusting his bullying manner. To her relief, Jake allowed her to walk the whole twenty feet to the waiting area.

This was so embarrassing. She'd thought she'd

been so brave, going aboard that plane without showing her fear, and then she'd actually fainted, scaring Jake witless. She felt a sharp pang of remorse as she looked sideways at him. He was staring straight ahead, his jaw clenched and his hand tight around hers. He had been terrified. He still was.

She should just tell him she'd fainted out of fear, and stoically face his incredulity and shock. She really should. But she was already here, waiting for the doctor. The easiest thing was to talk to the doctor, explain things, get a clean bill of health so Jake would be reassured.

And then she wouldn't even have to tell him the truth, that airplanes scared the hell out of her. Escaping that was very tempting.

"Well, hello again, young man. You're back."

An old woman with a cane hobbled over to Jake and was in the process of taking a seat next to him.

"Amelia!" Jake stood up and helped the old lady sit down. She smiled gratefully and then peered past him at Sarah. "Is this becoming the hot new in-place for young couples?"

"Not exactly," Jake muttered, sitting down again and reclaiming Sarah's hand. "This is Sarah. Actually, she's responsible for my first visit here. It was her cat that gave the redhead the allergy."

Amelia chuckled, her cheeks creasing like two small accordions. She winked at Sarah. "That was very clever of you, young woman. All is fair in love and war, as they say."

"Well, she didn't do it on purpose," Jake began,

even grinning a bit as he glanced at Sarah. Then he did a double take.

Sarah looked away and cursed her face. She could lie easily, that was not a problem. The problem was that her face always gave her guilt away. She got red, she bit her lip and according to Jake her eyes got a "shifty look." Whatever that meant.

Judging from the astonished look on Jake's face, she was radiating the guilty triad of red face, bit lip and shifty eyes right now.

"Sarah?" He cursed softly and shook his head. "I don't believe this. Did you come to me with that cat deliberately to do that to Roxy?"

"I'm sorry," she muttered. "It was a stupid, dangerous, selfish, irresponsible, reprehensible…"

Jake clamped his hand over her mouth. "I get it. I don't want excuses. Just tell me why."

Amelia gave a dry cough, that on closer inspection turned out to be laughter. "Men can be so dense, dear. Better get used to it. They never grow out of it. Take it from me. I buried one husband and dumped the other." She leaned across Jake and whispered to Sarah. "Between you and me, though, you just might have keeper material there."

Sarah smiled at the old lady, although those words hurt in unexpected places. She ignored Jake's waiting gaze and his question and then returned her attention to the floor as he and Amelia began friendly banter.

Jake had to know why she'd done what she did. It was obviously out of jealousy, no matter how she might try to disguise it. There was no need to spell it out to him and add to her humiliation.

It wasn't long until Sarah's name was called and she jumped gratefully to her feet, looking forward to getting this over with. She'd just explain to the doctor and leave. She hurried to the door and didn't notice Jake right behind her.

"Are you her husband?" the orderly asked, blocking his access. Sarah opened her mouth to deny it, but heard a resounding "yes" from behind her.

"Jake…!"

"Come on, darling." He put his arm over her shoulder and walked her down the hallway, following the orderly. Sarah groaned. Nothing was ever easy.

"Are you pregnant?" was the first question the harried-looking young doctor asked her as he grabbed her wrist to time her pulse. Sarah flushed slightly and shook her head. "You're sure about that?"

She glanced at Jake, standing there brooding with his arms crossed, his gaze not leaving her for a moment. "I'm sure. I haven't… I can't be pregnant."

"Okay. Have you been eating?"

"Yes. I had breakfast and lunch."

"Dizziness, headaches, nausea, recent illness, allergies?"

She shook her head. "Nothing like that. I've always been very healthy."

"So you've no idea why you fainted?"

She hesitated, and watched Jake's stance change into attack mode.

"Sarah?" he asked in a low voice. "You know what caused you to faint?"

"I'm sorry," she said to the doctor, her face burning now. "I've wasted your time. There's nothing wrong with me. I fainted because..." She looked at Jake, defeated. "I'm afraid of flying, Jake. Absolutely terrified."

Jake's eyes narrowed and he shook his head slightly. "What?" He took a step closer as the doctor shook his head and pointed toward the exit as he hurried out of the room. Jake put his arm around Sarah and led her out, then headed straight for the waiting area. Amelia was gone. They sat down in a secluded corner.

Jake was still looking astonished. "You mean you fainted from fear?"

Sarah covered her red face with her hands. "I know, it's silly. Not logical at all. I know the statistics. I'm in more danger in the car than in the plane. And I know you're an excellent pilot. It's just a silly phobia I have."

"Why haven't you ever told me?" Jake shook his head. "I've been flying planes for years and years. Even before, it was all I ever dreamt of doing, and you never mentioned you were terrified of flying!"

"It wasn't relevant," she muttered.

"Not relevant?" Jake sputtered. "Well, if it wasn't, it sure as hell became relevant the minute you decided to go up there with me!"

"I thought I could do it," she mumbled miserably. "I really wanted to. I even tried self-hypnosis." She shredded a piece of tissue between her fingers. "Obviously, it didn't work."

Jake put his arm over her shoulders. "You should have told me, Sarah. If you wanted to fly despite your fear, I could have helped you. We could have started easy."

"I didn't want you to think I was a wimp."

"Hell, Sarah." He hugged her, her nose pressing into his chest. She kind of liked that. He smelled nice. She burrowed deeper into his shirt until her nose was squashed against him. She liked that even better. "I know you're not a wimp. You've shown me every day of your life." He kissed her brow. "And then you come here with me, strap yourself into that seat, and let me fly you up in the air. That's heroic."

That was so sweet! She looked up at him and saw the concern in his eyes, and it seemed the most natural thing in the world to reach up and run her fingers across his cheek, brush the hair away from his forehead. And then to press her fingers against the nape of his neck and pull his head down until she could kiss him, at long last. She smiled as their lips met, forgetting everything about techniques and methods as his scent, his touch, his presence filled her world. She wanted to kiss him forever, but all too soon he was pulling away from her. She looked into his eyes, disoriented and then remembered where they were.

And they had quite an audience, too. Even a bawling preschooler with a huge cut on his forehead was now sucking his thumb and staring with interest at them. Sarah hid her face again in Jake's shoulder and he pulled her to her feet. They held hands to the car and once there she couldn't wait any longer, but leaned toward him, seeking his mouth again.

"Jake?"

"Yes?" He loved the way she sought reassurance by saying his name in that tentative manner. It had become a ritual with them—she would speak his name and he would reply "yes" to let her know she had his attention.

"I love kissing you."

He smiled. "Ditto."

She reached up and caressed his check.

"I want to sleep with you."

Jake stopped breathing for a minute. Then he chuckled weakly, even as all sorts of body parts reacted without humor to her words. He was relieved when there was an answering smile on Sarah's face. "I don't suppose you mean you want to crash on my couch tonight?"

Sarah shook her head. "No. I want to sleep in your bed."

"Right. And…I suppose you don't want me on the couch, either then?"

"Jake!" Sarah clenched her fists and beat at his shoulder. "I don't really care where you sleep or where I sleep as long as it's the same place."

He opened his mouth, but she beat him to it. "And no, I don't intend to just sleep, either."

"Just getting this clear," he chuckled. "Wouldn't want any more misunderstandings."

"Well?"

Jake hesitated. He was confused, unsure. Everything seemed new and fragile, including Sarah. Was she sure? Would it be okay?

Her eyes pierced his, waiting and suddenly everything was simple. She loved him. It was obvious. Why hadn't he seen it before? He smiled gently. Had he really considered saying no? He bent his head and kissed her, gently nibbling at her lips until she tightened her arms around his neck and responded eagerly.

When she drew away, her face was flushed. "Jake, can we try again, soon?"

"Try what again?" he asked, his mind less than clear.

"Flying."

He laughed. "Sure. You might want to try and just sit in the plane first, and see if both of us survive *that* experience."

"Actually," she looked up at him, "it wasn't so bad at first. Then we were all of a sudden off the ground..." She bit her lip. "And I kind of don't remember anything after that. But I really do want to try again."

Her reward was in the warm hug he gave her. "Anytime, Sarah. I love to fly. It would be terrific if you could learn to enjoy it, as well."

Not to mention useful, Sarah thought sadly, as she remembered the distance that soon would separate them. Visiting Jake in Florida would be all but impossible unless she flew there.

She postponed those worries and smiled, as she fastened her seat belt. "Shall we go?"

"Sure." He started the car and began finding his way out of the huge parking lot. "Where are we going?"

She smiled at him.

"To bed, of course."

7

DURING THE DRIVE HOME, Jake suffered alternate bouts of pure lust and pure panic. Sarah didn't help with her intermittent questions and comments, her analytic mind plotting every possible action they would take that evening. When she asked if her sex guides were still at his house, he had had enough.

"Sarah, stop it!" He grinned at her look of surprise. "Sorry, but at this rate you'll give me performance anxiety and then we'll *really* have trouble. You're not bringing those manuals to bed this time, okay?"

Sarah giggled. "Okay. But then you'll have to be more forthcoming with information than last time."

Jake groaned. If he could stop being so nervous, he knew it would be fun teaching Sarah. If this was anything like other things he'd taught her over the years, he would end up learning more than she did. Sarah was a very quick study.

Once they were home, Sarah became nervous. As usual, when anxious about something, she approached it head-on, determined to get it over with. He had barely removed his jacket when she started dragging him upstairs, directly to the bedroom.

"Hey!" he said, laughing. "Slow down." He tried to kiss her, but she was too busy getting their clothes off. He grabbed her hands and imprisoned them in his. "Relax, Sarah. We're not running a race here."

"I just want to get the first time over with," she said, a frown of determination of her face. "I mean, it can hurt and all. We'll just hurry up and get it done and then we can have some fun the second time around."

Jake grabbed her wandering hands again, and firmly held her wrists behind her back. He threw back the covers and pulled her into bed. Still keeping her hands captive, he kissed her, and when he released her hands, they went around his neck instead of tearing at his clothes to "get it over with." His hands roamed over her face and hair. It was as if he'd been let out of a cage, at last free to touch her and kiss her, to show her how he felt.

Sarah was in another universe, delirious in her pleasure at being able to touch him. She couldn't get enough of just burying her hands in the thick warmth of his hair, or of kissing his face. She traced his dimple with her tongue and pressed herself against him. His pulse pounded under her palm as she curved her hand around his neck, echoing the frantic beating of her own heart.

Then someone walked all over them.

Sarah squeaked and Jake tightened his hold on her as he glowered at the intruder.

"Go away!"

Bohr curled down on the pillow, ignoring him. He stuck his head between his paws and purred. Sarah giggled. Jake shook his head and got out of bed. He lifted the pillow, cat and all, and deposited the whole thing outside the bedroom door. Then he closed the door and locked it for good measure.

"Bohr can't turn the handle, Jake."

"I wouldn't count on it. That creature boldly goes where no cat has gone before."

Sarah was beaming, the covers pulled up to her chin. Jake stopped when he noticed her clothes scattered on the floor. How had she managed to undress in the few seconds it took him to get rid of Bohr?

"Hey," he chided with a smile, "I wanted to take your clothes off!"

An embryonic frown appeared on her face and he flung himself beside her on the bed to kiss it away. "Just kidding. You'll let me do the honors next time, okay?"

She didn't answer, but he didn't notice because she rolled on top of him, pulling the covers with her, and started kissing him again, and then her fingers found the buttons of his shirt and undid them. He ran his hands up her bare arms, and down her back and buttocks. Yep. She was stark naked, and judging by the speed with which she was undressing him, he would be too in just a few seconds.

His shirt was unbuttoned and as she rose above him to explore his chest with her hands, her breasts fell naturally into his hands, fitting into them perfectly. He was still wondering at the feel of them in his palms when she yanked his jeans down and moved over him.

Jake suddenly felt he'd stepped into the path of a freight train. This was not at all happening like he'd planned. They were supposed to take it slow and easy, not try for speed record of the year. He tried to grab hold of her and squirm away at the same time.

"No, Sarah, wait. Not yet."

She didn't listen. Instead, she squeezed her eyes shut and then jammed herself down in sort of the right spot.

"Ow!" She practically flew off him and landed on the floor. "Ow, ow, ow!"

Fear grabbed at his heart, but vaporized as she let out a string of curse words she'd probably learned from him a long time ago. She obviously wasn't too badly hurt if she could cuss like that. "That hurt!" she accused, clutching herself and glaring at him as if it was all his fault.

Reassured that she wasn't badly hurt, he couldn't contain his laughter. In just a few seconds it had escalated until he was moaning in pain and clutching his stomach trying to stop it.

"Of course it did," he managed to gasp at last, feeling terribly guilty for laughing at her. "You weren't ready." He sat up and smiled gently at her, hoping he was forgiven for laughing. "Ever hear of foreplay?"

She wasn't listening. Her eyes widened and her

mouth opened in a round O. "I have vaginismus. Oh, God. I'll never be able to enjoy sex."

"Vagi…what?"

His enjoyment at watching her pace the floor naked was somewhat ruined by her panicky words.

"Vaginismus. It's a sexual dysfunction. The vagina cramps so there isn't enough room for…" She waved a hand. "You know what." She sank heavily down in a chair and rested her head in her hands. "That's it. I'm frigid."

"Frigid?" Jake cursed. "Sarah…" He stood up and adjusted his jeans. "You're really okay, aren't you?" He knelt before her, his hands on her knees. "Let me see. You're not bleeding, are you?"

"I'm certainly not letting you see!" she screeched in indignation as she grabbed the pillow from the floor and clutched it in her lap for good measure.

He rolled his eyes. "What's all the modesty about all of a sudden? A few minutes ago you were doing a lot more than letting me see."

"That was before I found out I was frigid."

A new brand of Sarah-logic. Jake didn't even try to follow her reasoning. "I'll be right back," he muttered and exited to the bathroom, taking care not to step on the sleeping kitten. In the bathroom, he started running water into the tub. And he added a drop of vanilla bath gel to set the mood, courtesy of his mother's remaining bath paraphernalia. Maybe the hot water would make her too drowsy to be nervous.

When he returned to the bedroom, she was back in bed, under the covers, looking just as disgruntled as Bohr in one of his better moods. He crawled under the covers beside her and hugged her.

"Do you still hurt?"

She shook her head against his shoulder. "That was just for a moment."

"Why are you in such a hurry to blast your virginity into outer space?"

Sarah groaned. "It doesn't matter. Now we know I'm frigid."

"Come on." He lifted her easily out of the bed and carried her out of the room.

"Where are we going? Eeeks, Jake, the curtains aren't drawn! People will see us. *Mom* will see us."

"We're taking a bath."

"A bath? Together?" Intrigued, she almost smiled, but then the worrying frown returned. "That's no good. I'll still be frigid."

Jake pushed the bathroom door open with his foot and entered. "You're not frigid." He kissed her on the nose, then lowered her into the large tub.

Sarah gasped at the touch of the warm water, then slid down, trying to hide under the bubbles. She didn't quite succeed. The rosy tips of her breasts were just visible and he could barely keep his eyes off them. He did manage to pull away long enough to fetch towels from the cabinet. When he returned, he shrugged off his unbuttoned shirt and went to unzip his jeans when a wet hand stopped him. "You're not...coming in, are you?"

He paused. Her eyes were large and round, almost frightened. For the first time, she actually acted virginal. Without answering, he lifted her hand and kissed it, then removed his jeans and entered the tub. There was no question of letting her back out now. She'd be put off sex for life, and that was definitely something he didn't want to take responsibility for.

Sex for life was just what he wanted with her.

She moved as far away as possible, which admittedly was not very far.

"Come here, Sarah." He pulled her between his knees and kissed her nose. Hurriedly, Sarah grabbed an armful of bubbles and used them to cover her chest. He chuckled.

"You don't have any sexual disorder. You just went too fast and were too nervous." He shook her gently. "You want me to be your mentor, perhaps it would be a good idea if you actually listened to me once in a while."

She eyed him with distrust, then gestured underwater, banishing the bubbles with splashes so she could take a peek. "You're not even...turned on anymore."

"Watching my lover in pain is kind of a turnoff." He grinned. "Even if it was hilarious."

He was ready for the small fists coming down hard on his shoulders, but he winced anyway. Anything to please his lady.

"Well, don't think I'm going to turn you on again." She moved off his lap and back into her own corner of the tub. Jake turned off the water and

her loud voice echoed in the tiled bathroom. ''I'm
going to soak until I look like a prune, and then dry
off, get dressed, buy some yarn and start my new
career as a spinster.''

The pout was so adorable that he almost didn't
have the willpower to wipe it off her face. ''I don't
think so.'' He grabbed her foot and pulled it in his
lap, gently stroking her ankle with his thumb, until
she stopped trying to pull it back. ''You'd make a
lousy spinster. For one, you can't knit worth a
damn.'' His hands moved to her calf. ''Second,
you're too sexy to be a spinster. You turn me on
without even trying, so that plan of yours won't
work.''

Her head lifted from the brim, the curls already
damp from the steam. ''I'm sexy?''

He nodded, her vulnerability tugging at his heart
in a way that her brashness never had. ''Yeah. All
it takes is that smile.'' He slowly moved forward
until he could wrap his arms around her waist and
pull her back into his arms.

''Oh, Jake...''

''Now, Sarah, I'm going to kiss you. Will you
promise me something?''

''What?''

''Don't talk into my mouth. It tickles.''

Soon she began responding to his kisses, and he
felt her hesitation melt. He began to run his hands
over her slick body, thrilling when he felt her forget
her nerves. His focus on her pleasure, he bit back
his own need, his rising passion at seeing her natural

response and feeling her touch on his body, first hesitant and then bolder.

And when her teeth nipped at him and he felt her body tremble against his, the bathtub became too confining.

"We'll make your sheets wet," Sarah gasped as he placed her in the middle of the bed and himself on top of her.

"Terrible," he murmured, smiling at her, then set to work at kissing the droplets from her forehead and working his way down. He spent a lot of time getting her breasts dry, but that was only because she kept clutching his head to her, causing the moisture from his hair to ruin all his hard work. The way she wrapped her leg around his hips to keep him close was absolutely irresistible.

As his mouth moved over her belly and below, she grabbed his hair and stopped him.

"Jake…" Her voice was breathless, but not convincing. "You can't do that."

"Oh. I'll keep that in mind," he murmured, grinning up at her as his gently stroking fingers coaxed another moan out of her. She was so responsive to his every touch. He lowered his head, and her fingers entangled in his hair.

"Jake…" she muttered and he kissed his way up her body to her mouth, then knelt and reached for the foil package on the bedside table and ripped it open with his teeth.

"Let me…" She grabbed the condom away from him and sat up, the rosy look of sensual excitement suddenly replaced by a serious look of determination. "I know how. I practiced on a cucumber."

"A cucumber?" He gritted his teeth as she commenced to put her studies into action. "I thought the traditional practice tool was a banana."

"Tried that first. But then Lisa said you might be bigger than the average banana."

Jake raked a hand through his hair as he digested that. In the morning he had a scheduled flight to London. He would be flying with a crew that, no doubt after serious debate and careful consideration, had decided he might be bigger than the average banana.

He made a mental note to get Lisa transferred. It was too bad that posts on Saturn weren't an option yet, but Greenland or Antarctica would do in a pinch.

"So I upgraded to a medium cucumber."

"A medium cucumber," he repeated tonelessly.

Sarah had sat back on her knees and was examining her handiwork. "Yeah, but I think it was still somewhat bigger than this," she said seriously.

With a growl, Jake grabbed her and pulled her under him. Any more buckets of cold water, and Sarah would be keeping her virginity, at least for one more night, if not indefinitely. "I just thought of something very, *very* kinky, Sarah. Are you feeling adventurous?"

"Kinky? Okay. What?" Her pupils dilated and he could almost see the possibilities marching across her inventive little mind. "You want to tie me up? Spank me? Be spanked?"

"Close." He cradled her breasts in his hands and laved them with his tongue until her body went pliant under him. "I want to ban Lisa and her overactive imagination from our bed for the rest of the evening. Think we can do that?"

Sarah buried her hands in his hair, as her body reminded her of the pleasure he could give her. "'Kay," she breathed.

THE SILENCE OF AFTERGLOW lasted all of three seconds. Jake felt her mouth open against his shoulder and prepared himself for the onslaught of words.

"Wow..." she muttered. "Lisa was right."

Feeling indulgent, exhausted, and very much in love, Jake hugged her close and kissed her forehead. At least Lisa had stayed out of their bed for...well, he had lost track of time. Quite a while, anyway.

"Right about what? About sex?"

"No, about you."

His hand stilled on her back. "About *me?*"

"Yeah. She said you'd be an amazing lover."

"What?" To his chagrin, a blush crept up on him. How could his colleagues be rating his lovemaking skills? Were there theme-based staff meetings he didn't know about? Did the airline host international conferences on his sexual prowess? Did they have slide shows and visual aids, including bananas and cucumbers freshly flown in?

She craned her head to look up at him. "Well, if

you want her exact words, she said you'd be 'dynamite in bed.'" The smile was that of a satisfied woman and her next words were almost a purr. "She was right."

Jake stared up at the ceiling. *Women.* They were a species in their own right. "As much as I appreciate the sentiment, I hope you don't intend to fill her in on the details."

"Nah. I'll just tell her she was right." She yawned.

"Wonderful," Jake informed the ceiling with just the right touch of sarcasm, but Sarah didn't hear. She was already fast asleep.

JAKE WAS ALMOST LATE FOR his flight the next morning. Not because he didn't wake up, but because he lost track of time, watching Sarah sleep. There was a tiny crease between her eyes, as if she were concentrating on her dreams. She had said she was a deep sleeper and he couldn't decide whether to wake her up to kiss her goodbye or to allow her to sleep in peace. Finally, he decided to let her sleep, remembering how difficult it could be to get her to full consciousness. Instead, he tenderly stroked her hair and kissed her forehead, hoping the gesture translated into her dreams. He grabbed a pad from the bedside table and scribbled a short note to leave on his pillow. He kissed her sleeping face once more and then fled before he succumbed to the temptation of staying with her. How would she greet him when he came back? With shyness, passion, humor, regret?

He hadn't told her he loved her yet, and he fidgeted by the door, stealing one last glance at her. It didn't feel right to leave without telling her, without her having at least that reassurance to wake up to, should there be any regrets. He would do it as soon as he got back.

He wasn't really sure why he hadn't said the words. He hadn't felt they were lacking as they'd demonstrated their love in other ways. He smiled to himself as he rushed down the stairs. She loved him back. He was *almost* sure of it.

HE WAS STILL GRINNING TWO hours later when his plane was safely on course. He turned the reins over to Karen and walked to the back of the plane for a cup of coffee and a showdown with Lisa, stopping to chat with a few passengers on the way.

Lisa welcomed him with a mischievous smile and handed him a cup of strong coffee.

"You look tired this morning, Captain. Did you have trouble sleeping?" Her words were innocent enough, but the glow in her electric-blue eyes did not match her tone.

He shrugged, biding his time. Another flight attendant was within earshot, and as soon as she had disappeared, Lisa pounced again.

"Did you and Sarah have fun last night?"

"As a matter of fact, we did," he replied, leaning against the wall as he stared at her over the rim of his cup. He had not forgotten about her bananas and cucumbers, and absolutely not about her scheduled exile in Nuuk. Not for a second.

"Good."

"Actually, your name came up several times."

To his satisfaction, Lisa dropped a basket of rolls to the floor. She swore as she bent to retrieve them. "My name?"

"Uh-huh. Sarah told me all about your interest in the fruit and vegetable industry, as well as explosives."

"My...what?"

Jake raised the plastic cup to his mouth and stared her down as he drank the black liquid. Gradually, she turned a becoming shade of crimson as the meaning of his words sank in. For once, she seemed at a loss for words.

Jake chuckled, satisfied. "You really should have known, Lisa, that Sarah is refreshingly innocent when it comes to complex social issues such as the rules for girl talk." He winked and patted her shoulder before kissing her on the cheek. "I do appreciate your confidence in me. I will strive not to disappoint anyone." He turned away and swaggered down the aisle, laughter bubbling in his throat. That would teach her.

"Jake?" He turned around and reflexively his hand shot up to catch something she hurtled his way. "Have a banana."

Laughing, he winked at her. He made his way back to the cockpit and slid into his seat. Seeing the grin plastered all over his face, Karen sent him a strange look. He curbed it somewhat, just so she wouldn't think he'd gone completely out of his mind. He leaned forward and stared out the window at the ever elusive horizon, as if willing the plane to go faster. All he had to do was get this mountain of metal to England and back, and then he'd be back home with Sarah.

Sarah. He savored her name, feeling ridiculously happy.

She was the best thing that had ever happened to him.

8

SHE WAS THE WORST THING that had ever happened to him.

Sarah paced the floor of Jake's bedroom, dragging with her the sheet that had been wrapped around them during the night. Bohr was sitting on the windowsill, washing his face with a paw as he watched his mistress wear a groove in the floor. She was still holding the note that had been on Jake's pillow. Although a silly smile had taken up residence on her face when she'd read the note, a blissful minute later it had been replaced by a panicky scowl that was not going away in a hurry.

Love, Jake.

The signature was bold and strong, the message above it short, but tender. *I'll miss you. I'll be thinking about you. Until Tuesday.*

Love, Jake.

What did he mean? Love as in "I love you," or love as in "catch you later"? It was an innocent enough signature, and she used it often enough herself, but that word written in Jake's scrawl was stirring her love-softened brains as if they were soup. Jake had written her notes over the years, usually in response to small or not-so-small missives she'd left in his mailbox when he was away for work. She didn't think he'd ever signed them in that way before. *Cheers,* yes, *Later,* yes, *Behave yourself,* yes, *Your humble servant,* yes. *Love,* no. Never. Until now.

She stopped pacing and threw herself into what she was already thinking of as Jake's side of the bed. She buried her chilled toes under the blanket at the foot of the bed and hugged her knees. How did he mean that? How *could* he mean that? And if it was "I love you," was it just the regular love he'd always felt for her, or did he mean something else? She whimpered and huddled back on the bed, staring at the note as if she could decipher its true meaning by analyzing the way the ink marked the paper.

Why couldn't people be more like computers? The only logical system for these things was binary. On or off. Love or not love. None of this mucking around in the middle.

She punched the mattress with her fist and felt like screaming in frustration. Then she did. Bohr let out a grumpy whine at the sudden noise. He glared at her for a minute, one paw still at his ear, then jumped down to the floor and left the room, tail held high in contempt.

"Sorry, Bohr," Sarah muttered. She wasn't used to screaming out her frustrations. She was used to tackling them head on, analyzing them, working on them, solving them, and taking pride and pleasure in the process, each time adding her tiny piece to the jigsaw that was knowledge.

Of course, her frustrations so far hadn't had anything to do with the warm, fuzzy, confusing emotions that were cluttering her heart—her limbic system, she amended, reminding herself the heart was nothing but a blood-pumping organ. But she could deal with that. What she couldn't deal with were those same emotions in Jake.

After endless minutes of thinking in circles, her panic only increasing each time she passed Go, she gave a big sigh. She needed to get dressed. She might think better dressed and back in her own home, not sitting on the bed where she and Jake had made love and slept clutched in each other's arms.

Love, Jake. Why not *See you later,* or *Take care,* or even *Yours?* Why did he have to write *Love,* and mess up her whole life?

After one last look at the note, she folded it and held it in her palm as she threw off the sheet and hunted for her clothes. She found them draped over a chair, which was definitely not how she'd left them last night. Jake had actually taken the time this morning to collect her clothes. She pulled on her underwear, refusing to acknowledge that there were a few tears rolling down her cheeks at his thoughtfulness. Even as she dressed, she didn't let go of the note, not for a second. Having it in her palm was almost like holding hands with Jake.

Holding hands with Jake. Her movements slowed as she thought back a few hours. She'd made love with Jake. Her insides quivered as the memories pulled at her. He had smiled so tenderly as their bodies had joined for the first time. He'd been so careful, so thoughtful. He had touched her as if she was something infinitely precious; held her as if he wanted to protect her from all evils of the world, and in the early hours of the morning he had even sought shelter in her arms, allowing her to protect him in turn.

She had accomplished a lot in her short life, but she'd never felt more proud than when Jake lost control in her arms, his heart pounding under her hands, his body trembling as she explored him. *I can do this to him,* her body had sang, and she'd grown bolder and bolder seeing how much she thrilled him.

It had truly been a magical night. She floated halfway down the stairs before stopping short, remembering that this was all a disaster. A magical night it might have been, but nevertheless a disaster. She stomped the rest of the way down, pausing when she saw the grumpy kitten sitting on the lowest step. She picked him up and cuddled him to her chest, then took one last glance around before leaving the house.

"No, Bohr," she chided the struggling creature as she climbed over the fence. "You're coming back home. You don't live with Jake anymore." She put the kitten down close to Dead-or-Alive, who was sunning herself by the back door and pretending not to be stalking the birds.

"You know, Bohr," she said with a small sigh. "Jake doesn't even like cats."

A hiss was Bohr's disgusted reply and two seconds later his tiny gray body was a blur on the other side of the fence. Sarah shook her head and entered the house after bending down for Dead-or-Alive's morning scratch-and-purr. The windows of Jake's house were closed. Bohr wouldn't be able to find his way inside again. He'd be back when his empty stomach started complaining.

Her mother was arranging flowers, freshly cut from the garden, and didn't blink an eye when she arrived through the back entrance directly from Jake's house. After all, she had been spending the night over there almost all her life.

"Morning, darling. Did you have a nice time with Jake yesterday?"

"Yes." She sat heavily down at the kitchen table. The world had shifted on its axis. Everything seemed different now. Even her mother looked different as she stood there with her flowers, humming a tune along with the radio.

"Do anything fun?"

"Yep." Fun was one way of putting it, she supposed. "I slept with him."

Her mother glanced up at that, meeting her eyes for a second. Sarah read shock in her eyes, and knew that was not caused by her being intimate with Jake, but rather the fact that Sarah had confided anything personal to her.

Her mother looked away quickly and coughed. To

buy time, Sarah thought, amazed at how easily she was able to read her mother. "I see. In that case, I'm really glad it was...fun." She continued busying herself with the flowers for a while before asking hesitantly. "First time?"

Sarah nodded and fetched a bowl and some cereal. She wasn't hungry, but her confused brain needed glucose if she was to figure out what do to about the catastrophic situation. "I think he's probably in love with me," she muttered as she poured the milk and began spooning the cereal into her mouth.

Her mother gave up on arranging the flowers and pushed the vase away. She sat down and rubbed her hands together. "Are you...in love with him?"

Sarah nodded.

Her mother smiled. "That's wonderful, darling. You've always been good together."

Sarah shook her head, her mother's acceptance making her even more uncertain and confused. She pushed the cereal bowl away. "No," she protested. "Don't you see? It will never work out." She had to steel herself to keep her voice steady. "I'll embarrass him and cause nothing but trouble. I'm enough trouble just as his friend. It's best if we can just stay friends."

Her mother was silent for a minute, then she shrugged. "If you think so, dear. I'm sure you know best."

Sarah felt like screaming in frustration for the second time this morning, but she restrained herself.

Her mother might not share Bohr's stoic attitude toward hysterical females. Instead, she concentrated on calling forth that inner calm, as she did when she needed to focus all her mental energy on a complicated problem. She took a deep breath. Since they were having the first mother-daughter conversation of their lives, she better get some things out in the open.

"Mom...about this...brain of mine..." She searched for the right words and found none. She settled for a metaphor instead. "It's like a car. It's fast and powerful, but that doesn't mean it always goes in the right direction. I may be the driver, but I still need a map or directions."

Her mother nodded slowly, confusion clouding her face. This new theory of functional brain anatomy seemed to be giving her some trouble.

"Don't you see, Mom? I may be able to solve complicated problems and think quickly, but I nevertheless need advice. My brain doesn't automatically know what's right or wrong, what works and what doesn't." She clenched and unclenched her fists. "Ever since I was a child, I only had to say my opinion and you immediately agreed that I knew best." She laughed shakily. "So I stopped...relying on you. I relied on Jake instead."

Somewhat to her surprise, her mother seemed to be slowly understanding. She was silent for a while, a faraway look in her eyes. Before she spoke, she reached out to cover one of Sarah's hands with her own.

"Neither I nor your father were much good at school, Sarah. We could never figure out where that genius gift of yours came from. I guess it intimidated us from the start." She sighed before carrying on.

"I don't think I ever told you about the first time I realized how different you were. You were three years old and we were discussing household expenses. It was just before Christmas. Your father was talking about how much this and that cost, and I was writing the figures down and adding them up and then I told him how much it was."

She smiled tenderly at Sarah. "And you were on the floor quietly playing with some blocks, and then you looked up, and said in your baby voice. 'No!' and then you named another figure." She paused. "And it turned out you were right. You had calculated our Christmas expenses in your curly little head."

Her eyes slowly cast off the sheen of the past. "I know what you mean, Sarah. We never treated you like a child who needed us. You seemed too high above us, so unreachable with all your understanding of things we had never even heard of. We were never your map." The resignation in her voice told Sarah her mother knew what she meant.

"Exactly, Mom. And Jake..." Sarah gritted her teeth. Now it hurt just to say his name. "You left all that to Jake. He was just a kid himself, and he became the only person I could lean on, the only one who would guide me." She shook her head in frustration. "Jeez, Mom, do you know who told me about menstruation?"

Her mother shook her head. "No. I'm sorry I never did. You never asked me. I assumed you'd know from all your books or from school." She sat down and reached out to Sarah, stroked her cheek with the back of her hand. "Oh, honey, I'm sorry. I suppose your medical books were no substitute for a mother's advice. Did you find a woman who could tell you about it? Or a friend from school, perhaps?"

Tears welled in Sarah's eyes. "No, Mom. Jake did."

"Jake?"

"Yes, Jake." Unsuccessfully she tried to swallow the lump in her throat. "He was sixteen years old at the time. How many sixteen-year-old boys do you think would even give a twelve-year-old girl the time of day? But Jake spent days with me pouring over library books on female anatomy." She smiled wryly. "And not even the interesting parts." She took a deep breath. "He even helped me get my first pads. I was too embarrassed to buy them myself, and you only had tampons in the house."

Her mother's mouth was hanging open. "Jake bought you those?"

Sarah giggled through the tears. "No. He pilfered them from his mom. And he got caught, too."

She sobered up as she remembered the embarrassed look on Jake's face as he had leaned on the fence that afternoon and told her his mother wanted to speak with her. Mrs. Benford had calmly discussed the subject in a matter-of-fact tone her mother would never have dared take with her prodigy daughter. Then both of them had accompanied Mrs. Benford to the local supermarket where Jake's mother had helped her choose the feminine products. She wondered who had squirmed more at the checkout counter, her or Jake, but Mrs. Benford had resolutely handed her the money and then disappeared into the frozen food section. And Jake, sweet wonderful Jake, had stayed with her, although as a sixteen-year-old boy he had a lot more reason to be embarrassed than she had.

Of course, nobody had even given them or their purchases a second glance and Mrs. Benford's lesson had been successfully taught.

Sarah sighed deeply as her heart contracted with love for Jake. He'd always been there for her, no matter what. She couldn't allow him to keep sacrificing himself for her.

"And now?" her mother probed gently. "You and Jake?"

Sarah was abruptly yanked back to the present and the nostalgic smile vanished from her lips. "I've been nothing but trouble for him."

"I think Jake might like that kind of trouble, sweetie." Her mother took a lock of her hair and moved it behind her ear, an uncharacteristically motherly gesture. "He's a big boy, Sarah. Don't lock him out. Don't make this kind of decision for him."

Sarah stared at her mother. Okay, she had wanted

Mom to say something other than "Yes, you're right, dear," but she was not supposed to defect from Sarah's side and help Jake mess up his life. Mom was supposed to be sensible about this and see that there was no way Jake could be allowed to keep sacrificing himself for her. That he shouldn't have to keep paying the price for her inadequacies.

Mom was supposed to say... Sarah whimpered and put her head down on the table, allowing her mother to stroke her hair.

Mom was supposed to have said, "Yes, you're right, dear."

SARAH DIDN'T GET MUCH accomplished at work that day. She was slumped over her desk, staring at an article she'd been trying to read all morning, but the words were not getting through to her brain except as random black images against white background. It could've been Arabic for all she knew.

And it was only German.

"Sarah?" William was knocking on her open door, looking unusually enthusiastic. "Come take a look at something."

Glad to be interrupted, Sarah jumped to her feet and walked with him to the labs. "Our female chimp got here this morning," he explained, "and she turns out to be an old pal of Cosine. He was thrilled to see her. It's amazing to see them together."

It was. The two chimps were happily hugging each other, exchanging stories in Chimp, completely oblivious to the observing humans.

"She's named Sine and the two of them have spent most of their lives together. They've only been separated since Cosine came here." William smiled almost paternally as he watched the two chimps. "They obviously haven't forgotten each other."

"They're in love," Sarah said faintly, watching the two chimps cuddle each other. William looked at her quizzically.

"I suppose you could say that," he replied.

After getting to know Sine for a while, Sarah returned to her office almost in a daze, and fell down into her battered beanbag, curling up into a fetal position. This had been a huge mistake. She groaned and beat her head against her knees. Of course Jake loved her. He had to. Making love with him had been selfish of her. Had she really believed he would do that without deep feelings on his part?

Had she really imagined that she could have a one-night stand with Jake, of all men?

She had been incredibly stupid. He was going away, and that would be the end of any romantic feelings between them. It would have to be, despite Lisa's claims to the contrary. Now, everything was more complicated than ever. Jake wouldn't want to leave her. He would be imagining their future together. He would be planning all sorts of things that could just never be.

Sarah bit her knuckle, a nervous habit from childhood she still wasn't completely cured off. She had three days to decide what to do. Three days before

Jake would return and she would have to face him again.

Three days to figure out how to save Jake from himself.

9

JAKE WENT STRAIGHT TO Sarah's house when he got home, without even bothering to change clothes first. He wanted to see Sarah. He *needed* to see Sarah. He needed to reaffirm what had happened between them, reassure himself it hadn't just been a dream.

Ellen greeted him at the door, her smile telling him she must know something about what was going on between him and Sarah. And that she didn't disapprove of it.

"Hello, Jake. Straight from the airport, are you?"

"Hi, Ellen. Yes." He smiled broadly, not the least interested in keeping anything from his prospective mother-in-law. "I couldn't wait to see Sarah."

"Right." She looked toward the stairs and then closed the door quietly behind him, stopping him with a hand on his arm as he started for the stairs. "Just a moment, Jake."

Surprised, Jake waited. Sarah's mother had been a friendly but distant person in his life. He didn't remember ever really talking to her, beyond answering the customary questions, which had slowly changed from "How's school?" to "How's work?". Obviously, there was something else on her mind now.

"Is Sarah okay?" he asked.

"Yes. More or less, anyway." Ellen rubbed her hands nervously together and again glanced toward the stairs. "I've tried not to interfere in her life, Jake, and I'm beginning to think that was a mistake." She looked him squarely in the eye. "It may not be the most appropriate time for me to become an interfering mother, but…" She shrugged. "Sarah told me what happened between you two."

Uh-oh. Jake couldn't quite look her in the eye anymore and distinctly felt his ears warm. He hoped Sarah hadn't been as free with the details as he feared she might have been. He fidgeted. Sarah kept making him feel like he was fifteen-years-old.

"I think it's wonderful, Jake. She loves you, I know. She told me so." She put her hand on his arm. "She's got some strange ideas now. She'll try to push you away. You've been a good friend to her all this time, don't allow her to push you away now."

"Never," Jake assured her, as worry began to gnaw at his stomach. What was Sarah thinking? He swore under his breath. Couldn't she have spent her brain power on nuclear physics or something and just let their love alone? Some things didn't need analysis.

The newly tied knot in his stomach relaxed as the first part of what Ellen had said sank in. *Sarah loved him.* It would be okay. Sarah might be having some convoluted second thoughts, but she loved him. Everything would be just fine.

He impulsively kissed Ellen on the cheek and bounced up the stairs toward Sarah's room. He wanted to grab her and kiss her senseless. Sleep had eluded him the last few nights, stuck in a hotel room on the other side of the world. After only one night together, his bed seemed cold and empty without her in his arms. He had missed her something awful.

He should have woken her up and gotten a good-bye kiss and a sleepy smile. His steps slowed as he approached her open door. Hell, he should have skipped breakfast and woken her up with soft kisses and softer caresses, for a quick, but sweet reminder of what they'd shared during the night. He should've told her he loved her and made sure she wouldn't have any second thoughts.

Sarah was sitting at her desk, a small mountain of papers and books in front of her. Her back was turned to him and her unruly black curls fell to her shoulders. He paused for a moment and drank in the sight of her. Her head was slightly turned so he saw her face in profile, a small frown on her brow as she concentrated on her reading, with a pen between her teeth. Even with the noise he had made running up the stairs, she hadn't noticed his approach.

Sarah did that, he thought affectionately. She could tune out the entire world and just concentrate on the universe inside her head. He shut the door carefully, just in case they got up to something that didn't need an audience. He hugged her from behind and kissed her neck, burying his face in the sweet warmth of her hair.

"Did you miss me?" he breathed, savoring the feel of her for a second before noting her unresponsiveness after the initial startled response. He opened his mouth to ask her what was wrong, but closed it again. He'd pretend not to notice, and she might let it go. If he could just get to that mouth of hers... He stuck his head to the side of hers, seeking her lips, but she turned away. He tried the other side, and she turned the other way again.

Fine. Mentally he shrugged. Her mouth was not available, but there were plenty of other interesting places. He could, for example, start by nibbling her neck. He opened his mouth and gently sank his teeth into her skin. She tasted like sunshine. He felt a shiver go through her and smiled, ending his soft bite. He pushed himself between Sarah and the desk and perched on its edge facing her. Love punched into him as one last sunbeam sneaked in between the drawn curtains and touched her nose and cheek, and he realized there was probably a silly smile on his face.

Sarah was not smiling. Personally, he thought he made a fine substitute for the pile of dusty books that had formerly occupied this space. She didn't seem to agree. She was staring quite resolutely at the third button on his shirt, her hands folded primly in her lap.

She was beautiful. He took her hands and held them against his chest, hoping she could feel how his heart had picked up speed just at seeing her again. "I missed you, Sarah."

Sarah swallowed and for the first time glanced up at his face. Then she pushed her chair back and gestured to the second chair. "Sit down, Jake. We need to talk."

"No."

She frowned at him in that adorable way, her nose wrinkling slightly. "No?"

"No," he repeated. "We don't need to talk. We need to kiss."

She held out a hand as he leaned toward her, holding him off. "We do need to talk. I'm serious, Jake."

She *was* serious. Very serious. Too serious. Jake pushed himself away from the desk and fell down into the chair she'd pointed at. He glared up at her. He suspected he was pouting, but he didn't really care. "You better have a good excuse for depriving me of my kiss. I've been waiting for days and I really need that kiss."

As usual, she wasn't even listening to him. She stood up and began pacing the room. "I'm really sorry about all this, Jake. Really, I am. We need to stop this before it gets to your system."

Jake frowned, confused. "Stop what?"

She gestured aimlessly between them. "This. You and me. Our...affair."

"Our *affair?*"

"Yes."

Jake digested that for a minute. "We're having

an *affair?* Sounds so...forbidden. Very enticing.''
He felt like laughing, but she was so serious that he
curbed his impulse. ''You *are* in my system,
Sarah,'' he said gently, wishing he could just kiss
her frown away. ''And that's where you're staying,''
he added more firmly. ''Learn to live with it.''

''But...''

''No buts. You wanted to talk, we talked. Now
it's my turn. Come kiss me.''

''No!''

He grabbed her around the waist and pulled her
between his legs. ''Yes! Teach me, Professor. Have
you been studying the technical aspects of kissing
like you promised me you would?''

He simply loved the blush that crept up her face
as she stared down at him.

''I can't make you happy, Jake.'' Her tone was
wretched, her eyes moist with tears. Where had that
come from?

''You do make me happy,'' he said, allowing his
happiness to show in his smile. ''You make me very
happy, Sarah.''

''I mean it.'' She pushed herself away from him
and sat down at her desk, grabbing a pen to fiddle
with. He recognized the nervous gesture. ''I hope
we can go back to being friends, but if not, that's
just a loss we will have to face. You were right. A
man and a woman can't become lovers and expect
nothing to change.''

''Things will only change for the better. Trust me.''

She looked at him for a minute and hesitated before opening her mouth to what had to be the most ridiculous sentence he had ever heard emerge from there.

"I think you and Lisa should get together."

"Me and..." Jake sputtered after a few moments of stunned silence. "Are you absolutely out of that brilliant mind of yours?"

"Why not?" Sarah leaned forward, earnestly looking at him as if to convince him this was a suggestion worthy of the Bright Idea Award of the year. "She's beautiful and funny and smart, you like each other, even if you bicker all the time. It's perfect."

Jake stared at her for a minute, then pushed himself to his feet and yanked the curtains apart to look out the window. His ears were trying to convince his brain that yes, indeed, it *was* what she'd said.

"What are you doing?"

He turned around and glared at her. "I was just checking if we're still on planet Earth, or if you beamed us up to your spaceship."

"Oh, Jake." Wretchedly, she tapped her knees with the heels of her hands before turning away from him and bowing her head over her desk.

"Oh, hell." He was at her side in a split second. "Stop it, Sarah. Don't you dare cry." He leaned on the edge of the desk and grabbed her by the shoulders, shaking her slightly. "Don't you dare!" There was only one thing he hated more than seeing Sarah cry, and that was knowing he had caused her tears.

And right now, he didn't feel like comforting her, he felt like shaking some sense into her.

"Don't you see, Jake? That's just it. I *am* from another planet. That's why you need a mate...of your own species, so to speak."

"A mate of my own species?" He cursed colorfully. "How can someone so smart be such an idiot?" He raised a hand. "I do mean that in the nicest possible way."

"You wouldn't stay happy with me, Jake. I'm too...alien. You'd get tired of constantly standing between me and the world."

"I'm going to stand *with* you in the world, not between you and the world." He cursed and stared out the window, his whole body tense. "I'm not making sense." He spun around and pointed at her. "No, I'm making perfect sense. *You're* the one not making any sense. What are we talking about, anyway?"

"It won't work, Jake. You and me, it won't work. It can't work."

It was time for his trump card. "I love you, Sarah."

His words did not have the intended effect. His woman did not smile tremulously and fall into his arms with a shriek of happiness. Instead, she smiled sadly. "I love you too, Jake. I've loved you ever since you raided your mother's bathroom cupboard for me." She reached out and traced the curve of his ear with her finger, pressed her thumb to his cheek where his now well-hidden dimple frequently was. "Before that, I only adored you."

Jake saw the stars in her eyes, brighter than any he'd seen high above the clouds. She loved him. She'd told him she loved him. Everything in the world was perfect now. He hadn't thought it would be that easy.

He frowned. This was a bit *too* easy. His muscles tensed again as he resigned himself to the possibility that the struggle was not over. He frowned, then decided to hope for the best. "I love you, you love me. I'm seeing happily ever after here."

"No."

He sighed, exasperated. "Sarah, I'm really sick of hearing that word. And just so you know, I'll never, ever accept that." He needed to kiss her. If he could just kiss her and hold her and touch her...

She moved away. "That's just sex, Jake. It won't change my mind."

Had he spoken aloud? "What's just sex?"

Sarah frowned at him. "It was obvious that you wanted to convince me by pulling me down on that bed with you." Her eyes glazed over as she grabbed a notepad and jotted something down. "Amazing. Can it be that telepathy is real and somehow connected to people being hormonally in tune? Or did I simply read your body language?"

Jake pulled the notepad from her and tossed it along with the pen on the desk, then picked her up from the chair and carried her to the bed.

"What are you doing?" Sarah protested.

"I'm going to get my kiss. You owe me."

He tossed her down on the bed and joined her, throwing a leg over hers to prevent her from scrambling off. "Be still, angel. Kiss me first, protest later. I need my kiss. Please?"

His voice was a low growl and she couldn't resist the need that was honestly reflected in his eyes. She loved him. She loved him too much to allow him to stop loving her, to fall out of love with her once the novelty wore off, to watch disillusion replace love in his eyes when he looked at the strange creature he was stuck with.

But he was right, she told herself, there was no harm in allowing him his kiss. She smiled suddenly and wound her arms around his neck and opened her lips against his when his tongue pushed against them. She wanted a deep and furious kiss, a vivid reminder of their long and intimate night together. Jake groaned and his hands moved to her breasts, gently stroking them as their tongues played together.

"I missed you so much," he panted, as there was at last half an inch of empty space between their faces. His hand moved down her torso, again brushing over her breasts and she impatiently pulled at her shirt, wanting nothing between them. His laughter fanned her face and he helped her, pushing off his jacket and opening his shirt so he could press his bare chest against her breasts. Then his mouth was on her nipple, suckling through the thin fabric of her bra, when there was a loud sound from behind the closed door.

Sarah's flushing face broke out in a grin. "Did you miss Dead-or-Alive, too? It sounds like she missed you."

Jake rested his forehead against hers. "Is there any cat left at my house?"

She shook her head. "Not even one. Bohr really wants to live there, though. He's probably negotiating with every window, but I closed them all so he shouldn't get in."

"Good. Let's go over there." He nibbled on her eyebrow. "Not only will we be cat-free, we can make all the noise we want."

"Did I make noise?" she asked shyly, peering up into his face with those incredible gray eyes of hers. He kissed her once on the lips, quick and hard. He needed her. He needed her naked under him, above him, anywhere, as long as there was not even an inch between them and not a single cat in the room.

"Only when I did something right," he grinned back and pulled her to her feet.

That was a mistake. The minute she was standing upright, the frown reappeared and she pulled away from him and picked up her discarded shirt.

Jake sighed, and braced himself for what was coming. When she hesitated, her fingers trembling as she tried to fasten her buttons, he said it for her.

"I suppose you want to tell me again that we aren't good together and that you want me to shack up with Lisa and make babies with her?"

Sarah nodded very slightly. "Something like that," she said timidly.

Jake put his hands on his hips and tried to stare her down, but she looked squarely back. He folded his arms on his chest and leaned back against the wall. If she wanted war, she'd have war.

"Close your eyes, Sarah."

She shook her head, and he shrugged impatiently. "What are you afraid of? I'm not going to touch you. Just close your eyes for a moment."

She bit her lip, but then did as he asked.

"Okay, Sarah. Do some of that imaging stuff you're so good at. Picture this—Lisa in my bed. We are kissing, touching, making love, just like you and I did."

Sarah's face scrunched up in a frown and she whimpered, then turned away, her hands over her ears. "Don't do this, Jake."

He grabbed her arms and turned her to face him. "You don't want me with Lisa. You don't want me with another woman. You want me with you."

"I can't have you, Jake," she cried, "you know how I am. I'm different. I'll always be different. I'll always be saying the wrong thing and doing the wrong thing and I'll embarrass you. You deserve better." She looked at him, imploring. "I know it's hard for you to imagine now, but you may realize later that Lisa is right for you. She's everything I'm not."

"Just like you, Lisa is beautiful and funny and charming," Jake said between clenched teeth.

"She's pretty smart, too, from the perspective of the average mortal. But she's not you. And you're the woman I love. Like it or not, you're stuck with me."

"No, Jake." Her voice was serious. A chill went through him as he realized just how final that tone was.

"Why the hell did you sleep with me, Sarah?" he asked, the tone sharper than he'd intended.

"I wanted to…before you went away," she whispered.

"Went away? Where am I going?"

"Florida, Jake. Remember? Your transfer came through."

Jake shook his head, confused. "I haven't heard about that."

She shrugged. "Did you check your mail? Lisa told me."

"So, your virginity was my going-away present?"

Sarah still wasn't meeting his eyes.

"Something like that. I'm sorry, Jake. There was this really primitive feeling inside me, that I wanted to…possess you, just once, before it was over."

"*Over?*" Jake practically howled the word. "Sarah, you've been my other half since you were in diapers. Do you really think anything between us can ever be 'over'?"

Sarah bit her lip, then resolutely continued. "Do you remember how I met Lisa?"

"Sure. It was right after that date I had with her. What's that got to do with anything?"

"I met her at your house, after your first and only date."

She sounded as if this clinched the case. Jake raised his gaze to the ceiling and called upon the extra reserves of patience he always had for Sarah. "I repeat— What has that got to do with anything?"

"Think back, Jake. You went on a date with Lisa, and then you brought her home."

"So?"

"Something might have happened between you then, if I hadn't been there."

Jake rolled his eyes. "Nothing would have happened. There was this show on television we discovered we'd both wanted to see more than we wanted to be out on the town. All we had plans for was television and popcorn."

Sarah shook her head. "I remember it very well. I had something important to tell you, something from work, and when you weren't home, I crawled in through your window to wait for you." She was lost in thought for a second. "I remember now. It was my theory about the chemical basis of anger. And then I fell asleep on the sofa, and woke up when Lisa tried to sit down on me."

"I remember." He did. He'd been in the kitchen, throwing a bag of popcorn into the microwave when a bloodcurdling scream had sounded from the living room. When he got there, Sarah was sitting on the sofa under a blanket, her clothes and hair rumpled from sleep, and a very startled Lisa staring at this strange apparition.

"Lisa came home with you, to find another woman in your bed. No wonder your relationship became platonic."

"It didn't become platonic. It never was anything else. Plus, it was my sofa, not my bed. Plus, she knew from the start you and I were only friends."

"She says she knew all along that I was in love with you."

"Really? She should have told me. We could have been playing with condoms for years if she'd told me."

"Don't be silly, Jake."

Jake turned to the window again and grabbed the windowsill as he tried to calm himself. She was telling *him* not to be silly?

"Lisa isn't interested in me that way, Sarah. Nor I in her. If there was attraction between us, don't you think we'd have done something about it a long time ago?"

She didn't even blink. "I was always in the way."

Two hours later Sarah was feeling exhausted and Jake wasn't looking his best, either. He had talked, growled, cajoled, and generally tried every venue of attack. Resisting the look in his eyes, resisting the need to hug him and reassure him, wasn't getting any easier.

But now he was silent. His shoulders were slumped and he seemed to have finally understood how serious she was about this. He was giving up.

The thought gave her no sense of relief. Instead her heart ached even more at seeing how lost he looked.

"I'm going home to get some sleep, Sarah." He walked to the door, then turned back and dug in his inner pocket. "By the way, I got you something." He tossed an envelope on her desk. "I hope you can use it. They claim a 95 percent success rate."

Sarah nodded, her vocal cords paralyzed. His footsteps down the stairs echoed in her skull and long minutes passed until she reached for the oblong white envelope. She opened it slowly, pain wiping out all curiosity of what Jake could be giving her. She was right, she chanted to herself. She was saving Jake a lot of pain and heartache. Perhaps some day they could be friends again. Perhaps distance would lessen the hurt. Perhaps some day they'd laugh at all this.

Perhaps. She sighed. But not likely.

Inside the envelope there was a single sheet of thick parchment paper, folded in two. She opened it and for several seconds stared at the large cursive lettering.

And then the tears came, raining down on the cream-colored document as she clutched it to her chest.

It was a gift certificate to a fear-of-flying course.

10

"MY, YOU'RE LOOKING cheerful this morning."

Work had not come soon enough, but Jake had forgotten he'd have to face Lisa, along with the comforting ritual of flying.

"I have a headache," he grumbled. He did have a headache of a sorts, although the pain was more in his mind than in his actual head.

Lisa took up her usual stance by the mirror to tame her hair. "Is your headache named Sarah, by any chance?"

Jake grunted in affirmation. If he had been a drinking man, a bottle of something strong would be in his hand right now. As it was, he was clutching an empty paper cup of the dreadful cafeteria coffee. He'd actually drunk it all, instead of his one ritual masochistic sip before throwing it away.

And as if that wasn't bad enough, it wasn't even his first cup. It was his second. Might even be his third. He'd lost count. Cafeteria coffee—and Sarah—did that to you.

"You look terrible, Jake. I take it our resident alien has been messing with your mind again?"

"Yep." He brought the empty cup to his lips and

took a long swallow of nothing. If nothing else, it would give Lisa the visual image of a man at the edge of his rope. He needed sympathy. Heck, he could even use pity. God knows, he deserved both. "Get this— She wants you and me to live happily ever after."

"You and me?" Lisa laughed. "Are you serious?" She sat down and patted his arm. "As much as I adore your charming personality and terrific body, I have other plans for the rest of my life." She whistled something altogether too cheerful for Jake's frame of mind. "They might even involve a certain biologist who's probably pretty yummy underneath those glasses and that scowl."

Jake groaned as he slumped in his chair, tearing at the edge of the paper cup. "William? Don't go there, Lisa. He'll just take his extra IQ points and stab you through the heart with them. Take it from me. Been there, done that, bought the slide rule."

Lisa snatched the cup away from his clutched fist, brushed the torn paper ribbons into it and tossed it in the waste basket. "Now. Stop feeling sorry for yourself. What you need to do, Jake, is fight Sarah on her own level." She crossed her legs, grabbed her diary from her purse and then slapped him hard on the thigh.

"Ouch!" Jake straightened from his slouch and went bolt upright in his chair. He gave her a hurt look. "What was that for? Am I not in enough pain already?"

"Never indicate to Sarah that you're about to give

up. Keep her guessing. That's better. Sit up straight. Look confident. Send out waves of masculine energy and self-assurance." She winked. "And look sexy while you're at it."

Jake narrowed his eyes in the most threatening manner he could muster, sending out waves of masculine irritation and annoyance as he rubbed his still-smarting thigh. There was only one woman's hand he wanted on his thigh and it definitely wasn't Lisa's.

She glared right back, unintimidated. "Well, do you want my help or not?"

"I guess I don't have a choice," he muttered. "It's not like I've got anything to lose. Do you really have a plan?"

"Yep." She wielded a green ballpoint pen over her diary. "Tell me all the reasons she has used to try to drive you away."

Jake rolled his eyes. "How much time have you got?"

"That many?"

"Yep. Let's see." He counted on his fingers. "One—she loves me, I love her, but that's irrelevant and we'll get over it, cause love is just…blah blah. You get the idea. Typical Sarahese. Two—she'll ruin my life, because she's not Miss Average. Three—she thinks you and I would be happily married with 2.6 kids by now if she hadn't been asleep in my house after our date. Four—" he waved a hand "—something about our kids turning out just like her and that being a disaster. Five—I'm moving away, never mind I told her I'd rather be with her, even if it meant moving to the Klingon homeworld. And then there was something about her fear of flying, although how that is an insurmountable obstacle is a mystery only known to people who understand the theory of relativity on first, second or third reading.''

''Mmm.'' Lisa was busy scribbling. She looked up, pen still posed over the diary. ''That's it, or did you just run out of breath?''

''I think that's it. It's difficult to follow her convoluted reasoning.'' He stood up to fetch yet another cup of fake coffee, but Lisa pulled him back by his sleeve. She put her huge purse on her lap and dug deep, then triumphantly emerged with a small metal thermos. ''I've got real coffee here, Captain. How much will you pay?'' She looked at his face, and made a sympathetic noise. ''Never mind. You're a man in pain. I won't charge you this time.'' She unscrewed the thermos and poured him a cup. The aroma was heavenly, but it reminded him of Sarah. He stared glumly down into the obsidian liquid. Everything reminded him of Sarah.

''Coffee is a stimulant drug, you know. A synaptic enhancer. Alcohol has the opposite effect, it's a tranquilizer. Only it sort of tranquilizes inhibitions first so the effect initially looks like that of a stimulant.'' He bent over the coffee, his elbows on the table and his hands supporting his temples. A pulse pushed against his fingers, so he was probably still alive, despite everything. He wasn't sure if that was a good thing or not. "Or something like that, anyway."

Lisa wasn't even listening, let alone admiring his nearly fluent Sarahese. "Okay. Well, this is our plan. We countermand every one of Sarah's arguments. Then you throw in a smoldering look with those killer blue eyes, an adorable smile, hurt, yet hopeful, and a masterful seduction robbing her of all her sensibilities. Dr. Sarah won't know what hit her. In short, my friend, you sweep her off her feet." She threw him a brilliant smile and with three fingers, turned the diary to face him. She had listed every venue of attack in green ink, with an empty check box by each one. "Think you can handle that?"

Jake stared at the list and at the empty check boxes, and saw in his mind an endless row of obstacles receding into the horizon. "You meant it when you said you were going to bring me to my knees, didn't you?" he muttered, his head spinning a bit.

"You betcha, darling. Don't look so miserable. We'll crack her yet."

"Sarah *is* a nut, but I'm not so sure she's that easily crackable. I like to think that my last attempt was pretty thorough."

"It obviously wasn't good enough." Lisa chuckled. "She really thinks you and I should be together? That's so funny."

Jake wondered whether to take this personally,

but decided not to bother. "Are you really going to stalk poor William?"

"He's 'poor William' now? You seemed ready to put him six feet under last time I looked."

"That's when I thought he had designs on Sarah," he replied. Then he shot to his feet so fast the table shook. Lisa narrowly managed to rescue her open thermos as it teetered on the edge of the table. "What's wrong?"

"Sarah. William. Compatibility. Research."

Lisa understood immediately his incoherent key phrases. "She wouldn't."

"She might," Jake said grimly. "Even if only to convince me. She doesn't know you're really interested in him, does she?"

"The nerd is mine!" Lisa screwed the lid on the thermos and stuffed it into her purse. "How long before that flight leaves?"

Jake looked at his watch. "Two hours."

"I'm calling in a favor." Lisa strode to the pay phone. "I'll get someone to fill in for me. There is no way both of us are flying to another continent leaving those two alone together. No way."

Jake tugged at his hair, then turned on his heel and ran out in the hallway toward another pay phone. He would bribe, threaten or beg his way out of this flight. William could be Lisa's available mouth. He'd not be Sarah's. Jake growled as he punched in the numbers. Not if he wanted to keep his teeth.

TWO DARK HEADS WERE BOWED together over a mouse cage when Lisa and Jake barged into the room like a pair of charging elephants in airline uniforms. Both looked up, startled at the intrusion.

"Jake? Lisa? What are you doing here?"

There was nothing but surprise in Sarah's voice, no guilt or even irritation at the interruption. Jake and Lisa looked at each other, and then at the two scientists, then around at the roomful of students who were all staring at them.

Jake slumped against the door and decided he never should have woken up this morning.

"Hi!" Lisa chirped. "We just decided to drop by and pay you guys a visit."

Sarah wasn't buying it. Of course she wasn't. Not even the chimpanzees would buy that story. "At nine in the morning?" she asked doubtfully. "In your uniforms? Aren't you supposed to be on your way to Europe in an hour?"

Jake continued to keep the door company and refused to meet Lisa's imploring gaze. She could handle this. She was much better at making up lame excuses for ridiculous behavior than he was. She had more experience, although he was rapidly evening out the score.

"Well, we were, yes. But now we're not. The flight was canceled."

"Why?"

Lisa shrugged. "You know. One of those things that can cause flights to be canceled. Weather and whatnot."

Jake rolled his eyes. The weather? There was

nothing wrong with the weather and insulting the intelligence of the white-coated pair probably wasn't a good idea.

"A bomb threat," he supplied. "False alarm probably, but they had to check it out."

"A bomb threat?" Sarah paled. "Oh, my God."

Lisa gave him one of her rolling-eyes looks. "Not a real bomb threat, Sarah. It was just a silly prank. It's nothing to worry about. Anyway…" She linked her arm through William's and smiled at Sarah. "We came to ask you out on a double date."

William backed away in a hurry, but Lisa was quite determinedly stuck to his arm. She pulled him back, a move that succeeded only because in that corner, backing farther away than two feet was impossible.

"Um. Double date?" Sarah looked warily between the three persons present, and behind her, a group of students was watching the developing drama with fascinated expressions. "Who is dating whom?"

"Who cares? We'll all go. It'll be fun."

Jake noticed Sarah's eyes move between him and Lisa and knew exactly what she was thinking. "Couldn't just you and Jake go?" she asked hopefully, and Lisa rolled her eyes. "That wouldn't be a double date, silly. We need four people for a double date. Two times two, you know."

William coughed at Lisa's display of advanced mathematics. "Count me out. I'm busy. Sorry."

"Nonsense," Lisa said. "Sarah, aren't you his boss or something? Tell him he has to go."

Sarah looked at William, her lower lip caught in her teeth. "Would you mind, William? I'm sure it would be fun."

"I don't think so," he protested.

Sarah pulled him to the side, and to Jake's horror whispered something into his ear. William hesitated, then nodded reluctantly and Sarah returned to them, smiling.

"Okay, double date it is."

The students cheered.

THE DOUBLE DATE was somewhere between a failure and a disaster. Jake and Sarah were both quiet, while the witty and not-so-witty remarks flew between William and Lisa. It turned out Sarah had bribed William on the date by promising to clean out the chimpanzees' cage for him.

The things we do for matchmaking, Jake thought sarcastically. Sarah had repeatedly tried to push him and Lisa together, pointing out things they had in common. She had even tried to prod them out onto the empty dance floor together. At least Lisa was on his side. She was very clearly staking her claim on William and that would ensure that Sarah wouldn't turn to that guy with any strange plans.

"Jake?" Sarah leaned toward him, once again pointing at Lisa. "Lisa doesn't like cats that much either," she said triumphantly. "She's a dog person."

That was it.

He stood up and grabbed Sarah's wrist, pulling her with him. "Come on, genius. Let's dance." He didn't listen to her protests, knowing she would allow him to pull her out on the dance floor rather than cause a scene. Once there, he put his arms around her and pulled her close, even if the song wasn't exactly a slow one.

At first, Sarah was stiff in his arms but then she rested her head against his shoulder and Jake melted. He moved slowly, just rocking back and forth, enjoying having her more or less relaxed in his arms.

"It's not going to work, Sarah," he said softly into her ear. "Lisa and I will never be an item. Besides..." he shifted them so that their table was in her line of view "...she has designs on someone else."

Sarah nodded. "I noticed. I'm sorry." She patted his shoulder. "You'll find someone, Jake. I know you will."

"I've already found someone. You."

She was silent.

"I'm not going away, Sarah. I won't move to Florida unless you come with me."

She pulled back and he saw tears glittering in her eyes. "Don't do this, Jake. I won't change my mind." She moved away and walked back to their table, her head bowed.

Feeling utterly depressed, Jake followed. It was time to go home. He had one last plan, but it wasn't a very sophisticated one. He was just going to drop

Lisa and William off, then corner Sarah and try to convince her, using Lisa's green list of advice. One last shot at knocking sense into Sarah.

"That was fun," Lisa said, patting Jake's and Sarah's respective shoulders from the back of the car. "We should do this again sometime." A loud kissing sound echoed in the car and Jake looked in the mirror just in time to see William rub lipstick off his cheek with the expression of a little boy just attacked by an overly affectionate aunt. He stored that image away. Perhaps he'd be able to laugh at it in ten years or so.

They dropped William off, and then there was silence in the car as they drove back home. Usually Jake stopped the car outside Sarah's house and let her jump out before pulling into his own driveway. This time, however, he passed her house and only stopped inside his garage, effectively blocking any escape she might be thinking of. He walked around the car and opened the door for her, then led her into the house.

"I should be getting home, Jake."

"We need to talk first." Where was that note Lisa had written? His palms were sweating. This was important. Perhaps his last chance at convincing her. He excused himself to the kitchen and ransacked his pockets until he found the list. He perused it for a minute, memorized it and then shook his head in frustration, balled the note in his fist and tossed it on top of the refrigerator.

"Look sexy!" was one piece of Lisa's sage advice, with a smiley face check box. At least someone was enjoying this farce. He blew out a frustrated breath. Look sexy? How the hell did a man go about looking sexy, anyway? Now, if he were a woman, he had a few ideas, but he didn't think those tricks would work to make Sarah realize she was an indispensable part of his life.

Seduction he could do, and Sarah did tend to be more agreeable in a horizontal position. The bad part was that common sense trickled right out of her brain as soon as she was upright again.

He retrieved the note from the top of the refrigerator and read it again. He would give it a try. One more try wouldn't hurt.

An hour later he was back in the kitchen, fetching a fresh supply of drinks. Nothing had changed. She wasn't even budging. He felt absolutely powerless as he shuffled back into the living room and passed the can to Sarah. "Is there nothing I can say to change your mind?"

Sarah rolled the cool can on her cheek and shook her head without meeting his eyes. She looked miserable. She had looked miserable all evening, but she did love him. She didn't deny that she loved him. That was the only positive thing about this evening.

Jake opened his mouth but shut it again. He had already recited all his best arguments at least twice, tried everything short of emotional blackmail. He should have known. He'd known Sarah all her life, and he knew well enough that nothing could sway her once she had made her mind up.

So much for Lisa's plots. He felt totally dejected as he fell down on the coach, yet the plea Sarah's mother had voiced was echoing in his head. "Don't let her push you away."

But there was only so much rejection a man could take.

"Jake?" She sat down beside him and tentatively put her hand on his. Jake didn't bother getting his hopes up. She'd bashed them down too often for that. "I wanted to talk to you about Bohr. He already thinks he's your cat. When you go away, would you like to take him with you?"

Another goodbye present? Jake turned his head and looked at her. Her head was bowed, and the hand resting on his was trembling. This was taking just as much out of her as it was him. He sighed.

Why did she have to be so stubborn?

"Yes, Sarah. I'll adopt Bohr."

"It didn't work?"

Jake shook his head without elaborating.

"Darn. She's more stubborn than I gave her credit for."

"When she makes up her mind, she rarely changes it," Jake sighed glumly.

"I've got one more idea." Lisa hummed to herself. "And the good part is that it involves the cooperation of my own prey."

"How are you going to drag poor William into

this?" Jake was beginning to develop a certain sympathy for William. Fortunately, Sarah's colleague did seem able to hold his own against Lisa's attacks.

Lisa grinned. "How's your geometry?"

He gave her a wry look. "We're going to calculate our way out of this mess?"

"Exactly. We're going to use Sine and Cosine to create a beautiful equation."

Jake groaned. "Stay away from mathematical metaphors, Lisa. They don't become you."

"You don't appreciate me. You never have, which is why I never got to find out if you're any good at kissing. Just as well that I've got Sarah to spill the beans." She shook a finger at him as he opened his mouth. "Now stop sulking and listen. I've got a foolproof plan. You see, your Sarah is a romantic at heart. We can use that."

SARAH STARED AT WILLIAM. "What? No! You can't separate the chimps!"

"I don't like it either, Sarah, but there's no choice. We'll have to send Sine back." William shrugged and turned his back to her to peer at something on his monitor. "You were right, they are in love, or at least the chimp equivalent of love. They only think about each other and aren't concentrating on their tasks. It's quite impossible to work with them like this."

"No," Sarah pleaded. "They've just found each other again. Let them be together. It's not fair to separate them.'' She almost whimpered. ''Just look at them.''

Inside the huge cage, Sine and Cosine were huddled together on the wooden bench, long hairy arms wound around each other, their big eyes focused on the white-coated humans. She could almost see large chimp tears teetering at the edges of their eyes, ready to roll down leathery cheeks.

''We can't do this to them,'' she muttered again. She stared at the chimps for a while and almost felt the bricks move and fall into place in her mind, shifting from being an unclimbable wall to forming an inviting stairway.

What had she been thinking? How crazy was it to push Jake away because of her own fears and insecurities? How insane was it to try to drive Jake away because of her gifts and her shortcomings, because of her personality, the way she was? Jake knew all there was to know about her. He had always accepted her as she was. Jake *loved* her just the way she was.

''Oh, Jake...'' She looked at the clock and clenched a fistful of hair in her hand as she ran Jake's flight schedule through her mind. ''William, I have to go. Promise me you won't do anything about the chimps until we've talked again?''

''Okay.'' William nodded. ''I can wait. But don't take too long.''

''Thanks, William. I have to go see Jake. I've been so stupid.'' She tore off her coat and left it in a heap at the door before running out. No, she wouldn't take too long. She was lucky if she wasn't too late already.

Once outside, she jumped on her bike and stood on the pedals, pushing hard as she flew down the streets. A million things were speeding through her brain, regret and fear, hope and joy.

Breathing hard after the furious bike ride, she left the bike unchained on its side in the grass near Jake's front door. After a small struggle with her conscience, she let herself in with the key she still had. She didn't want to meet Jake on his doorstep. She wanted to be inside.

Jake was on his living room sofa, slumped there with Bohr purring away on his stomach and the television blaring a sitcom rerun.

"Hi, Jake." She hesitated for a moment in the doorway, but then walked slowly toward him. "You're here."

"Where else would I be, Sarah?" His voice was gentle, only softly sarcastic. "Reading baby name books with Lisa?"

She knelt down by his side and put her hand on top of his as he stroked the kitten. "I love your hands, Jake. They're so big that they should be clumsy, but they are so gentle and careful."

She looked up and Jake's eyes held hers, his gaze thoughtful and probing. She swallowed. "I'm not gentle and careful, Jake. I'm constantly putting my foot in my mouth and making terrible decisions."

"Can't argue with you there," Jake muttered. "One of those dreadful decisions nearly ruined both our lives." He lifted the sleeping kitten and gently deposited it on the next chair. "Come here."

A second later she had taken Bohr's place on top of Jake, receiving the same sort of purr-inspiring strokes.

"I love you, Jake. I've been very, very stupid. And cruel to us both."

"I love you too, Sarah."

So simple. For a moment she felt completely content, but then remembered she hadn't explained everything to him. She raised herself up and looked into his eyes. He was smiling. She smiled back, then snuggled down on his shoulder, loving the feel of his body under hers and the warmth of his hands on her back. Perhaps there was no need to explain.

"Did you go see Sine and Cosine, Sarah?"

Her head snapped back up. "How did you know about that?"

He grinned. "Our friends thought you needed some sense knocked into you with a pair of smelly chimps."

She stared at him for a moment and then she laughed. "I should have known something was up."

Jake smiled tenderly at her, causing her heart to dive down for a cozy chat with her liver.

"Jake?"

"Yes, Sarah?"

The sound that emerged from her was somewhere between a plea and a whimper. Her sigh told him everything he needed to know, but he settled for staying where he was, listening to her words.

"Jake—you scramble my brains when you look at me like that."

Jake chuckled, reveling in knowing he did that to her. "I like your brain, Sarah. Scrambled or not. And I adore every one of your IQ points."

His tender words contrasted with the exasperated rolling of his eyes as her automatic faucet system switched on. "Don't cry, Sarah!"

"I'm sorry," she sniffed, "I can't help it. It must be biological. This love stuff is messing with my hormones and my neurochemistry. It's probably causing some major changes in my cerebral cortex." She hiccupped. "The process may be irreversible."

"Really?" He kissed her forehead. "That sounds kind of romantic. You know, a man and a woman, floating on a rosy cloud of happiness as they inflict irreversible brain damage on each other."

Sarah giggled, her tears swerving to slide into the small caves of her dimples as she looked up at him. Her face was wet, but she was laughing. Joy swept through him. It had been far too long since he'd heard that sound.

"When you and Lisa came to the labs, still in your uniforms, I almost couldn't resist you," she confessed. "I loved you so much I nearly ran straight into your arms."

Jake grinned, ridiculously happy. "I think you have a uniform fetish, Sarah."

She blushed and her red cheeks looked so cute he just had to kiss one, then the other. She looked down at him, head tilted in the way that always told him she was in deep thought.

"You have a fetish too, Jake."

"I do?" He thought. "I don't think so." He tightened his hold on her. "Unless you're talking about Sarah fetish. I have that one. Bad."

"Nope, that's not it." She was smiling. "Wanna guess again?"

Jake thought. He thought hard, and the harder he thought, the wider she smiled.

"Okay," he muttered. "I admit it. I have this thing about you in your lab coat. How did you notice?"

Sarah giggled, her eyes alight with pleasure. "Really? That wasn't it."

"What?" Jake drew his brows together in a mock frown. "You mean I confessed to that for nothing?"

"I wouldn't say for nothing. I'll bring a lab coat home tomorrow for you to play with."

"I don't want to play with the coat. I want to play with you in the coat. In nothing but the coat."

She grinned. "Fine with me."

"What's that other fetish you think I have then?"

Sarah backed a few steps away. She put her hands in her back pockets and for the first time he felt comfortable allowing his eyes to rove over her.

"See? You have a hands-in-back-pocket fetish."

Jake squirmed, feeling as if he'd been caught red-handed. "Well, I wouldn't call it a fetish exactly..."

Sarah held her pose and turned around in a circle,

then curtsied. "Lisa said you couldn't resist me in this pose."

"Lisa said that?"

"She said it befuddled you and I could use that to my advantage."

He held up a finger. "Did I tell you about my plan to drop Lisa out the window on our next flight?"

"You'll give her a parachute, won't you?"

"She doesn't need one. She'll just bully a stray bird into carrying her down."

"She's nice. You do like her, don't you?"

"I like her a lot better when you're not trying to marry me off to her."

"That was kind of stupid of me."

"Kind of?"

"Okay, it was very stupid."

"Can we stop talking about Lisa now, and talk about us?"

"Okay," Sarah said meekly. She sat down in his lap and linked her arms around his neck, and the look in her eyes suppressed all need he might have had for talking.

"Scrap that. Can we stop talking altogether and do something more interesting?"

"What? And me without my lab coat?"

"Mmm... Know what other fetish I have?"

"No."

"You in a wedding gown."

Sarah's eyes glowed. "Is that just a comment, or are you proposing?"

"I'm leading up to the proposal."

"Oh." She got comfortable. "Propose away, then."

"Do you promise to say yes?"

"You haven't asked me, yet."

"I'm not proposing unless you promise to say yes."

"Okay, I promise."

"Mmm…"

There were no words for a while as their mouths communicated their love in other ways.

"What about my proposal, Jake?"

"I'm getting to it."

"Uh…Jake, I hate to break this to you, but I don't think you'll find it there."

"Don't be too sure. There are all sorts of treasures there. I know, I've been there before."

"Jake!" She slapped his hands away, then sat up and straightened her clothes. "I'm not going to be proposed to in the nude. Our grandchildren would be shocked."

Jake accepted her sudden chastity and cuddled her instead. He trailed kisses down her cheek toward her mouth. "Mmm…grandchildren. I like the sound of that. How many babies shall we make?"

"Not a single one until I get my proposal."

"Bossy woman," he muttered. "You do promise to say yes?"

"I promise."

"In that case…" He rolled out of the sofa and knelt on the floor, taking one of her ankles in his hand. It was narrow and smooth and his hand fit perfectly around it. He fought the urge to nibble on it. Proposal first. He looked up at her, and mirrored her smile. "I love you, Sarah. Will you marry me?"

Her arms went around his head and she hugged him so fiercely against her chest that he could hardly breathe. "Oh, Jake. Thank you. That was beautiful!"

"You didn't say yes," he protested, but she was already gluing herself to his mouth. He pushed away from her. "Sarah! Say yes! You're not having your wicked way with me until you've said yes."

"Yes," she muttered at last, working on the buttons of his shirt. "Yes, yes, yes. Now, let's rehearse our wedding night. I've got some new ideas."

Jake looked at her suspiciously as she pushed his shirt off his shoulders. "Something Lisa suggested?"

"Nope." Her smile lit up the room. "Something I read about."

Jake kissed his way up her jean-clad leg, over her stomach and chest, up the side of her neck and to her forehead, climbing back on the sofa as he went along. "And is this cutting-edge science?"

"Absolutely. State-of-the-art research."

"I'm intrigued."

"Good. Because I intend to do some follow-up studies." She climbed on top of him, pushing and pulling their limbs this way and that, maneuvering them into some ridiculous position. God, he loved this crazy creature.

"Um, Sarah, I'm not complaining or anything, but what exactly are we doing?"

She craned her neck and looked at him, smiling. "Number ninety-three, of course. Only with our clothes on."

GET FREE BOOKS and a FREE GIFT WHEN YOU PLAY THE...

Lucky 7

SLOT MACHINE GAME!

Just scratch off the silver box with a coin. Then check below to see the gifts you get!

YES! I have scratched off the silver box. Please send me the 2 free Harlequin Duets™ books and gift for which I qualify. I understand I am under no obligation to purchase any books, as explained on the back of this card.

311 HDL DRRR

111 HDL DRR7
(H-D-03/03)

FIRST NAME	LAST NAME

ADDRESS

APT.#	CITY

STATE/PROV.   ZIP/POSTAL CODE

7	7	7
🍒	🍒	🍒
♣	♣	♣
🔔	🔔	🍒

Worth TWO FREE BOOKS plus a BONUS Mystery Gift!
Worth TWO FREE BOOKS!
Worth ONE FREE BOOK!
TRY AGAIN!

Visit us online at www.eHarlequin.com

Offer limited to one per household and not valid to current Harlequin Duets™ subscribers. All orders subject to approval.

© 2000 HARLEQUIN ENTERPRISES LTD. ® and TM are trademarks owned by Harlequin Enterprises Ltd

DETACH AND MAIL CARD TODAY!

The Harlequin Reader Service® — Here's how it works:

Accepting your 2 free books and gift places you under no obligation to buy anything. You may keep the books and gift and return the shipping statement marked "cancel." If you do not cancel, about a month later we'll send you 2 additional books and bill you just $5.14 each in the U.S., or $6.14 each in Canada, plus 50¢ shipping and handling per book and applicable taxes if any.* That's the complete price and — compared to cover prices of $5.99 each in the U.S. and $6.99 each in Canada — it's quite a bargain! You may cancel at any time, but if you choose to continue, every month we'll send you 2 more books, which you may either purchase at the discount price or return to us and cancel your subscription.

*Terms and prices subject to change without notice. Sales tax applicable in N.Y. Canadian residents will be charged applicable provincial taxes and GST.

If offer card is missing write to: Harlequin Reader Service, 3010 Walden Ave., P.O. Box 1867, Buffalo NY 14240-1867

POSTAGE WILL BE PAID BY ADDRESSEE

BUSINESS REPLY MAIL
FIRST-CLASS MAIL   PERMIT NO. 717-003   BUFFALO, NY

HARLEQUIN READER SERVICE
3010 WALDEN AVE
PO BOX 1867
BUFFALO NY 14240-9952

NO POSTAGE
NECESSARY
IF MAILED
IN THE
UNITED STATES

The Maid
of Dishonor

Tanya
Michaels

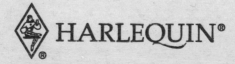

HARLEQUIN®

TORONTO • NEW YORK • LONDON
AMSTERDAM • PARIS • SYDNEY • HAMBURG
STOCKHOLM • ATHENS • TOKYO • MILAN • MADRID
PRAGUE • WARSAW • BUDAPEST • AUCKLAND

Dear Reader,

I had the most amazing month—I gave birth to my first child, a beautiful little boy, and then sold my first book to Duets! Good timing, since motherhood has reminded me how important a sense of humor is. Mine has always allowed me to see things a bit differently.

Weddings are so romantic, right? Unless the bride is really in love with her gardener, the groom has no idea what love is (because he hasn't met the right woman yet!) and the maid of honor is trying to break the whole thing up. The last thing she expects is to fall for the groom herself, or to be the perfect person to teach him what love is.

I hope you enjoy watching Samantha and Ethan fall in love, and have a few laughs along the way. I truly believe laughter is the best medicine (unless you're giving birth, in which case I personally vote for a good epidural).

Best wishes,

Tanya Michaels

Thanks Mom, Dad, Lara, Kathy and Jane for encouraging me to write. Thank you to my critique partners, fabulous writers and even better friends, and to the ladies of the GRW.

Special thanks to my husband, who actually knows what it's like to live with a writer but has always supported me anyway—every day you remind me that happily ever after isn't fiction.

1

_____

I'M GETTING MARRIED. Ethan Jenner stood in line at the airport, holding his breath and hoping for a surge of joy or excitement or anything resembling an emotion. Unfortunately, his strongest reaction was, *I can't believe I'm missing that meeting in Denver for a wedding rehearsal.* Not exactly a sentiment they printed on Hallmark cards.

He glanced ahead at the airline ticket counter and took a step forward, murmuring the words to himself again, testing them. "I'm getting married."

Maybe if he said it like he meant it, louder with confidence.

"I am getting married!"

Okay, that was too loud.

People turned to stare. A little girl in pigtails regarded him with wide eyes, and the woman waiting in front of him swung around in surprise, nailing him with her floral tapestry shoulder bag. "Well, congratulations, mister."

He managed a weak smile that disintegrated as soon as she turned back around. Great. He could see the headlines in the *Journal* now. "Renowned businessman loses mind five days before wedding. Last seen talking to himself in LaGuardia Airport."

The uneasiness made Ethan want to gnash his teeth. He brokered multimillion-dollar deals with complete confidence. Why the schoolboy nerves at the thought of marrying Jillian? This marriage would be the best business deal he'd ever made.

Still, when he reached the ticket counter, he had to wrestle the urge to ask for a ticket to Los Angeles or Miami. Or Iceland. He'd heard it was lovely in December.

But years of practiced self-discipline prompted him toward Dallas, Texas, and the five-day wedding extravaganza that awaited him.

SAMANTHA LLOYD BOLTED from her seat as soon as the attendant announced the first boarding call. Sam couldn't wait to get out of New York. Not even a city of eight million people was big enough for both her and her parents.

Since most of her students took time off for the Thanksgiving and Christmas holidays, Sam had obligingly come to New York to visit her parents and hear her mother play at Avery Fischer. But her trip had degenerated into a series of arguments followed by expensive bribes for peace, and Jillian's rescuing phone call had come not a moment too soon. When Jillian begged her to rush back to Texas to be maid of honor at the wedding, Sam had been so grateful she'd forgotten to ask the crucial question—what wedding? Last she'd heard, her girlhood friend had been nursing a broken heart.

Sam stood behind the other waiting passengers at the purple-and-orange podium and pondered her friend's situation.

Maybe Jillian went back to Peter. Maybe he swept her off her feet. In which case, Peter had better marry her before Jillian let her parents talk her out of it. Sam and Jillian had been best friends since meeting at the exclusive all-girl boarding school they'd attended, and she loved Jillian like a sister. But Jillian did have an annoying habit of letting her parents run her life.

At the opposite end of the spectrum was Sam, poster child for parental disappointment. Her mother had married into old money and made a name for herself as a concert pianist. She expected similar success from her daughter. Instead, Sam bounced from one dating disaster to another and taught kids to play the piano. She loved her job, even though both her parents bemoaned its lack of prestige and its meager salary.

Happy to put this trip and her parents' complaints behind her, she handed her pass to the uniformed East-West Air employee and boarded the plane.

Moments later, she located her aisle seat in first class. Her father had insisted on upgrading her coach ticket when he dropped her off. Knowing that arguing wouldn't accomplish anything more than an increase in his blood pressure, she'd acquiesced, silently counting the seconds until she'd be in the air and flying to freedom. She dropped her belongings and slumped into her seat, emotionally drained from the last few days of defending her life choices.

Staring with unseeing eyes at the back of the seat in front of her, she tried to imagine the turn Jillian's life was about to take, tried to imagine what her friend must be feeling. Excitement, eagerness to embrace her future, love... Years ago, Sam had informed her parents that she wouldn't marry for money or connections or social status. She wouldn't marry at all unless it was for love.

So far, life had mocked this decision. Pickings for true love were slim, and she had the boyfriend-roster from hell to prove it. Brad the Kleptomaniac, who ended all their dates with a steamy kiss and a cash withdrawal from her wallet. Gregory the Sensitive Artist, who'd wowed her with his depth, his evocative paintings, his scorn for all things material. Until he'd run off with Adam, a fellow sensitive artist. Most recently there had been Ted.

Nice guy, Ted. Statistics analyst. Decent-looking, ready to settle down, polite, and—big plus—not interested in dating other men. Perfect, as long as she overlooked his neurotic attention to *every little detail*. Which had been easier in theory than practice.

So here she was, once again unattached. Not that she was in a hurry to find someone else. No telling what would be wrong with the next guy she fell for.

"Excuse me, ma'am."

She glanced up and her heartbeat suddenly shifted to rapid sixteenth notes. *I fell asleep. That must be it. I nodded off while thinking about men and dreamed up the perfect man.*

Everything about him exuded raw masculinity. Black-as-sin hair, piercing green eyes, a face that was all planes and hard angles. None of the boyish softness she saw so often in the male models and actors that other women drooled over. This man had a strong, stubborn jaw and full sensual lips. In spite of his Armani suit and wine-colored tie, something about him refused to be civilized.

"Ma'am?" He gestured to the empty seat next to her and then to her belongings, which she still hadn't pushed under the seat in front of her. "I need to get by you."

Heat suffused her cheeks. "Right, sorry." She moved her carry-on bag and oversize purse to let him by. Here in first class, she got to enjoy quadruple the leg room of the poor slobs sitting behind her, but on East-West Air, first class still meant close quarters.

Close enough that the man's body brushed hers as he passed, and the scent of his cologne, somehow distinguished and subtle at the same time, filled her nostrils.

The pilot interrupted her thoughts, greeting passengers with forced cheer and recycled airline jokes over a static-filled intercom. Then the plane was taxiing down the runway and a male flight attendant stood in front of the curtained cockpit, explaining the safety procedures. Sam actually paid attention to the familiar demonstration, hoping it would distract her from the mysterious and sexy man who sat inches away from her.

The space between them seemed to grow smaller and smaller. She'd never reacted so viscerally to a stranger; maybe it *had* been too long since her last boyfriend. Jittery with hormones and uncharacteristic shyness, she drummed her fingers on the armrest.

"Nervous flyer?" The man's voice matched his appearance—deep, dark, somewhere between rough and silken.

"Not at all. I've been flying all my life." Flying alone on planes bound for various schools. At first, she'd resented the way her parents shipped her off, angry that they didn't want her. But over the years, she'd realized that family harmony was better kept with hundreds of miles between them.

He eyed her fingers, which tapped the rhythm to

her favorite Beethoven symphony. "You *seem* nervous."

"I am." The truth tumbled out of her mouth before she could stop it. She'd rather have a baby grand dropped on her from eighteen stories up than admit *he* was making her nervous, so she belatedly clutched at the excuse he'd offered earlier. "I hate to fly."

"But you just..." He bowed his head, running a hand through his hair and muttering something about women. Under the circumstances, she couldn't blame him.

Cheeks warm with embarrassment, she reached for the seat pocket in front of her and rifled through the slim selection of in-flight magazines. She grabbed a dog-eared copy of *Influence,* the high-profile magazine about movers and shakers in America's economy, and leafed through the pages. Not because of an overwhelming interest in market trends, but out of a need to distract herself from her traveling companion.

But smiling back at her from the glossy pages was her alluring stranger, searing her with his forest-green gaze!

A small, startled cry escaped her and a heavyset man across the aisle jerked his head toward her, eyes round with alarm.

"Is something wrong with the plane, miss?"

Next to him, a snoring blue-haired woman awoke with a start. "There's something wrong with the plane?" she hollered.

Half a dozen hands reached up for the stewardess call button, and Sam slunk down in her seat. She wasn't usually this high-strung, but she'd been feeling off balance for the past few days. First it had been the emotional roller coaster that always accompanied visits to see her parents, then Jillian's surprising marriage, finally the handsome stranger seated next to her.

The same stranger, identified in the magazine as Ethan Jenner, who now regarded her warily. "You're worse off than I thought. Maybe you should order a drink, soothe your nerves before you cause a stampede to the emergency exits."

"It wasn't the plane, I was just surprised." She folded back the magazine and held it up. "That's you, isn't it?"

His forehead wrinkled in a perplexed frown. "No. That's Sir Elton John."

Sam glanced down at the Got Milk? ad featuring the pop star. "Wait, wrong side." She flipped the periodical over and showed him the opposite page. "*That's* you, right?"

"Yep. Vice president of Peabo-Johnston Brokerage. Not as exciting as performing 'Crocodile Rock,' but it's a living." He turned back toward the window, clearly uninterested in further conversation with the crazy lady.

Considering the number of celebrities she'd met at her parents' gala functions, it made no sense for her to be so impressed with Ethan. But she read with growing admiration the story of how he'd gone to school on a hard-earned scholarship and built himself up from meager beginnings in a small Southern town. Recently promoted as the youngest vice president in Peabo-Johnston history, Ethan often headed up community charity events and had graced New York City's Sexiest Man list twice.

"But be warned, ladies, your chances to catch Mr. Jenner are dwindling. Rumor has it he will be married by Christmas."

Disappointment stabbed her, catching her off guard. Why feel a sense of loss? It wasn't as though she knew Ethan Jenner or would ever see him again.

Telling herself it didn't bother her in the least that he was getting married, she squared her shoulders. "Congratulations."

He glanced at her, one eyebrow raised in question.

"Says here you're getting married."

He clenched his jaw, but then he smiled. She would have bet money that his smile, despite its charm, was fake. "As a matter of fact, I am." He took the magazine from her and riffled through the pages, stopping on 167, where there was a profile of Jordan Winthrop, Texas media magnate. "I'm marrying his daughter. Jillian."

"Oh, my Lord!" The involuntary shout was louder than her other small outburst and brought a flinty-eyed stewardess barreling down the aisle. People in nearby seats murmured their apprehension and the heavy man across the aisle reached for his airsickness bag.

Sam turned to Ethan Jenner—*Jillian's fiancé!* "Um, air turbulence. I think I *could* use that drink you suggested."

ETHAN STARED OUT THE WINDOW. Ironic that the unending stretch of cloudless blue sky should be so serene when he felt as if he were hurtling to earth in a thousand-foot free fall. He wished he had someone to tell him he was making the right decision. Stupid for a thirty-two-year-old man who lived by his own rules and instincts to suddenly need outside guidance.

If his parents were alive, he knew they'd both try to talk him out of his upcoming marriage. His mom and dad had loved each other wholeheartedly.

They'd also been dirt poor. Maybe they wouldn't approve of his every decision, but they would have to admit that his choices had resulted in financial success. When Ethan had children, they would never miss a meal or go without shoes in the summer.

Marrying Jillian is the right decision. He'd be a fool not to ally himself with the wealthy Winthrops. Jordan Winthrop, one of Peabo-Johnston's biggest clients, had introduced Ethan to Jillian and made it clear he favored a match between them. Ethan had to admit, Jillian was perfect wife material. Lovely, well-spoken, familiar with big business, a great hostess. With a wife like Jillian at his side and the contacts he would make through the Winthrop family, Ethan would never again have to worry about living a life like his parents if something happened to his present job.

His engagement to Jillian had worked out perfectly. He'd get everything he needed, and Jillian would get what she wanted. Although he hadn't known his bride-to-be long, he'd seen that she craved a better relationship with her parents, longed for their approval. They'd made it clear that they completely approved of the engagement and that nothing would make them happier than Jillian's marrying a successful man and eventually giving them grandchildren.

So Ethan had no reason to feel guilty about marrying Jillian. She wanted this wedding, too, for her own reasons. And he'd give her respect, support and fidelity, being a good husband in all the ways that mattered.

You're just experiencing pre-wedding jitters.

And he must be going through that panicky syndrome where an almost-married man starts to notice how good other women look. Except he hadn't noticed women, plural. Just the redhead seated next to him, asleep after her two shots of scotch and a stern talking-to by one of the flight attendants.

Since her eyes were closed, dark lashes sweeping the tops of her ivory cheeks, he took the opportunity to study her. Undisciplined red curls spiraled around her face and shoulders, more attractive in their disarray than chic, hundred-dollar hairstyles he'd seen. She wore a long, rose-colored dress that should have clashed with her hair, but instead lent a becoming pink blush to her high cheekbones. Her features were bold, a high, patrician forehead, a wide mouth that looked as though it laughed a lot. He remembered that her eyes were the dark blue of quality sapphires.

Too bad she was so unpredictable…contradicting herself from one breath to the next and reacting fiercely to what had been barely discernible turbulence. He'd heard that redheads were temperamental and passionate.

But Ethan had always been more interested in pragmatism than passion. And now, as he was poised on the edge of the security and success he'd dreamed about growing up, all his practicality, all his sacrifices and hard work were about to pay off.

SAM PEEKED ONE EYE OPEN, half hoping she'd find herself on a different plane. Or at least next to a different man.

No such luck.

Ethan Jenner sat next to her, still more handsome than was humanly normal and still engaged to her best friend.

Maybe I should introduce myself. I am going to be the maid of honor at his wedding, after all.

No, better not to say anything until she'd had a chance to talk to her friend. The minute Sam's cab dropped her off at the hotel, she was calling Jillian. The bride-to-be had some explaining to do!

The pilot announced their impending descent, giving the temperature at DFW as sixty-five degrees, thirty degrees warmer than it had been in New York.

Ethan grinned wryly at her. "The plane will start going down now. Don't panic, we aren't crashing."

She bit back a grimace. *He probably thinks I'm the biggest fruitcake ever to board a plane.* "I'm fine. I really *don't* mind flying. I was just a little tense earlier."

"Uh-huh. So, are you going to Dallas on business?"

Since he didn't strike her as a small-talk kind of guy, she assumed his sudden interest in conversation was to distract her from her "fear of flying." "Business? Hardly. I'm a piano teacher. Not much out-of-state travel involved in that."

"So you're visiting Dallas to...?"

"To be—" in a wedding, *your* wedding "—with a friend."

"You live in New York?"

"Actually, no. I live here in Texas, in Austin. I was in New York visiting family."

Minutes later, the plane skidded across the runway, wheels squealing, then pulled up to the gate. Sam grabbed her carry-on bags and got in line behind the other deplaning passengers, eager to put distance between her and the disturbing Ethan Jenner.

A purple-polyester-clad stewardess stood at the entrance, distributing cheery greetings. "Bye-bye. Thanks for flying East-West Air. Enjoy your stay in Texas. Bye-bye."

Sam noticed that when *she* deplaned, all she got was a narrowed gaze and the telepathically relayed command to never darken the door of East-West Air again. Ready to put this bizarre flight behind her and get a taxi to the hotel, she hurried down the skyway.

Zigzagging through the assembled crowd, she passed a uniformed chauffeur holding a sign for Bennett Electronics and swerved around a heavily pregnant woman hugging a tall man. But on the other side of the expectant mother, Sam crashed to a halt, slamming into a blonde in a pale blue suit.

"I'm so sor— Jillie?"

The blonde spun around, surprise and joy on her delicate features. "Sam? *Sam!*" Jillian leaned forward and gave her friend a one-armed hug and a kiss on the cheek. "You were on this flight? I don't believe it! I know you said you'd take a cab when you got here, but since I'm here, anyway, picking up Ethan…"

The rest of Jillian's words were inaudible over the sudden buzzing in Sam's ears. Ethan! He'd be along any second. Even though she knew she'd have to face him again, she wasn't quite up to it yet. She still hadn't had a chance to talk to Jillian and find out what was going on.

"I'm beat from traveling and not very good company right now. Why don't you just let me go on to the hotel and call me toni—"

Her words were cut off by Ethan's already-familiar voice behind her. "Jillian. Good to see you again."

Both women turned, but it was Jillian who spoke. "Ethan. I hope your flight was uneventful."

"Actually, it was…interesting." He stared at Sam with quizzically raised eyebrows.

"You'll never believe who you were on the plane with. This is my dearest friend in the world, Samantha Lloyd. Sam, meet Ethan Jenner. I'm marrying him."

Forcing a smile, Sam raised her hand and waggled her fingers in a weak wave. "Nice to meet you."

His unbelievably green eyes widened. "*You're* Sam? Sam, the notorious rebel?" He glanced at Jillian. "The way you talked about her, I expected someone in leather, maybe riding a Harley." A snort of amusement escaped him. "Not a piano teacher in a pink dress."

What had Jillian said about her to make someone think of motorcycles and leather?

"Didn't I mention she was a piano teacher?" Jillian frowned. "And if I didn't, how'd you know?"

"We, um, kind of met on the plane," Sam interjected. "We sat next to each other, but didn't exactly introduce ourselves."

"That's right. We had no idea we were your best friend and fiancé." Ethan spoke to Jillian, but pinned Sam with his gaze, obviously wondering why she hadn't spoken up when he'd revealed the identity of his future wife.

Sam smiled again, hoping it looked more sincere than it felt. "Well, I'm going to grab that taxi now and head to the hotel. I'm sure the two of you would like some time alone."

"Don't be silly," Jillian insisted, her grip uncharacteristically firm on Sam's elbow. "Ethan and I were going to join my parents at the club for dinner. You'll come with us."

The only thing worse than enduring Jillian's parents was eating at the country club. Still, Jillian was obviously desperate for her to come. Sam was going to have bruises on her arm from her friend's fingers.

"That sounds…fun."

"Great, it's settled." Jillian's sky-blue eyes held an odd amount of relief. Sam knew Jillian had never liked being alone with her browbeating parents, but she wasn't alone now. She had Ethan.

Although, Jillian didn't seem all that pleased to see her fiancé. She hadn't even spared a hug for him, the way she had for Sam. *Well, maybe they just saw each other a few days ago. She hasn't seen me in almost a year.* That could be it.

Still…there were a lot of unanswered questions, not the least of which was what had happened to poor Peter?

Sam could probably answer that herself—Jillian's parents had finally chased off the stubborn suitor. Imagine the nerve of a lowly gardener falling in love with Jillian Winthrop. Then again, maybe Jillian had simply had a change of heart. It was easy to see how Ethan Jenner could turn a girl's head.

At Jillian's prompting, Ethan retrieved Sam's luggage from the baggage carousel and then returned to the two women. "Are we ready?"

It should've been an uncomplicated question, but Sam was no longer certain just what she should be ready for.

2

WHEN JILLIAN'S LEXUS rolled to a stop in front of the country club, Sam didn't know whether to feel dread at the impending dinner or relief that the awkward ride was over. Barely a word had been spoken during the drive. She assumed Ethan and Jillian would've had more to say to each other if she hadn't been along as a third wheel.

Ethan handed Jillian's keys to the valet, and Sam followed the engaged couple inside the club. Almost immediately, the walls closed in around her. One of the things she enjoyed about living in Texas was the state's distinctive, unique personality. But here, surrounded by the cherry-paneled walls and the art prints that were far more expensive than aesthetically pleasing, she could have just as easily been in her parents' country club back east.

A tuxedoed maître d' hurried forward, hands outstretched. "Miss Winthrop, delightful to see you. You look enchanting this evening. Your parents are in their usual private room."

Jillian thanked him and led the way to a small room in the back where her parents sat at an ornately sculpted oval table, sipping coffee from fine china cups. Sam mentally rolled her eyes. Her mother would have been immediately able to name the pattern, but to Sam a teacup was a teacup was a teacup.

Claire and Jordan Winthrop hadn't aged a day since Sam had first met them more than a decade ago. Jordan still had the distinguished brush of silver at his temples, but the rest of his thick hair had kept its chestnut color. And Claire looked more like Jillian's sister than mother. Sam shivered, thinking of Oscar Wilde's *The Picture of Dorian Gray*. Maybe somewhere in the Winthrop mansion there was a portrait of a wrinkled Claire and a balding, overweight Jordan.

Jordan rose to hug Jillian, and Claire turned her attention to her future son-in-law.

"Ethan." She bussed his cheek with an air kiss that wouldn't smear her perfect lipstick. "How lovely to see you again. I was just saying to Jillian the other day that—" She stopped abruptly, nervously tucking one strand of ash-blond hair behind her ear. "And...is that *Samantha* lurking back there?"

Jillian nodded. "She and Ethan came in on the same flight. Isn't that a wonderful coincidence?"

"Wonderful," Claire echoed. Only the tiny frown lines on her forehead revealed her intense displeasure at seeing Sam. Claire Winthrop letting her face wrinkle was the equivalent of any other woman throwing herself to the floor in a kicking, screaming tantrum.

In earlier years, Jillian's friendship with Sam had been the only area in which Jillian defied her parents. They'd never approved of Samantha's outspokenness, and they frequently expressed sympathy for her parents.

Jordan hid his dislike better, behind the hearty joviality he was known for. "Good to see you again,

Samantha. You've certainly grown up. Why, you're almost as lovely as our Jillie.'' He indicated the gold brocade-covered chairs around the table. ''Sit, sit. Now that we're all here we can go ahead and order.''

Mournfully, Sam wondered if burgers were on the menu. Though she'd been raised in an old-money community, she'd never developed what her parents considered good taste. Pizza and blue jeans worked just fine for her.

''Miss Lloyd?''

Sam's gaze shot to Ethan Jenner, her heart beating ridiculously faster because he'd singled her out. ''Y-yes?''

He glanced meaningfully toward the hovering waiter, and she realized everyone was waiting for her to place a beverage order. *Wow. Today is not my day to make good impressions.* A cold beer sounded good—wouldn't Claire just die?—but she settled for iced tea.

As the waiter walked away, she became aware that Jillian was talking about her. ''So you should call her Sam. You'll be seeing a lot of her during our marriage. I'm sure the two of you will become close friends,'' Jillian concluded.

Ethan's fathomless green eyes fixed on Sam, and she wished she could guess what he was thinking. She knew what *she* was thinking—she didn't want to be his close anything! The man gave her heart palpitations, and each palpitation made her feel lower than a worm. *He's Jillian's husband. Practically. You have no business reacting to him like this!*

For once, Sam was grateful the Winthrops discussed nothing but business. It gave her a chance to sit quietly without exposing how uncharacteristically tongue-tied she felt.

Noticing that Jillian was also excluded from the conversation, Sam caught her friend's eye. "Could you show me where the ladies' lounge is?"

Jillian rose and Sam felt an unwelcome surge of admiration for Ethan Jenner when he stood, too, pausing in his assessment of TexCom Enterprises to smile at Jillian. Sam quickened her steps, wanting to get at least a room away from that smile.

The moment the two women entered the door to the lounge, Sam plopped down on the velvet-upholstered settee. "Talk fast and tell me *everything*."

Jillian sat next to her. "There isn't much to tell. Ethan came down this fall to do some business with Daddy, and I met him at one of my parents' parties."

Sam remembered the Winthrops' parties well. They seized any excuse to show off their wealth and hobnob with important people.

"Ethan visited me on the weekend a few times," Jillian continued, "and proposed not long after we met. He's smart and successful, always the gentleman. My parents adore him."

"And you adore him, too?"

"What's not to adore? He's smart and successful, always the gentleman. What about you? Do you like him?"

Sam bit her lip, worried by her friend's flat tone of voice. "I don't really know him, Jillie. But he is gorgeous."

"You think so?" Jillian tilted her head to the side. "Sometimes he seems a bit...much. When he

smiles, he almost makes me nervous. Not like P—"
She broke off abruptly, her light eyes clouded with
hurt.

"Oh, Jillian." Sam paused, wanting to speak her
mind without starting an argument. "Do you still
have feelings for Peter?"

Jillian stood. "Well, of course, I'll always have
feelings for him. He holds a special place in my
heart. You know how it is with old loves."

"That's not what I mean. Do you—"

"Sam, they're waiting on us. I want to catch up
as much as you do, but you know you aren't my
parents' favorite person. My mother will think it's
rude if we stay holed up in here."

Not that the Winthrops showed any sign of even
noticing she and Jillian had been gone. They were
far too engrossed in their future son-in-law.

"And I'll introduce you to the Sterns," Jordan
was telling Ethan. "They aren't flying in until the
afternoon of the wedding, but I can set up a meeting
for you the next day. Between your market knowledge and a little friendly persuasion from me, I think
you can convince Randolph Stern to invest in that
California deal."

Ethan pushed away his bowl of vichyssoise and
pulled a small black object that looked like a cal-
culator from his pocket.

"His PalmPilot," Jillian whispered in response to
Sam's puzzled expression. "He never goes anywhere without it or his cell phone."

"Randolph Stern," Ethan muttered. "California
merger. Day after the wedding."

"But won't you be busy then?" Sam blurted.

All eyes turned to her.

Ethan consulted his PalmPilot. ''No, I don't have anything scheduled.''

Heat flooded her cheeks. Sam looked to Jillian for help, but her friend looked as puzzled as Ethan. Was she really going to have to spell this out for them? ''Your honeymoon?'' she prompted.

Jillian waved a hand. ''Our flight to Aruba doesn't leave until that night. Ethan has plenty of time for his meeting.''

Sam scanned her friend's face for some sign that she was kidding. She leaned toward Jillian, whispering, ''But aren't the two of you anxious to, ah, *be together?*''

''Wh—oh, no! Not at all!'' For a second, Jillian looked positively horrified by the prospect. But then she recovered, adding casually, ''We have our whole lives to…be together. No hurry.''

No hurry? If Sam were marrying a compelling, sexy man like Ethan she'd waste no time in engaging in honeymoon activities. And she didn't mean snorkeling. Then again, Ethan seemed more passionate about his PalmPilot than his bride.

The waiter returned with the salad course, but Sam's appetite had withered. *What's my problem? She's my best friend, and I should be happy for her.* Which would be easier if Jillian herself seemed happy.

Claire, on the other hand, was positively jubilant. Whenever there was a lull in the men's business conversation, she regaled everyone with wedding details. ''Of course, it *should* have been the social event of the season,'' she said, managing to frown and somehow keep her face smooth and unwrinkled at the same time. "I don't see why it has to be so small."

Sam wondered how many thousands of guests fit the Winthrop definition of a "small" wedding.

"If we invited more people," Jordan added, "Ethan would have the opportunity to network that much more at the reception."

Jillian's lips compressed into a thin line. "But everyone agreed that we should have the wedding before Christmas. It's hard to arrange a huge wedding that fast. Besides, a small wedding is better for Ethan. You know he has no f—" She broke off when she saw the thunderous expression on her fiancé's face. He clearly didn't like being discussed as though he weren't there.

Has no f—? Sam wondered. No fun at weddings? No friends? No family? No funnel cake? What?

And if this wedding should have been the social event of the winter, why *was* it so rushed? Could it be that the Winthrops wanted to act fast before Jillian changed her mind?

Ethan cleared his throat. "You ladies do whatever you think is best for the wedding, but your father's right, Jillian. I could always take the opportunity to make more connections. You want us to be financially secure, don't you?"

Years of boarding school etiquette crammed down her throat were all that kept Sam from snorting in disbelief. *Financially secure?* Jillian drove a Lexus and Ethan wore Armani. These were not two people who would be cutting coupons and eating macaroni and cheese to get by. So what really motivated Ethan?

As if she didn't know. He was just like her parents. Like Jillian's parents. Greedy and materialistic.

She shot a disappointed glance his direction. Planning a meeting the day after his wedding night and treating his wedding reception as a prospective client cocktail party. Didn't the man have a heart?

As though he felt her eyes on him, Ethan turned to capture her gaze, and she shivered. If he had a heart, it certainly wasn't reflected in his glittering green stare.

Sam suspected Jillian still loved Peter, and that was bad. But worse was that Ethan Jenner didn't even look capable of love. Unless the *Wall Street Journal* had featured an article about it, he'd probably never heard of the emotion.

"Samantha?"

Sam jumped as Claire's wintry tone sliced through her. "Yes, ma'am?"

"I was asking how your parents were, dear. We saw them in the Hamptons over the summer. They said you were finally dating a promising young man. Ned, I believe."

"Ted. But we broke up."

Claire tut-tutted and shook her head, but Jillian grinned. "So you're single? Now that I'll be a married woman and can't date, I'll have to live through you. Maybe we could set you up with someone Ethan knows."

Sam cringed, picturing herself trapped with a man who couldn't carry on a conversation unless it involved stock quotes. Across the table, Ethan cringed, as well, probably scandalized by the suggestion of one of his friends with a woman whose mental stability he questioned.

Unexpected laughter bubbled up inside her. She knew she should be offended by Ethan's obvious distaste for the idea, but the way his reaction perfectly mirrored hers struck her as funny. Their eyes met for a second and although he didn't laugh—or even smile, if one were to be completely accurate— the corner of his mouth lifted. The private moment of shared amusement caused his eyes to sparkle, and his face suddenly appeared younger. Likable.

But then Claire jerked Sam back to reality with a murmured "Jillian, dear, I doubt Samantha needs your help finding dates. From what I've heard, she's gone through a string of men."

Sam clenched her jaw. Claire's wording made her sound like a…like a… "I wouldn't say a *string* of men, but I do date a lot," she admitted. "How else can a girl find the right man?" With a smile so sweet she hoped it would send Claire into sugar-shock, she added, "This isn't the fourteenth century after all, where a girl's parents get to pick the groom."

Jordan choked on his wine and Ethan's dark eyebrows shot up so high they disappeared into his hairline.

A sharp, stinging pain in Sam's shin suggested that Jillian had just kicked her under the table. Apparently, her friend didn't appreciate the editorializing or thinly veiled accusation. Sam didn't get it. Why would Jillian throw the rest of her life away on a marriage that would make only her parents happy? Jillian was entitled to happiness of her own.

Then again, no one knew better than Sam how much Jillian, the only girl amid three adored Winthrop sons, longed for some attention and approval from her parents. When Jillian had agreed at sixteen not to cut her hair because her father told her it looked classier long, that had been one thing. But agreeing to spend the rest of her life with a cold-hearted suit if she still loved Peter was something entirely different.

Inspiration struck and Sam seized the opportunity to get Jillian out of her parents' clutches for a little while. "Jillian, how would you like to stay at my hotel suite with me? We can catch up. I know your brothers are in town and doubtless other relatives will be staying at the house, too. If you come with me—"

"Out of the question," Claire interrupted. "She's the bride and there are lots of last-minute wedding details—"

"Which I'm sure you have completely under control," Sam contended. "No one's more of an expert than you at handling social events and making sure they're flawless."

Claire lips parted wordlessly—her dainty version of gaping—and Jillian stared at Sam with undisguised shock.

Hey, it wasn't as though she didn't have any social skills, she thought defensively. Just because she chose not to go around kissing butt didn't mean she couldn't be tactful. Once every couple of years or so.

Sensing her temporary advantage, she pressed on. "If you stay with me, Jillian, I'll be sure to give you some time to yourself. The last thing a bride with pre-wedding jitters and last-minute doubts needs is a herd of relatives underfoot."

In a voice that made Sam think he'd stepped in

something, Ethan Jenner inquired, "Are you saying Jillian has doubts?"

Imagine that. Somehow she'd offended the man with no feelings. She shrugged, forcing a casual smile. "I thought all brides had doubts right before the wedding. And grooms, too."

"Well, I certainly have no d—" Ethan coughed. When he spoke again, he was studying Jillian with more warmth than Sam had seen from him previously. "Are you having second thoughts?"

"Of course not!" Jordan Winthrop blustered, firing Sam one of the this-is-all-your-fault glares she knew so well.

"I was asking Jillian," Ethan said, his tone soft but adamant. The encouraging look he gave his fiancée and the way he stood up to Jordan made Sam wonder guiltily if her assessment of him had been too hasty.

Jillian held her head high. "Of course not. I look forward to being your wife. And you? Do you have any doubts?"

Unlike Jillian, he actually paused, eyes narrowed in concentration as he considered. Finally, he shook his head. "This is the smartest thing I've done since buying Intel stock."

In her mind, Sam disemboweled him with her butter knife. He compared marrying sweet and vulnerable Jillian to a cash transaction? Nope, she hadn't been too hasty in her assessment of him. If anything, she'd been too kind.

SAM SHUFFLED HER LUGGAGE and punched the elevator button.

"You know, we could have let the bellboy help us with our bags," Jillian said.

Sam shrugged. "I'd just as soon do it myself."

"Thanks for inviting me to stay with you, by the way. Space from my family is exactly what I need."

Yeah, like thousands of miles and a few continents. "But I thought Claire and Jordan couldn't be happier now that you were marrying the man they deem perfect for you."

Jillian either missed or ignored the sarcasm. "Oh, they're very happy. It's just that wedding preparations are stressful."

"Speaking of which, can I ask you a question?" The elevator doors parted and the two women padded down the hall in the direction of their room. "Over dinner, when you and Claire were discussing guests and why the wedding was so small, you said Ethan had 'no f—' I couldn't help wondering what you were going to say. Family? Friends?"

"I was going to say family." Jillian pointed at a door. "Room 603. This is us."

They stepped inside a hotel suite that had the standard two beds, replete with floral comforters and bad paintings hanging over them.

Sam sat her luggage on one of the beds. "So," she prompted, "Ethan doesn't have any family?"

"Just an uncle." Jillian shrugged. "But I'm not sure he has any close friends, either. His groomsmen are my three brothers."

"*No* friends?" Unimaginable. "Everyone has friends."

"Ethan has acquaintances. When we put together the list of invitations, he gave me mostly names of business colleagues. I asked if there wasn't an old friend he's kept in touch with, like a college room-mate or something.''

"And?"

"He said he was busy working during college, not socializing," Jillian had explained.

Certainly in keeping with what I saw at dinner. Work appeared to be not just his first priority, but his only priority.

"So, the groom's side at the wedding will be con-spicuously small," Jillian said. "I keep trying to scale down the guest list. I thought it would be more appropriate since Ethan will know so few people. But my parents..." She hung her garment bag in the closet and opened her duffel, pulling out items which she neatly arranged around the room. "At least it will be an elegant wedding. I have pictures to show you of the decorations we've chosen, and swatches."

Oh, boy, swatches. "I'd love to see them," Sam lied. "I wanted to talk about the wedding tonight, anyway."

"What about it?"

"Well, it seems...sudden. The last I heard, you were dating Peter, and then—"

"You know what? I could really use a hot bath, if you don't mind." The bathroom door slammed shut before Sam could respond.

SAM HAD NEVER LIKED alarm clocks, but right at the moment, she'd have preferred an alarm clock to Jil-lian's perkily chirped, "Rise and shine! Day's awas-tin'."

Sam pried open one eye and glared through it. "Who the hell says 'awastin'?"

"I suppose 'get your butt moving' is more your style?"

"It does have a certain directness to it," Sam agreed, smiling despite herself. She freely admitted that she lacked Jillian's charming nature. Everyone liked personable Jillian.

But there was a difference between being likable and being a doormat. "Jillian, are you sure you aren't getting married bec—"

"Don't start. We covered all that last night."

Actually, they hadn't. Outside of deep, meaningful topics like the color of the reception tablecloths, Jillian wouldn't discuss the wedding. Which made Sam even more suspicious that this marriage was a bad idea.

"Sam?" Jillian's voice jerked Sam from her musing. "We have to get moving. My mother will kill us if we're late."

There was an early-morning fitting for all the bridesmaids and then a brunch. Sam dragged herself out from under the comforter, but continued to shoot longing glances at the bed as she rounded up her clothes and the necessary toiletries. She wasn't surprised to see that Jillian's bed was already neatly made. You could probably bounce quarters on it, Sam thought, as she shuffled across the soft taupe carpet.

After a brief shower, she dressed in a cotton wrap-around skirt appropriate to the ridiculously warm December weather and a melon-colored top. She dabbed on a minimum of makeup, including her favorite cranberry lipstick, but chose to let her hair dry naturally. She'd learned long ago that trying to tame the wayward spirals into behaving was an exercise in futility. Probably the same way her parents felt about her.

She took one last look in the mirror and called out, "Okay, I'm ready." While she wasn't as crisp and beautiful as Jillian in her tailored slacks and linen blouse, children wouldn't stop on the street to point and laugh, either.

When the two women reached the small boutique where the fitting was scheduled, Sam asked, "So this is where you found your wedding dress?"

Jillian's laugh was dry and brittle. "You think my mother would allow her only daughter to wear a domestic bridal gown? My dress came from Paris."

The fitting seemed endless, but that was probably just because Sam hadn't had any coffee yet. She stood with her arms outstretched and her patience running thin as the seamstress's deft hands worked on the midnight-blue satin. Sam suspected Claire had slipped the woman an extra twenty to stab her a few dozen times with the pins. She hoped the blood would come out of the dress.

Sam had to admit the dress was gorgeous. Backless, A-line, with a drape of chiffon falling gracefully across the neckline. Very elegant. The entire winter motif for Jillian's wedding was elegant. The colors were to be dark blue, white and silver, and the pictures Jillian had shown her last night of the floral arrangements were breathtaking.

Sam had teased, "Heck, you think Claire would plan *my* wedding?"

But instead of laughing with her, Jillian had replied somberly, "I never pictured you getting married. A loner like you? Awfully conformist, isn't it?"

Now Sam played the words over in her head. A loner? That's not how she saw herself. *Unlike that work-obsessed Ethan Jenner, I have friends.* Well, she had Jillian. And she kept in touch with some classmates from Juilliard, classmates who had gone on to fulfill grander destinies than teaching piano lessons to kids. But Sam loved her kids.

Aha! Her students. She spent tons of time with them. She wasn't a loner at all. Not that her kids were much for going out for coffee and discussing current events, but still…

"Ouch!" Sam shot the evil eye at the seamstress, who responded disdainfully, "Don't move, and you won't be poked."

"If you would quit poking me, I'd quit moving," she muttered, but kept the retort under her breath. No point in provoking the needle-wielding maniac.

When the fitting was over, Sam joked that the bridesmaids should go to the emergency room for stitches instead of to brunch. Only Jillian laughed. Claire glared in disapproval and the three brunette bridesmaids looked confused. Sam had concluded earlier that confusion might be the natural state for the girls, whose names were somewhere in the neighborhood of Bitsy, Muffy and Sofie. The cream of the debutante crop.

Half an hour later, the entourage sat in the private room of a posh restaurant decorated as a greenhouse. The thick, sweet smell of bunched flowers competed with the rich aroma of coffee and French pastries. Sunlight streamed through endless glass windows, illuminating a floral rainbow of colors, and Mozart played softly through hidden speakers. If Sam were the one getting married, she would have planned the wedding here.

"Nice, isn't it?"

She turned to find one of the other bridesmaids—Buffy? Candy? Sleepy? Grumpy?—smiling. Her expression was so openly friendly that Sam choked on her mental condescension. If she weren't careful, she'd turn out to be a worse snob than Claire Winthrop. Just a different type.

"It's beautiful," Sam concurred.

"Everything around Jillian is. She always looks so perfect, the church is perfect...have you seen their engagement picture? A perfect couple," the woman enthused, a romantic, dreamy look in her hazel eyes. "The groom's especially stunning, if he looks half as good in person."

"Oh, he does," Sam blurted. She may not have liked Ethan Jenner, but even she couldn't deny his masculine appeal. Dammit. "I mean, I haven't seen the picture, but I met him last night."

"Lucky girl," the bridesmaid breathed. She pulled a rolled-up newspaper from her designer bag. "Here, it was in today's society section."

In the photograph, Jillian stood at Ethan's side, fashionable in a long-sleeved dress and with her hair smoothed into a demure, conservative bun. Her pale beauty contrasted sharply with Ethan's dark suit and somber expression.

Actually, Jillian's expression, while not as fierce as her fiancé's, was unsmiling, as well. Sam frowned at her tingling sense of déjà vu. What did this remind her of? Ah, yes, the yuppie version of *American Gothic*. Only thing missing was the pitchfork.

Jillian and Ethan inarguably looked good together, but they didn't look happy together.

So they took a lousy picture, Sam thought. Some people just aren't photogenic.

But Sam had seen dozens of great pictures of Jillian, and judging from the magazine spread on Ethan Jenner, he was no slouch, either.

"Sam, I need to talk to you." Jillian peered over her shoulder. "What do you think of the portrait?"

Don't ask. "Reminds me of something I saw in a museum."

"Yes, the photographer was a real artist. Look, I need to ask you a favor," Jillian said, tugging Sam off to the side.

"Anything," she agreed automatically.

"I need you to spend the day with Ethan."

Anything but that.

3

SAM WASN'T SURE WHAT her expression looked like, but it couldn't have been encouraging.

Jillian immediately switched to her soothing, reassuring tone, the one she frequently used to try to win over her parents. "Well, not all day. Just a few hours."

That's a few too many.

Delicate blond eyebrows arched, Jillian frowned at Sam's lack of response. "It's just a small favor so I can go with my mother to the caterer's. There's been an emergency."

"A *catering* emergency?"

"Don't laugh. You probably wouldn't care if I served pigs-in-blankets at the reception—"

"What's wrong with that? Got your protein, your carbs—"

"—but it's important that I make the right impression on the guests at my wedding. I need to take care of this, so I can't go with Ethan this afternoon to…his lesson."

Suspecting that she'd regret asking, Sam echoed, "Lesson?"

"Dancing." Jillian sighed. "Don't make jokes. He's a little touchy about it. Ethan's not the type of man who likes to admit he can't do something, but there hasn't been a great need for ballroom dancing in his life. And he's determined to make a good impression at the reception.''

It was the second time Jillian had mentioned impressions; the desire to make a good one seemed like the only thing the bride and groom had in common.

''I—''

Jillian pressed her hands to her temples. ''Things are hectic right now, and I could use your help.''

''You know I'll help.'' That's what the maid of honor was for, wasn't it? To be the bride's right hand? Make sure there was as little stress as possible surrounding the wedding? ''Where are these dance lessons?''

A sunny smile broke across Jillian's face. ''Thanks, Sam. And don't worry about finding your way. Ethan'll pick you up here. He's on his way over to meet me, and now he can just take you instead.''

I'm sure he'll be delighted.

''Thanks again,'' Jillian gushed, squeezing Sam's hand. ''This gives you a chance to get to know him, tell me what you think. It'll be great.''

Right. ''Just let me get my purse and say goodbye to—'' Bobbie, Brittany and Bunny? ''—them,'' Sam concluded, gesturing toward the gaggle of bridesmaids.

Why couldn't Jillian have asked one of the other women? They probably would have jumped at the chance to spend the afternoon—*don't think it*—in Ethan's arms. *You thought it.*

Sam pushed the image away. Deep down, she knew exactly why Jillian had come to her. Jillian *always* came to her. That's the way their friendship had been from the beginning. And Sam always agreed to help. She had a lot of flaws, but she prided herself on being loyal.

Unfortunately, her loyalty was telling her that she needed to add "break up my best friend's wedding" to her maid of honor duties.

TURNING TO THE PASSENGER next to him, Ethan attempted the type of charming, jolly smile his future father-in-law could always pull off.

His facial muscles tensed and contorted with the effort.

"Are you all right?" Sam asked, looking as though she might reach for the door handle and throw herself from the moving vehicle.

Okay, so the smile had backfired. But he didn't feel like smiling. He felt like growling. The *last* thing he wanted was to be saddled with this woman for the rest of the day.

"I'm fine," he lied. "I was just thinking how…grateful I am for your help this afternoon."

Her husky peal of laughter startled him. Almost as much as his response to the infectious sound. Ignoring the strange heat in his veins, he tightened his hands on the steering wheel of Jordan's BMW. "Something funny?"

"Yes. I understand that in business one should be able to bluff, but you are a lousy liar."

"You're calling me a liar?" The fact that she was right didn't dim his disbelief or indignation. "Hardly fair, since you don't know me at all." Which hadn't stopped her from passing judgment last night. Considering the looks she'd thrown him over dinner and the way she'd hinted that Jillian should be having doubts about the wedding, Samantha Lloyd didn't have a high opinion of him.

But he'd survived lower opinions than hers. From the kids he'd grown up with who looked down on him to the uncle who hadn't wanted to be saddled with his dead sister's kid. Shaking off the shadows of the past, Ethan told himself he couldn't care less what Samantha Lloyd thought of him. It wasn't as though he held her in particularly high esteem, either. Troublesome, erratic and unconventional, she was the exact opposite of what he desired in a woman.

Well, maybe not the *exact* opposite. Not if he took into account the sound of her laugh, the sparkle in her eyes and the way she filled out a skirt. The woman had legs that—

He increased his grip on the steering wheel again, then realized he'd cut off circulation in his fingers. Life wasn't a fairy tale and Jillian might not be the princess he'd been destined by birth to wed, but she would be his wife. He owed it to her not to ogle another woman's legs. Even if they *were* truly spectacular.

Unfortunately, the rest of Sam's body lived up to her legs, and he was going to spend the afternoon way too close to that body. The dance lesson that had seemed mildly embarrassing before now promised to be unbearable. He'd attended many elegant events, even a few that included dancing, but he'd remained on the sidelines, discussing business. There would be dancing at the reception, though, and how would it look if the groom didn't dance with the bride?

Not wanting to dwell on the idea of dancing before a crowd of important onlookers, he studied Sam. "Based on Jillian's descriptions of you, I didn't know what to expect."

"At least she described me. I'd never even heard of you. Short engagement, I take it?"

Was that disapproval in her tone? From all he'd heard and seen, she wasn't a stickler for convention. "Is there a point to long engagements? When you know what you're going to do, it's best to proceed accordingly."

"'Proceed accordingly'? Very romantic." She quirked one auburn eyebrow. "Do you love Jillian?"

The social polish he worked so hard to cultivate slipped for a moment, and his own forthright nature surfaced. "My feelings for Jillian are none of your business."

"Most bridegrooms wouldn't hesitate to say that they loved the woman they were about to marry."

"Claire mentioned you had a habit of sticking your nose where it didn't belong."

She wrinkled the nose in question. "Claire's just afraid I might encourage Jillian to think for herself. I'll bet it didn't take Mommy and Daddy long to bully Jillian into this marriage, did it?"

"Are you saying a woman would have to be *bullied* into marrying me?"

She surprised him by opening and closing her mouth several times, unable to reply.

Mark this date on your calendar, folks. He was willing to bet she wasn't at a loss for words often.

"I am sorry." She sounded as though she genuinely meant it. "I crossed the line. I didn't mean to imply you were…"

"Undesirable?"

She swallowed. "I definitely didn't mean that."

He glanced from the two-lane road to her sapphire gaze. Her eyes were frankly apologetic—she was as candid in remorse as she was in rudeness—but there was something else there, too. Something suppressed but not quite buried, and for a reckless moment, he considered asking if *she* found him desirable.

Lord. One day with her and I'm as unbalanced as she is. He hadn't realized insanity was catching. Feeling unprepared for further conversation, he switched on the radio to a public station where he could get market updates and hoped she'd take the hint. But not talking to her didn't stop him from thinking about her.

Growing up as an outcast, the poorest boy in school, he'd had a lot of time to study people. He used that talent now when sizing up investors and figuring out how to maneuver them into deals. But Sam was hard to figure.

On the plane, she'd made very little sense—he still didn't understand why she hadn't said something when she discovered he was marrying Jillian. In the car after leaving the airport and at the beginning of dinner, she'd been subdued. But between the soup and the first course, she'd turned combative. Though he didn't understand the nuances of everything she'd said, there was no doubt she'd been challenging Claire and Jordan. And even him.

Why did she think he wasn't good enough for her friend?

Well, to hell with all the people who'd never thought he was good enough. He'd accomplished a lot through his own hard work, and he was about to ally himself with one of the most powerful families in the Southwest. By this time next week, he'd have a beautiful new wife and dozens of influential connections.

And that's going to make you happy?

He didn't recognize the small voice in his head, but it reminded him unpleasantly of Jiminy Cricket.

Happiness was fleeting, unpredictable and didn't pay bills. If happiness were a commodity on the market, Ethan would advise every one of his clients to stay away from it. It was unstable, liable to crash at any moment and leave you with nothing.

Had his parents' happiness done them any good? When his father had died after a prolonged illness and his mother worked herself to death trying to pay off a pile of medical bills, Ethan had been sent to his uncle—a crusty SOB who'd never claimed to love Ethan or anyone else. But his uncle taught him the value of hard work, the value of security. The same principles that had gotten Ethan where he was today.

Yikes. The maudlin introspection was unlike him and unproductive. Maybe he should have just kept talking to the nutcase.

If he wanted to mentally review anything, it should be his recent promotion, not his past. The youngest Peabo-Johnston employee to ever become vice president, he planned to hit the ground running and prove he was equal to the task. Start building a foundation now for one day being president. The connections the Winthrops provided and the refinement Jillian would help bring to his life were a step in the right direction.

Thinking of Jillian, he took a deep breath and smiled. Around her, his composure was safe and he never felt the need to defend his own actions. She was good for him. Relaxing. The antithesis of her friend.

Once again confident in his decision, he addressed Sam almost smugly. "You seem to have a problem with my engagement to Jillian, but I'll have you know she's the perfect wife for me."

Instead of arguing with him, she nodded. "It's good you feel that way."

There. Guess I showed her. So why did he feel something like disappointment? It wasn't as though he wanted her to debate with him.

Not a moment too soon, the dance studio came into sight. A short while ago he'd been dreading the lesson, but now he relished having something to occupy his mind. He drove through the intersection and turned into the small parking lot.

"We're here," he announced, killing the engine.

Inside, a petite blonde who looked about thirteen sat behind a chipped and scarred oak desk. Ethan waited impatiently, shifting his balance from one foot to the other, while she finished her phone conversation. *Let's get this over with.*

He took perverse joy in noticing that Sam looked as uncomfortable as he felt. She absently twirled strands of her hair in a nervous fashion he doubted she was even aware of.

Finally, the leotard-clad pixie receptionist hung up the phone and stood, extending her arms in a welcoming gesture that looked choreographed. "Afternoon," she drawled in a thick Texas accent. "I'm Madame Anastasia."

You've got to be joking.

A funny noise burbled out of Sam—something that had obviously begun life as a laugh—and she faked a sneeze to cover it. "Nice to meet you," she managed to say.

Anastasia consulted an open appointment book. "Jenner party, here for private ballroom instruction?"

Ethan merely nodded, thinking the girl looked a lot more like a Miss Anna than a Madame Anastasia. She led them down a narrow tiled hallway to a large studio room with a hardwood floor and wall-length mirror. Parallel to the mirror was a long bar, and Ethan's unease doubled. If anyone so much as mentioned a weird French word like *plié* or *pirouette,* he was out of here.

Anastasia glided to the stereo at the front of the room and hit Rewind on the tape deck. "Y'all stretch, get comfortable. I have to return a call, and then we'll begin. With a waltz, something simple to start."

She left them alone, shutting the door behind her. Ethan turned to Sam, prepared to offer her a cash bribe to look the other way while he hauled ass out of this joint.

Sam was grinning. "*She's* Madame Anastasia? With a name like that, you'd expect a gaunt European woman in her sixties. Wearing a turban. She looks more like she should be named for one of Jillian's bridesmaids. Sandy, Sunny or Sissy."

"Is that really what their names are? For the life of me, I can't keep them straight."

Spots of color blossomed on her cheeks. "I hate

to admit it, but I can't, either. Daphne, Dilly and Daisy? Does that sound right to you?''

He shook his head, but gave it a shot of his own. "Freddie, Farrah and Felicity?''

Sam laughed, and the sound cut into him in the painful, poignant way really good music sometimes did. She laughed so naturally, so freely. Since his parents' deaths, few people laughed around him. Jillian smiled politely and his co-workers guffawed when clients told jokes.

When was the last time *he* had genuinely laughed?

"I know that two of them are her cousins and the other's a lifelong neighbor of the Winthrops,'' she said, derailing his train of thought.

"Hmm?''

"The bridesmaids. Two are cousins, one's a neighbor.''

"Oh.'' He filed away the information, but doubted he'd ever be able to tell the women apart. The three attractive bridesmaids looked and sounded pretty much the same to him. There was a brunette with long hair, a brunette with short hair and a brunette with curly hair. Thank God Jillian was a blonde, or he might not be able to pick her out of the crowd.

He winced immediately. What a horrible thing to think. Jillian was beautiful. She'd stand out anywhere, and he was lucky she'd agreed to be his wife.

"Ethan?'' Sam snapped her fingers. "You okay? I dated a guy who had that same look on his face once. It turned out to be appendicitis.''

"I appreciate your concern, but this is just my natural reaction to dancing.''

She shrugged a shoulder. "It's not so bad. Of course, Jillian and I had years of comportment and interschool cotillions, so I'm used to it. I imagine you weren't the cotillion type."

"No, I didn't grow up a rich kid like you."

Her half smile faded at his harsh tone. "That's not what I meant. I only—"

"You're right. I snapped at you, and it was uncalled for." He hated feeling rattled, but *rattled* was the best word to describe what this woman did to him. Time to put an end to it. "We didn't get off on the right foot, but I'd like to change that. Maybe we could start over, try to be…friends?"

Her midnight-blue eyes darkened with something akin to apprehension, then she shook her head.

His teeth clicked together so hard it hurt his jaw. He wasn't even good enough for her to temporarily befriend in the name of civility?

"I'd like to accept your offer," she ventured, "but it would make me a hypocrite. You see, I don't think you and Jillian are really in love—"

"I told you before that's none—"

"Of my business, I know. But she's the closest thing to a sister I've ever had. I don't want her in a marriage she'll regret later."

"I'm flattered that you're so sure she'd regret marrying me." But there was no heat to his words. Against his will and better judgment, he respected Sam's loyalty and candor. He'd had to bite his tongue so often in the business world that he'd probably caused permanent scarring; her openness was refreshing. "Would it ease your mind to know that I'll try to be a good husband?"

She caught her full lower lip between her teeth.

"I'm afraid not, no. There are other…issues. To be perfectly frank, I plan to talk Jillian out of marrying you before Saturday. So I couldn't in good conscience claim to be your friend."

Momentary shock at her blatant announcement gave way to his innate stubbornness—the part of him that was most motivated by people telling him he couldn't achieve something. "Then I should tell *you* in all good conscience that I have no intention of letting you wreck my future."

"Fair enough."

What now? He shoved his hands into the pockets of his khakis. He was on unfamiliar territory. A gauntlet thrown between himself and an adversary he almost found himself liking at the moment. "Well, then, I guess we can't be friends. But we can stop baiting each other. I really didn't mean to snap at you earlier."

He held out a hand. "Truce?" Jillian was unlikely to change her mind at this late date, and how much damage could Sam do if he kept an eye on her? "A limited one, anyway," he qualified with a smile.

She met his gaze, nodding finally and sliding her hand into his grasp. Her skin was warm and smooth, and a small spark shot from her fingers to his.

It's just static from the carpet.

A moment later, as Madame Anastasia reentered the room, Ethan remembered there wasn't any carpet in the building.

4

ETHAN TWIRLED HER AROUND the floor, but Sam feared that wasn't the only reason her head was spinning. After a painful beginning—especially painful for her toes—she and Ethan had fallen into a rhythm. Even Madame Anastasia, who'd spent the first half hour of their lesson cringing and muttering under her breath, nodded her approval.

But Sam almost wished Ethan would crunch her foot again, distract her from the muscular contours of his shoulder under her hand and the easy strength of his fingers locked with hers. Denying his masculine appeal had been much easier before he'd offered his version of the olive branch. Granted, they still weren't the best of friends, but most men wouldn't have been nearly as calm about her announcement that she intended to ruin their plans.

One thing she could say with absolute certainty: Ethan Jenner was *not* most men.

"We seem to have reversed roles," he murmured near her ear.

His voice, low and unexpected, startled her. "What?" She focused on his face and realized he was grimacing.

"My foot," he clarified.

"Sorry. My mind wandered."

His lips curved into a self-mocking smile. "I figure you're entitled to a little payback. A toe for a toe.''

The music she'd barely been listening to stopped, and Ethan dipped her. Madame Anastasia clapped her hands together.

''Super. Y'all aren't ready for anything complicated, but you certainly have the basics down. If you'd relax a little, you'd move like you were made for each other.''

Simultaneously, they released each other and sprang apart.

''Actually,'' Sam spluttered, ''I'm just a stand-in. A practice partner since his fiancée couldn't make it. But he'll be dancing with her.''

''Oh.'' Anastasia frowned. ''But you—never mind. Well, our time is up. You can pay up front and schedule any future appointments.''

''Thank you, but no,'' Ethan replied, his eyes on Sam. ''This was strictly a onetime thing.''

SAM SCRUNCHED DOWN FARTHER in the hotel bed, wishing she had a pint of rocky-road ice cream. But tonight, comfort was limited to her favorite flannel pajama shirt, a cold washcloth over her forehead and an incredibly bad horror movie on cable. Good thing Jillian was out with Ethan; she'd never have been able to sit through *Return of the Surfer Dude Zombies*.

By the time Jillian had finished at the caterers, she'd had to leave almost immediately for dinner with Ethan and potential investors, so the two women hadn't yet discussed the dance lesson. What would Sam have said if it had come up?

''The dance lessons? Well, the doctors said I

should be out of the walking cast in about a month...."

"He can't tango, but he has the waltz down smoothly. Oh, and I mentioned my plan to nix your wedding. He took it pretty well...."

"Jillian, did you ever notice how when you look in his eyes you forget where you are?"

She groaned. Better to concentrate on the dialogue in *Surfer Zombies*. Witty, insightful lines like, "Dude, let's go unarmed into the dark basement and check on the guy we sent to investigate those creepy noises."

The phone on the nightstand rang, and she hit the mute button on the remote control. "Hello?"

Silence. But the kind of silence where someone was obviously on the other end. Sam's gaze flickered nervously to the TV screen and the two young men in the shadowy basement, moments from certain, badly acted, death.

"Hello?"

A man cleared his throat and asked hesitantly, "Is Jillian there?"

"No, she's— Who is this?" Female intuition sparked. She'd have recognized Ethan's voice and no way was this one of Jillian's brothers. None of the Winthrop men were ever hesitant. "Peter?"

"I'll call her some other—"

"No, wait. It's okay, I'm Sam. Is there a message I can give her?"

His dejected sigh broke her heart. "I don't know. I can't think of anything to say that I haven't said already. And nothing's worked."

"How did you know she was here?"

"I had my sister call the Winthrops and pretend

to be a friend of Jillie's. They gave her the hotel and room number, said she was with you. I was hoping that if I could catch her away from her parents she might listen to reason."

Sam smiled, thinking of her similar strategy in inviting Jillian to stay here. "There's nothing I'd like more than for you to talk some sense into her, but she isn't here right now."

"Do you know what her schedule's like this week? I have to see her before the wedding. If she can tell me she truly wants to marry this guy, then I'll wish her the best, but..."

Yeah. But. Sam felt the same way. "She's driving out to some spa tomorrow for a day of bridal beauty." He made a small, pained noise at the word *bridal,* and she rushed on. "Tomorrow night is a big barbecue at her parents'. They're keeping her busy." The day after was the wedding rehearsal, then came the day of reckoning.

Time was running out. She racked her brain, trying to remember just how big that barbecue tomorrow was. "If I could help you get a few minutes alone with her tomorrow night, do you think her parents would notice her absence?"

He snorted. "Those parents of hers don't notice her at all unless there's something they want from her. They spend all their time with her brothers or showing off their future son-in-law."

Good point. "I'll see what I can do."

"Thank you. You know, Jillian speaks very highly of you. She looks up to you."

"Thanks. She's told me great things about you, too."

"Really?"

The hope in his voice made her ache inside. He so clearly loved Jillian that Sam experienced a twinge of envy. No man had ever sounded so determined to win *her*. Then again, she hadn't been involved with anyone special enough that she'd wanted to be won.

"Peter, I really believe she loves you."

"You don't think she'll marry this Jenner guy, do you?"

"I hope not." *But I guess we'll know in a few days.*

A STRANGE CHIRPING interrupted Sam's dreams—not that she minded; she'd been plagued all night with odd visions of waltzing surfer zombies moving in time to Anastasia's steady counting. She groped blindly for the alarm clock on the nightstand, trying to shrug off the bizarre dreams. But pressing the buttons on the little clock did nothing to stop the chirping…no, ringing.

"Sam, could you get that?" Jillian's request, called from the bathroom over the sound of running water, cut through the last of Sam's slumber-induced fog.

She sat up, yawning, and stared at the blinking red light that accompanied each of the phone's rings. It took her a minute to get the message "Answer it, dummy" from her brain to her fingers, but she finally grasped the receiver and lifted it to her ear. "'Ello?"

"Did I wake you?"

Ethan! Hearing his voice, she suddenly had the disturbing feeling that not all of her dreams had been about zombies.

He sounded self-possessed and faintly amused. And so *awake* that there was no way she could admit to having been asleep.

"No, you didn't wake me." Technically, Jillian had been the one to wake her up.

"You sure? Because you sounded like—"

"Jillian's just getting out of the shower if you'd like to talk to her," Sam interjected. "I assume that's why you called."

"Just goes to show why people shouldn't make assumptions. It was you I wanted, actually."

It was you I wanted. Good thing she hadn't stood up yet. His words effectively liquefied the lower half of her body.

Get over it. He means he wanted to talk *to you.*

Surely if she'd been more awake, she wouldn't have had such an inappropriate reaction to his words or his deep, rich voice. Willing herself to sound casual and collected, she asked, "What did you need to speak with me about?"

"Your plans for the day."

"I thought you said the dance lessons were a one-time thing."

"Trust me. They were."

She grinned, clearly picturing the disgruntled expression that went with his tone. "Okay, so no dancing."

"Nope. Today it's golf."

"You need golf lessons, too?"

"I could *give* golf lessons," he rejoined, obviously offended by her ego-bruising suggestion. "It's a golf partner I need. I asked Jillian about it last night. Unfortunately, she'll be at the spa and unable to help me, but she assured me you were free for the day.''

"Oh, she did, did she?" This made two days in a row Jillian had done this to her. Sam might be the first maid of honor to throttle the bride.

"Our tee time is ten-thirty. I figure I can pick you up at—"

"Hey! I never agreed. Actually, I was thinking about going with Jillian to the spa and pampering myself today." And maybe using the time to mention Peter's call and the fact that he was still very much in love with Jillian. Sam had wanted to bring it up last night, but Jillian had come home so tired and cranky that Sam hadn't broached the subject.

"Okay," Ethan sighed, "forget it, then. I just realized you probably don't have anything appropriate to wear on the golf course, anyway."

"What's that supposed to mean?"

"Nothing. Besides, I never asked Jillian if you could even play." His skeptical tone made it clear that he thought he knew the answer to his own question.

"I am an excellent player." He'd had the nerve to chide her about making assumptions? "I bet I can run circles around you on the green."

"Wonderful. I'll meet you in the lobby at ten, then."

He hung up, leaving her with the dial tone bleating in her ear and no chance to rebut his quick and blatant manipulation.

Too late to save Sam from disaster, Jillian emerged from the bathroom, wearing the thick white robe provided by the hotel and towel-drying her honey-blond hair. "That wasn't my mother, was it?"

Worse. "Your fiancé."

"Oh. Did he invite you to play golf with him?"

"Invite? More like issued a summons. I can't believe you told him I'd go without even checking with me." She knew she sounded petulant but, darn it, this was the second morning in a row she'd been forced into human interaction before she'd had coffee. She was used to living alone, waking up at her own pace.

"I didn't tell him you would go with him," Jillian protested. "I told him you were an excellent golfer and it wouldn't hurt to ask."

"Wait a minute." She recalled his roundabout questioning of whether or not she could even play. "You *told* him I was an excellent golfer?"

"Well, you are."

Her earlier plans to throttle Jillian shifted direction. She should throttle that conniving Ethan Jenner. And then pummel him and hang him by his thumbs, too.

Sam sighed. "Why's he so desperate to find a partner, anyway? And what's wrong with your dad? Your father practically lives on the links."

"I think Ethan wanted a female partner." Jillian shrugged. "He's meeting with a potentially huge investor who's bringing his wife along, so Ethan wanted a foursome. He asked me to go last night."

"He didn't know you were busy today?"

She shrugged again. "We don't feel it necessary to keep tabs on each other."

"But don't you think that's because—"

"*Anyway,* I told him he could ask you if he

wanted. I'm just glad it wasn't my mother calling. She's driving me crazy." Jillian held up her thumb and index finger, pinched together with almost no space between them. "I am this close to losing it."

"I know what you mean," Sam mumbled.

Either Jillian didn't hear or she chose not to comment. "Oh, Sam, speaking of my mother, I should probably tell you that you're throwing me a bachelorette party tonight."

"I am?"

"Just a small one. You, me and the bridesmaids. I told my mother it was tonight so we could duck out of that barbecue at a decent hour. Besides, it's been a while since we had a wild crazy evening."

Sam wasn't sure they'd ever had an evening that qualified as wild and crazy. Jillian normally went more for the "quietly enjoyable" forms of entertainment, but why not? Sam could certainly throw a bachelorette party. How hard could that be to arrange between playing eighteen holes of business golf, providing covert assistance to a lovesick exboyfriend and sabotaging a wedding?

"I AM A GENIUS." Normally, Ethan wouldn't have made such a boastful comment, but since no one else was in the BMW to hear it, what the heck? He really had done some slick maneuvering.

First, he'd convinced the elusive Walter Matthias to take a meeting, disguised as recreation; Peabo-Johnston had been trying to talk Matthias into investing for months. Then Ethan had had his brilliant brainstorm and invited the family-oriented Matthias to bring his wife, Glenda, to the course. According to Jordan, Glenda and Walter—though married almost thirty years—were as devoted as newlyweds. The way to win over Walter was definitely through Glenda. And once Ethan had determined Glenda would be present, he had his excuse to keep an eye on Sam.

Knowing that his fiancée had plans for the day and guessing that both women had been raised around yuppie sports like tennis and golf, he'd asked Jillian to come with him. She had responded exactly as he'd hoped—she couldn't do it, but maybe Sam...

No way he was trusting the meddlesome maid of honor to the hour's drive out to the spa and a full day of girl-talk with his bride-to-be. Entirely too much opportunity there for her to stir up trouble. Now, thanks to him, the only trouble she'd be stirring up would be on the golf course—far, far away from Jillian.

As he turned into the hotel parking lot, a horrifying thought struck him and his self-satisfaction evaporated. Oh boy. What if she *did* stir up trouble on the golf course? Matthias was a very important potential client. Sam wouldn't deliberately do anything to make Ethan look bad, would she?

This is the same woman who boldly assured you she planned to terminate your wedding, and she's had all morning to get good and mad that you railroaded her into golf today.

He banged his hand against the steering wheel. Why hadn't he thought of this before? Usually, business was his top priority, but he'd been sidetracked by thoughts of Sam. That is to say, sidetracked by thoughts of how to minimize her chances of corrupting Jillian.

Taking a deep breath and telling himself not to panic, he parked the car, then strode into the lobby.

Sam stood right inside the doors, dressed conservatively in a crisp blue top and beige slacks with her hair pulled back in a bouncy ponytail. She looked the part of the perfect golf partner. Well, except for her glare, the arms folded angrily across her chest and the mutinous angle of her chin.

"Great," he said, opening with a conciliatory smile, "I see you're all ready to—"

"You lied. You said you didn't know if I could play."

A lesser man would be caught off guard by the immediate attack. "No, I said I didn't ask Jillian. Which is true, she volunteered the information."

"Semantics."

"And you were 100 percent truthful when you said you were awake this morning?"

She blinked. "Don't try to change the subject. I don't know what you're up to, but I'm sure it's sneaky."

"All I'm up to is trying to put a stop to what *you're* up to," he retorted, jabbing his index finger in her direction. "We need to go. I don't want to be late for the Matthiases."

"Are they filthy rich socialites used to people kowtowing? It would probably do them some good to wait a few minutes."

Her out-of-hand disdain for his potential clients reminded him unpleasantly of what a loose cannon she was. He chose his words carefully. "You understand, don't you, how critical these people are to me?"

"To *you*, yes." She arched an eyebrow and smiled.

All his instincts told him to be afraid. Very afraid. And he might have been if some strange, undisciplined part of him wasn't looking forward to the challenge her dark blue eyes promised.

5

"NICE DRIVE."

Sam looked over her shoulder, half prepared to find sarcasm in Ethan's expression. But his eyes held only sincere admiration. Well, why not? It *was* a nice drive. Still, she hadn't expected admiration. Just as she hadn't expected rich and powerful Walter Matthias to be warm and fatherly. Or expected workaholic Ethan to look so relaxed and confident.

Ethan clearly enjoyed golf and seemed in his element wooing clients. His eyes, brought out by the deep green of his polo shirt, crinkled at the corners when he smiled, and he played with an easy athleticism she found mesmerizing. A man who moved with such deliberate grace probably knew exactly how to—

Samantha! Thoughts like that were no more productive than hitting herself repeatedly in the head with her rented nine-iron.

Hoping her guilt didn't show in her expression, she stepped away from the women's tee to let Glenda Matthias take her swing. Abrupt and cold, Glenda at least had been as expected. Sam couldn't understand why Walter looked at his aloof wife with such open affection.

After all four of them had landed balls on the fairway, they headed forward in their two separate carts. Sam had suspected, watching Ethan shoot the first three holes, that her partner was holding back. Not in an obvious-enough way to insult their opponents, but still...

He quickly confirmed her suspicion. "Jillian didn't exaggerate, you are a great golfer. But maybe, just for today, you could..."

"Could what?"

"Well, Glenda isn't the world's best player, and she's obviously upset about the way she did on the first couple of holes. I thought—"

"You thought we could throw the game to keep her happy and thereby make her husband happy enough that he'll turn his millions over to you?"

She expected a denial, or at least an angry reminder of how important these people were. Once again, her expectations failed her. Ethan threw his head back and laughed.

"Did I say something funny?" she asked.

"You certainly have a knack for cutting to the chase," he said. "There I was trying to figure out how to delicately phrase the situation, and you summed it up in a nutshell."

"And that's funny, how?"

He just shook his head, still smiling. "You're something else."

Oddly enough, the way he said it made her go all warm and tingly inside. Feeling too unsettled to carry on the conversation, she was relieved when he stopped the cart and hopped out.

Unfortunately, she was also too unsettled to putt well. Her score for the hole was substantially worse than any of her first three.

As they headed for the fifth tee box, she glared

in Ethan's direction. "I had an off moment, but I am not throwing the game."

"Everyone's entitled to an off moment."

"I just didn't want you to think I was doing it for you."

He grinned. "Sam, I don't think you'd spit on me if I were on fire."

It was the first time he'd ever called her by name, and shivers danced up her spine.

That's ridiculous. It's your name, not an endearment. Her favorite teachers all called her Sam. Heck, her great-uncle called her Sam. Nothing special about it.

Except when it was said in Ethan's deep, sexy voice.

Her score for the next hole was even lower.

This was shaping up to be a very long afternoon.

Unable to concentrate on her game, Sam focused on Ethan's conversation with Walter Matthias. The investment Ethan wanted the man to make was in a pharmaceutical company needing money to research and produce a new treatment for childhood leukemia. As Ethan talked about his investigation of the company and his actual visits to a hospital to spend time with afflicted children, she could see he cared more about the kids than he did about the money he'd make off of Matthias's investment.

A memory niggled at her and she belatedly recalled reading about his many charitable contributions—especially to children's organizations—on the plane. Before she'd learned who he was or who he was marrying. Come to think of it, she'd also read that he'd grown up poor. A little fact she'd forgotten when she'd later painted him with the same brush as her parents and the Winthrops. She hadn't considered that his dedication to work and comments about financial security might be motivated by something more than simple greed.

Feeling smaller than the golf ball she was trying to hit, Sam reassessed his engagement to Jillian. If she'd been wrong about Ethan, might she be wrong about trying to talk Jillian out of marrying him?

No. Even if he were a saint, which was unlikely, Jillian didn't love him. She loved Peter. And Ethan Jenner may be much nicer than Sam thought, but he didn't love Jillian, either.

She mulled over the situation as Ethan drove the cart, trying to reassure herself she was doing the right thing.

"You seem pensive all of a sudden. Should I be worried?"

"Just the opposite," she blurted. "You should be flattered. I was thinking nice things about you."

"What?" Clutching his chest with one hand, he cautioned, "Careful shocking me like that. I almost drove us into a tree." A beat later he asked, "What were these nice things, exactly?"

She wasn't sure she wanted to have this discussion. But she'd been so evident in her disapproval of him that she owed it to him to be equally vocal in her newfound appreciation.

"Those kids you mentioned—the ones who are sick?—you really seem to care about them. More than the money, I mean."

He clenched his jaw and singed her with seething emerald eyes. "*Seem to?* Exactly what kind of heartless bastard do you think I am that I'd care more about money than critically ill children?"

"I—"

He stepped out of the cart before she could finish her sentence and she was left feeling even lower than before. He may not be the most sentimental man in the world, but he did have feelings. And she'd thoughtlessly hurt them.

Nice going. At this rate he'll call off the wedding himself, figuring Jillian can't be too great if she's friends with someone like you.

Wait a minute, that's what she wanted, wasn't it? For the wedding to be called off? She'd help Jillian and Ethan come to their senses, then go home, never to see Ethan Jenner again. The thought should have given her some sort of satisfaction.

It wasn't until after their bantering between rounds stopped that she realized how much she'd been enjoying the day. Ethan drove the next few holes in angry silence and played with such single-minded vengeance that he must have forgotten his goal to go easy on the client. After one particularly successful swing, he smirked in Sam's direction, silently daring her to do better.

Self-flagellation had never been Sam's style. Sure, she felt bad about insulting him, but it hadn't been intentional. Plus, she'd tried to apologize. She wasn't so mired in guilt that she couldn't rise to his wordless challenge. Each hole she hit better, and he did, too, until they were spurring each other on to furious perfection. Their team score got lower and lower until the Matthiases stood almost no chance.

Walter managed some decent scores, but seemed more interested in the interteam competition unfolding before him. Glenda continued to hit badly. Her comments became increasingly whiny as she blamed

Sam for messing up her concentration on one green and the groundskeeper for doing a lousy job on another. Sam even noticed that on the eleventh hole, Glenda moved her ball almost a foot when she thought no one was watching. Not that Sam cared. Glenda wasn't the opposition.

Sam had to restrain an undignified whoop of victory when she eagled on the twelfth after Ethan birdied. She glanced in his direction, aware that a "take that" expression radiated from her eyes.

Walter clapped her on the shoulder. "Nice job, young lady. You ever thought about playing on the women's pro tour?"

Before she could answer, Ethan interrupted with "Oh, don't encourage her. She's already insufferable."

She rounded on him. "*I'm* insufferable? You—"

He herded her toward the cart, not allowing her to finish the thought. "Come on, there's a group behind us waiting to play."

"You can't keep doing this, you know."

"Shooting birdies? Sure I can, although I'm hoping for a few eagles. You aren't the only one who can do that."

"You can't keep bullying people. Is that how you deal with anyone who gets in your way?"

"Maybe you should stay out of my way, Samantha."

She ignored the advice. "What about your marriage? Will you bulldoze over Jillian whenever there's a problem?" *Lord knows her parents do.*

"Jillian and I shouldn't have any problems. *She* is a very reasonable woman."

"Going along with everything suggested to placate the people around her doesn't make her reasonable. It makes her—''

"I'm getting tired of your unsolicited opinions on my marriage and soon-to-be wife. In fact, I find it odd that a woman with your history of failed relationships feels qualified to give her opinion at all.''

Thick black anger boiled up inside her, choking her and rendering speech impossible. Just as well, because the obscenities she would have otherwise yelled at him would get her permanently banned from the course. Her mood and her golf game both grew progressively worse. To think earlier in the day she'd been feeling benevolent toward the man! Now she entertained visions of mowing him down with the golf cart.

All she wanted was to go home, take a long bath and congratulate herself on not having a man in her life. But the game was interminable. Time slowed to a crawl, each second adding to her irritability.

Which was probably why she finally snapped at Glenda, who had hit her ball out of bounds, but dropped another one from her pocket onto the fairway while the men discussed business.

"Okay! That does it,'' Sam announced. "We aren't playing for money or some championship. So why is it so important for you to keep cheating?''

Glenda's patrician face flushed a mottled red. "What did you say to me?''

Ethan jerked his head up at the heated tone of Sam's voice and the contrasting chill of Glenda's. What now? He'd been within moments of closing a deal with Matthias and had temporarily forgotten about the women's presence. But then Sam's voice had penetrated his "zone," and he slowly realized that she'd just called Glenda a cheater.

Oh, no. Please, Lord, don't let her be doing this. She was ticked off at him and ruining a potentially huge business deal. One that could help a lot of children, a deserving new company and his career. He glared at her, silently willing her to back down even though he knew she wouldn't.

"I said," Sam continued in a deceptively soft voice, "that I don't understand what's so important that you have to cheat on every other hole."

Glenda spun toward her husband. "Walter! Are you going to let her talk to me that way?"

His expression pained, he reached out to pat his wife's arm. "Honeybunch, I don't want you upset, but you have to admit that today you've been a little—"

Just when Ethan thought that Walter and Glenda's marriage was over and his investment deal was going down for the long dirt nap, Sam intervened. When she opened her mouth to speak, he braced himself for the worst.

"Glenda, I'm sure you're very talented at a lot of things. There's no shame if golf doesn't happen to be one of them. In fact, didn't I see in a newspaper article that you recently won a Junior League charity cook-off?"

Glenda's eyes widened. "Why, yes, I did."

"And I'll bet you're great at lots of other things, too," Sam cajoled.

"She does our taxes," Walter volunteered. "I used to pay an accountant, but she's got a better head for numbers than anyone else I know."

Between the two of them, Walter and Sam defused the situation and had Glenda smiling so broadly that she looked ten years younger. Ethan couldn't believe it. Sam had completely smoothed over the situation and was now getting Glenda to promise her some recipes.

Glenda clucked her tongue. "I'm so ashamed of myself. I've been peevish all day, and it wasn't because of you, dear," she assured Sam. She shot her husband a pointed glance. "It was Walter's fault."

"*My* fault?"

"The first day you take off work in three months and this is how we spend it? Doing business on the golf course instead of us spending some time alone?" Her voice wavered and Ethan looked away, noticing that Sam did the same.

Walter's voice, low and gruff, still reached Ethan's ears. "I didn't realize I'd hurt your feelings."

"You've been working so hard lately, and I've… I've missed you."

Their voices dropped to bare murmurs, and Ethan studiously pondered each individual blade of grass at his feet. What was happening here? His business meetings on the greens had never gone like this before. The whole day was topsy-turvy, and, dammit, he was feeling rattled again. He really, really hated that.

Ethan lifted his head when he realized Walter was speaking to him.

"Son, I'm sorry to do this to you, but I think the missus and I are going to turn back. You and Samantha finish out the eighteen holes, and give me a call tomorrow about how much cash we're talking to start."

Ethan grinned and reached out to shake the other man's hand. "That's wonderful, sir. Thank you." He glanced over at Sam. "Would you like to finish, or do you want me to take you back to the hotel?"

She shook her head. "I like to finish what I start."

"Me, too." Their eyes locked, and it was with great difficulty that he turned back to Walter. "It was a pleasure meeting you, sir."

Walter nodded. "Nice meeting you and your friend. She's something, isn't she? Pretty, spunky, and a helluva golfer to boot."

"Um, I guess so."

"You guess? Shoot, if I were twenty years younger and single…but I suppose you're too enamored with your fiancée to notice how special Sam is."

Ethan tried not to grimace. Not notice her? He'd give his left arm to notice her a lot *less*. Well, his left hand, maybe. His little finger for sure. Point was, he noticed much too much about Sam already—her spirit, her unique beauty, her sense of humor. Before they'd argued this afternoon, he'd been truly enjoying her company. So much that he'd temporarily forgotten why he'd really brought her here.

Walter elbowed him in the ribs. "She seeing anyone? I have a son I wouldn't mind introducing her to."

Annoyance surged through Ethan. He told himself it was because only Samantha could call the client's wife a cheat and still come out smelling a rose. It was not—repeat, *not*—because he felt in any way jealous of Walter's son.

Glenda steered her husband toward their golf cart, so Ethan was spared having to play matchmaker for

Sam and the unknown Matthias offspring. Come to think of it, though, maybe if Sam had her own romance, she'd be less inclined to meddle in his and Jillian's.

Your relationship with Jillian isn't romance, it's...

What? Business? For once, it sounded cold even to him. Funny, he'd never thought of the arrangement as cold before, merely convenient. When he'd first been hired at Peabo-Johnston, he'd quickly made up for all the dates he'd missed as the awkward poor kid in high school and the college student working all hours to hold on to his scholarship and land a great post-graduate job. But none of Ethan's brief affairs had developed into anything important; the women he'd seen weren't willing to put up with his intense work schedule. Even though he really wanted children and had always planned to get married, he had trouble making time for dating.

And then Jillian had more or less dropped into his lap. Her father had introduced them, clearly wanting them to become a couple, and it had worked out perfectly.

Perfectly for him, at least. What about Jillian?

Obviously she wasn't madly in love with him, but that made things easier, less complicated since he wasn't in love with her, either. Love wasn't part of his pragmatic nature, and Sam had no right to judge him for it.

He didn't realize he'd muttered the thought until Sam asked, "What was that?"

Angling a look over his shoulder, he answered, "I said, you have no right to judge me."

He could see from the glint in her eyes that she

wanted to spout off a retort, but she paused, inhaling deeply. "No, I suppose I don't. But I do have a right to my opinions. And my opinion is you're not the man for Jillian."

"I'm not good enough for her, you mean?"

Her mouth widened and the blood drained from her face. "I never thought that for a minute." She looked so genuinely appalled by the suggestion that he couldn't help believing her. "It's just that...I can't really say any more. It's not my place."

He smiled dryly. "I never thought that would stop you."

"I had that coming. Look, it's nothing personal. Maybe it was at first, but...you're right. I shouldn't judge you. After all, what do *I* know about relationships?"

"I only said that because I was angry."

"That doesn't make it any less true."

The next few holes passed quietly, and they used the game to fill the awkward silence. They each played their best, but without the earlier bloodthirsty competition.

Ethan putted on the sixteenth hole and made par. "I have to ask, how did you know about Glenda's victory in the Junior League cook-off? I can't imagine you reading the society pages. No offense."

"None taken. Jillian gave me a quick briefing on the Matthiases before she left this morning. She wanted to help you secure this deal."

"She'll be the perfect business wife."

Sam retrieved her ball from the hole. "Is that what attracted you to her?"

He knew his answer wouldn't impress her, but why lie? "Yes. Jillian understands the world I work in and will be an invaluable asset. She's so refined, so tactful; and she helps bring out those qualities in me. In a lot of ways, we're perfect for each other. Even if we do have such different backgrounds.''

''The only person who cares about your difference in backgrounds is you. Even Jordan and Claire, those card-carrying snobs, are too enchanted with your success and potential to mind.'' She shot him a sideways look. ''But your childhood really bothers you, doesn't it?''

''You wouldn't understand. When you live your whole life with a certain stigma—''

''But you aren't living your life with it now,'' she insisted softly. ''Nobody sees you that way. Give yourself more credit.''

''What do you know about how people see me?'' *And why do you suddenly sound so concerned about me?* He was more comfortable with her antagonism than her compassion.

Sam, too, must have grown uncomfortable with the turn in conversation because she smiled and taunted playfully, ''I know how I see you—a sorry-ass golfer who has no chance of keeping up with me on the next two holes.''

''You're on. Forget the first sixteen, all the glory goes to he—''

''Or she!''

''—who does best on the last two. Loser has to buy a late lunch back at the clubhouse.''

''Deal.''

In the end, Ethan won by a single stroke. Wearing a deliberately self-satisfied smile, he stroked his chin. ''Let's see…what do I want? Does the clubhouse sell lobster at this time of day? And maybe a bottle of fine wine to go with it.''

"Whatever you want. A bet's a bet, and you earned it.''

"You're not going to be a sore loser?'' He walked to the cart and slid his club into his golf bag. "You're ruining this for me.''

"Why should I be a sore loser? I gave it my best and have nothing to feel bad about,'' she said sweetly. "Besides, you played beautifully.''

"Ack! You're *really* ruining this for me. Could you be a little less gracious?''

She brushed past him, grinning. "Nope. This is more fun. I enjoy sucking the thrill out of your victory.''

"Cruel woman.''

"And don't you forget it.''

He climbed in the cart beside her. "Don't worry. There's nothing about you I'm likely to forget.'' The words tumbled out more serious, more meaningful, than he'd intended.

Her startled gaze collided with his, and time froze. For a second, the world narrowed down to Sam, inches from him, her eyes wide and luminous, her lips slightly parted.

Forget business. Forget this wedding. It's not too late to do something you want for a change and not something you planned.

That annoying Jiminy Cricket voice was back! Only, wasn't Jiminy supposed to act as a conscience and talk people *out* of inappropriate behavior? The images Ethan struggled to block of himself and Sam were definitely not appropriate.

He envisioned a small green cricket and then

mentally jumped up and down on the evil insect. The wedding was in two days. Now was not the time to lose his mind.

CLOSING THE MENU, Sam placed her order and wondered what she would do after the waiter left. Playing golf with Ethan was one thing, they'd had the game to distract them. But sitting across the table from him, a table set only for two, she suddenly worried about long pauses in conversation and further incidents of foot-in-mouth disease as she'd had when she'd insulted him earlier on the course.

She wrapped a strand of hair around her finger, realized what she was doing and stopped abruptly. Only to start fiddling with her silverware. Should she talk about the wedding? Considering their opposing views of the marriage, probably not. Maybe when the food came, they wouldn't have to talk at all.

Ethan rescued her with an opening gambit. "You know, I saw your mother play once in concert."

Her mother. The accomplished, socially polished opposite of Sam. "Mmm-hmm."

"She was wonderful."

"Yes, she is great with the piano."

He set down the glass of water he'd been drinking from. "Meaning?"

"I don't understand your question."

"You said 'She's great with the piano.'"

Sam shrugged, wishing they'd hurry up with that food. "I meant just what I said—she's a gifted pianist."

"But the way you said it implied she wasn't so great with other things."

Where the heck was the food? She'd only ordered a Greek salad. Did they have to go all the way to Greece to get it? "If it's all the same to you, I'd rather not discuss my family."

His eyes took on a knowing gleam, an I-knew-I-was-onto-something look, but then he nodded. "I guess I can understand that. My family wasn't exactly a Rockwell painting, either."

They had something in common? "You didn't get along with your parents?"

"My parents were great, but after they died, my uncle raised me. And let's just say that, while he accepted the burden, he made sure everyone knew what a burden it was." The rusty, halting rhythm of his words made it clear he was as unused to discussing family as she was.

She propped her chin on her fist. "Maybe we should talk about current movies or something?"

"I don't go to the movies."

Of course he didn't. A workaholic like Ethan was probably far too busy with client dinners and late nights at the office. "Assuming you have any spare time," she said, "what do you do with it?"

"Read. I love books."

Ah, a subject she could sink her teeth into. "Me, too." They'd been her closest friends growing up, and staying home with a good book beat going out on a bad date any Friday. "I just finished Don Scarlatti's last thriller, and I can't wait for the next one."

"Comes out in May. Although my favorite was his second book."

"His second one?" she echoed. The waiter approached, setting down Ethan's chicken quesadillas and her salad, but she ignored the food in front of her, too intent on making Ethan see the error of his ways. "The second one was a good book, I grant you, but compared to his fourth one..." As she argued her case, she realized that long, awkward silences weren't going to be a problem after all.

"YOU SURE YOU DON'T want it?" Sam asked.

Ethan shook his head. "Help yourself."

So she popped the last tortilla wedge of his spicy quesadilla into her mouth and listened as he finished telling her about the Harrington deal he'd closed last summer. She hadn't anticipated finding his job intriguing, but it entailed more than just numbers and sucking up to customers. There was also the research, the risk-taking, knowing enough about people to match the right investors up with the right opportunities. To hear him describe his work, it could be fascinating.

"I've probably talked too much about my job," Ethan said.

"Actually, I was thinking that it's surprisingly interesting," she replied. "I mean, when you first started describing your work, I just listened to be polite and told myself to stay awake, but—"

"Thanks a lot." He grinned. "I'd withhold quesadillas as punishment, but since you ate them all..."

"Hey, you said you weren't going to finish them."

Ethan gestured to their waiter for more drinks. "So tell me more about what you do. Any aspirations to play onstage like your mother?"

Sam's smile became strained, matching the tightening sensation in her stomach. "No, I'm not much like my mother. I'm not quite as talented," she admitted, "but few people are. I make a good teacher, if I do say so myself. The rewarding part of my job is the kids."

"I know what you mean. The president of my company makes sure we keep involved in high-profile charities. He does it for the publicity, but I love the time I've spent working with kids."

Her stomach tightened again, but this time in a completely different way. The warm, happy light in his eyes when he talked about children...well, it was enough to make any red-blooded woman offer to be the mother of those children.

"I can't wait to have kids of my own," he said.

"Really? As hard as you work, with the hours you keep, I just assumed..."

He stared at her blankly. "But kids are part of the reason I work those hours. I have to make sure I can provide for them. Really provide for them. They'll be able to afford the best schools and food whenever they're hungry and whatever clothes they like."

Sympathy tugged at her as she imagined a young Ethan, hungry and wearing tattered jeans and threadbare sweatshirts. He was obviously talking about his own childhood, the insecurities that still plagued him. Would he ever feel confident enough to slow down at work and have those children he wanted? Didn't he realize that many people raised families on much less than what he already made?

Deep sadness washed through her as she considered Ethan's plans for a family. Was it the disturbing certainty that he'd never have his own children because he'd constantly be setting new goals, telling himself that when he achieved the next one, *then* he'd be satisfied?

Or, was she simply bothered by the idea of he and Jillian having children together?

6

WHISTLING, SAM PULLED back the pale peach
shower curtain and stepped gingerly out of the tub.
The shower had invigorated her. She loved the way
her skin tingled, the way the floral shampoo smelled.
She felt extraordinarily alive.

Probably just all the fresh air today. And the exercise did her good. She spent too much time sitting
alone inside at the piano.

Well, not always alone. She had her students.
They were enough. Sam wasn't really a "people
person." Although, she'd sure enjoyed her afternoon
talking to Ethan. Was it because of his company, or
simply because indulging in adult conversation was
a welcome change? She suspected it was the first,
but really hoped it was the latter.

Just how much time did she spend in solitude?
Growing up an only child with very busy parents,
she'd spent most of her school vacations amusing
herself. At school, though, she'd been well liked,
she'd stood apart from the other girls. Maybe because she'd thought that lessons on which spoon to
use and how to walk while balancing a book on her
head were asinine while many of the other young
ladies had taken them seriously. And as an adult, it
seemed as though most of her time—

Why was she thinking about all this now? What

she really needed were a few carefree hours not dwelling on her dating habits or her unsettling feelings toward Ethan and this mistake of a marriage. Knotting an oversize towel under her arms, she promised herself a big drink tonight at Jillian's bachelorette party.

Sam had done some quick research before her shower and decided on a bar called Jungle Jim's for the improvised party. But before she could get to Jim's and her self-awarded drink, she had to make it through the Winthrops' "barbecue." Anywhere else in Texas, a barbecue would mean a lively gathering of friends, dressed in variations of denim, enjoying beer and steak. A gathering where they offered veggie trays and chips and dip rather than hors d'oeuvres.

She opened the bathroom door and marched toward her closet. Since this evening definitely fell into the "hors d'oeuvres" category, she'd better find something to wear.

"Hey." Sam stopped short at the sight of Jillian sitting on her bed, knees tucked up under her, puffy eyes full of misery. "You're back."

"Yep."

Sam sat on the edge of the bed next to her friend. "You okay?"

"Yep."

"You sure? Because I thought the spa was supposed to leave you glowing and revitalized."

Staring straight ahead at the wall, Jillian asked, "Don't I look revitalized?"

"More like a cast extra from *Night of the Undead.*"

"You and your grade-B horror movies." Jillian

rolled her eyes. "I'm just tired. You know how stressed brides can get right before the big day."

Especially brides who don't want to get married and are in love with someone else, Sam thought.

Jillian changed the subject before Sam could say anything. "I see you survived your afternoon with the Matthiases."

"The who?" It took her a moment to recall that there'd been anyone there besides Ethan. "Oh, them. Yeah, they were okay. They left early, but not before Ethan closed his deal."

"Good for him. See, I told you it wouldn't be so bad."

"You were right," Sam admitted. *But I'm afraid you're wrong about so many other things.* She took a deep breath. "I haven't really had a chance to talk to you, but you got a phone call last night."

"I did?" For the first time, signs of animation showed in Jillian's expression. She nervously tucked her hair behind her ears and regarded Sam with a combination of dread and hope. "Who called?"

"Peter."

Joy flashed in the soft blue depths of her eyes, but was washed away by the tears that rose to the surface. "I'm surprised he called. We don't have anything left to say to each other."

"Then I guess he'll be wasting his time tonight."

"Tonight?" Jillian gripped Sam's shoulders. "What do you mean, 'tonight'?"

"He's coming to see you. At your parents'." Too bad Sam hadn't known last night about Jungle Jim's. She could have told Peter to drop by the bar and meet Jillian, but she didn't know how to reach him now.

"He can't come to my parents' house. They hate him."

"I don't think it's their feelings he cares about. Won't you at least try to get away and talk to him for a few minutes? I can cover for you."

"I don't know if this is a good idea, Sam."

Sam stood, relenting. "Okay. If it won't bother you for the rest of your life that you didn't at least listen to what he had to say, then don't meet him." Leaving Jillian with that food for thought, Sam turned to the closet. "You want to help me pick out something to wear?"

"Aren't you just going to put on something shockingly indecent?"

"Of course not." She looked back, surprised. "Why would you think that?"

"Don't you remember the gala my parents hosted on my sixteenth birthday? The skirt you wore probably wasn't even legal."

Sam flinched. She'd forgotten all about that. Perhaps Claire Winthrop did have reasons for branding her a troublemaker. Sam had wanted to reject everything her parents and people like them stood for. As a teenager, she'd been proud of her status as a fearless rebel and independent loner. But she wasn't a teenager anymore. Even though she didn't particularly like the Winthrops, showing up in something outrageous would only make her look and feel foolish.

She selected an ankle-length jacquard sheath in mint green from the closet, then changed in the bathroom. When she returned to the bedroom, shrugging into a matching shirt jacket that was a shade darker, she consulted Jillian. "How's this?"

"Fine," she answered, not even glancing her direction.

"I'm serious. Does it look okay?"

Jillian raised her eyebrows. "You get dressed every day without my help. Why so nervous about your appearance tonight?"

Why, indeed? It wasn't as though she had anyone special she wanted to impress.

WIDE FRENCH DOORS OPENED onto a well-manicured lawn, and Sam hurried through them, anxious to escape the cloying, suffocating atmosphere of the room. Each conversation opener she'd heard tonight had been a blatant status announcement. Why didn't the guests just lay their bank statements and family trees out on the enormous mahogany dining room table and give up the pretense of small talk?

Thank God this is not the life I lead. Despite the condescending gazes she'd drawn when she told people she was a piano teacher, she'd never trade her job to be one of the wealthy elite inside. How many long, dry evenings like this would be in store for Jillian?

Sam strolled under the twinkling white lights strung in the trees and admonished herself not to think about Jillian. Because thoughts of the bride inevitably led to thoughts of the groom, and Sam was already thinking about Ethan too much. How odd that a man she'd only recently met occupied so much of her mind. It felt as if he'd been there forever.

You're doing it again. Quit thinking about him!

She approached one of the buffet tables, set up outside to perpetuate the illusion of a barbecue. The red-and-white checkered tablecloths fit the image, but somehow the tuxedo-attired catering staff didn't.

"What may I serve you, ma'am?"

Sam smiled at the young woman on the other side of the table. "It all looks good." The glazed ham, the crisp tossed salad, the steaming potatoes au gratin—

Potatoes au gratin? Whatever happened to potato salad?

Before Sam could make her selection, a man she recognized as one of the parking attendants hurried toward her. "Excuse me, miss, but are you Samantha Lloyd?"

She nodded, wondering why one of the valets would be looking for her.

"There's a gentleman out front who asked if you would come speak with him."

Peter. Sam rushed—trying hard not to look like a woman rushing—to the front of the Winthrop mansion. A man cloaked in shadows stood along the sculpted hedges lining the circular driveway.

"Peter?"

At her urgent whisper, he stepped forward and Sam got her first glimpse at the love of Jillian's life. Tall, but not overly so, and lean. He had sandy-blond hair, several shades darker than Jillian's, and gentle brown eyes currently filled with anxiety.

He *looked* right for Jillian. Like a sensitive man who wouldn't inadvertently take advantage of her acquiescent nature.

"You must be Samantha." He extended his hand and she shook it, thinking that his rough callused grasp was so at odds with his soft voice and tender expression. "Does she know I'm here?"

"Not yet, but I told her you were coming."

"Does she…does she want to talk to me?"

She bit her lip. "She was still thinking it over last time I talked to her. But stay here and I'll find her. Just try not to let anyone see you."

Bitterness hardened his features, making his face an incongruous mask of itself. "Right. Mustn't let anyone see me or I'll embarrass the Winthrops."

Sympathy squeezed Sam's heart. "Trust me, I don't give a damn if they're embarrassed or not. I just don't want them chasing you off before you get the chance to talk to Jillian."

He smiled. "You're a good friend to her."

She forced herself to return his smile. *If I'm such a good friend, why did I spend this afternoon chatting and laughing and—admit it—flirting with the man she's supposed to marry?* No, the man Jillian *planned* to marry.

The man she was *supposed* to marry was a gardener who stood in the shadows hoping for a chance to talk to the woman he loved.

SAM APPROACHED THE well-dressed cluster of people in time to hear Jordan Winthrop drag out his old joke about the three men in the desert—honestly, was there anyone here who hadn't heard it already? And didn't anyone find the joke offensive besides her? If they did, they all hid it behind polite laughter.

She waited until the laughs had died down to tap Jillian on the shoulder. "Jillie, could I borrow you for a second?"

Jillian turned with a welcoming smile—a smile not mirrored by her scowling father or a wary-looking Ethan. He looked suspicious of Sam's reasons for dragging Jillian away, and considering what her reasons actually were, she didn't blame him.

Jillian nodded to Sam, then faced the group of guests clustered around Jordan. "This is my maid of honor, Samantha Lloyd. Sam, I'd like you to meet Mr. and Mrs. Ridenhour, Judge Loomis and you've already met the Fosters. If you all will excuse me…''

They hadn't made it two feet away before Jillian's gracious smile dissolved into a weary grimace. "I can't thank you enough for getting me away from them. Judge Loomis is drunk again, Mrs. Ridenhour is throwing herself at Ethan, and my father was about to tell the joke about the elephant. Why on earth he thinks it's funny is beyond me."

"But everyone laughs, anyway."

"Of course."

"Is this what you want for yourself? In fifteen years, aren't you afraid it'll be Ethan standing with important people telling bad jokes?" The image filled Sam with despair, but Jillian shrugged it off.

"I doubt it. Ethan doesn't joke around."

Sure he does. He was funny at lunch. But that wasn't what Sam had come to talk about. "Don't get mad, but I have to tell you something. Peter is here."

Jillian turned her head from side to side, her gaze scanning the room.

"Not in here. Outside, waiting to talk to you. I didn't know if you'd meet him or not, but I think you should."

"What if my parents notice I'm gone?"

Sam closed her eyes for a minute, willing herself

not to shake some sense into her friend. "I'll tell them you're upstairs taking a phone call."

"Okay." She took a deep breath and squared her shoulders. "I'll do it. I'll be back as soon as I can."

But Sam wished Jillian wouldn't come back at all. It would be so much better if she and Peter just rode off together into the proverbial sunset.

Better for whom? a snide inner voice asked. *For her and Peter, or for you because you wouldn't have to watch her walk down the aisle and marry Ethan?*

ETHAN'S FROZEN SMILE had begun to hurt his cheeks. If Mrs. Ridenhour sidled any closer to him, he was asking Judge Loomis to issue a restraining order. And Jordan's jokes grew more annoying by the minute.

Desperate to flee, Ethan held up his empty glass. "I think I'm going to get another drink."

He headed for the bar and food tables outside. Breathing in the sweet, fresh air, he felt the tension melt from his muscles.

Are those people back there really the ones you want to impress?

The damn cricket had returned! *Shut up and leave me alone,* Ethan commanded.

Don't worry about that. If you spend the rest of your life—how did Sam put it?—"kowtowing" to these people, I'm out of here.

Look, I know what I'm doing. And don't mention Sam to me. She has nothing to do with—

Sheesh. Now he was *conversing* with the imaginary bug? Maybe he had been working too hard.

The smell of grilled food drifted across the lawn, making his stomach rumble, and he abandoned his excuse of getting a drink in favor of checking out the buffet. This being a barbecue, maybe he could scare up some real food for a change. As part of his strategy to overcome his background and fit in the upper echelons of society, he'd been trying to cultivate a taste for dishes like caviar—unpalatable salty stuff—and vichyssoise—unpalatable cold stuff. But give him a plain steak and fries any day.

He loaded up a plate with what looked like reasonably satisfying food—unlike the tiny, overcooked bird he'd paid thirty dollars for last night to carve up, searching for enough meat to form a bite— and scouted for a place to sit. If anyone remarked on his not returning to the party, he could truthfully answer that he enjoyed the evening's warmth. The night was soft and balmy, much different than the stinging-cold New York winters to which he'd never quite adjusted.

At a table on the edge of the lawn sat Samantha. Even in the dark at this distance he had no trouble recognizing those telltale red curls. Instead of enjoying his own company, why not enjoy hers?

His step faltered, and he blanched at just how good her company sounded right now.

He had to keep an eye on her and make sure she wasn't causing trouble, he reassured himself. That's all. Like the saying, Keep your friends close and your enemies closer.

But Sam, such a refreshing change from many of the pretentious guests inside, felt like the first true friend he'd made in years. A wave of unexpected loneliness washed over him. Why hadn't he taken the time to make more friends?

Because security was more important, because

he'd been working so hard to fill the gnawing hollow place inside him, to ease the fear that he'd once again be poor and awkward and unwanted.

Shaking off bitter childhood memories, Ethan told himself that was ridiculous. If he was a loner now, it was only because he'd spent most of his adolescence alone and was comfortable keeping his own counsel. Still, he couldn't seem to move fast enough across the lawn to join Sam.

He stopped a few feet from her table and angled his chin at one of the padded wicker chairs. "This seat taken?"

"You won't tell any bad jokes, will you?"

Balancing his plate and glass with one hand, he placed a palm over his heart and shook his head. "I swear on my life."

"Then have a seat."

He sat, struck by the sudden proximity to her. Though the chairs were comfortable enough, the table was tiny, more decorative than functional, meant to give the impression of intimacy. His legs grazed hers under the table, and she jumped.

Rather than sit across from her, he scooted his chair toward her so he could kick his legs out to the side, but that only brought him closer to the smoky vanilla scent of her perfume.

The food. Concentrate on the food and don't think about how she smells. Or looks. Or—

He jabbed a forkful of ham into his mouth. He was practically a married man. It wasn't right to be so aware of Sam. And he certainly had the self-discipline not to think about her like that. He hoped. "Wasn't Jillian with you?"

"She was. But she's upstairs. On the phone.

That's why I was looking for her. The housekeeper told me she had a long-distance phone call. One of our old friends from school. To congratulate her.''

''Ilene?''

She frowned. ''I don't think we went to school with an Ilene.''

''No, I meant Ilene, the housekeeper. I didn't see you talking to her, I saw you with Pedro.'' Too late he realized that he'd admitted he'd been watching her. But she didn't notice his slip.

''Who's Pedro?''

''He's Claire's chauffeur, but he works as a valet when they have big events at the house.''

Sam set her glass on the table and leaned forward, studying him with oceanic eyes he could happily lose himself in. That is, could happily lose himself in if he weren't engaged to be married.

Nervous and trying to cover up the unfamiliar emotion, he lifted a napkin to his chin, trying to make a joke of her intense expression. ''What? Do I have something on my face?''

''No, I was just… You know the names of the housekeeper and chauffeur?''

''Well, sure.''

''I've never heard the Winthrops use their employees' first names. I don't even think they realize their employees *have* first names.''

''Oh. It's no big deal.''

But she was looking at him as though it was. And he liked the way she looked at him.

Food, he reminded himself. That's what he was interested in. Not soft, dusky vanilla-scented skin or limitless indigo eyes. He picked up his fork and ate as though it were his last meal, not even glancing in her direction. She concentrated on her own plate, and they fell into a peaceful silence broken only by the music from inside and the voices of other party-goers.

As dinner wore on, the tension ebbed until Ethan was half convinced he'd imagined it. He polished off the last of his food and leaned back in his chair. "That was pretty good."

She nodded. "Much better than the last meal I had here. I feel sorry for people who don't occasionally have something as simple as a burger or corn on the cob."

"A woman after my own heart."

"Hmm. I would have pegged you as someone who liked fancier fare."

"Are you kidding? I grew up eating sixty-five-cent canned ravioli. But I'm trying to cultivate a more sophisticated palate."

"Best of luck to you." She twisted her face into a comically exaggerated scowl. "I was raised on the sophisticated stuff, and I envy you your ravioli."

Normally his hackles would have risen—how dare a person from privileged birth make such a flippant comment?—but tonight he just laughed. Sometimes he missed the ravioli, too. "I have a question for you. How did escargot become an accepted food? I mean, I've tried it and it's not that bad, but who woke up one day thinking, You know what would be good right now? A snail."

Intoxicating laughter bubbled out of her, reminding him of champagne. Warmth and satisfaction curled inside him. Her natural, unaffected response encouraged him to continue.

"You know what else people order that I don't

understand? Steak tartare.'' He wrinkled his nose for effect. "Raw beef. At least I can figure out how that one originated. Some bachelor too lazy to actually cook the cow before eating it."

"Stop it," she commanded laughingly. "You'll make me lose my appetite."

He eyed her untouched plate of cheesecake. "Does that mean I can have your dessert?"

She brandished her fork in his direction. "One move toward my cheesecake and you may not live to regret it."

"Fair enough." He signaled a passing waiter. "I'll get my own." He placed his request and turned back to Sam, who was studying him again with those fathomless eyes. "What now? I didn't know *his* first name."

"You're really funny. And I mean that in a good way."

"Think I should give up my gig at Peabo-Johnston and tour comedy clubs?"

"Seriously. J—someone said you don't joke around, but you have a great sense of humor."

"Actually, your source was right. I don't joke around much."

She tilted her head to the side, and he tried not to notice the graceful curve of her neck. "But over lunch, and now…"

He locked gazes with her, realization punching him in the gut. "I'm different around you."

Cautiously, she asked, "Is that good or bad?"

I wish I knew.

7

WHO NEEDED MEN WHEN SHE HAD chocolate-marble cheesecake? Sam mused. She dug into her slice as the waiter set down a piece for Ethan. Best that she concentrate on the rich dessert instead of dwelling on Ethan's comment.

I'm different around you.

The statement wouldn't have been as heady or as frightening if *she* weren't also different around *him.* She'd never reacted so strongly to a man before. She'd been attracted to some, laughed with others and a few had made her angry. But when had just one man evoked so many emotions?

Forget men. You have the cheesecake, remember? She licked the corners of her mouth to make sure she got every last crumb. "Cheesecake is definitely my favorite food. What about you?"

"Mine is probably homemade pancakes." He paused, fork halfway to his mouth. "When my mother was alive, she always made them for me on my birthday. One of my earliest memories is her singing 'Happy Birthday' to me with this splotch of pancake batter on her face." He stared out into the night. "She had a pretty face."

Sam almost laid her hand over his, but thought better of it. "My earliest memory of my mother is her standing over the piano telling me that my Mozart sounded like a train wreck.'' Good thing that Sam, unlike Jillian, wasn't hung up on parental approval. *I don't live my life to please anyone but me.*

Maybe because there *wasn't* anyone to please except herself? For a moment, her eyes stung. She blinked away the burning sensation.

''Sam?'' His voice was a caress, soothing the frayed edges of her nerves. ''I'm sure you play the piano beautifully.''

Swallowing, she nodded. ''Oh, thanks, I know my playing is good. Heck, it got me into Juilliard. I just…'' Words evaded her, and she had to look away to regain her composure. ''Wow. Not exactly your cheerful, meaningless party conversation, is it?''

''Strange.'' He sounded as dazed as she felt. ''Meaningless small talk I'm used to. Opening up to someone is new.''

She considered alleviating the tension by joking that it must be something in the cheesecake or pointing out that he'd only shared an isolated memory with her, not revealed a state secret. But she couldn't make light of what had passed between them. The single disclosure she'd made about her mother was more private than anything she'd ever told a boyfriend.

''I know what you mean,'' she admitted. ''Most of my interaction is with kids, and that's…safer.''

He nodded. ''My conversations are all business-related, not personal.''

''Not even with—'' She bit her lip, hating herself for wanting to make the comparison.

His green eyes arrested hers. ''No. Not even with Jillian. She's sweet and attentive and able to speak intelligently about dozens of topics, but she…we don't…''

"You don't click?"

"Right. There aren't any sparks." He slanted her an odd look, half amused, half intense. "Do you know that until recently I thought sparks came from carpets?"

She overlooked his odd comment. "If there are no sparks, you shouldn't marry her." It wasn't as much an opinion as a plea.

"You just don't give up, do you?" He ran a hand through his dark hair. "I've met dozens of people through her father, important potential clients who expect me to get married this weekend. How will it look to those people if I go back on my word?"

Her fingers tightened into involuntary fists in her lap. "I was wrong. You and Jillian *are* perfect for each other, so concerned with other people's opinions. She's been trying to win her parents' approval all her life, and she's sacrificing her own happiness to do it, when what she should do is tell them to take a flying leap and run off with—" Reason asserted itself. Abruptly, but too late.

"Run off with?" When she didn't answer, his eyes narrowed. "What aren't you telling me, Sam?"

"I was going to say run off with the circus," she mumbled.

He cupped her chin in his hand and lifted her face. "Not a very convincing lie."

Instead of flinching away from his probing gaze, she met it straight on. "At least I don't lie to myself. You honestly think that a future as Jordan Winthrop's son-in-law will erase your past? You believe this is what you want?"

"What I want..." He rubbed his thumb slowly over her skin, and a thousand tiny bursts of light pulsed through her. "This marriage is what I need. I gave it a lot of careful, rational thought. I know you think the engagement was rushed, but I've planned out my life. I don't do things impulsively."

Somehow she found enough voice to squeak out the words "Maybe you should."

He leaned forward, an imperceptible inch at a time, until suddenly he was so close that their breath mingled and the heat from his body warmed her. "You of all people don't want me acting impulsively right now."

What he may have meant as a warning, her body took as a promise. Her heart thrummed in her chest and her senses spun dizzily, drinking in the raw richness of his cologne, the rough velvet of his voice, the pulse-accelerating sensation of his touch against her face.

She leaned closer, too. "Ethan, I—"

"There you two are!"

Ethan pulled away so fast she might as well have been toxic waste. Sam was slower to react, having to refocus her eyes and sluggishly come out of her dazed state before she realized that Jillian's oldest brother had just interrupted them.

Considering what Jordan Winthrop Jr. had interrupted, she wasn't sure whether *hallelujah* or a different, four-letter word was in order.

She sat back in her chair, nodding coolly to Jillian's brother. "If you haven't had the cheesecake, you should. Ethan and I were just discussing how good it is."

Ignoring her completely, Jordan Jr. cast a rebuking glare Ethan's way. "Father went to a lot of expense to throw you this party so you could mingle, get to know people. You may have noticed the people arc *inside*."

Ethan indicated his empty plate. "Wc were just headed that way, weren't we, Samantha? But I'm so used to the New York winters that I couldn't resist eating out here. The warm weather's terrific."

Jordan Jr. narrowed malevolent eyes—the same pale blue as Jillian's, but with none of the geniality. "Yes, I'm sure the *weather* can keep a man quite warm. Nonetheless, it would be best to go inside."

Ethan's face clouded, but he said nothing more. Sam found she couldn't speak in her own defense. Not while she was choking on guilt. As much as she wanted the wedding called off, until it was, Ethan belonged to Jillian. Sam had no business drooling over him. No matter what she told herself, she'd never wanted a piece of cheesecake the way she'd wanted Ethan in those bare, electric seconds before Jordan Jr. interrupted.

She rose, manufacturing a smile for the two men's benefit. "Shall we?" She pivoted on her heel and strode toward the house. As soon as she walked through the French doors, she realized the party had kicked up a notch. Very few people had eaten dinner, but plenty of guests were taking advantage of the well-stocked bar.

Liquor flowed, the hired band had moved from staid, classical pieces to livelier tunes, and people were dancing and laughing. With very little effort, Sam could imagine they were all laughing at her.

Behind her, Ethan observed, "The party seems to be a success."

Without turning, she replied, "You're supposed to be mingling. Or was Jordan Jr. too subtle for you?"

His hand curved over her shoulder, and she envisioned what it would be like to lean back against him—ridiculous, really, since she never leaned on anyone.

"Dance with me."

"Are you crazy?" She spun around. "Jillian's brother all but insinuated—"

"Acting guilty and avoiding each other will only feed into those insinuations. Besides, this is a fast waltz, isn't it? I need the practice."

She should suggest he practice with his bride-to-be, but Jillian was nowhere to be seen. Sam had promised to cover for her, and pointing out her conspicuous absence wasn't the way to accomplish that. So she let Ethan lead her out among the other waltzing guests.

They began to dance, free of the toe-crunching awkwardness of the other day. She could hear only the music, and the people spinning around her in a colorful blur barely registered. Tonight, the two of them moved with ease, practically gliding as their bodies molded to each other's movements. She glanced up to congratulate Ethan on his improvement, but when their eyes met, the words died in her throat.

His gaze smoldered, hot and tense, and she shivered, surprised the ceiling didn't glow with heat lightning—the kind that silhouetted the clouds on sweaty, sultry Texas nights.

She hastily released his hand. "You're a natural. I don't think you need any more practice."

The corner of his mouth twisted into a self-deprecating smile. "How ironic. Because I was just thinking that I don't have a clue what the hell I'm doing."

Claire Winthrop fluttered toward them, and it was probably the first time Sam had ever been happy to see the other woman.

"Glad to see you two are enjoying the party." Having obviously talked to her eldest son, Claire scrutinized them, as though assessing whether or not they'd enjoyed it too much.

"You're just in time to dance with your future son-in-law," Sam said. She stepped into the crowd, eager to get away, and bumped into another guest. When she turned to apologize, she found Jillian, her face flushed, lips swollen, eyes stricken.

"What if I gather up the girls and we head for that bachelorette party?" Jillian whispered. "I don't know about you, but I'm ready to get out of here."

"Race you to the door." Definitely time for that drink at Jungle Jim's.

Sam and the other four women stood outside, waiting in line until a bouncer with a grim smile and no neck waved them in. The raucous rhythm of pulsing techno music met them even before they'd crossed the threshold.

Inside, the noise intensified. Sam paused in the entrance, her senses on overload. The scents of colognes and liquors and shampoos and smoke combined to give Jungle Jim's its own fragrance—not so much unpleasant as it was overwhelming. The club was dark, but climbing neon green vines illu-

minated each wall, and at the end of every vine blossomed glowing orange-and-blue tropical flowers.

Stopping mid-scan, she zeroed in on the main bar.
Aha. Their destination. She waved her hand. "Follow me, girls, and let the festivities begin."

The bar was crowded, but it didn't take long for
a group of five reasonably attractive women to catch
the bartender's notice. In his mid-twenties with
slightly arrogant good looks, he sauntered toward
them, a towel slung over the shoulder of his denim
button-down shirt. "Welcome to Jungle Jim's. What
can I get you, ladies?"

The bridesmaids and Jillian had daringly agreed
to forgo their normal glasses of wine and spritzers.
"What's the house specialty?" Sam asked.

"Jungle Monkey punch," he said.

"What's in it?"

He winked. "You're better off not knowing,
love."

She slapped her credit card down on the counter.
"We'll take a pitcher. And run a tab, please." While
she waited, she looked around, trying to spot the
table she'd reserved earlier by phone. White helium
balloons danced over a booth in the back, and Sam
directed her party that way.

Within minutes, the five of them were ensconced
in a dim booth with a condom centerpiece on the
middle of the table, and Sam poured drinks for
everyone. She took a tentative sip and blinked as the
surprisingly potent fruity drink blazed a trail down
her throat. By her calculation, the beverage was a
little bit of Kool-Aid powder, a splash of coconut
flavoring and about a case of rum.

Good stuff.

The curly-haired bridesmaid to her left took one drink and promptly choked, coughing loud enough to be heard over the pounding music.

Sam patted her on the back. "You okay there, Mandy? Mimi? Okay, I give up. I'm afraid I have trouble remembering your names."

The woman offered a wobbly smile. "Y-you were close on two of them." She coughed one last time. "Mitzi, Millie and Bambi. I'm Bambi, which, believe me, is a lot better than my real name."

"Your real name?"

The brunette grinned. "Bertramette. My parents' desperate attempt to inherit Grandfather Bertram's money."

She's right. I'd probably let people call me Thumper before I went by Bertramette.

Bambi laughed. "So you can see why I use the nickname even though people assume I'm a stripper or a truck stop waitress."

Sam swallowed some more of the Jungle Monkey punch. "What do you do for a living?"

"Assistant D.A." She flashed Sam a mischievous grin.

The two discussed a case Bambi had worked on last year, and Sam reached a startling conclusion: she liked Bambi. Mitzi and Millie weren't so bad, either. *Ain't that a kick in the pants?* She'd even liked the rich, influential Matthiases.

And, despite her initial objections to him, she really, really liked Ethan Jenner.

The only person I don't like is me.

She claimed to be Jillian's best friend, but she was trying to break up her wedding. She was the worst maid of honor in history. What had started out as such a noble goal seemed far uglier now. Sure, she told herself it would be best for Jillian, but might it also have something to do with the fact that Ethan had almost kissed her tonight?

Hadn't he?

When he'd leaned closer to her like that, for a moment, she'd thought... Of course, she was relieved it hadn't happened. Kissing her best friend's fiancé was unconscionable. Yes, this was definitely relief pooling inside her, not regret that they'd been interrupted.

She groaned. Thoughts along these lines required more Jungle Monkey punch.

When the three bridesmaids decided to scope out the action on the dance floor, Sam declined, choosing to baby-sit the pitcher instead. Jillian surprised her by not only staying behind, but pouring herself a second glass.

"You finished the first one already?"

"Yep." Jillian swigged some of the punch.

Sam held up her own glass. "Cheers. You want to talk about what happened with you and Peter?"

"Nope."

The two women drank in a grim silence more appropriate to a wake than a bachelorette party. But Sam felt obligated to speak up when Jillian poured a third glass.

"Jillie, drinking won't make you forget him." As Sam knew all too well. A glass and a half of this stuff hadn't dimmed the memory of Jillian's fiancé.

"Sam, you've always told me what I should do. In fact, I always come to you specifically because you'll help me figure out what to do when I'm too wishy-washy to decide. But tonight—and please

don't take this the wrong way—shut the hell up.''
With that, Jillian took another generous swallow.

Sam sagged against the vinyl bench. "I don't
know if I'm offended or proud. I've never heard you
talk like that.''

"I know. If I'd learned to talk like that years ago,
Peter and I never would have broken up and this
whole mess—''

"It's not too late to fix it.''

"Yes. It is. I gave my word.'' She held up her
left hand, and the large diamond she wore glinted
ominously under the colored neon lights. "I accepted a ring. Mailed invitations. Asked people to
spend time and money to fly here for a wedding.
They have every right to that wedding.''

"What about you?''

Jillian shook her head resolutely. "I gave up my
rights. As they say, I made this bed, now I have to
lie in it.''

With Ethan. Real jealousy, the hot-red kind with
jagged teeth, ate at Sam's insides.

She pushed the jealousy away, but the guilt and
self-loathing that replaced it were just as bad. He
was going to be Jillian's husband. He was not available, even for fantasies. And if he were, he'd still
be all wrong for her. His life was business, net-
working parties like the one tonight. She would be
miserable and she wouldn't be an asset to him the
way Jillian would.

Polished, patient Jillian really would be an asset.
Sam stuck by her belief that her friend should call
off the marriage if she loved Peter, but her original
assumption that Jillian and Ethan were completely
wrong for each other might not have been as accu-

rate as she'd thought. After all, she'd been wrong about lots of other things.

Sudden giggling distracted Sam. She looked up to find the bridesmaids huddled at the edge of the booth, with Millie grinning mischievously. "Sam, when Jillian told us you were throwing this bachelorette party, the three of us decided we wanted to pitch in, too. So—"

The trio of women parted, and for the first time Sam saw the tall, broad-shouldered blond man standing behind them, wearing a white lab coat over his clothes and a stethoscope around his neck.

Bambi nudged Jillian. "This is Dr. Love, our gift to you."

No sooner had the introduction been made than the deejay in the corner booth announced over the loudspeaker, "This next song goes out to Jillian, who's getting married this weekend. Enjoy your last nights of freedom!"

Sensual, throbbing music filled the club, and "Dr. Love" began gyrating. Jillian turned wide, questioning eyes to Sam, who shrugged. Nothing to do now but enjoy the show.

Except she didn't. The man shimmied out of his lab coat and shirt, and the three bridesmaids oohed at the sight of his—she supposed—impressive chest. But Sam was unimpressed by the slickly oiled muscles.

I bet Ethan has hair on his chest. Dark and—Stop it!

Dr. Love lowered his hand teasingly to the zipper on his pants. Petite, well-bred Mitzi waved cash in the air and hollered "Take it off!"

Sam's jaw dropped. *It's always the quiet ones.*

The slacks fell to the floor, uncovering bulky, rock-hard thighs and a very bright pair of red Speedos. Sam considered pulling sunglasses out of her purse. He revolved slowly, flexing his butt cheeks in the direction of the booth.

Not particularly in a butt-cheek-admiring mood, Sam was tempted to offer him money to put it all back on.

Lighten up! she thought. She was here with her best friend, whom she didn't get to see often enough, she had Jungle Monkey punch and a stripper. What more did she need?

Unfortunately, she was starting to think she knew the answer to that question.

8

"GOOD NIGHT. AND THANKS AGAIN." Sam handed the driver an extra ten, one dollar for every time Jillian had moaned "I think I'm gonna be sick" from the back seat of the cab.

The taxi sped away, and Sam dragged her friend through the hotel lobby. "Work with me. It's not that far to the elevator."

Once inside, Jillian clasped a hand over her mouth and the other to her stomach as the elevator lurched into its ascent. "No more Jungle Monkey punch, *ever*," she vowed from behind her fingers.

"Good plan," Sam agreed, shouldering her friend's weight when the elevator halted.

"Or alcohol of any sort. Including cough medi— medishu—med—" She gave up trying to pronounce *medicine* and added, "Not even food marinated in red wine."

"Well, at least you can still say *marinated*." Sam guided Jillian toward their room. "Which, I believe, is what you are."

"Pickled," Jillian said with a hiccup. "Hey, know what's funny? Peter Piper and peppered pickles."

"Hilarious, but I think you mean pickled peppers." Sam fumbled in her purse and found the key card. Seconds later, she dropped Jillian onto her bed. "No offense, but you aren't as dainty as you look."

"Sam, I have a secret to tell you." She struggled to sit, but gave up after two failed attempts. "I don't want to marry Ethan."

"I know you don't. Actually, I have a secret of my own. A confession, really." Sam hadn't planned on saying this, but since they were sharing admissions and she was feeling emboldened by her share of the Jungle Monkey punch... "It's not fair of me to tell you while you're in this condition, but if you get really mad, I have a good shot at defending myself."

"I couldn't be real mad at you. Yer like a shishter."

"And you're like a sister to me. Which is what makes this so awful. But Jillian..." Lord, how to say this? She squeezed her eyes shut, unable to look at her friend while she admitted the terrible truth. "I, um... It's about Ethan." *Okay, on the count of three. Just spit it out. One. Two. Three.* "He makes me laugh and he makes me crazy and he makes me want to... I think about him all the time. Jillian, I'm falling for your fiancé."

Jillian was clearly stunned into silence, and Sam waited, muscles rigid, for the righteous anger to burst forth. When none was forthcoming, she opened one eye. "Jillian?" Then both eyes. And saw that Jillian had curled up on top of her comforter, eyes closed, face serene.

"Did you hear what I said?" Sam asked.

A drunken snore was her only answer.

ETHAN TURNED THE CORNER, slowing out of respect to his cramping calf muscle. He ran every day, but not usually with this intensity. This morning, it was as though he was trying to outrun something. Or someone.

He walked briskly up the sidewalk, past a newsstand and small café serving breakfast, surprised he had any energy since he'd hardly slept a wink. His little friend the conscience cricket had shown up about one in the morning. Armed with a bullhorn.

What could he possibly have been thinking last night? He'd barely stopped himself from kissing Samantha.

Don't kid yourself. Jordan Jr. is what stopped you.

Even now, he wasn't sure how he felt about the kiss that hadn't happened.

Reaching the end of the block, he rounded another corner. He'd always known what he wanted. He was decisive. He outlined his goals, formed a battle plan and took action. But Sam—confusing, alluring, maddening Sam—had taken the single grain of disquiet he'd been feeling and turned it into an entire field of uncertainty.

He'd been attracted to women before and respected them and even liked them. With Sam, he felt all those things multiplied by…some number not yet known to man. Even though she came from a radically different background and held different priorities, he shared a strange affinity with her. He *got* her. And, maybe more importantly, she got *him.*

Not at first, perhaps, and she still didn't always agree with him, but he couldn't shake the feeling that she saw him for who he was. Not the boy from the wrong side of the tracks. Not the brightest stu-

dent in his college class. Not a successful businessman who could help her win parental approval. Just
as Ethan.

A horn blared. In the nick of time, he staggered
to a stop, realizing that he'd almost plowed into the
path of an oncoming beige minivan.

*Great. Then my physical condition would match
my emotional one.*

See? This was the problem! Until this week, he
wasn't the type of man who *had* an emotional condition. Sighing, he leaned against the building and
waited for the minivan-induced adrenaline to sub-
side.

Tapping on the glass behind him caught his attention, and he glanced over his shoulder. A balding
shopkeeper was moving his mouth and making
shooing motions. Ethan couldn't make out the exact
words, but the gist of it was clearly that the man
didn't appreciate Ethan's sweaty body up against his
display window. Ethan moved, studying the display
of jewelry and expensive knickknacks.

One particular item caught his eye. An exquisitely
fragile, blown-glass grand piano. A little girl in a
blue dress and yellow braids sat at it, and the morning light illuminated the colors brilliantly. The stat-
uette glowed.

*It would make a perfect Christmas present for
Sam.* He smiled at the thought of handing her a
wrapped box Christmas morning, waiting impatiently for her to open the gift and tell him how
much she absolutely loved it.

Odd, since he wouldn't be spending Christmas
with Sam. Odder still since Christmas presents had
never been part of his life. Well, his parents had

exchanged homemade presents, but that had stopped once he went to live with his uncle. And Ethan was in the habit of giving his employees bonuses instead of personal items, and treating his girlfriend du jour to an expensive date rather than bestowing anything with sentimental meaning.

Jillian would be his *wife*. He probably couldn't get away with taking her to the theater or handing her a Christmas bonus check. What the devil would he get her? When he tried to picture their first Christmas together, only a couple of weeks away, his mind went blank.

But his vision of Samantha had been so vivid, he'd almost been able to smell the pine of the Christmas tree.

Suddenly his feet were moving again, and soon he was running full-out. He had to get back and shower.

And then he needed to talk to Jillian.

SAM FUMBLED WITH THE coffeemaker in the room, trying not to wake Jillian. Her friend was going to have a doozy of a headache. Sam had been a bit foggy herself this morning, but a shower had brought her most of the way back to life.

But not so much that the sudden knock at the door didn't reverberate in her tender skull. Whoever stood on the other side better have a good reason for being there.

After managing to shuffle toward the door, she slid aside the security latch and opened it, leaning against the jamb for support when she saw who waited in the hall. "Ethan." After thinking about him all night, it was a little spooky to find him standing here now, devilishly handsome in dark slacks and a maroon shirt that contoured a well-defined chest. "Wh-what are you doing here this early?"

"Early? It's almost nine. I assumed you'd both be up by now." He studied her eyes, which she knew were bloodshot and puffy. "Long night?"

She muttered a derogatory response under her breath, conveying her unwillingness to ever attend another bachelorette party.

"What was that?"

"Nothing."

"You sure? Sounded like you mentioned monkeys and someone named Mitzi going home with a dancer." He raised an eyebrow, his expression full of amused curiosity. "I'm particularly intrigued by the monkey part."

"But that's not what you came to discuss. Which brings me back to my original question."

His smile melted, and his green eyes darkened. "I need to talk to Jillian."

"Ah..." She checked behind her to see if the knock and subsequent conversation had awakened her roommate. Jillian had piled both bed pillows over her head and was curled into a ball, snoring softly. "Maybe it could wait until later? I'd hate to wake her up right now."

He shifted his weight. "It's kind of important...."

"She won't be in any condition to have an important conversation for at least another three hours. Trust me. Let her sleep the worst of it off."

He poked his head inside in time to hear the latest snore. "You aren't trying to tell me that Jillian's hungover? She doesn't drink."

"Not very well, she doesn't. Hey, as long as

you're here, would you mind giving me a lift to pick up the car? I called a cab to take us home last night.'' It was a legitimate request. Not just a pathetic excuse to spend time with him.

For a moment, she thought he was going to insist on speaking with Jillian, but then he nodded. ''Sure, let's go. I can always…talk to her later.''

''Great, thanks.'' She retreated long enough to grab her purse off the dresser before stepping into the hallway and pulling the door shut.

''You're going like that?'' He sounded like a man trying not to laugh.

She ran a hand self-consciously through her damp hair and regarded her faded jeans and oversize chenille top. ''I realize it's not high fashion, but—''

He pointed to her feet. ''I just meant you might want shoes.''

''Oh.'' Heat climbed in her face.

''Nice toes, by the way. Who would have thought the tough, challenging Samantha Lloyd favored delicate pink polish?''

Somehow the intimate timbre of his voice made it sound as though he were commenting on her naked body rather than her feet. She barreled into the room, looking for thick socks and the clunkiest shoes she could find.

ETHAN STARTED THE CAR and, recalling their brief discussion of Beethoven yesterday, flipped the radio to a classical station he thought she might like. She rewarded him with a bright, appreciative smile that made him glad he was a man.

Squirming uncomfortably in his seat, he asked, ''So where's the Lexus?''

"Are you familiar with a bar off the loop called Jungle Jim's?"

He laughed. "No. But judging by the name, I'm surprised that's where you were. I can't imagine—"

"Jillian in a place like that? I know. And after last night, I see why she stays away from bars."

"I was going to say I couldn't imagine *you* there. Sounds loud and crowded, not your style." He couldn't picture Jillian there, either, but she hadn't been his first thought.

Sam shot him a sidelong glance. "What's 'my style'?"

"A quiet evening out. Simple dinner served at a cozy table, with lots of cheesecake for dessert, of course."

"Of course."

"And then maybe a symphony concert. But not an indoor one at a hall where everyone is formal and uptight. Outside. In the dark, on a blanket, where the music and the stars…" He trailed off. Was he describing her idea of a perfect evening or his idea of a perfect evening with her?

"Go on," she urged in a husky whisper.

He cleared his throat. "You get the idea."

"I think so."

He made it onto the interstate loop, grateful when she changed the subject by giving him detailed directions. She pointed to a large building that looked eerily deserted in the daylight, and he turned by a tall sign featuring a monkey-and-coconut-infested palm tree. A couple of cars sat in the huge parking lot, and he pulled up beside the Lexus.

Sam unfastened her seat belt. "Thanks for the

ride. I'm, um, glad you dropped by this morning. Well…bye."

At the last minute, he reached out, lightly gripping her arm. "Wait. I went running this morning and haven't had breakfast yet. Since you said Jillian will probably be asleep for a few more hours, if you haven't eaten, maybe—"

"I'd love to."

Two hours later, they'd finished brunch and leaned back in their respective chairs, neither in a hurry to end their political debate—not surprisingly, they were on completely opposite sides, but he couldn't remember ever enjoying disagreement this much. When Ethan's cell phone rang, he jumped. Somehow, around Sam, he tended to forget the rest of the world existed.

He flashed her an apologetic smile. "I should get that."

Nodding, she reached for the bill the waitress had left. Ethan covered her hand with his. "I invited you, I'll pay."

"I'm big on equality," she said, as if he couldn't have guessed that, "and I think women should pay sometimes."

"Good. Then you pay next time."

She blinked, making him aware of how incongruous his statement sounded. Would there be a next time?

He quickly moved his hand off hers. "Sam, I—"

"Your phone," she reminded him.

"Right." He answered more abruptly than he'd intended. "Jenner here."

"Ethan?" It was his assistant calling from New

York, and judging by her agitated tone, this wasn't a casual check-in.

"Barbara, is something the matter?"

She explained that the firm had just dismissed one of its top employees, Bob Hunter. Hunter had been Ethan's chief competition for the vice presidency and had been fired yesterday when several of the deals he'd put together simultaneously fell apart. Peabo-Johnston had lost a lot of money all at once, and the company tended to be unforgiving about that.

"The worst part is that Hunter was supposed to bring in a number of investors for the California merger. You know that's Peabo's pet project."

Ethan nodded absently into the phone. "I have a meeting with Randolph Stern the day after the wedding about the merger. Maybe with Jordan's influence, I can convince Stern to invest heavily."

"Great. As soon as you get back from Aruba," Barbara said, "the big guy upstairs wants to talk to you about damage control. I suppose you're going to be working even longer hours than normal until things stabilize around here?"

"Of course. I'll give the situation some thought and come back with a strategy for helping us recover."

"Your poor wife. What a way to start a marriage."

"Trust me, Jillian understands how important business is." And he suddenly remembered with stark clarity why she was the perfect woman for him. He'd never been able to put romance ahead of business, so he'd managed to find a relationship that combined the two. His romantic involvement with

Jillian *was* business. Right now, he needed the benefits of that alliance more than ever.

"I hated to bother you with this the day before your wedding," Barbara apologized.

"I pay you to bother me with stuff like this. I'll touch base with you before I head to Aruba. Anything else?"

She passed on a few messages, then said goodbye. He hit the end button and glanced up to find Sam watching him.

"You look grim," she commented. "Anything wrong?"

"A co-worker lost his job," Ethan answered, a little dazed. Bob Hunter. Ethan's corporate peer. Hunter was great at his job, had seemed unbeatable.

Ethan had deliberately picked his career because the risks made it possible to advance quickly. But failure was just as quick. Tomorrow, could he find himself behind Hunter in the unemployment line? The image sent a chill up his spine.

He shook his head to clear the unexpected memory of himself in fourth grade, wearing clothes two sizes too small and trying to pretend he didn't care. Once again the cold, empty feeling left by his past spiraled through him, pounding him with a need to do everything in his power to assure he was never again uncomfortable and helpless. Never again someone that life could bully around and others could feel sorry for.

"Ethan?" Sam's voice came from far away. "Are you okay?"

"Fine. It was just a...reality check."

She checked her watch, then glanced back at him,

concern shadowing her face. "Well, if you're sure you're okay, I should be going. Want me to tell Jillian you need to talk to her?"

"No. I'm not sure I need to anymore."

9

"BREATHE, BREATHE, BREATHE," Sam chanted. "You can do this, just breathe."

Jillian glanced up from the vanity in the church's bridal room. "You sound like a demented Lamaze coach. I'm getting married, not having a baby. Besides, this is just the rehearsal. I'm not that nervous."

I am. Deep down, she'd never thought it would get this far. How was it possible that two people who didn't love each other were about to walk into that ornate sanctuary and practice exchanging vows of eternal love?

"Jillian, you should really talk to Ethan—"

"I swear if you start up with that again, I'm locking you in the janitor's closet and asking Bambi to be my maid of honor." Her blue eyes paled to the silver of steel.

Sam immediately backpedaled. "I just meant you should talk to him. Like I told you, he seemed to have something important to say this morning."

"Oh, that. I asked him about it, and he said to forget it. Couldn't have been that important." She turned to the mirror and applied the finishing touches of mascara and lipstick.

The two women had come up to the bridal room on the pretext of Jillian showing Sam the newly delivered wedding gown and freshening up, but Sam suspected Jillian just wanted to get away from Claire. The crazed mother of the bride was barking orders like a platoon sergeant and had made the wedding coordinator cry.

Unfortunately, there was no escaping Claire. A fact proved when she barged into the room, a beleaguered Ethan in tow.

"Jillian! We need to discuss the photographer and the pictures tomorrow. I was just telling Ethan that—"

"Mrs. Winthrop?" A man in green coveralls spoke from the corridor. "Those marble urns you ordered for tomorrow are here."

Claire spun on her heel. "Oh, good. But let's call them vases, shall we? A bit less morbid. Ethan, be a doll and go make sure they're placed in the exact locations we settled on."

Sam would've bet money that the "we" was used in the royal sense, with Claire alone dictating location.

"I'd be happy to," Ethan answered with what sounded like gallantry but was probably relief.

"Wait, I'll go with you," Sam volunteered.

Jillian's expression was clear: *Traitor.*

She shot back her own telepathic message: *Hey, she's not my mother. You deal with her.*

Sam and Ethan followed the man in coveralls through the church's back exit and onto the black asphalt of the small service parking lot. Blinking against the late-afternoon sunlight, Sam spotted an orange van. Next to it sat the two largest vases she'd ever seen.

The man nodded toward them. "I'd hate to see

the size of the flowers going in those. Well, where do y'all want them?''

Ethan gave the man explicit directions, ending with, ''Sure you don't want to write this down? If they're even slightly out of place, I'm afraid I can't be responsible for Claire's actions.''

Which would be violent and swift.

The man grinned. ''We handle the decorations for most of Mrs. Winthrop's parties. Don't worry, we know better than to screw up. We still haven't found the head of the man who sent the wrong shade of peonies to her Valentine's soiree.'' He drawled out the last word in his good ol' boy accent so that it became ''swaaar-*ay*,'' reminding Sam of a pig call and making her grin. ''You folks want to stand aside. These things are damn heavy.''

They both stepped back and watched as the man and several coveralled co-workers navigated the vases into the church. Sam wasn't sure how she felt about being left alone in the deserted lot with Ethan, but they were only alone for a second before Jordan hurried toward them.

''Son, I've been looking for you.'' The father of the bride jogged up to Ethan. ''The housekeeper took a phone message for you. Your uncle won't be coming to the wedding, after all. Didn't want to spend the money for the trip, but wished you best of luck on your nuptials.''

A dark flush stole over Ethan's chiseled cheeks. ''But I wired him the money for airf—'' He clamped his mouth shut.

Oh, Ethan. She knew from the way he'd talked about his uncle that the two men weren't close, that his uncle had barely tolerated the little boy who'd needed a home. But she also knew his uncle was all the family he had, and the blasted man was pocketing the airfare instead of coming to his nephew's wedding! Her heart breaking, she watched Ethan school his features into a stoic expression that didn't quite mask the pain in the green depths of his eyes.

Jordan, however, was either blind to the pain or too insensitive to care. "Just as well. He wasn't our type of people. Can you imagine explaining his background to the other guests?"

"His background is the same as mine," Ethan said stiffly.

"Well, yes, but you overcame it pretty well, didn't you? You have real potential. Why, in a couple of years—"

Sam couldn't bear another word. "Shut up, Jordan. Don't condescend to tell him he has potential when he's already ten times the man you'll ever be!"

Jordan's trademark heartiness flickered and then blanked out like cheap satellite reception. His mouth thinned to an angry slash, and his eyes narrowed. "I will not have you talk to me that way. As soon as this wedding's over, I want you out of here and away from Jillian for good. Why she couldn't have just asked Flopsy, Mopsy or Cottontail to be her maid of hon—"

She marched forward to jab him in the chest with her finger. "Their names are Bambi, Mitzi and Millie. *You* of all people should know that, since two of them are your nieces and the other one's lived next door to you for twenty years. The minute Jillian wants me out of her life, I'll go. But not a second before. Maybe she loves you enough to let you bully her instead of telling you to stick it, but trust me, I'm not about to let you order me around.''

Jordan's face turned purple. Very few people dared speak that way to a Winthrop. Too bad for him Sam was one of the few. ''Why, you—''

She raised one eyebrow.

Rather than continue the verbal battle with her, he strode toward the church. ''Claire! *Claire!*''

She watched with feral satisfaction as he disappeared inside, but strangled sounds from Ethan's direction distracted her. She turned slowly, afraid he was choking on outrage over her performance.

Instead, when he finally found his voice, it was full of laughter. ''Oh, that was worth more money than I'll ever see in this lifetime.''

''You aren't mad?'' She was accustomed to people reproaching her for her behavior, and she would have guessed Ethan'd be the first in line to do just that. Especially since she'd lost her temper with his future father-in-law.

''Mad? A few days ago I might've been, but...nobody's ever stood up for me before.''

She licked her lips nervously. ''Probably because you can take care of yourself without anyone's help.''

''True.'' He advanced toward her, his voice lowering. ''But it was nice, having you defend me. Really nice.''

''It was?''

He nodded, a half smile playing on his face. ''I'd be flattered that you think I'm ten times the man Jordan is, but, knowing your opinion of him, ten times probably only puts me even with pond scum.''

"No, that's not how I see you at all. I think you're a *hundred* times the man he is, I think—"

"Sam." He brushed a strand of hair away from her face. "I was joking."

"Oh." Her breath caught in her throat.

Instead of chastising her, he was teasing her. Instead of storming off in a huff over her ill-bred behavior, he had moved even closer. So close she could hear his heart beating. Or was that hers?

She inhaled deeply to steady herself, but only drew in more of his sharp, clean male scent. His hand, which had been toying with her hair, cupped her cheek. She should do something, say something, but when she looked up, her gaze crashed into his heated one. Speech capabilities vanished.

Mayday, mayday! Do not look directly into his eyes. Abandon ship, get out of here while there's still something left of your heart.

She scrambled backward but caught the heel of her shoe on the lip of a small pothole. Waving her arms at her sides in a vain scramble for balance, she tumbled back. She squeezed her eyes shut and braced herself for the impact of her butt on the bumpy ground.

But the only impact was of her body being hauled against Ethan's chest as he grabbed her and pulled her to safety.

Her eyes flew open to find him closer than he'd ever been. "Th-thank you. You rescued me."

"I don't think you're the one needing rescue," he murmured, his voice more gravelly than the ground below. Then his head descended, closing the bare inches that separated them, and his lips claimed hers.

Most of Sam was stunned, but part of her was thrilled and eager. Her sigh of satisfaction parted her lips just enough for him to delve into her mouth, and she welcomed the sensual exploration. Tightening her hold on his shoulders, she leaned into him, standing on her toes to get closer.

If she could think, she'd probably be reminding herself of the many reasons this shouldn't happen. But he sucked lightly at her bottom lip, slid his tongue over hers, and thinking became impossible.

Ethan couldn't hear any of his own mental objections over the pounding in his ears. Electricity jolted through his body, stemming from where his mouth connected to hers. Had anything ever felt this good, this powerful? What if nothing ever felt this good again?

Slightly desperate at the thought, he angled his head and deepened their kiss, reveling in the taste of her. Feminine and buttery and soft. She met each thrust of his tongue with her own, wrenching a groan from him.

Sam always gave 100 percent of herself, and kissing was no exception. His body hardened at the question of how giving she'd be during—

What the hell was he thinking? He broke off the kiss. Kissing her while he was engaged to her best friend? Samantha and Jillian both deserved more respect than that. What sort of unscrupulous jerk had he become?

"Sam, I—"

"Whatever you say, please don't tell me that was a mistake. I know it was." She slid her hands off his shoulders and looked down, her breathing ragged. "Hearing you say it will only make me feel worse than I already do."

"Well, you *should* feel horrible!" Claire's shrill voice startled them both, and they sprang apart.

Ethan silently apologized to Sam for putting her through this humiliation. "Claire, what you just saw—"

She whirled on him. "Do not attempt to tell me what I saw. I know good and well what I saw. This little hussy has been causing trouble since the minute she came into Jillian's life."

Ethan clenched his jaw. "Don't—"

"It's okay," Sam interrupted softly. "She's accused me of a lot of things before, but this time I deserve it."

Guilt swamped him. Okay, she'd been an active and intoxicatingly willing partner, but the kiss wasn't her fault. And no one had the right to call her a hussy or anything else derogatory. "Sam shouldn't take the blame for th—"

"Well, no," Claire conceded. "You take some blame in it, too. But you're only a man, after all. Subject to base urges and bad decisions. Since I'm sure she threw herself at you, I won't mention this to Jillian or her father."

Ethan opened his mouth to defend Sam, but she cut him off. "Claire's right. I've been meddling since I got here, and it's time I stopped." She glanced up, meeting his eyes in silent apology. "You and Jillian are getting married. You have my word that I won't interfere again."

Then she was gone, rushing toward the church. He took an involuntary step forward, but Claire grabbed his arm.

"I assume this was some last-ditch, pre-wedding fling, but I promise you, if anything like this ever happens again, there will be repercussions. *Severe* repercussions." Her voice and eyes were matching shards of ice. "Don't forget that my husband and your boss have been friends for years."

Guilt and the memory of Bob Hunter, one day on top of the world and the next day cut adrift, kept him from responding to the implied threat. Claire did have a right to be angry over what she'd seen, and she could, at the very least, damage his reputation and career. But that bothered him less than the wounded look in Sam's eyes right before she'd fled.

Anxious to get away from Claire and the condemnation in her pinched expression, he said, "I think we should go in now."

They found everyone else gathered inside, including Sam, who managed to look remarkably calm. Except for the way she was nervously toying with her hair, but he doubted anyone else noticed that. He stood close to her, hoping to whisper some words of comfort, but she cut him off.

"I meant what I said out there," she told him. "I know what this marriage means to you, and I believe you will make Jillian a good husband. It's completely inappropriate for me to interfere now. I'll just have to trust that whatever decision you make is best."

After all her insistence that the wedding be canceled, after the amazing kiss they'd shared, he couldn't believe his Sam was giving up.

She wasn't *his* Sam. And wasn't giving up what he'd wanted her to do?

The question ate at him. He should be happy she'd backed away gracefully, made it easy on him. Thank goodness she was being logical for both of them. If he took a moment to examine the situation rationally, he'd see that Jillian made sense. Sam made his blood boil.

A cultured, tactful woman like Jillian and influential in-laws like the Winthrops—these were part of The Plan. The plan to make something of himself, the plan he'd been working on since he was old enough to understand the scornful looks of his classmates and the pitying glances of his teachers.

Unpredictable Sam with her untamed beauty and opinionated frankness was *not* in The Plan. How understanding would Sam be with late nights at the office? How patient would she be during necessarily sycophantic business dinners?

"People!" The wedding coordinator clapped her hands together. "We are running late, and it is time we get started!" She glanced timidly in Claire's direction. "Isn't it?"

At Claire's nod, the coordinator arranged the men at the front of the altar and shooed the bride and her attendants out of the sanctuary to practice their entrance. Ethan stood at the front of the church, feeling as though he were suffocating, buried alive in the high-ceilinged room that seated several hundred.

Marrying Jillian was for the best. Even Sam saw that now.

And even if it weren't... It was the night before the wedding. What kind of man dumped his bride at this stage? He'd given Jillian his word, and he owed it to her to honor that promise.

Still, tomorrow the minister would charge both of them with the responsibility of admitting any reason why they shouldn't wed. And what would Ethan do then?

10

HER LIPS STILL WARM from Ethan's sexy kiss, Sam stood alongside the other women, unable to meet Jillian's gaze. The wedding coordinator issued instructions, but Sam was transfixed by her own racing thoughts. *How could I have kissed him?*

As inexcusable as her behavior had been, another question plagued her even more. *How can I let them get married?*

But she couldn't interfere, not if her motive was that she wanted the groom for herself, not after she'd promised Ethan she was finished meddling. Besides, the choice wasn't hers to make. If Jillian was really determined to live her life to please her parents, if Ethan really couldn't see that having money wasn't as important as having love...

Oh, no. Did she love Ethan? Maybe the dizzy, breathless eagerness she felt whenever she saw him was something else. Some sort of chronic respiratory condition.

And the way he made her so angry she couldn't see straight, when other people, like the Winthrops, merely annoyed her? True, she didn't like them, but normally it was with a detached sort of aversion—frustration and sympathy for Jillian, nothing more. Well, she had lost her temper with Jordan today, but that had been on Ethan's behalf.

And what about the way Ethan made her laugh? And that thrill she got when she made *him* laugh?

And she could talk to him. Over the last few days, when she'd been alone with Ethan, she'd discussed her parents, whom she never mentioned, several times. It had been a relief. Ethan was so strong, she wanted to let herself rely on his strength, to finally lean on someone in a way she hadn't since learning young to depend on herself.

"Do you all understand what to do?" the coordinator demanded—she tended to be more imperious when Claire wasn't nearby. "You there, Samantha, did you get all that? It didn't look like you were listening."

"I got it," Sam answered. It wasn't rocket science, after all. They just followed the straight line from the back of the church to the front. No surprises there.

"Good." The coordinator thrust out an oddly shaped, colorful cluster. "Now just walk down the aisle as soon as the wedding march plays."

Whoa! "Isn't that the bride's job?" Sam stared at the strange, lightweight mass she now held. Bows and ribbons stuck together. The practice bouquet, she realized. Belatedly, she recalled the tradition that the bridal bouquet used during the wedding rehearsal was made from the ribbons from bridal shower gifts.

She recalled the Southern tradition of practice *bride* at the same time the wedding coordinator said, "I thought you were listening. The bride doesn't actually walk down the aisle until her big day. For rehearsal, we use a stand-in."

"Right." Sam glanced in Jillian's direction. *I've*

made trouble for her since I got here and was kissing her future husband ten minutes ago; the least I can do is get the stupid rehearsal right.

When the wedding march blared through the mostly empty sanctuary, Sam took a step forward, then faltered.

After throwing away the last year on losers she could never love just to prove to herself she hadn't become a total recluse, she'd finally met the man she did love. And now she was marching straight down the aisle to be by his side in front of the minister and witnesses—in preparation for his marriage to her best friend.

Too bad Sam didn't have a finer appreciation of irony.

The aisle running to the front of the sanctuary led to her own downfall. *Dead maid walking.*

She forced herself to keep moving forward, trying to cheer herself up by insisting it wasn't possible to love a man she'd known such a short period of time.

You have to get to know a man, his likes and dislikes and habits, date him for a while, and...

And what? Because she had dated men. Yes, her most recent dates had been yahoos, but she'd dated some good men before. Good men who'd eventually wandered off when her feelings never matched theirs, when she hadn't needed any of them. She'd known men who were in theory perfect for her, but she'd never felt anything more than fondness.

She came to a halt directly next to Ethan. Her feelings definitely went beyond "fondness." Invisible sparks sizzled through the space between them.

Ethan ran a hand through his hair. "Sam, I—"

"Thank you," the wedding coordinator called out. "Jillian will take it from here."

LEAVING THE CHURCH AN HOUR later, Sam and Jillian walked to the Lexus to ride to the rehearsal dinner together.

Jillian unlocked the car door. "What's wrong? I know something's bothering you."

Sam tried to look her friend in the eye, but only made it as far as the bridge of her nose. "The same thing that's bothered me since I got here. This wedding—"

"Forget I asked," Jillian said as she climbed into the driver's side. "I'm starving."

"You're kidding." Sam's appetite was as nonexistent as her chances with Ethan.

"You forget, I'm a nervous eater. Besides, I've barely eaten all day. Aren't you hungry?"

"No, I—" *had a big breakfast with your fiancé while you slept off your hangover, and then I kissed him behind your back* "—have a migraine. Could you take me to the hotel?"

Jillian eased the car out of the parking space. "Sam! You're the maid of honor. You have to come to the rehearsal dinner."

"Oh, come on. I had dinner with your parents the night I got here and went to their ridiculously upscale barbecue gala last night. Surely I can miss their latest social shindig."

"Actually, Ethan's throwing the shindig. The rehearsal dinner is usually taken care of by the groom's family, but since he doesn't have any... He planned it himself and is hoping to make a good impression on—"

"Auugggggh!" Again with the good impressions on the important people?

"What was that about?"

"A cry of pain caused by my migraine."

"Well, I'm sorry your head hurts, but please say you'll come to the dinner. I need you there."

Sam bit her lip. "Promise we'll leave as soon as possible." They could leave during the appetizer and it wouldn't be soon enough.

But if the night promised to stretch on endlessly, the drive to the hotel where the dinner was being held ended much too quickly. Instead of yielding to the urge to curl up in a fetal position and hide on the floorboards, Sam got out of the car and followed Jillian through the arched doorway into the hotel's marbled lobby.

"Ethan reserved one of the ballrooms for dinner," Jillian said, "after reading an interview with the chef, Claude Brouchard. The hotel's famous for their citrus-seared tuna on mousseline potatoes, and Ethan said it would be a nice change from all that steak Texans are always eating. He wanted something memorable."

All Sam wanted was for the evening to be over. "Which way is the room?"

"Ethan said downstairs. We're in the Baines Ballroom." Jillian led the way to the elevators, and they got in alongside a man in a navy suit and a woman in a low-cut, high-hemmed red sequin dress that was eye-catching if not tasteful.

When the elevator doors opened, Jillian studied the sign on the hotel wall. "Which way is Baines?"

Sam squinted. Darn sign would be a lot easier to read if they hadn't used such fancy, elaborate script.

"To the left," the woman in the sequins answered. "We're headed there ourselves."

Sam exchanged glances with Jillian, but couldn't ask her question out loud. Traditionally, rehearsal dinners were limited to the bridal party and immediate family, but no doubt Ethan had expanded the guest list to include a few of Jordan's wealthy business colleagues. Which might explain the stranger in the suit, but the woman in sequins? For once there would be a woman in the room Claire disapproved of more than Sam.

The foursome walked down the hall toward the ballroom. Voices spilled out, raucous and laughing.

A stout man in a polyester suit and paisley tie stood outside the door, presiding over a folding table piled with brochures and name tags. "Evening, folks."

Navy Suit and Low-cut Sequins grabbed name tags off of the table and entered the crowded ballroom. Sam and Jillian hung back, exchanging puzzled looks.

The man behind the table asked, "You purty gals here for the salesmen appreciation dinner?"

"Salesmen?" Jillian echoed.

"This here's the annual appreciation dinner for top sellers for Goldwyn Insurance."

Sam leaned closer and saw that the man's name tag read *I'm Don. Ask me about my death-and-dismemberment clauses.* "Um, Don, is it? We're here for the Jenner-Winthrop rehearsal dinner. It's supposed to be in the Baines Ballroom."

He scratched his head. "Nope. This is the right room, but it's full of insurance salesmen. Speaking of which, let me talk to you about cars. I'm sure you both have the legally required liability coverage, but do—''

''Hotel management must have reassigned the rehearsal dinner to another room,'' Sam told Jillian. ''Let's go ask someone upstairs.''

They returned to the elevators, and, when the doors opened, Sam found herself looking at the person she'd most wanted to avoid tonight.

Ethan's gaze locked with hers as he stepped forward. A shiver shot down her spine all the way to her toes, which obligingly, traitorously, curled.

He cleared his throat. ''Ladies.''

Jillian placed a hand on his sleeve, and Sam realized it was the first time she'd seen the engaged couple touch each other. ''Ethan, am I glad to see you. Where's the rehearsal dinner?''

''Down at the end of the hall. The Baines Ballroom. Great facility.''

''But we were just there,'' Jillian said.

Her words were cut off by the ding of the second elevator. Claire and Jordan stepped out with Mitzi the bridesmaid, who clung to the arm of—

Dr. Love? It took Sam a moment to recognize the stripper without his stethoscope and red Speedos.

''This is Rupert,'' Mitzi said quickly, shooting imploring looks at Sam and Jillian ''I was told I could bring a guest.''

Sam shook her head to clear it. Their room had been taken over by zealous insurance salesmen and the blue blood bridesmaid was on a date with a man who had last been seen slathered in body oil. All the occasion lacked was a Rod Serling voice-over.

Claire smiled thinly. ''Well, is the party in the ballroom or out here?''

"Yes, let's move this into the ballroom," Jordan instructed. "I could use a drink."

"I think we've been moved to a different room," Sam told Ethan.

He shook his head. "No, we've reserved the Baines room."

Then you may want to ask for your money back, Sam thought. The Winthrops and Mitzi were already halfway down the hall. Shrugging, Sam turned to follow. Ethan would find out for himself the change in plans soon enough.

By the time Sam returned to where Don of the death-and-dismemberment clauses stood, Jordan had already stormed into the ballroom and was ordering people out. Claire, looking pained, hovered in the doorway, insisting to a woman in a green suit, "Yes, we have adequate fire coverage."

"This is what I was trying to tell you," Sam told Ethan. "There appears to be an insurance convention going on in here."

"Well, that's ridiculous," Ethan said. Beneath the annoyance in his voice, Sam heard fear—the fear that things were going wrong and he'd make a less-than-sterling impression on those around him.

She longed to comfort him, to tell him that he wasn't a poor, lonely little boy anymore, to tell him that other people's opinions didn't matter a damn, anyway. She wished she could make him see himself the way she saw him.

Then Jillian asked, "Ethan, what are we going to do?" and Sam was reminded that she didn't have the right to comfort him.

"I'll run upstairs and take care of this," Ethan promised.

But he never made it that far. A small, nervous-looking man with a pencil-thin mustache and wearing a gold badge with Hotel Manager written on it was rushing toward them. "Mr. Jenner! I am so sorry! My staff has only just realized there was a double booking. People have been coming to the front desk, asking where the Jenner-Winthrop dinner was, and I...there's obviously been an error."

"Obviously," Ethan agreed. "My question is what are you going to do about it?"

The manager wrung his hands. "There's nothing I *can* do. All of our large rooms are booked for tonight."

"Yes, and I was one of those bookings," Ethan pointed out. "We're supposed to be in this room here, preparing to eat citrus-seared tuna."

The hotel manager winced. "I am afraid we are out of tuna for the evening, sir. We have a large crowd and most everyone has ordered that dish. We're famous for it, you know."

"Yes. I know." Ethan's eye began twitching. Not a good sign.

Hating the tension she saw in Ethan's expression and hoping to avert any murderous thoughts he was having about the hotel manager, Sam attempted to mollify Ethan. "I'm sorry about the tuna, but I'm sure everything Chef Brouchard makes is wonderful."

"But Chef Brouchard has tendered his resignation," the manager piped up. "Last night was literally his last night. He left to host his own cable cooking show, *What's Brewing with Brouchard?* His replacement, Chef Jackson, grills a great steak."

Sam glared at the wiry man, entertaining a few murderous thoughts of her own.

Jordan stormed back into the hallway. "What the hell is going on? We're hungry and our room is full of these life-insurance hawkers. Do you know who I am?"

"Daddy," Jillian insisted, "lower your voice. There's no reason to ruin these people's dinner just because our own plans are in question. Let's discuss this more privately."

Sam was grudgingly impressed by the way Jillian maneuvered Ethan, Jordan and the manager to the other end of the hall to talk about alternative arrangements. It had been a small step, but Jillian had stood up to her father.

She was willing to stand up to him to avoid making a scene, but not to preserve her own happiness? It was the eleventh hour. If Jillian couldn't stand up for herself, and Ethan couldn't reorganize his priorities…

The migraine Sam had claimed to have earlier was more than just an excuse now.

Moments later, Jillian returned, shaking her head. "The best we can do is a large meeting room, so it looks like my rehearsal dinner is going to be held around a conference table. But the hotel is throwing in free drinks, not that I plan to have any. Lord, my head is killing me."

"You took the words right out of my mouth," Sam agreed.

From his post outside the Baines Ballroom, Don said, "I couldn't help but overhear." He pulled a small yellow bottle out of his jacket. "This here's a Chinese herb guaranteed to cure headaches. It's only been available in the West for a few weeks, and for a mere $19.95 a bottle you can be one of the first to try it.''

Sam scowled. ''I thought you sold insurance.''

''I do, ma'am. But I also freelance. Herbs that prevent hair loss, that promote weight loss—not that either of you purty ladies need it. Even got a herb here to increase potency if the man in your life isn't—''

''He's *plenty* potent,'' Sam burst out. Any more so and she'd suffer heatstroke just from being in the same room with him.

Jillian's eyebrows shot up. ''I didn't think there was a man in your life.''

''What?'' Guilt speared Sam. ''There isn't, really.''

''You sure?'' Jillian prompted. ''You seem—''

''Are you girls coming?'' Claire demanded from behind them.

Jillian nodded over her shoulder before telling Sam, ''We can talk about this later, okay?''

Since Sam was in no hurry to have that conversation, she hastily followed her friend to the elevator, joining the other disenfranchised rehearsal dinner guests on their way to Conference Room D for some steak. Too bad there was no Chinese herb to cure heartbreak.

11

ETHAN STOOD NUMBLY in the center of the room, listening to the well-wishes of his groomsmen, Jillian's brothers. How could it be time already? Jordan Jr. had picked Ethan up this morning for the Winthrop family breakfast and the momentum of nonstop activity since had pushed him here. Now he stood in his tuxedo, ready to be married.

This was it. The beginning of his future. The smartest merger he'd ever participated in. All his goals and dreams coming true, right?

Somehow, he hadn't expected it to feel as if he was being strangled with his own bow tie.

FROM THOUSANDS OF MILES away, Sam heard Bambi tell the bride, "You look beautiful. It'll be the perfect wedding." An elbow to Sam's side. "Won't it, Sam? Talk to her, for heaven's sake, she's sitting there looking petrified."

"Bambi's right," Sam said dutifully. "It'll be, um, perfect."

Jillian turned her head slowly so as not to mess up her veil or two-hundred-dollar topknot of curls. "Sort of ironic, you being the one to tell me this will be perfect."

Sam gave her best if-you-can't-beat-'em-join-'em shrug.

Bambi frowned. "The two of you do know this is a wedding, right? A traditionally *joyous* occasion?"

Jillian cleared her throat. "Ladies, if everyone's about ready, could I have a few minutes alone with Sam?"

The bridesmaids obligingly filed out of the room, leaving the two friends together.

"So..." Sam smoothed her long blue skirt and stared at the plush carpet of the bridal room. "You got your something old, something new and all that?"

Jillian, pale underneath her artfully applied cosmetics, leaned forward in the replica Louis XVI chair. "You've tried to tell me not to marry Ethan, and I disagreed with most of your reasons. But if he were a horrible person, if I thought he'd be a terrible or unfair husband... Can you give me a strong reason to turn him away?"

Guilt wormed through Sam. What about the fact that he kissed another woman? But it had just been one kiss, as much her fault as his. Besides, she trusted Ethan's honor enough to know that nothing like that would happen once the vows had been said. Still, she longed to admit her sin to Jillian.

At what cost, though? Sam's conscience would be somewhat lighter, but she'd be poisoning a marriage on its very first day.

"Sam, can you think of *anything* horrible to say about him?"

She thought of how he'd lost both his parents at such a young age and how hard he'd worked to be successful; she recalled his passionate determination when he talked about kids and the way his eyes crinkled at the corners when he joked about the foods rich people ate.

"No. I can't." The best reason she could give for Jillian not getting married today was Peter, but Jillian had to make her own choices. If she wasn't willing to stand up for love, Sam couldn't make her.

I should at least give it one last shot.

No. You promised Ethan you wouldn't.

A knock outside the bridal room removed the choice from her hands, and she opened the door to admit the photographer, a slim, balding man with rosy cheeks and a perpetual smile.

"Ah, there's the beautiful bride! I just love weddings. Don't you?"

"Yeah," both women chorused heavily.

The photographer's smile faltered for a moment, but then he recovered. Holding up his camera, he said, "I wanted to get a few last shots of the bride. Maybe one or two with her looking out that window over there, contemplating her big day." He gestured toward the gold-curtained window that overlooked a small copse of trees.

Unable to endure any more of the wedding preparations, Sam excused herself. She joined the bridesmaids outside the sanctuary, listening halfheartedly to their comments on how many guests there were, how beautiful the flowers were, how dashing Ethan was in his tuxedo.

Sam forced herself not to peek through the large glass windows at the front of the church. The *last* thing she needed right now was to see for herself how incredible Jillian's groom looked.

Swells of organ music, accompanied by a majestic trumpet, filtered out into the hallway. The music, like the arranged flowers and stylish guests, was perfect. Claire would get the wedding she'd envisioned, Jillian would obtain her parents' approval, Jordan would gain a business-brilliant go-getter for a son-in-law, and Ethan would finally have the security he'd craved.

If I were a better person, I'd be happy for all of them.

But she was fixated on her own misery. So fixated that the wedding coordinator's anxious whispering escaped Sam's notice until Bambi tapped her shoulder.

"Sam, where's Jillian?"

"With the photographer," Sam answered, wishing people would leave her alone in her numb cocoon.

The wedding coordinator snapped her fingers and pointed. "*That* photographer?"

The photographer stood in the corridor, snapping shots of a preening Jordan, who waited to escort his daughter down the aisle. "I guess Jillian is still upstairs." She seized the opportunity to get away from the crowded entryway and the reality of what was about to happen. "I'll run get her."

Upstairs, Sam turned toward the bridal room, then knocked on the closed door. "Jillian? They're ready for you." No one answered as Sam twisted the knob and opened the door. "Did you hear m— Oh, Lord, Jillian, have you lost your mind?"

Sam had to address this last comment to a petticoat-swathed backside and two dangling feet. The voluminous, bell-shaped skirt of the bridal gown was wedged in the open window, leaving Sam with a view of Jillian's bottom half framed by the gold curtains.

The feet wiggled. "Sam, is that you? I'm stuck."

"No kidding." She closed the door behind her and advanced toward the layers of satin, crinoline and taffeta. "I suppose it would be a stupid question to ask what you thought you were doing?"

Jillian's muffled voice came from the other side of the window. "Getting out of here, that's what. I can't go down there. If I do, they'll make me marry that man."

Sam didn't know whether to pull her friend back in or shove her out the window. "Well, what did you think was going to happen when you sent out all those wedding invitations and reserved the church?"

"I thought I could do it," answered the plaintive voice. "But I can't. I just can't marry him."

She's not going to marry Ethan. Relief, so piercingly sweet it hurt, exploded inside Sam. But a hint of annoyance followed. It was all well and good that Jillian wasn't going to marry him, but did she have to wait until *now* to decide that?

"Sam? You're quiet. What's happening back there? I'm still stuck."

"I'm thinking," Sam replied.

"What is there to think about? Help me get out of here. I think I can reach that tree and shimmy down. It's really not that far."

Shimmy, in a several-thousand-dollar gown? "Jillian, are you sure this is how you—"

"Positive. I called Peter on my cell phone to tell him. You've been right all along."

Sam tugged on the sides of Jillian's skirt, trying

to free her friend. "I'm happy to hear that, but don't you want to tell Ethan?" An image of him waiting, unsuspecting, at the front of the church stabbed her. "He deserves to hear it from you."

"I know…but if I have to face him, if I have to face my parents, I'll chicken out. You know I will. You'll handle it for me, won't you, Sam? I need you. You must think I'm so weak. You've never needed anyone. You're l—"

Lonely.

"Lucky," Jillian concluded.

Sam sighed. "Of course I'll help you. Hang on a second, I've almost got this skirt unwedged." Her declaration was followed by a horrible ripping sound and the sudden disappearance of Jillian from the window.

"Aaahhh!" Thank heavens the sanctuary was on the other end of the building or hundreds of guests would have heard the bride crashing the short distance to the ground.

Sam poked her head out through the curtains. "Jillie! You okay?"

Jillian stood, wobbling on one ankle, and brushed leaves away from her torn veil and two-hundred-dollar hairdo. She held up the A-OK sign. "Never been better."

Then she limped off through the trees, leaving Sam with a jagged shred of French wedding gown and bad news to deliver to soon-to-be very angry people.

CLAIRE LIT HER FOURTH cigarette, despite the wedding coordinator's repeated insistence that there was no smoking allowed on the church premises, and stalked across the carpet. "I can't believe you've done this to us, Samantha. After all the times you've come home with Jillian and we treated you like another daughter…"

Resisting the urge to point out that the way *they* treated their daughter was why Jillian had ultimately run away, Sam repeated, "I'm just the messenger here." *And we all know what happens to the messenger.* "She was unhappy."

Jordan looked up from the incongruously dainty chair he'd sprawled in. "She seemed plenty happy till you got here."

Sam focused on Jillian's father; it was easier than risking a glance at Ethan, who stood in the corner, silent since marching into the room. *What must he be thinking?* "You know she wasn't happy. You both knew she loved Peter."

"Who the hell is Peter?"

Sam jumped at Ethan's fierce tone.

Jordan waved his hand. "Nobody. A gardener. Jillian had a fling with him a while back."

"It wasn't a fling," Sam insisted. "She loves him. She never stopped loving him. She only stopped seeing him to try to please you."

Ethan stepped away from the wall he'd been leaning on, staring at Sam. "And you knew about this Peter?" She heard his unspoken question, *And you never told me?*

"It wasn't my place to say anything about him, and what if I'd been wrong? Jillian kept insisting it was over between them. I didn't want to—"

"We know what you wanted to do," Claire interrupted before dragging in another puff of nicotine. "You've always been jealous of Jillian, and you set out to ruin her wedding. You must be very proud of yourself. What did you say this morning to convince her to leave?''

"I—"

"*Did* you say something to her this morning?" Ethan narrowed his eyes, obviously recalling her promise yesterday not to interfere. And doubting that she'd kept her word.

Claire laughed, a harsh, grating sound, and spoke before Sam could. "Is that why you kissed him yesterday, Samantha? Hoping Jillian would find out and call off the wedding?"

Everybody's eyes were on her, and she felt like a bug pinned under a microscope. Miserable, she tried to hold Ethan's gaze, tried to silently assure him that breaking up the wedding had been the last thing on her mind when she'd kissed him.

But Jordan shot out of his seat, coming between her and Ethan. "You kissed my daughter's fiancé! I can't believe you have the gall to…" By the time Jordan blustered through his tirade and Sam was able to step around him, Ethan was gone.

ETHAN INSERTED THE KEY CARD into the door and staggered inside the ironically named honeymoon suite. Not that the name had been ironic when he'd originally booked the room.

Maybe this was an odd place to come, but he couldn't be around Jordan and Claire right now. And Sam…best not to think about her yet. Besides, the suite was already paid for and the hotel was close to the airport. If he wasn't going to Aruba tomorrow, he might as well fly back to New York after the meeting with Stern and start repairing the fallout from Bob Hunter's bad business decisions.

He felt deep empathy for Hunter—most of Ethan's decisions this week had been pretty bad, too.

After setting his laptop and garment bag on the king-size bed, he advanced on the wet bar. Ethan had always believed indulgences and vices weakened a man, interfered with his goals. He drank on occasion, but never because he *needed* to; tonight might be the exception that proved the rule. He downed a glass of whiskey on the rocks, but the liquor didn't burn with the same intensity as Sam's unforgettable kiss.

He sat heavily on the edge of the bed. Yesterday, she'd looked so sincere when she'd sworn not to interfere. And yet this morning, he'd found himself standing in front of hundreds of guests, looking like an ass when no bride walked down the aisle.

Acrid humiliation churned in his gut. He hated humiliation more than anything else in the world. He'd worked hard to gain respect and status, mostly so he could avoid the same type of biting shame he'd felt today. The shame Sam had caused by sabotaging his wedding. She'd betrayed him.

Of all the people he knew, he would have bet she'd be the least likely to go back on her word.

If you'd made that bet, you would've lost. You would've been a sucker. A fool.

Never one to stay silent, the cricket spoke up. *You would've been an even bigger fool if you'd married Jillian.*

Oddly enough, that cricket's voice was beginning to sound more and more like Ethan's. And the bug made sense. He *hadn't* wanted to marry Jillian, he just hadn't known how to call it off at the last minute. Though he doubted he would've been able to actually say the vows.

Okay, yes, today had been embarrassing. But wasn't a few minutes of embarrassment better than a lifetime of regret?

He'd narrowly escaped his own stupid plan today. He was free.

A knock sounded at the door. "Room service," a voice called. "Complimentary champagne for the happy couple."

Laughter surged up in Ethan, unpredicted and uncontainable. Much like Sam's presence in his life. "Come on in," he managed to say between laughs. He'd learned when he was young not to turn away anything complimentary. Besides, he had something to celebrate, and he might as well do it with champagne.

KNOCK, ALREADY. YOU MUST look ridiculous standing in the hall with your fist raised. Sam sighed. Pushing her fist toward the suite's door was as physically difficult as trying to lift a piano by herself. Ethan probably didn't want to see her.

Okay, "probably" was being optimistic. Doubtless, she was the last person he ever wanted to see. But she hadn't been able to stop herself from coming after him. Too many things still needed to be said.

After taking only the time to change into a blouse and slacks—showing up in her bridesmaid's dress would just be salt in his wound—she'd hurried to his hotel. They needed to talk. Well, unless she planned on talking telepathically through the door…

Taking a deep breath, she finally banged her hand against the door. Maybe he wasn't even here. *Would you come to your honeymoon suite hours after your wedding fell apart?*

No, but apparently Ethan would. He swung the door open and peered down in surprise. "Sam. I didn't—"

"Ever want to see me again?" she ventured.

"Expect you." He waved her inside. "Come join me for a drink."

She didn't know what surprised her more, the invitation or his appearance. He wore his tuxedo shirt unbuttoned over a pair of jeans—Ethan owned jeans?—and his hair was sexily rumpled. No sign of his jacket or tie. Better that she concentrate on the missing components of his tux than stare at what was revealed of his muscular chest.

"I'm glad you're here," he told her as he walked toward the wet bar.

She swallowed. "Because this saves you the trouble of tracking me down and wringing my neck?"

"You think I'm mad at you?"

"Well, earlier, you did look sort of—" *enraged? ticked? hacked off? homicidal?* "—mad, yes."

He poured two flutes of champagne and turned to face her. "I was embarrassed. And I don't like being embarrassed, Sam."

Nobody did. But she knew that this proud man who'd worked so hard to impress others and overcome a past of pity and disdain truly hated it. "Ethan, I'm sorry if anything I've done caused you pain." And she meant it. She'd been opposed to the wedding, but she hadn't wanted to hurt him.

"You don't owe me an apology." The bed

creaked under his weight as he sat next to her, and her heart kicked into double time. "If either of us owes each other anything, it's that I owe you my gratitude."

Blinking, she took her glass. "Kinda lost me there."

"I'm trying to say thank you."

She choked on her first sip of champagne. "Thank you?"

"For getting me out of this mess. I have to admit that at first I was angry you'd lied to me, gone back on your word when you'd said—"

She pressed a hand to his lips. "I'm glad Jillian left today, and I don't even mind taking credit for it. But I want you to know I stuck to my promise. She made up her own mind this morning, with no help from me."

Maybe it would've been better for his male pride to think she *did* have something to do with Jillian's leaving, but it was too important for him to know she wouldn't lie to him like that.

"Oh." The warm rush of air reminded her that her fingers were still against his mouth.

She jerked her hand into her lap and concentrated on the champagne flute she held.

"If you stare any harder at that glass, it'll shatter," Ethan teased.

"It's easier than looking at you." Probably an unwise thing to admit, but wisdom was overrated. She held up the flute. "If you're so grateful, how come you're here alone drowning your sorrows?"

"Actually, I was celebrating. And I'm not alone. I have you."

I have you. Yes, he did. But did he realize yet to what extent?

I am alone in a room, on a bed, with the man I love, who also happens to be the sexiest man I've ever met. Should she be counting her blessings or making tracks for the door?

"What an odd day," Ethan marveled. "You, being quiet. Jillian, being even braver than I am—"

"Some people would call the way she ducked out cowardly," Sam argued, still a little irritated at the way her friend had left her to take the rap for everything.

He laughed ruefully. "Maybe I'm more of a coward for *not* doing it myself. I should have called this off days ago. I'm glad she left. I don't think I could have gone through with it, but no gentleman jilts the bride at the altar. Jillian might have made me look bad by standing me up, but I would've made myself look worse by rejecting her in front of all her family and friends."

Sam's thoughts spun dizzily, and she didn't think it was from the sip and a half of champagne. "Re-reject her? Why would you have done that? Marrying her was what you wanted."

He took her champagne flute and set it next to his on the nightstand. "No. What I wanted...what I *want* is—" his lips brushed hers "—you."

12

CHILLS RACED UP SAM'S spine while at the same time, heat pooled in her abdomen. Overwhelming, contradicting sensations engulfed her as Ethan deepened the kiss. But not even the expertise of his mouth on hers could compare to the sexiness of his words.

I want you.

She kissed him fervently, hoping to convey that the sentiment was mutual. She did want him. Wanted him in her life, wanted to make him laugh, wanted to debate opinions with him, wanted to fan the flame she saw in his eyes when he looked at her.

Threading her hands through his hair, she tilted his head closer, tasting him, savoring his unique flavor combined with the tart sweetness of the champagne.

Champagne!

Groaning, Sam pulled away. "Um, Ethan—"

"Yes?" He leaned closer, his tone and sensual expression every bit as compelling as his kiss.

"I, well, about that kiss...I'm flattered. Thank you—"

"You're thanking me?" He raised one eyebrow, and the passion in his gaze dimmed. His mouth quirked as though he hadn't yet decided whether to be annoyed or amused.

"Yes. Thank you. It was lovely. But...I have to ask, exactly how much champagne have you had?"

His jaw went slack, and, for a moment, he only stared. Then he grinned. "Are you worried that you're taking *advantage* of me?"

She ignored the warmth climbing in her cheeks and the certainty that he was laughing at her. "Well, not exactly. It's just that some people would say it's a little odd, you kissing me after I helped destroy your plans for the future."

"Everything's been odd lately." He ran a hand through his hair. "The things I've been feeling aren't at all normal. But I don't think it's the champagne, I think it's you."

Her heart fluttered. "Should I take that as a compliment?"

"I'm not sure. I'm tired of not being able to sleep because I spend every night thinking about you. And it's very infuriating that not only did you insist I was making a huge mistake, you were right. And don't think I'm at all happy that when I'm with you, I practically forget about business when I should be focused on making the most of this promotion. You're a huge pain in the backside, Sam."

Tears misted her vision as she smiled. "Really?" He couldn't sleep because he'd been thinking about her? She made him forget about business and money? No one had ever said anything so romantic to her. "Putting up with you hasn't exactly been a picnic, either."

He clasped her hand in his. "I guess that makes us even. I'm going to kiss you again, but just so we're clear on this, it's not because of the champagne. Trust me, what I feel for you is scary enough to be sobering.''

His mouth captured hers, wooing, marauding, persuading. All the kisses that had come before in her life had only been practice for this moment. She wished it could go on for hours. Although, when he ended the kiss to explore her neck and earlobe and the acutely sensitive spot at the base of her collarbone, she had to admit that was just as good. He ran his finger down the neckline of her blouse, and she sighed, eager for his touch in other places.

"Sam?'' He paused at the top button.

The hunger in his green eyes and the raw beauty of his masculine features stole her breath. "Y-yes?''

"Just making sure you wanted this.''

She brushed her knuckles across his cheek. "I've never wanted anything more.''

"You don't know how relieved I am you said that.'' He leaned her back against the comforter, pressing his weight over her as he rained kisses across her face and throat, pausing once to claim her lips in a deep, soulful kiss.

Ethan told himself not to rush. He desperately wanted to be with her, but there was no reason to hurry. *None except that I may spontaneously combust soon.* With fingers that trembled like a teenage boy's, he unhooked the buttons on her silk blouse. He tucked his hands in the sides of her shirt and parted the material, touching skin even softer than the silk that covered it.

He managed to tear his gaze away from her full, blue-lace-covered breasts long enough to meet her eyes. "You're beautiful.'' He palmed one firm globe. Beneath his hand, her nipple immediately stiffened, and he groaned. She was the most responsive person he'd ever known.

Savoring each ragged breath and small moan, he traced delicate circles over her skin, watching her face and loving the way she closed her eyes and bit her lip and raked her nails over his back. But he could only tease her for so long before it became torment for him. He pulled her half sitting into his arms to reach behind her and unfasten the lacy bra.

She smiled a siren's grin as she shrugged out of the bra and unbuttoned shirt. "Unfair. What about you?" She slid the tuxedo shirt off his shoulders slowly, her fingers lingering on his skin, branding him with their heat.

Sitting up straighter, she ran her hands over his chest in light, inquisitive touches. He closed his eyes, happy to let her set the pace. Until her tongue flicked across one nipple, shooting lightning bolts of desire through his body.

He laid her back on the bed, reaching for the waistband of her slacks as he did. He tugged down the zipper and kissed her flat abdomen, working his way up to her breasts, loving each of them in turn, kissing and suckling until she writhed beneath him, gasping his name.

Everything blurred together, creating a passionate haze of the feel and taste of Sam under him, the sound of her shallow breathing, erotic music to his ears. He was barely aware of skimming her slacks down her long legs or shrugging out of his own jeans.

He ran his hands up her calves and the insides of her supple thighs. "Have I told you what incredible legs you have?"

She shook her head against the pillow.

Pressing a kiss above her knee, he trailed his fingers from midthigh to the soft juncture between her legs. He smoothed his hand over her light blue panties, torn between wanting this to last forever and wanting to bury himself inside her. Easing one hand under the waistband, over the feminine curls beneath, he found the damp, waiting core of her.

She arched her back. *"Ethan."*

The naked longing in her voice obliterated his intentions to make it last forever.

Together, they shed the last of the clothing that separated their bodies, and his mouth caressed hers as he fumbled for a condom in the nightstand. Wanting to make sure she was as ready, as frantic for this, as he was, he reached between them, stroking the slick, intimate folds of her skin.

The whimpering noises she made in her throat made him feel strong and powerful and weak and humble all at once. She was exquisite.

Stilling his hand with her own, she stared into his eyes. "Now, Ethan. Your touch feels incredible, but I want *you.*"

Placing his hands on either side of her and balancing his weight, he flexed his hips and thrust forward. Her body wrapped around him, welcoming, seducing. *Home.* Never before in his life had he experienced the sensation of being exactly where he belonged.

Sam's nerves thrummed with satisfaction when he entered her. This was what she'd wanted. *He* was what she wanted. But the satisfaction quickly gave way to restlessness, to the promise that something even better was within her grasp.

She bucked her hips, meeting his thrusts, finding a rhythm that was meant only for the two of them. Ethan's loving was intense, all-consuming and generous. She wanted to reciprocate, to make him experience all the sensations rioting through her.

Pressing her hand against his shoulder, she shoved gently. "Roll over?"

He grinned. "Happy to." He locked his arm around her waist, taking her with him as he moved to his back.

She smiled down at him, memorizing every line of his face. Straddling him, she began moving. Slowly, up and down, rocking her hips. But then Ethan propped himself up, nibbling and sucking at her breasts until urgent desire flooded her. Moving faster, she clung to him, unable to think or breathe.

Deep within her, something squeezed so tight she knew she would shatter. And then she did. Shuddering waves rocked her body as her orgasm spiraled through her. From far away, she heard Ethan's hoarse cry and knew he'd joined her over the edge.

SAM CAME AWAKE UNWILLINGLY, not wanting it to be morning because that would mean the most perfect night of her life had come to an end. But then the knock echoed through the room again. Yawning, she opened her eyes. Who was knocking this early?

Ethan grunted "Go 'way" in his sleep, and she turned to nestle closer to his warmth. They'd made love repeatedly and then held each other, talking and teasing and sometimes just cuddling silently, yet she still couldn't get enough of him.

Another insistent knock. "Ethan? Are you in there?"

Jillian. Sam bolted upright, assaulted by an onslaught of unpleasant feelings. Should she feel guilty
for being here? Jillian hadn't wanted Ethan, but
surely there was some kind of grace period one
should wait before sleeping with the ex-fiancé of
one's best friend?

Next to her, Ethan also sat up, frowning at the
door. "What is she doing here?"

Good question. Jillian was supposed to be off living life with Peter. Why would she be here first
thing in the morning? Oh, Lord, what if she had
changed her mind? What if she did want to marry
Ethan? Sam would crawl under a rock and die.

"Ethan, I know you're probably mad at me," Jillian called, "but please open the door. We need to
talk. About us."

Us? Sam's eyes burned with threatening tears.
Last night, she'd been given the most precious gift
of her life; would it be taken away this morning?
And had she jeopardized a lifelong friendship?

Trying to shrug away the morbid thoughts, she
mumbled, "You really should go talk to her."

Ethan nodded, already pulling on his discarded
jeans. He tugged a polo shirt over his head, then
kissed Sam's cheek. "She and I can talk in the
lobby."

Sam hunched down under the sheets, listening as
he opened the door to the suite and exchanged wary
greetings with Jillian. The door closed with a loud
click, and she winced at the finality of the sound.

Guilt and uncertainty churned in her stomach.
Had she made a huge mistake by sleeping with
Ethan? She loved him, but she'd neglected to men-
tion that fact to him. And although he'd seemed like

a man in love last night—smiling tenderly, laughing freely, touching her passionately—what if she were wrong?

What if he thought their lovemaking had only been... She swallowed, suddenly nauseous. Despite the fact that some people still branded her with the "rebel" label she'd acquired as a teenager, she was plenty conservative when it came to sex. She never took it lightly, didn't act impulsively, and now she remembered why. It wasn't worth the vulnerability and insecurity that followed.

She didn't find it easy to allow people to get close to her. In fact, now that she thought about her roster of boyfriends, she wondered if she hadn't deliberately chosen some of them because she'd known they'd never get close. But last night, she had given Ethan her body and heart and soul without knowing for certain that *he* wanted them.

What if he went back to Jillian? Or simply went back to New York, considering last night nothing more than a fond memory?

Despite his convenient revelation that he hadn't wanted to marry Jillian, he'd still been humiliated yesterday. What if last night had only been a salve to his ego? She was due to go home today, and neither of them had mentioned when they would see each other again. She'd been too filled with love and desire to ask.

In the harsh reality of the daylight, she considered their two lives, where they lived, what they wanted, which priorities mattered the most to each of them. Although she knew now that Ethan was motivated by a need to distance himself from his impoverished past and not greed, he still placed money and business above relationships. He had a meeting later to-day for crying out loud, scheduled between his would-be wedding and honeymoon! She'd grown up second to social status in her parents' affections, and she couldn't be content with second place again.

Sam, you're a fool.

Last night had been incredible. Magical. And an intensely painful mistake. She dreaded his return, when he'd no doubt confirm just how big a mistake.

I have to get out of here. She glanced at the clock. If she rushed, she could catch an early flight home.

ETHAN TOOK A SEAT IN ONE of the overstuffed green chairs in the hotel lobby. Jillian sat across from him, huddled inside a man's denim jacket, drumming her fingers on the small, decorative table between them.

Perhaps he should say or do something to put her at ease, but he was more concerned with getting back to Sam. He hadn't liked the appalled expression on her face when he left. Was she regretting what had passed between them?

God, he hoped not. Last night had been amazing; he felt *happy*. And if she took that away by telling him it never should have happened or—heaven forbid—wouldn't happen again... He had to get this over with and hurry back to Sam, convince her that last night was only the beginning.

He bent forward, hands braced on his knees. "What do you want?" When Jillian blinked wide, watery eyes at him, he realized his words had spilled out much more abruptly than intended. "I'm sorry, Jillian, I don't want to bite your head off, it's just that—"

"You're angry. I understand. I deserve it."

"No, I'm not angry. Honestly." Should he tell her the truth, or would it hurt her to know he hadn't wanted to marry her? Assessing the self-reproach in her pale eyes, he decided to relieve the burden of her guilt. "Jillian, I'm *relieved.*"

"Relieved?" The startled word echoed off the columns decorating the lobby, catching the attention of several passersby. Lowering her voice, she asked, "Are you saying that to make me feel better?"

"No, the truth is, you and I were both going through with the wedding for the wrong reasons. You're a bright and wonderful woman, but I don't think I could've said 'I do' at that altar yesterday. You saved me from making a painful decision."

"Painful, huh?" She grinned impishly. "I thought marrying me would be the smartest thing you'd done since buying Intel."

He laughed at her audacious humor—it reminded him of Sam—but groaned, too. "I'm sorry I ever said that. I honestly believed that's what relationships should be. Smart, well thought out, mutually lucrative…"

"And now?"

"Now I think the really great ones are unplanned, unpredictable pains in the butt."

"Bingo. They certainly aren't convenient." She stared at a point past his shoulder, obviously lost in her own thoughts. He wondered if she was thinking about Peter and the problems he would pose to her goal of parental approval.

Then again, as Ethan had learned only recently, love was more important than goals. He blinked. *Love?* Is that what he felt for Sam?

Of course it was. Why had it taken him so long to figure out?

"Ethan?"

He squinted at Jillian, trying to recall what she was doing here. "Yes?"

"You okay? I've never seen that look before."

"What look?"

"You had a big, goofy grin on your face. You never smile like that."

He had a feeling he'd be smiling a lot more from now on. "I don't mean to run you off, since it was courageous and decent of you to come here this morning, but there's not much else for us to say. You don't need to apologize or explain."

"Thanks, but it's time I grow up and take responsibility for my actions. I've always deferred to my parents or relied on Sam or Pet—" She broke off, a horrified expression on her face.

"It's okay," he assured her. "I know all about Peter."

"I'm sorry. I didn't mean to lie to you, I honestly thought I could get over him."

"I wish you both all the best." He stood, eager to send her on her way with a clean conscience and return upstairs to the woman who occupied his thoughts and heart.

Jillian stood, too, favoring her bandaged left ankle. "I suppose it's too much to hope that telling my parents will be this easy. Peter and I are going to see them this afternoon, tell them we're going to Mexico. Eloping, and I don't care what anyone thinks about it."

"Good for you." He suddenly realized he liked Jillian right now more than he ever had before.

Maybe because he wasn't confronted with the prospect of spending the next fifty years with her. "But if you don't care what anyone thinks, why are you stopping at your parents before eloping?"

"Because they spent a lot of money and time on that wedding, and I should have the guts to explain my decision face-to-face. How can I ask them to respect me if I don't respect them enough to tell them honestly how I feel?"

Impulsively, he pulled her into a hug. "Jillian, I sense good things in your future."

"Thank you." She kissed his cheek and pulled away. "What about you?"

He hesitated. Sam would probably want to be the one to break the news about their relationship. "Don't worry about me." *I sense even better things in my future.*

"DAMMIT." ETHAN QUIT HIS pacing and dropped onto the bed, no longer able to deny the truth: Sam wasn't coming back.

When he'd first come up to the hotel room earlier and discovered it empty, he'd assumed she would be returning soon. She wouldn't just leave after what they'd shared. Not without saying goodbye. He'd rationalized that she'd gone downstairs for coffee or the newspaper or run to her hotel for a change of clothes. But she'd be back. Or she'd call.

But now, with ten minutes left before he was supposed to meet Randolph Stern and three other potential investors downstairs, he realized Sam wasn't coming back.

Yesterday he'd been left publicly, by the woman he'd planned to spend his life with. And it hadn't hurt half as much as this unwitnessed abandonment by a woman he'd known barely a week.

How could she do this? No phone call, no explanation, no chance for him to tell her how he felt.

What if he had told her how he felt?

He sprang to his feet again, remembering the stricken look on her face this morning, the vulnerability in her ocean-blue eyes. Had she been worried he and Jillian would reconcile? Or what if she'd simply feared that she was second choice, that he'd chosen to be with her only because being with Jillian had no longer been an option?

"You idiot. You should have said something to her before it was too late."

A shrill, chirpy sound came from his discarded jacket across the room. He dived for his cell phone. "Sam?"

"Ethan, is that you? This is Barbara."

"Oh. What can I do for you?"

"The big guy upstairs has already heard about yesterday. You were jilted at the altar?"

Yesterday, he would have hated having to face everyone, having to return from his own wedding minus a blushing bride. This morning, all he cared about was that Sam wasn't here. "I'm fine, if that's why you're calling."

"Actually, old man Peabo wanted me to relay the message that if you won't be taking your honeymoon this week, get your butt back in the office as soon as the meeting with Stern is over. Some of our big clients are nervous after Hunter's mistakes and they need hand-holding."

"Right. See you tomorrow, Barbara." He hung

up the phone and told himself to focus, forget about Sam for at least a couple of hours.

Peabo-Johnston was in trouble, and Ethan needed to do his part to secure the future of the company. The job would be harder than he expected now that he wouldn't be bringing in all those extra connections through Jordan. Hell, Jordan himself would probably fire the firm after yesterday's debacle. The meeting with Stern was more important than ever.

Ethan grabbed a set of folders off of the small table and headed for the door. He could do this presentation. He'd done thousands of client presentations. But no business meeting had ever been as important as his feelings for Sam.

What if I can still catch up to her? What if it's not too late to let her know how I feel?

The sharp, fearful feeling he'd grown up with stabbed at him. Was he panicking now because his future was in question?

No. The panic was only because his future with Sam was in question. Ethan's past came into view with more clarity than he'd seen it in years. He and his parents had been poor, true, but he hadn't been unhappy while they were alive. It wasn't until he'd moved in with his uncle... It wasn't financial security he needed to make him feel secure and once again at peace with life. It was love.

In the lobby, Ethan passed the small room he'd booked for the meeting. Instead, he marched right outside and hailed a taxi, giving the driver the name of Sam's hotel.

13

THE CAB PULLED UP to the Winthrop estate, and Ethan jumped out of the car while it was still moving, tossing a handful of bills at the driver.

Please let Jillian be here.

She'd said she would be talking to her parents this afternoon, and, if she hadn't already headed south of the border, maybe she could help him. He'd been to Sam's hotel, but the desk clerk told him Ms. Lloyd had checked out. Jillian might be his only chance to find Sam.

Asking the woman he was supposed to marry less than twenty-four hours ago to help track down the woman he loved wasn't exactly normal behavior.

Yeah, well, neither was jumping out a window on your wedding day. If anyone would understand, it would be Jillian.

He rapped on the front door, bulldozing inside when Ilene opened it.

The plump housekeeper wrung her hands. "Oh, Mr. Jenner, I was so sorry to—"

"Is Jillian here?"

She took a nervous step backward. "Yes, Mr. Jenner, but I don't think—"

At that moment, he heard raised voices coming from the study. "Thanks, Ilene." He strode toward the sound, only half aware of the housekeeper trailing him.

He knocked once at the study, then opened the door to find Jillian and her parents in various states of agitation. Jordan stood behind the minibar, drinking what looked to be scotch. Claire was pacing the Oriental carpet and screeching. Jillian sat ashen-faced on the antique loveseat. A blond man—the controversial Peter?—stood behind her, rubbing her shoulders encouragingly.

"Am I interrupting?" Ethan asked.

Four pairs of eyes focused on him. Jillian looked confused, her parents looked relieved, and Peter struggled not to look extremely nervous.

Jordan gestured toward the doorway with his glass. "Ethan, thank goodness you're here. Come in and talk sense to my daughter. We've tried till we're blue in the face, but she's being as stubborn as that crazy friend of hers."

Ethan grinned despite himself, knowing that both Sam and Jillian would be pleased with the comparison. "You've been talking to her, but have you listened to her?"

Claire sniffed. "She's babbling about true love. What a load of— Ethan, talk to her."

You won't like what I have to say. He knew his refusal to "reason with" Jillian would definitely cost Peabo-Johnston Jordan's business. Then again, what did he care? After he blew off that meeting this morning, he probably didn't work there anymore. Instead of feeling alarmed, he felt liberated. His grin widened as he stepped toward Jillian.

Peter quickly inserted himself between them. He was shorter and leaner than Ethan, but he held his

ground. "This is the woman I love. I know we ruined your wedding day, and you have a right to be
angry, but—"

"Relax, Pete." He clapped the younger man on
his shoulder. "Jillian's parents want my opinion,
and here it is—you two get out of here and go get
married. But I need a favor first."

"What?"

Jillian, smiling gratefully up at him, was the only
one in the room who didn't shout the stunned word.

"Have you taken leave of your senses?" Jordan
demanded.

"Nope. I've finally come to them. You really
think I'd want to force your daughter into a marriage
she doesn't want? She loves someone else." Looking at Jillian, he added softly, "And so do I."

Jordan's glass crashed to the floor. "Not Samantha! That obnoxious, ill-bred—"

Ethan's terse "Shut up" competed with Jillian's
"Daddy, don't say another word."

Silence filled the room, and Jillian gaped at Ethan.
"Is that true? Are you in love with Sam?"

His face flushed—he felt a little silly admitting
his feelings in front of these four when Sam herself
didn't know yet—but he nodded. Behind him, Claire
ranted and Jordan raved. Ethan ignored them. "I do
love her, but I need your help convincing her of
that."

Peter glared. "You were going to marry my Jillian when you loved someone else?"

Jillian sidestepped her true love. "Peter, I appreciate your outrage on my behalf, but don't you think
it's a touch hypocritical, considering?"

"Sorry," he mumbled.

"I can't believe I didn't know," Jillian mused. "I thought I knew her so well, but I didn't even... I've been pretty self-absorbed lately."

"You aren't mad at Sam, are you?" Ethan asked worriedly. "I know how important your friendship is to her."

"Mad? Not at all. I've always thought she belonged with someone strong. Someone as stubborn and determined as she is. Don't take this badly, but you were a bit...much for me. What can I do to help you?"

He shoved his hands in his pockets. "I've lost her. She took off before I could tell her how I felt."

Jillian nodded. "I saw her leaving her hotel this morning. I stopped in to apologize for the way I left her to face the music yesterday. She seemed distracted and in a hurry, but I had no idea... She's gone home to Austin."

A fresh ache throbbed in his chest. He wouldn't give up yet. He knew where she was now, he just had to talk to her. "Will you tell me how to get there?"

"I can do better than that. We'll take you to her on our way to Mexico."

ETHAN BIT THE INSIDE of his cheek to keep from asking "Are we there yet?" His impatience to see Sam aside, he wasn't sure how much longer he could stand being in the car with the two lovebirds.

When they'd stopped at a gas station to fuel up, Ethan had returned to the car just in time to hear Peter tell Jillian, "I need you like a geranium needs fertilizer with an N-P-K analysis of 5-10-5."

A few weeks ago, Ethan would have called Peter's comment fertilizer. Now Ethan had a better understanding and patience for being in love, but still, a guy could only take so much. The murmured comments and shared glances in the front seat were nauseating. Not to mention the way Ethan's muscles tensed every few minutes when he realized how often Peter watched Jillian instead of the road. *Wonder if I'll reach Austin in one piece.*

It was a real eye-opener, though, to see Jillian with the man she loved. Refined, detached, proper Jillian now blushed, giggled and occasionally whispered suggestions that made Peter redden and grip the steering wheel of the little Toyota Corolla.

She swiveled in the passenger seat. "Austin city limits, Ethan. We're almost there."

He released a deep breath. *I'll be with Sam soon.*

As though she'd heard the thought, Jillian reached back to pat his hand reassuringly. "Not too much longer now. But...wouldn't you like to stop and get something first?"

"Something?" he echoed in confusion.

"Something romantic. Like a card that says you love her?"

"Why do I need that? *I'm* going to say I love her. Isn't paying Hallmark a couple of bucks to do the same thing redundant?"

Sighing, she turned to Peter. "Help me out here. Talk to him guy to guy."

This should be interesting. Peter was likable enough, but Ethan doubted they were on the same wavelength.

Peter glanced in the rearview mirror, his expression earnest. "Women like romance. Jillian is my world, and if you feel even half of what I do for your Samantha, you want a romantic way to express it. Not that you have to ride up on a white horse—"

"That would be a nice touch," Jillian interjected.

"—but you could at least take five minutes out of your day to do something simple. Wouldn't it be worth it to stop and buy some flowers if it would make Sam happy?"

Hmm. The gardener had a point.

"Okay. I can do flowers."

Jillian directed Peter through the streets of Austin, and they pulled up to a flower shop several blocks from where Sam lived.

As he parked the car, Peter suggested, "What about something from the *Iridaceae* family?"

"Whose family?" Ethan asked.

"An iris," the younger man clarified. "I was thinking a miniature tall bearded. They make graceful, elegant arrangements that resemble bouquets of butterflies."

"Miniature tall?" Ethan glanced in Jillian's direction. "Does that make sense to you?"

She shrugged, and the three of them entered the shop. Ethan's nose twitched at the sweet, cloying scent of dozens of varieties of flowers.

He pointed to a cellophane-wrapped bundle right inside the door. "We can grab those."

"But they're prone to leaf rot," Peter objected. "Leaf rot is not romantic."

Whatever Ethan bought her would be dead in a few days, and he didn't see how that was romantic, either. Then again, Peter knew his flowers. Maybe Ethan should consider the man's advice.

"What about roses?" he asked. "Will they work?"

Peter and Jillian exchanged glances. "Not the most original idea," Peter said, "but certainly a classic one. Hard to go wrong with roses."

Jillian nodded. "Women love roses."

"Great." Ethan walked around the store until he spotted a bouquet of deep pink roses with perfectly shaped petals and nary a hint of leaf rot. "I'll take these."

"Wait!" Peter shook his head. "Are you sure you want those?"

"You just said I couldn't go wrong with roses."

Peter shot him a look that said "and yet you found a way." "I think you want red. It symbolizes love. True, soul-deep love like what I feel for my Jillian. The kind of love that lasts forever. *That* color—" he pointed to the offending pink roses "—means gratitude and appreciation. You sure that's what you're going for?"

Ethan hesitated. Should he get the kind that symbolized forever? Iffy, considering he had no idea whether Sam shared his feelings or even wanted to see him again. Then again, the whole point of this "romantic gesture" was to show her he loved her, so maybe the red...

But then he recalled the dark pink dress she'd been wearing the first time he'd seen her on the plane, the one that should have clashed with her red hair but only heightened her beauty. And the delicately feminine pink toenail polish that was such a contrast to her feisty exterior. He knew firsthand she was more delicate and feminine than she let on.

"I like the pink," he insisted. "Besides, every guy in love gets a woman red roses. Sam deserves something different. You say they mean gratitude and appreciation? I appreciate the way she showed up unexpectedly in my life and I'm grateful she taught me what love was before it was too late.''

Jillian blinked. ''I think you've figured out what to write on the card.''

''You *are* a romantic,'' Peter said with a proud grin.

Ethan fidgeted. ''Don't say it so loud, okay?''

Sheesh. A romantic. He used to be a well-known cynic. A shrewd, determined businessman. Smart and savvy, unfettered by sentimentality. What had Sam done to him?

He had no idea, but he couldn't wait to see her again and let her do some more of it.

SAM WINCED AT THE FLAT NOTE, but tried to cover it with a smile. ''Nice job, Ana. Why not try it one last time?''

Ana enthusiastically launched into a third rendition of ''Do You Hear What I Hear?''

Sam didn't have any official lessons scheduled this week, but she sometimes gave free lessons to Ana Kramer, the thirteen-year-old only child who lived next door. Ana had watered all of Sam's plants and brought in the mail while she was gone, and Sam had given into the girl's plea for a quick lesson this evening.

Anything to get Ethan off my mind. Not that the impromptu lesson had done anything to eradicate him from her thoughts. She should have handled things better with him. At least left a note or something. But what could she possibly have said— *Whoops, I fell in love with you?*

Ana finished the song and turned around on the piano bench. "I'm getting better, aren't I?"

Sam nodded. "You sure are. But why don't we take a short break? I can make some hot chocolate." It wasn't really cold enough for hot chocolate, but it never felt like the Christmas season without it.

Not that this year would be very jolly, anyway. Since she'd been gone for the last few weeks, she didn't have a tree or any of her usual decorations up. And it would be hard to get in the festive spirit with a broken heart.

Determined not to think about it, she stood abruptly. "That's what we need. Hot chocolate with lots of marshmallows."

Ana trailed her to the small kitchen, painted a sunny yellow and decorated with sunflower accents. "Did you have fun at that wedding you went to?"

More fun than she should have and the consequence was a broken heart. "Er, yes." Sam pulled down two mugs, then busied herself pouring milk into a pan.

"Was the bride beautiful?" Ana sat at the square kitchen table. "I'll bet the bride was beautiful. I hope I'm beautiful at my wedding. I hope I have a wedding."

"I'm sure you will, sweetheart. And you'll be gorgeous. By next year, the boys will be begging to go out with you."

Beneath Ana's round glasses and last vestiges of baby fat were porcelain-fine skin, a stunning smile and wide green eyes. It didn't hurt that she never had a bad hair day, either. Yep, Ana would catch the boys' notice soon enough. Sam stopped herself right before warning the girl it might be best to stay away from the boys.

Far, far away.

But the teenager was still caught up in the romance of a wedding and hadn't given future heartache a thought. "I'll bet the groom was handsome, too. Did he wear a tuxedo?"

"Yes," Sam managed to say past the lump in her throat. But she wasn't thinking of Ethan at the church in his debonair tux. She was recalling the way he'd looked at the hotel, in the unbuttoned tuxedo shirt. And the way he'd looked out of the tuxedo shirt.

"The milk!" Ana pointed to the pan on the stove, where the contents were beginning to boil over.

"Thanks." Sam shut off the heat to the burner, wishing she could shut off her memories and feelings as easily.

"Do you think you'll ever get married?"

A spoonful of cocoa missed its intended mug and landed on the pale yellow counter. "I don't know." She filled the mug and handed it to her guest, hoping the hot chocolate would prevent further questions.

No such luck.

"Well, have you ever been in love?"

Sam started to answer no, but what was the point in lying? The truth was inescapable. "Yes. But we wanted different things."

"Like what?" Ana blew across the top of her steaming mug and looked up expectantly. "Like you wanted kids and he didn't?"

Sharp pangs raked Sam's chest as she remembered the look on Ethan's face when he talked about children. About wanting to be a good father fiercely determined to make sure his kids knew they were loved. Adamant that they never felt unwanted, the way his uncle had made him feel. "No, we both wanted kids."

"Did he have a stupid sense of humor? Jenny Bartholomew and Chad Akins were going together, but she broke up with him because he was always telling dumb jokes and thought fart noises were funny."

"No, Ethan had a great sense of humor. We laughed together." She missed his laugh.

"Oh." The girl silently contemplated the mysteries of love and all the reasons men and women didn't end up together. "Was he a bad kisser?"

Sam choked on her hot chocolate. After swallowing, she assured Ana. "His kisses were fine."

"Jenny said Chad had squishy lips. And they were too wet."

Not a thing wrong with Ethan's lips. Or any other part of his anatomy. "Wow, sounds like Jenny and Chad were all wrong for each other."

"Doomed from the start," Ana said sagely. "But I don't get why you and Ethan broke up."

"We weren't exactly together. It's...complicated."

"I hate when grown-ups say that, like I'm too young to understand. I'm *thirteen*."

"For one thing, he lives in New York, and I live in Texas."

"So one of you has to move," Ana concluded with a shrug.

The doorbell pealed, and Sam said a quick prayer of thanks. Most likely Ana's mom coming to tell her it was dinnertime. Sam had thought being alone was a bad idea, but solitude was probably healthier than discussing Ethan with the adolescent relationship guru.

Sam flung the door open. "Come on in. We were just having some—" The words died in her throat as she realized Ethan probably wasn't there to tell Ana it was dinnertime. "You."

He shifted his weight. "You were expecting someone else. Is this a bad time?"

"I—" If she said yes, would he go away? Did she want him to? No, she wanted him to stay forever, but since that was out of the question, it was better to send him away before she was hurt any more.

"Who is it?" Ana piped up from behind Sam. "Is it my mom? Oh, hello there. You aren't my mom."

Ethan smiled over Sam's shoulder at the girl. "Nope. My name's Ethan."

Ana gasped. *"You're—"*

"Just in time for some hot chocolate," Sam interrupted, hustling Ethan inside and shutting the door. "Ana, we're all done for today. Your mom's probably waiting for you, so maybe you should gather up your sheet music and—"

"He has flowers," Ana said, clearly uninterested in sheet music.

Sam turned back to see that Ana was right. She'd been so shocked to see Ethan that she hadn't taken any notice of the gorgeous bouquet he carried. Long-stemmed pink roses. He held them out awkwardly.

"They're for you. Aren't you going to introduce me to your pretty friend?" He glanced in Ana's direction. "Sorry I didn't know you'd be here or I would have bought flowers for you, too."

The girl giggled, instantly smitten. Sam knew the feeling. She recalled the way her heart had raced when Ethan had sat down next to her on that plane. It seemed forever ago, yet her heart still had the same reaction every time she saw him.

A little voice in her head told her she was staring, but it was hard not to. Had he actually become *better*-looking? His khaki slacks were rumpled and obviously in need of ironing and his eyes had a bleary, tired look to them, but his tousled state only made him sexier.

"Sam." He groaned the single syllable. In a low whisper, he added, "If you keep looking at me like that…"

The unfinished sentence galvanized her into action. "One hot chocolate, coming up." She marched toward the kitchen, dismayed but not surprised when Ana followed closely.

In a not-so-quiet whisper, the girl commented, "He's *hot.* I'll bet he's a much better kisser than Chad Akins. Are you sure you want to break up with him?"

Sam sighed. "I told you, we weren't really together."

"I'd like to fix that."

She jumped when Ethan joined the conversation. Whirling around, she asked, "You would?"

"That's why I'm here. That, and to find out why you left in such a hurry."

Not sure how to answer, she stalled by searching for a vase to put the roses in.

Ethan leaned against the counter, filling her small

kitchen with his masculine presence. "I should have bought you sunflowers instead," he said, studying the decor.

"No, these are beautiful." She glanced his way to reassure him and realized her mistake too late when his gaze captured hers. His eyes burned with emotion and passion and accusation. She *did* owe him an explanation as to why she'd left without even a goodbye. But she hadn't expected it to bother him so much. Actually, her deepest fear had been that he'd be relieved.

"Sam says you live in New York," Ana piped up, reminding Sam that she and Ethan weren't alone.

Ethan raised an eyebrow. "What else did she say about me?"

"That you laughed together and that she's in l—"

"Ana! I think Ethan and I should probably talk alone. Why don't you come back over tomorrow?"

Ana glanced from Sam's nervous expression to Ethan's curious one. "I can have lessons tomorrow?"

"Yes."

"What about the day after that?" the little black-mailer asked.

"And the next day, too. But you should go now."

"Okay." She skipped out of the room, calling over her shoulder, "Nice to meet you, Ethan."

"You, too," he answered before turning his grin Sam's way. "You told her about me?"

"Er...hot chocolate?"

"That's the third time you've offered."

The front door banged shut, and Sam jumped. "Maybe we should skip the chocolate and see if I have anything stronger."

His fingers curved over her shoulders, and he guided her toward the kitchen table. "First, why don't we sit down?" He pulled out a chair for her, then sat much too close in the seat next to her. Her nerve endings pinged and sizzled at his nearness, and his familiar scent invaded her senses. "You look confused, so I'll start. When I got back to the room this morning and found you gone, I was... well, unhappy is a massive understatement."

"I apologize for that. I know I didn't handle things well, but I sort of panicked." Not a dignified admission, but the truth. She'd fled blindly without due consideration to how it would affect him.

"You panicked because Jillian showed up?"

"That and...I wasn't sure what would happen with us. I didn't know if last night meant anything. To you." And even if it had, she hadn't known where to go from there.

"If it meant anything?" He stood suddenly. Pacing back and forth, he addressed his words to the tile floor. "Sam, I've fallen in love with you."

The world disappeared from under her. She was falling into an endless black hole, spinning weightlessly. When she tried to respond, only a squeak came out.

"I know what you're going to say," he told her. He did? Because she had no idea. "This doesn't make sense. My marriage to Jillian would have made sense. I mapped out my life and chose a bride accordingly, but I would have been miserable. You certainly don't fit into the life I'd mapped, but you make me happy. I love you."

"I love you, too." The response spilled out of her.

Ethan froze, his eyes blazing bright. "Say that again," he said softly, taking both her hands in his.

"I love you. Wow. I never thought it would be so easy to say. The few serious boyfriends I ever had who said it to me, I always had to respond with things like 'me, too' or 'thanks.' Love wasn't really a concept I grew up with."

He nodded. "Me, neither. Doubt my uncle's ever said the word."

"Oh, my parents said it constantly." She pulled her hands free of his grasp, uncertainty filling her. "My mother *loved* the dignitaries she met, *loved* the fall collections she bought every year, *loved* the people at the club. She just didn't…"

Ethan knelt in front of her. "I'm sure she did. Some people just aren't good at showing it. Some people don't even recognize it. Until you walked out on me this morning—"

"I'm sorry about that. I just didn't think there'd be a future for us. I do love you, but what if it's not enough? Your job will always—"

His laugh was the last thing she'd expected to hear. "You mean the job I lost when I blew off my meeting today to run around looking for you?"

"You did that for me?" Along with the shock, an unfamiliar warmth welled up inside her. She'd been his first priority?

"Losing my job worried me. Losing you terrified me," he said. "You're what's irreplaceable. So what do you say, can we make this work?"

The only thing remaining between them was the way she kept others at arm's length. She'd always prided herself on being self-reliant, but in the past week she'd realized that it was more a case of self-isolation.

"Sam?" Anxiety laced his voice, and she loved him even more for his vulnerability. He ran a hand over his face. "Aren't you going to say anything?"

Unshed tears filled her eyes. "I'm n-not sure I c-can."

"Are you crying?"

"No," she sniffed, wiping at the corner of her eye.

He cupped her face with his hands. "Sad crying or happy?"

"Deliriously happy. Of course we can make this work."

He exhaled in a whoosh. "Oh, thank God. I was starting to worry."

Unable to go another second without kissing him, she pulled him closer. She hadn't thought his kisses could get any better, but now, knowing that he loved her and being able to freely admit her love... She made a sound of protest when he pulled away.

"I hated losing you this morning. I never want to feel that way again," he told her. "I want to know that you're sticking around. Pete the gardener had a pretty good idea. How do you feel about running off to Mexico to get married?"

Her heart stopped. "Are you... Was that a proposal?"

He snapped his fingers. "Damn. That wasn't romantic at all, was it? And I can't very well expect you to marry a man who doesn't have his next job lined up yet, although I have quite a bit hoarded away in savings and I think that Walter Matthias—"

She pressed her hand firmly against his mouth.

When she had his attention, she enunciated slowly, "*Was* that a proposal?"

He nodded and asked beneath her fingers, "What do you say to Christmas in Cancún?"

She launched herself out of her chair and into his arms. "I say *sí*, Señor Jenner."

He pulled her to him, sealing their engagement with a hot, openmouthed kiss that left her knees trembling. Planning out the details would have to wait until later. Much later.

We've been making you laugh for years!

 HARLEQUIN®

Duets™

**Join the fun in May 2003
and celebrate Duets #100!
This smile-inducing series,
featuring gifted writers and
stories ranging from amusing to zany,
is a hundred volumes old.**

This special anniversary volume offers two terrific
tales by a duo of Duets' acclaimed authors.
You won't want to miss...

Jennifer Drew's You'll Be Mine in 99
and
The 100-Year Itch by Holly Jacobs

With two volumes offering two special stories every
month, Duets always delivers a sharp slice of the lighter
side of life and *especially* romance. Look for us today!

Happy Birthday, Duets!

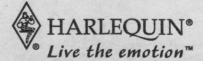

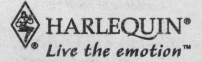

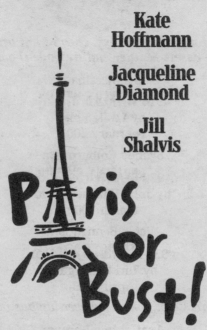